GHOSTLY DELIGHT

Valerian was about to mount the stairs to his bedchamber when he saw a ghost.

The apparition floated some distance above the floor, draped in white and wavering in the light of a single candle.

A shaft of icy terror held him in place, until he realized a ghost was the last thing he had to fear. By the rood, he *was* a ghost. But he couldn't bring himself to move, even when the spirit descended to the floor and advanced toward him.

"What in the name of heaven are you doing here?" Gwen Sevaric demanded. She set her candle on a side table and folded her arms, her small bare foot tapping as she waited for an explanation.

He broke out laughing. Now that he could see her clearly, he realized she had been standing on the stairs that led to the second floor. The white gown was her nightrail, an altogether pedestrian swath of flannel.

"Well?" Her foot tapped double time as he moved closer, still laughing. "Should I call a footman to search your person?"

That brought him up short. "Search my—? Oh, I see. You imagine I've been pilfering the family silver." With a smile, he held out his arms. "Rummage away, Miss Sevaric. Anything you find is yours for the taking."

ZEBRA'S REGENCY ROMANCES
DAZZLE AND DELIGHT

A BEGUILING INTRIGUE   (4441, $3.99)
by Olivia Sumner

Pretty as a picture Justine Riggs cared nothing for propriety. She dressed as a boy, sat on her horse like a jockey, and pondered the stars like a scientist. But when she tried to best the handsome Quenton Fletcher, Marquess of Devon, by proving that she was the better equestrian, he would try to prove Justine's antics were pure folly. The game he had in mind was seduction—never imagining that he might lose his heart in the process!

AN INCONVENIENT ENGAGEMENT   (4442, $3.99)
by Joy Reed

Rebecca Wentworth was furious when she saw her betrothed waltzing with another. So she decides to make him jealous by flirting with the handsomest man at the ball, John Collinwood, Earl of Stanford. The "wicked" nobleman knew exactly what the enticing miss was up to—and he was only too happy to play along. But as Rebecca gazed into his magnificent eyes, her errant fiancé was soon utterly forgotten!

SCANDAL'S LADY   (4472, $3.99)
by Mary Kingsley

Cassandra was shocked to learn that the new Earl of Lynton was her childhood friend, Nicholas St. John. After years at sea and mixed feelings Nicholas had come home to take the family title. And although Cassandra knew her place as a governess, she could not help the thrill that went through her each time he was near. Nicholas was pleased to find that his old friend Cassandra was his new next door neighbor, but after being near her, he wondered if mere friendship would be enough . . .

HIS LORDSHIP'S REWARD   (4473, $3.99)
by Carola Dunn

As the daughter of a seasoned soldier, Fanny Ingram was accustomed to the vagaries of military life and cared not a whit about matters of rank and social standing. So she certainly never foresaw her *tendre* for handsome Viscount Roworth of Kent with whom she was forced to share lodgings, while he carried out his clandestine activities on behalf of the British Army. And though good sense told Roworth to keep his distance, he couldn't stop from taking Fanny in his arms for a kiss that made all hearts equal!

Available wherever paperbacks are sold, or order direct from the Publisher. Send cover price plus 50¢ per copy for mailing and handling to Penguin USA, P.O. Box 999, c/o Dept. 17109, Bergenfield, NJ 07621. Residents of New York and Tennessee must include sales tax. DO NOT SEND CASH.

GWEN'S CHRISTMAS GHOST

LYNN KERSTAN

and ALICIA RASLEY

ZEBRA BOOKS
KENSINGTON PUBLISHING CORP.

ZEBRA BOOKS are published by

Kensington Publishing Corp.
850 Third Avenue
New York, NY 10022

First Printing: November, 1995

Printed in the United States of America

Prologue

Eternity was a bloody bore.

Valerian Caine didn't know exactly how long he had been in this not-heaven, not-hell, but he knew he'd had enough.

Unfortunately, no one had ever bothered to consult him on the matter. He was, not to put too fine a point on it, dead. And dead men had three alternatives—Heaven, Hell, and this remote antechamber of the Afterlife.

Time seemed to be irrelevant here, and consciousness an occasional thing. Now and again he would find himself engaged in some useless task, but nothing that gave him any excitement. He had vague recollections of monitoring the motions of a comet, and was marginally certain that he'd once been put to nursemaiding a troop of breeding sea-turtles. A profound waste of talent, in his opinion.

But then, death was a waste of his talent. He had been very good at living, and a notable failure since his life was cut short by a bullet.

Whatever assignments he was given, he invariably bungled them, or so he was informed whenever Proctor called him to account. That was never a pleasant experience. And now he had been summoned once again, from a place he could not recall to a place he didn't recognize, to hear yet another pious lecture on the subject of his imperfections.

'Struth, he had never claimed to be a saint. Indeed, he claimed, with some pride, to have reveled in all the Seven Deadly Sins and invented a few of his own. But Proctor held him to higher standards, enumerated in tedious platitudes that only confirmed his dedication to wickedness.

Usually Valerian listened with sullen incomprehension, but this time he intended to stand up for himself and get a few answers. This time he felt stronger, more truly himself, than he had done in a long time.

For one thing, he had some awareness of his body. Not much—an outline at most—but when he concentrated he could see his arms and legs. As he peered down at what seemed to be his body, he saw something appear below his feet. A floor. He looked up and saw that an office had materialized around him. There was a massive desk, a couple of chairs, and wisps of mist rather than the fog that usually enveloped this place. Something—no, someone—sat behind the desk.

Naturally, now that he was geared for battle, he was deprived of his opponent. Instead of Proctor, he was greeted by a sweet-faced, balding man wearing a long white robe.

"Won't you be seated?" Politely he gestured toward a chair. "I am Francis, your . . . er . . . Guardian."

Valerian slumped onto the chair, surprised that it felt solid. He ran his fingers over the carved wooden armrests. "Is this real? It looks transparent. So do you, by the way."

Francis sighed. "I was hoping to make you feel more comfortable, but I'm woefully inept at reproducing solid objects. Not many souls care about physical sensation once they have . . . moved on."

"Moved on? You mean died?" Euphemisms might be appropriate here in this translucent no-place, but suddenly Valerian wanted clarity. "And if you are my guardian, why haven't we met?"

"But we have, although you'd not be aware of it. I was assigned to you from the instant of your creation." Francis chuckled. He even managed a shake of the head, though it left long wavery trails in the air. "I was warned how much trouble you would be. But my last charge was Teresa of Avila, and I had little to do beyond modifying the content of her visions. When she Advanced, I was dispatched to the Major Challenges Department. You have proved to be that, I must confess. I did my best, but if anything, you have sunk below the point where you started."

Valerian had once been known for his expressive face, but now it took all his concentration to lift a quizzical brow. "Were you supposed to see to my salvation?"

"Something like that. Alas, my abilities are circumscribed. You see, only through your own free will can you move to a higher place. At most, I am permitted to nudge your conscience, and . . . rarely . . . protect you from harm." Francis folded his arms, looking sad. "I admit to having let you down in that regard. Do you remember how you passed from earthly existence?"

"Hell, yes."

Francis winced. More shimmers trailed from his face and dissipated into the mist. "That is *not* a word we like to use around here."

"My apologies. But if I was such a failure, why aren't I there? In Hell, I mean. Not that I'm complaining," he added hastily. "But I have to wonder if there even is such a place."

With a frown, Francis began to pace the room. The mist didn't so much part for him as slide through him. "There is indeed a state of eternal damnation. Fortunately for you, every soul is given many opportunities to choose good over evil. Now and again a creature is bent on perdition, and no amount of mercy can stay his course." Some emotion—regret?—flickered across his face. "Even angels can choose evil over goodness. Lucifer was like that."

Valerian nodded. He had heard of Lucifer, had, in fact, gone once to a club named for him. Just once, for the cards were marked and the dice were loaded. "He is real, then? Lucifer?"

"Oh, yes. Our greatest disappointment. We were friends once, you know."

It was hard to imagine the sweet, slightly dim Francis befriending the Evil Angel. "No longer, I take it."

"Oh, no. He never forgave me for not joining his band of rebels. I sometimes wonder if he attacks my clients for that very reason. Your earthly death is a case in point."

That was more interference than Valerian could accept. "Sounds like humbug to me. You think the Devil had some hand in my demise?"

"Possibly. You caused the duel, of course, by seducing Richard Sevaric's wife. But I assumed you would win—you always did—and I did not think to monitor the outcome. How was I to guess his bullet would ricochet off a stone and strike you in the temple?"

Valerian erupted from his chair, more slowly than he would prefer. But he ended up standing on the something-like-a-floor. "*You* caused my death?"

"Certainly not." Francis clucked. "But I might have saved you. At least, I could have moved that stone, although the bullet might have found it anyway. We Guardians never know when our efforts will have any effect. And accidents do happen. If it's any consolation, Sevaric died from a bullet to the heart."

Even after eternity, Valerian felt a certain vindication. "As I intended. So—where is he now?"

"That is none of your concern," Francis replied austerely. "Now pay attention, because Proctor will be here shortly. I have put my reputation on the line and asked an enormous favor on your behalf. For once, try for a little humility and make the most of this opportunity. If you succeed, you will get what you keep wishing for. Unfortunately, that is not what you ought aspire to, but as things stand now we are making no progress whatever."

What he kept wishing for? It couldn't be—he couldn't hope. "You're being as clear as mud," he muttered, just as another Presence manifested itself. An imposing Presence.

Proctor put him in mind of a Roman Senator. Tall and lean, with a stern face and penetrating eyes, he radiated authority. Valerian recognized him again, although he had no solid recollection of their previous meetings.

"You again," Proctor said in a resigned voice. "What is that Earth-proverb about a bad penny? Do sit, Valerian. So long as Francis has gone to the trouble of semimaterializing an office, we may as well use it."

Sullenly, Valerian lounged on the chair and folded his arms. "I suppose I have tripped up again. Damned . . . er . . . blast if I can even remember that last assignment."

"Irrelevant, but you botched it as always." Proctor glanced at Francis. "How much did you explain?"

"Nothing, sir. But I advised him to cooperate."

"That would be a refreshing change." The stern gaze transferred to Valerian and fixed there. "The fact is, Valerian Caine, you have been trouble from the moment you joined us. The only thing I can say in your favor is that with all these galactic storms, we have been too busy to diagnose the exact nature of your difficulties. However, Francis has suggested a solution. For his sake alone, I am considering a radical departure from the usual procedure."

"The usual procedure?" Valerian grimaced. "So far as I can tell, there is no 'usual' in this place."

"It isn't a place, and you are by no means ready to comprehend the slightest aspect of the Divine Plan." Proctor pointed a long finger in his direction. "Know only this. There are many paths a soul may take after a Transition, from physical reincarnation to a position here with the Directors. And you suit none of them."

"That's because you haven't let go your previous existence," Francis put in.

Proctor shot him a dark look, but didn't contradict him.

"Do you mean the life I led before that idiotic duel?" Valerian took a deep breath as memory flooded him. "Of course I can't let it go! I had everything a man could possibly want—good looks, position, money, women. All snatched away because a bullet bounced off a rock. Dammit, I was just twenty-seven years old!"

"And a fool," Proctor said curtly. "A useless, self-absorbed mortal, wasting gifts that should have been put to better use."

"Perhaps." Valerian slumped lower in his chair as that litany of flaws echoed in the mist. "Oh, very well, I made a few mistakes. But—" Cannily he introduced a term he had heard someone use around here. "I never had a chance to *repent.*"

"Death comes like a thief in the night," Proctor intoned.

"You don't say."

Proctor glared at him. Then, with what looked to be an almighty effort, he assumed a more pious face. "We have decided that you will never progress while your spirit continues to hunger for mortal animation. And frankly, we are weary of cleaning up after you here. Therefore, you will be granted one chance to reclaim your former existence. Complete the tasks assigned and you will find yourself in the garden seconds after the duel. This time, Sevaric's bullet will miss you."

Valerian felt a surge of exhilaration. To live again! To feel blood coursing through his body. To taste brandy, to laugh, to hold a woman in his arms. "I'll do anything," he vowed. "What will it take, to go back to what I was?"

"It won't be easy," Proctor warned. "Your dalliance with the Sevaric woman precipitated a feud that has endured, by Earthtime, a hundred years. Caines and Sevarics have been at daggers drawn ever since." He shook his head. "I cannot count the sins, on both sides."

"You hold *me* responsible?"

"In part. A soul is accountable for its own actions, and for the consequences of those acts. But judgment is not mine to pass."

"Thank God," Valerian muttered.

"Exactly." Proctor raised his eyes to the insubstantial ceiling, as if seeking divine patience. "Nevertheless, you are in my charge for what is beginning to seem like an eternity, so I suggest you practice the unaccustomed virtue of self-restraint while I rid myself of you. Otherwise, I shall put you to work hatching dung-beetles."

Valerian slid down an inch in his chair and lowered his head. He could restrain himself, even with Proctor, if he had hope of a return to life.

"Very well then," said Proctor with satisfaction. "We were speaking of the feud. Not long ago the most virulent of the antagonists, Basil Sevaric and Hugo Caine, passed into the Afterlife, and so far their heirs have not pursued the quarrel quite so diligently. We have some hope this matter can be put to rest before old wounds begin to fester in the younger generation. And that, Valerian, is to be your task."

"You expect me to end a feud? But I don't even know why they are fighting. I cannot credit that my affair with Blanche Sevaric was to blame, because heaven knows I was scarcely her first lover."

"Heaven," Proctor informed him dryly, "knows everything. But that does not mean it will all be explained to the likes of you. As a rule, we do not interfere in earthly matters, and you must not count on extraordinary assistance to acquire information you can discover for yourself. If you are to claim your reward, by God you will earn it."

"Whatever you say. So, if everyone, Sevaric and Caine, shakes hands and calls it quits, I may continue my former life?"

"Oh, we shall ask more of you than that." Proctor's patrician lips curled. "Now pay attention, because you will hear this only once. Turn your chair around."

Puzzled, Valerian obeyed and found himself looking at what appeared to be a blank wall. Suddenly it dissolved and he saw a man sitting at a desk, a pen in his hand. He was frowning.

"Maximilian Sevaric," Proctor said.

This was clearly a descendant of Richard Sevaric—darkhaired and dark-browed, with a powerful set of shoulders. He hadn't any of Richard's fashionable pallor, but otherwise, Valerian had to admit, he was better-looking than Richard. More formidable, at least.

A young woman came into view, carrying a cup and saucer, which she handed to Sevaric. He smiled at her warmly, and she perched on the corner of the desk. The girl was plain and petite, with short, curly, ginger-colored hair and a sprinkling of freckles across her nose. She had a stubborn chin, a pursed mouth, and large hazel eyes.

"Gwendolyn Sevaric is the baron's sister," Proctor said. "Until her father died, she kept house for him, and now does the same for her brother. She is unmarried."

"I'm not surprised," Valerian observed. "She's no beauty."

Francis made a tsking noise. "Do not be unkind, boy. It ill becomes you."

"Sorry. But she doesn't look dangerous either. Not like a woman engaged in a lethal feud."

"Appearances are often deceiving," Proctor chided. "If physical beauty reflected the soul, you would surely have been a saint. But—"

"I get the point." Mischief seized Valerian and he glanced over his shoulder at Proctor. "Have you considered that unattractive people may be virtuous only from lack of opportunity to be otherwise?"

"For shame!" Francis scolded. "Sometimes I despair of you, Valerian."

"I begin to think," Proctor said in a forbidding voice, "that this project is doomed to failure before it begins. Obviously you are more suited to marshaling dung beetles."

"It was only a question." Valerian tried, without much hope, to right the situation. "I thought we could be honest here in Heaven."

"Young man, you are so far from Heaven that a millennium of repentance would not open the gates."

The image of the two Sevarics faded, and the wall reappeared. Francis moved, or floated, to Proctor, and the two engaged in a long whispered discussion. Now and again Valerian heard words like "recalcitrant," "degenerate," and "hopeless case." His heart sinking, he wondered if he should go to his knees and beg another chance.

But he couldn't make himself do it. Not to Proctor, that

marble-hearted, censorious brute. Obviously Proctor had never experienced any of the things that made life worth living— passion, curiosity, the sheer excitement of not knowing what the next moment would bring. Proctor had never been human. And if he was an angel, he gave the species a bad name.

"For your sake only, Francis," Proctor said finally, and even in his defiant mood, Valerian felt relief shoot through him. "With a soul like his to guard, I, too, should be close to despair. And don't imagine I shall allow you to intercede on his behalf once we send him back. He must succeed, or fail, on his own."

As their voices lowered again, Valerian cocked his head, trying to hear their discussion. He wasn't altogether sure they were truly speaking; all he sensed was a flow of energy between them.

The energy flow increased, and Valerian could hear again. "Oh, very well, Francis, if you insist," Proctor said grudgingly. "Now and again you may play a part, but I shall monitor you carefully. And his motives must be pure. Given his usual attitude, I doubt you'll have occasion to take action."

Then, without seeming to move, Francis materialized at Valerian's side, placing a hand on his forearm. Valerian saw it without feeling his touch.

"Behave," Francis whispered urgently. "Proctor is losing patience with you."

Brandy. Women. *Life*, Valerian reminded himself, mustering a tone of humility. "I apologize, gentlemen. Only tell me what you expect and I shall do my best."

From behind him, Valerian heard a grunt of disbelief. But the wall dissolved again, and he saw a slender young man with his own green eyes, mobile mouth, and high cheekbones. There the resemblance ended. The youngster had a weak chin, dull brown hair, and the pastiness of a man who spent all his time indoors. Indeed, he was seated at a green baize table, holding a fistful of cards, and wore the grim expression of a loser.

"Robin Caine." To judge from the dry tone, Proctor disapproved of this young man even more than of Valerian. "Viscount

Lynton, the great-great-grandson of your elder brother. You see what a poor specimen your family has dwindled to. He is addicted to drink and gaming, not unlike yourself at his age. Indeed, he has no other interests. In our opinion he is a lost cause, at least in his current existence, and we shall not hold you responsible for salvaging him. But you will have to deal with him nonetheless, hence the introduction."

Robin's image faded, to be replaced by a lovely girl. Valerian sat up straight, something like a pulse thrumming in his veins.

"Dorothea Caine," Proctor said. "Robin's sister."

Like Sevaric, Dorothea was frowning, only this frown was more fetching, just a wrinkle between her perfectly arched brows. Wherever she was, the sun must be shining, because she raised her hand to shield her gray-green eyes. With the other hand, she brushed aside a windblown strand of auburn hair. What she looked at must have pleased her, for the frown dissolved into a sweet secret smile.

Now *this* is a Caine, he thought—full-blooded and true-bred. Almost, Valerian felt a twinge of desire. But a liaison with Dorothea would border on some sort of incest, even though a century separated them. Still, he always enjoyed the company of beautiful women, whether or not he could bed them.

His task, whatever it was, appeared more promising, or at least more interesting, with Dorothea in the picture.

The wall became a wall again and Proctor moved in front of him, a stern look on his gaunt face. "All four of these people are unhappy, for different reasons. It will be your responsibility to change that, except for Robin. He need not concern you." Proctor looked up, concentrating fiercely, as if communing with Something or Someone elsewhere. Then he nodded and focused his cold, colorless eyes on Valerian.

"You will be granted one month, by Earth-time, to fulfill your tasks. When you take form again, remember that on Christmas morning the feud must be at an end. Moreover, Dorothea Caine, Max Sevaric, and Gwendolyn Sevaric must be happy and at peace. And now, since I have far, far better things to do, I will leave Francis to explain the rest."

"You think I will fail," Valerian said flatly.

"Yes." Proctor's image began to shimmer. "I greatly fear that you will be back to torment me all too soon. But if it matters, no creature in the universe wants you to succeed more than I do."

In a blink, Proctor disappeared.

"Well." Valerian lapsed back in his chair with a sigh. "I'm glad *he* isn't God." His eyes narrowed. "Is there actually a God, Francis, or is this all some never-ending nightmare?"

Francis's face glowed brightly. "Of course God exists. He is, always was, always will be. What is the point otherwise?"

"I have no idea," Valerian said glumly. Brandy. Women. Life. That was the point, he told himself. "So, what happens next?"

"You will be returned to Earth, one hundred years after your last visit there. I shall provide you with everything you require to get started, but beyond that I must leave you on your own. To others, you will appear perfectly normal, and in most ways you can function like a mortal man. Alas, that means you are subject to all the foibles and temptations you experienced when you were truly alive. Your ability to resist and overcome your own faults will determine your success."

"You sound nearly as pessimistic about that as Proctor." Valerian stood. "If I've been dead for a century, Francis, how will I know how to go on? Surely things have changed."

"Human nature has not. As for the details, you must be clever and improvise." He stepped forward and placed his fingertips at Valerian's temples. "Are you prepared to go?"

"Yes. Wait! One question first. If God exists, why is Proctor in charge of everything?"

"But he is not," Francis said kindly. "Proctor manages a portion of Creation, nothing more. There are many others like him, appointed to deal with galaxies and worlds you cannot begin to imagine."

Valerian frowned. "But why would a deity leave a whole universe in the hands of stiff-rumped bureaucrats?"

"That you must ask Him, son, if ever you have the opportunity. For the most part, God communes with those who reach out to him in sincere and selfless prayer." Francis sighed. "There are few enough of those. Most who pray are greedy, and ask for foolish things. I've always suspected He devotes Himself to innocent babies because only they are pure of soul. I know that I would do that, given the chance."

"Instead, you are stuck with me."

Francis gazed solemnly into his eyes. "I do His will. Perhaps you will remember me, Valerian, when you return to Earth. I do not know. But I shall be with you, always praying for your success."

"Pray hard, Francis. I want nothing more than to reclaim my life just as it was when I left it."

Francis began to shimmer, and Valerian caught his last words from what seemed like a great distance.

"I want better for you than that."

One

November 1816

His nose was cold.

Valerian reached automatically to rub it and realized that he actually felt the touch of a leather glove against flesh. His eyes shot open.

The dark bare branches of a tree met his gaze. Beyond the tree, he saw the pale blue of a winter sky. He was seated on a wrought-iron bench in what appeared to be a park. Distantly, he heard the rattle of wheels, the clip-clop of horses' hooves, and the sound of human voices.

By God, he was alive!

For a few minutes he savored the pleasure of simple physical sensations. Sucking in a long breath of cool air, he expelled it and watched steam rise from his lips. He wriggled his toes, flexed his arms, and yawned deliciously.

Alive, sentient, everything intact.

It occurred to him that while all his parts appeared to be in place, they might not be the same parts that had presumably been entombed in the Caine family vault a century ago.

He was wearing a heavy, ankle-length coat with capes at the shoulders. Undoing the buttons, he opened it and stretched his legs. Supple boots, sporting tassels, reached to just below his knees. From there, a fawn-colored fabric was practically molded to his thighs. With some pleasure, he recognized his own well-shaped, muscular legs and the prominent, clearly defined bulge at their apex.

No complaints so far, he thought, examining a waistcoat which, to his astonishment, halted at his waist instead of reaching to midthigh. It was singularly devoid of embroidery. Over it, a dark-blue jacket with brass buttons was similarly plain.

English fashion had certainly declined since his previous lifetime. Still, his chest remained broad and his shoulders wide. He peeled off a glove. His hands had been among his chiefest vanities, and he was relieved to see once again the long slender fingers, graceful and strong, always admired by the ladies.

He felt his face and it, too, was familiar, but when he reached behind his neck to touch his hair, his hand met on a high collar. He removed his curly-brimmed, unadorned hat, horrified to discover that his thick, luxuriant hair was clipped to scarcely an inch in length anywhere on his scalp. He plucked a few strands and examined them closely. Chestnut brown, with a hint of auburn. Still his own hair, what was left of it.

Damn. He had loved the sensation of a woman's fingers loosing the ribbon at his queue, stroking his long hair as he kissed her and becoming entangled as he drove her to climax.

No lace at his wrists, and none at his throat—only a starched cloth wrapped around his neck. So far, he had no reason to admire the modern age. Or perhaps he had been revivified as a workingman, one who couldn't afford fancy dress. He supposed he should be grateful. Proctor might have materialized him as a beggar wearing rags.

But rubbing the coat's lapel between his fingers, he discerned quality in the fabric and cut. This was most certainly gentleman's garb.

The gentlemen of the nineteenth century, he concluded, were a benighted lot.

Once he rediscovered his physical form, he had time to wonder where he was. Coming to his feet, he followed a narrow path through the copse of trees until he came to an open patch of winter-brown grass. Just beyond was the curve of a busy road and with some relief, he recognized it immediately.

This was Hyde Park, the eastern edge near Park Lane.

But nothing else was familiar. The road was wider and the traffic heavier than he remembered. In his day, only the wealthiest Londoners could afford to ride rather than walk, but now he counted dozens of carriages rushing by. Perhaps in the century past, London had become more affluent, or the carriages had become cheaper as well as lighter and more graceful.

He did see a few pedestrians on the side paths, swathed in heavy cloaks against the chill. Even the gentlemen looked drab as sparrows. And where were their weapons? No courtier in Valerian's day would stride about the street without a fine short sword to ward off footpads or respond to an impromptu challenge.

London must have become damnably dull in his absence.

Across the way he saw a row of ground-floor shops. With windows. The weak winter sun glanced off the glass, turning it mirrorlike. Valerian felt a surge of excitement. Now he could see if he retained the good looks that his women all loved.

Of course, it meant risking his life. Cautiously, he approached the road edge. A coal wagon sped by, followed closely by an odd-looking contrivance drawn by two horses, the driver perched on a flimsy bench high above large, narrow wheels. Steeling himself, Valerian waited for the next break in traffic and then dashed across the street. He barely missed getting stomped by a rearing cart horse, but made it safely to the other side. Taking a relieved breath, he approached a shop window to examine his reflection.

And saw nothing. Or, rather, he saw people passing behind him on the walk, and vehicles in the street. He touched the pane of glass where his face should have been looking back at him. It was solid and ungiving.

By the rood, was he invisible? A ghost, in fact, even though he could see and feel his body when he looked directly at his hands and legs and feet?

Valerian planted himself in the middle of the walk to test the reaction of passersby. A gentleman took care to walk around him, and a pair of young women giggled and regarded him from beneath fluttering lashes before separating to go by. He turned and doffed his hat when he saw they had paused to look back at him. Giggling even louder, they scurried away.

Yes, indeed, other people could see him. But why could he not see his own reflection? He spied a haberdashery two shops down and entered. Immediately a clerk hurried to assist him, bowing obsequiously and nattering about the fine quality of Mason-David's headwear.

Valerian ignored him and marched directly to a large cheval mirror. He saw only an earnest young man holding out a tall-crowned felt hat for the approval, apparently, of the adjacent hat rack.

'Struth, he must be invisible only to himself. Others, like this shop boy, found nothing amiss. That was a relief. But his inability to see his reflection was a subtle reminder that he existed in this world only by the grace of Proctor—and only for a short few weeks.

In that time, he had to make the acquaintance of three people he wasn't sure he could recognize, assuming he was able to locate them at all in this teeming city. He had to get to know them well enough to end a feud he didn't understand. Then he must see to it they were happy by Christmas Day.

Suddenly aware of the awesome task that lay ahead of him, he walked past the disappointed shop attendant and back out into the chill afternoon. He stood at the street corner, gazing left and right, debating his next move. He had to track down the Sevarics and the Caines—and they might not even be in London.

A few yards away, a handsome black carriage lumbered to a halt. He was wondering how one went about hiring such a conveyance, when the door opened and three women emerged and walked toward him.

Valerian found himself face-to-face with the plain girl he had last seen on a blank wall, handing a cup to Maximilian Sevaric.

Gwendolyn. The freckle-faced sister. She was flanked on one side by a plump, elderly woman who regarded him with apparent approval. To her left, a beautiful and lissome blond lady gazed at him with even greater delight.

Automatically, he removed his hat and made a gallant leg. The blonde and the old lady smiled. The ginger-haired girl frowned, hooked her arms around the elbows of her companions, and drew them past, the heels of her half boots clicking on the pavement.

It was a miracle. Here was the very girl he had been seeking, walking away down the street. She would lead him to the others—and they would lead him back to his former life.

It must have been Francis's doing. No doubt Proctor would rather have revivified him in distant Devon, but Francis had his interests at heart. Here he was, at the right time, in the right place, and with the right girl in sight.

Turning on his heel, he followed the three women from a distance, pondering what to do next. Ladies of Quality spoke to no man before being formally introduced, at least when he had been t'other side of the grave. And if the lovely blonde seemed ready to violate that social rule, Gwendolyn did not.

He trailed them for several blocks, fading back into the crowd whenever they stopped to look into a shop window. When they turned into a side street, he halted, momentarily confused. There was nothing in that direction, was there?

But in the century he had been dead, everything had changed. Doubtfully, he approached the corner, and found beyond it a street where there had once been nothing but a rocky field. The ladies were a dozen yards ahead, just entering an establishment with a sign over the doorway that read Gunter's.

What sort of place was it? he wondered. Would a man go in there? He certainly didn't want to follow them into a shop that specialized in lady's undergarments. Crossing the street, he leaned against a brick wall and tried to look inconspicuous.

After a few minutes, it occurred to him to check his clothes for pockets. Sure enough, in the greatcoat he found a card labeled "Pulteney's Hotel," followed by an address. He recognized the street, but not the establishment.

Much to his astonishment, there was also a pocket in one of the odd, tail-like contrivances hanging over his buttocks. What had possessed men, he wondered, to abandon jackets that ended evenly at the knees, back to front? Glancing down, he couldn't help but admire the fitted breeches that sculpted his legs, but those tails! Most absurd.

The pocket held a slender wallet containing folded paper. Money, he decided after studying the notes, although he had no idea how much they were worth. Whatever happened to gold and silver coins?

With a sigh, he edged around the corner and folded his arms, deciding to wait out of sight until Gwendolyn emerged. Then he would follow her, at a distance, and discover where she lived. Now and again he saw people hailing coaches that were clearly for hire. What would he do if Gwendolyn did the same and made off before he could discover her direction?

Nearly half an hour passed before he saw the three women come out of Gunter's and stroll down the street, chatting happily. When Gwendolyn glanced over her shoulder, he ducked into a tobacco shop, and when he emerged they had disappeared.

Breathlessly, he hurried in the direction they'd been walking, but he had lost them. He went back to the closest intersection and tried three directions before spotting the plumed lavender hat of the blond beauty half a block ahead. The ladies had paused to look at something in a shop window. Once again he turned his back, pretending to examine a display of chamber pots in the window next to him. Those looked the same, at least in shape, he decided, although he wasn't sure he'd ever want to pizzle in a pot adorned with lilies and nymphs.

When the ladies moved on he edged closer, casting about for some excuse to approach Gwendolyn again. Devil take it, how was he to make contact? Any moment now she might hail a vehicle and disappear.

Recklessly, he wished for another miracle. If one of those

coaches swept down as she crossed the street, he could leap out and save her. The drama of it tickled his fancy, and it was several moments before he realized his fantasy was coming true.

At the next intersection, Gwendolyn moved ahead of the other women, speaking to them over her shoulder. At the same time, from a few yards away, something frightened a pair of matched grays pulling an elegant carriage. Panicked, they raced directly toward Gwendolyn.

He was almost too late. Barely in time he launched himself into the street and managed to shove her away from the stampeding horses. Something hit him hard aside the head and he rolled into the gutter.

As consciousness faded, he heard screams and saw the blond woman leaning over him. Not you, he thought with a twinge of regret. I don't need you.

Then everything went black.

Two

"He'll live," said a high-pitched male voice. "Beyond that I dare not prognosticate. Head injuries are unpredictable, and he has been unconscious a long time. That does not bode well."

Valerian lifted his eyelids a fraction. Slowly the room took focus—a bedroom, pleasantly furnished. It was late afternoon, to judge by the light slanting in through the window. He was lying in bed, covered with a soft blue wool blanket. At the foot of the bed was a short man in a black frock coat and bagwig. The sunlight glinted off the gold head of his cane. A physician, he realized, obscurely comforted to learn that at least the medical men still dressed properly.

The physician was speaking to a broad-shouldered man— Maximilian Sevaric. Careful not to move, Valerian peered at them through his lashes. Once the roar in his ears subsided, he could even hear them.

"So what are the possible consequences?" Sevaric's voice was deep, authoritative, and impatient. "He saved my sister's life, Dr. Murkin. I want him to have the best of treatment."

"I've cleaned the scalp wound," the doctor said calmly. "He has no other injuries, beyond a few scrapes and bruises. But if there is swelling in the brain, he may well be disordered mentally, for some time. Loss of memory, that sort of thing. Usually it is temporary, but complete amnesia is not unheard of. We'll know nothing more until he wakes up."

When Sevaric glanced in his direction, Valerian immediately closed his eyes.

Amnesia. The perfect solution! How better to account for his failure to know how the world went on during the hundred years he was dead? Casting back, he found no Proctor-implanted knowledge. The last he recalled, it was 1716, and George I was King of England.

"And my sister?" Sevaric's boots clicked as he paced the floor. "Was she hurt?"

"Just minor scratches and bruises. She insisted I see to the gentleman first, but I'll tend her wounds now. Where is she?"

Valerian heard more footsteps, the sound of a door closing, and low voices from an adjacent room. When he was sure he was alone, he opened his eyes and looked around curiously.

The bedchamber was small and simply appointed. No heavy canopy or brocade drapes around the bed, alas. And he was clad in a linen nightshirt—the first time he'd ever worn anything in bed.

His head throbbed abominably. Proctor's little joke, no doubt. Apparently he was to experience all the dire consequences of being alive, although he wasn't. Not really. Or was he?

Tossing back the covers, he stumbled to the dressing table and looked into the mirror. Still nothing. "Francis?" He pressed his hand to his temple to stop the pounding so he could hear better. "What are the rules?"

But all he heard were voices from the hallway, and as the door opened, he dove under the covers and lay like one dead.

"Do you know this man?" That was Max Sevaric.

"Never saw him until now," replied a haughty male voice. "Did I fail to make myself clear? The agency sent me to the Pulteney Hotel with instructions to present myself to a Mr. Jocelyn Vayle. His luggage had been delivered and a reservation secured, but the gentleman had yet to arrive."

Jocelyn Vayle? Was that supposed to be his name? And who was the man who arrived to meet this Jocelyn Vayle? Valerian decided it was time to regain consciousness. Emitting a low moan, he shifted on the bed and opened his eyes.

A pair of rather lovely hazel eyes, flecked with gold, stared down at him from a few inches away. Skeptical eyes, in a feminine face.

"Ah. I rather thought he was awake," Gwen said crisply. "His mouth was twitching."

It was not, he wanted to say, offended. Forcing a disoriented expression, he groaned deeply. There was nothing like a play for sympathy to win over the ladies.

Gwen, still bent over him for a close inspection, didn't seem impressed. "He looks fine to me," she declared, leaning back.

"Thank God." Max came to her side, and soon the bed was surrounded with people, all gazing at him from close range.

Valerian felt like a particularly interesting bug pinned to a blotter. "Wh-where am I?" he murmured.

"You were brought to my home after the accident," Max told him. "I am Max Sevaric."

"Accident?" Valerian reached to his head. This time he didn't have to fake the groan. "I don't remember. What happened?"

"A carriage nearly ran my sister down, and you pushed her out of the way just in time. You have no recollection of it?"

"Is she all right?" Valerian interrupted. "Your sister. Was she hurt?"

"I'm perfectly fine," Gwen put in. "Surely you cannot have forgot an act of supreme heroism?" Her voice was tinged with sarcasm.

He sighed soulfully. "I'm afraid so. But I am glad to have been of service, if indeed I was."

"I warned you," the doctor said to Max in an undertone. "Clearly his mind is uncertain."

The devil you say, Valerian almost retorted, but instead he brought his brows together in a frown of concentration. "Disordered? Is it? 'Struth, my head hurts like the devil, though I can see you well enough and your words make sense. But I don't know who you are." His brow furrowed. "Now that I consider it, I don't know who *I* am."

"Oh my." The pudgy woman from the corner of the bed laid

a hand on her heart and tilted her head as if praying. "The poor boy."

Valerian recognized the elderly lady who had been walking with Gwen before the accident. Her chaperone, he supposed. He could already tell she was much kinder than her young charge. He winced a bit in her direction, and she said, "Oh my" again and patted the coverlet over his leg.

"There is nothing to worry about just now. You'll be better in a trice." Despite his bracing words, Max wore a look of concern. "And your name is Jocelyn Vayle."

"Are you sure?" Valerian managed another frown, though all that manipulation of his brow made his bruised temple ache the worse. "It doesn't sound familiar."

"We found calling cards in the pocket of your coat, and the address of the Pulteney Hotel written on one of them. Apparently you were expected there. I sent a footman to inquire, and he has just now returned with your luggage and valet."

Valerian's gaze shifted to the slender man with a hooked nose and colorless eyes. He was standing behind Gwen, an expression of imperious indifference on his face. He didn't look like a valet, but perhaps in this benighted century, valets no longer looked like servants. "You are my valet?"

"If you approve." Only a fool would not, his tone implied. An insolent instant too late, he added, "Sir. I am Clootie. Sent by the Hobson Agency. You may be assured I have vast experience in all matters of proper attire and am wholly dedicated to fulfilling your every wish."

It was an odd thing for a manservant to say. But Clootie could only be an emissary from the Powers—such a haughty valet would appeal to Proctor's perverse sense of irony.

On pure instinct, Valerian disliked the man. He put it down to Clootie's association with Proctor. But there was nothing for it but to rub along as best they could. Heaven knew he required a valet, as he couldn't shave or dress himself without the use of a mirror.

Gwen bent over him again. It was a solicitous pose, but there wasn't a hint of solicitude in her narrowed eyes and pursed lips. "Do you truly remember nothing of the accident, Mr. Vayle? Not your name, or where you came from? What is the very last thing you recall?"

He made a helpless gesture. He could hardly reply *1716*, but he worried she might detect a direct lie. She had such sharp eyes.

"Gwen." Max tugged her away from the bed. Valerian warmed to him immediately. "Mr. Vayle has been injured. We must not press him."

"Exactly." The doctor stopped gathering up his supplies long enough to say firmly, "He must rest. Only with rest can he be expected to recover his memory."

"Perhaps there are clues in his luggage," Gwen said stubbornly. "I shall examine the contents and—"

"Oh my, that would not be proper," the older woman protested. Her voice dropped to a whisper. "You cannot rummage through a gentleman's unmentionables, Gwen."

"I'll see to it," Max said, "but only if you've no objection, Mr. Vayle."

"I have nothing to hide," Valerian replied, waving his hand. "At least, I hope that is the case. Do let me know what you find, because no one is more curious than I about my past." That was the right note to strike, he thought, concerned but admirably candid. "And where am I to go from here, Lord Sevaric? I cannot impose on your hospitality much longer. Did I perchance have any money in my pockets?"

"A hundred pounds," Max said, as if it were no great sum. "But you are not to think of leaving until your health is recovered. We are obligated to you, Mr. Vayle, and Sevarics always honor their debts."

Sevaric. Even after a century, that name unnerved him. Once, a man who looked very much like this Max had shouted, "Sevarics always avenge dishonor!"

The room suddenly felt close and hot. Valerian turned a wavering smile on the five people hovering over him. "Forgive me, but I fear I require a bit of privacy. And perhaps the services of my valet for a few minutes."

Max understood and gestured commandingly toward the door. Within seconds the room was vacated except for Clootie, who fetched the chamber pot from under the bed.

"I seem to be functioning normally," Valerian said when the valet had resettled him under the sheets.

"Whyever not?" Clootie inquired over his shoulder as he carried the ceramic container into the privy room.

Valerian had not realized he spoke aloud and reminded himself that he must be careful. What amazed him would seem ordinary to everyone else. They would not understand that he was feeling out the parameters of his new existence. But he could always invoke the head injury to explain his disorientation.

"Are you familiar with London?" he asked when Clootie returned.

"Of course." The valet's lips stretched into a thin, knowing smile. "Especially the sorts of places a young gentleman might enjoy visiting. You have only to inquire."

Apparently in this century valets functioned as panderers as well as dressers. It was something to keep in mind, certainly. "Perhaps later," Valerian temporized. "First we ought to come to terms, I suppose. I would like to employ you, but for some reason I expect my stay to be temporary."

"My wages were paid in advance," Clootie replied. Again he smiled in that knowing way, a smile that never made it to his eyes. "For precisely one month."

No doubt about it, this man had been sent by Proctor. Could Clootie be, in fact, his Guardian in disguise? It was quite a disguise, if so. "Would your first name happen to be Francis?"

Clootie's eyes flashed. "Indeed not. Why would you think so?"

Valerian settled back onto the pillows, oddly disappointed. Francis, he knew somehow, wouldn't lie. "I meant no offense. Perhaps you remind me of someone I once knew."

"That may well be true," Clootie said, his voice ominous. "But I can assure you, his name was not Francis."

Before Valerian could follow up on that curious statement, Max entered the room, his arms full of paper.

"I've brought a few newspapers, if you feel up to scanning them. A name, or an event, may prod your memory." He put them on the table beside the bed. "Clootie, a cot in the dressing room next door is being readied for you. You may go and unpack Mr. Vayle's luggage. And Vayle, the doctor says you are to sleep as much as possible. Use the bellpull if you require any service." He nodded and left.

A military man indeed, Valerian reflected as Clootie exited without a word. Max Sevaric knew how to give orders.

He stared at the ceiling. In the center was a plaster medallion of a star radiating beams. "Francis? Are things going as they ought?"

Silence.

Without pleasure, Valerian considered that he might have to accomplish his tasks without Heavenly Help. A nuisance, that. But he shouldn't forget Clootie, though the help he had suggested wasn't precisely heavenly—the addresses of places where young men enjoyed themselves. After a century spent nowhere, he was ready for a bit of enjoyment.

He was lying. About what, Gwen didn't know. But she trusted her instincts, and they were shrieking. Jocelyn Vayle, if that was his true name, was a liar.

The amnesia was suspect enough, and all those groans were a bit too theatrical to be plausible. Still, she might have dismissed her suspicions as fanciful if she hadn't been watching his face when Max invited him to stay. She couldn't mistake the gleam of triumph in her rescuer's green eyes—he had been planning on this very opportunity.

The hall was deserted as she waited outside the sickroom door. As soon as her brother came out, she took him by the arm and pulled him into the little sitting room she shared with Winnie. Max was clearly annoyed by her high-handedness, but he closed the door and with exaggerated patience, gestured for her to speak.

Gwen took a deep breath and launched into her prepared speech. Unfortunately, she was too upset to give it in the way she had prepared, in the quiet reasonable tone that worked best with her brother. "Max, what are you thinking, inviting him to take up residence with us? We don't know anything about him!" Even to her own ears, her question sounded more like an accusation.

And as she might have predicted, Max's face grew cold and stern. "He saved your life. That's all I need to know—and all you need to know."

Stay calm, she told herself. Reasonable. She sat down on the edge of the couch and clasped her hands in her lap in a penitent manner. "Yes, he did rescue me. And it's not that I'm not grateful, for I am. But Max, he could be anyone! He won't give us any information about his past, so that we might question his friends and family."

Impatiently, Max exclaimed, "He doesn't know his past, do you recall? He lost his memory—by taking the impact that might have killed you."

Her hands unclasped, and then tightened into fists. "Don't you think that was rather convenient, this loss of memory?"

"Convenient? Blasted inconvenient, I'd say. And if you're implying he's lying about it, you're wrong. I've seen the same thing many times after a battle. It usually doesn't last, this loss of memory, but it's disorienting. Went through it myself, after Ciudad Rodrigo. I knew my name well enough, but couldn't remember any of the events of the battle. Shock, you know."

"Perhaps."

Gwen couldn't disguise her skepticism, and her brother's face clouded over. "What are you suggesting?"

"If he's lost his memory, how is it he came to call you 'Lord

Sevaric'? You introduced yourself as Max Sevaric. How does he know you are a lord?"

Max shook his head. "What a mind you have, to seize on some detail like that. He might have seen a coat of arms somewhere. Or just looked around him and presumed this was a noble's house. Needn't be any suspicious reason at all."

"But I saw the look in his eyes when you invited him to stay with us. He was—almost gleeful. As if his plan had succeeded."

"His plan? What plan? Come now, Gwen, you can't think that he planned for that carriage accident? Threw himself in front of it? Risked his life just to insinuate himself into our household?"

Put that way, it did seem rather unlikely. But Gwen couldn't give it up. "He could be a criminal, in hiding from the law. Or he could be hoping to steal something from us—"

"What rubbish!" The sun was setting outside, and Max crossed to the table and turned up the lamp. In the glow that framed him, Gwen could see his jaw tightening. "He's an honest fellow, I can tell. And a courageous one, too, with quick instincts. I'd have him guard my back without a qualm."

Gwen sighed and let it drop. Her brother was a plain man— oh, not in appearance; he had, as their mother used to declare, gotten all the family's dark dramatic looks, and now, scowling at her, resembled nothing so much as one of Lord Byron's heroes.

But in his character, Max was plain, even simple. He had no patience with ambiguity. A man was good, or he was bad, and a bad man couldn't have a good trait like courage. Her rescuer had courage; therefore he must be entirely good.

Gwen sometimes wished that she shared her brother's idealism, but she had been born a skeptic. And life had done nothing to dispel her belief that appearances couldn't be trusted, especially where men were concerned.

And this man's appearance—so demonically tempting— couldn't be trusted. She knew that the moment when she first saw him, those startlingly clear green eyes narrowed at her in surprise and anticipation. He didn't look at her as a man might look at a woman he wanted—Gwen hadn't been the recipient of any of those looks, but she had seen enough of them directed at her friend Anathea to know the difference.

No, he had regarded her as if she was the prize in some mysterious quest. And she had seen that same look just now, when he thought he had won a place in their home.

She turned back to find Max regarding her with that annoyed masculine confusion. She knew she tested his patience and his devotion, for try as he might he couldn't ever make her fit his concept of what a little sister should be. But he loved her anyway, and she supposed she should be glad of that.

So she said, "Oh, don't mind me. That accident just overset me, I suppose. Mr. Vayle did me a service and was injured in the deed, and surely it's only right that we shelter him until he is recovered."

Max's scowl cleared away, and he smiled at her approvingly. She knew that she had managed to return to the sweet little sister he preferred. She didn't want to ruin this, so she took a deep breath and added in a conciliatory voice, "But we must help him determine his identity, and locate his connections. He won't want to stay here indefinitely."

Max nodded, frowning again, but this time not at her. "He seems rather foreign, don't you think? Oh, he's British-born, perhaps, but his accent is odd. Perhaps he's a colonial, recently come home to England. I should send notes round to the captains of ships arrived from India and Canada, to see if they recognize his name."

The prospect of taking positive action restored Max's good humor, and he dropped a kiss on her forehead as he headed for his study. "While I do that, you'll see to Vayle's comfort, won't you? The medico said he should have gruel—could you tell the cook to prepare that?"

Gwen only nodded. She had no desire to play Lady Bountiful to a man she didn't trust. But bringing the mysterious Mr. Vayle his gruel would give her a chance to observe him, and perhaps to interrogate him.

He was hiding something, she could tell, something more than just his supposedly lost identity. And she was determined to find out what that was, before he won over her brother entirely and started borrowing large sums from him, or used him as an introduction to society.

Three

As the sun set and evening gathered outside, Valerian sat up in his bed and took stock of his predicament. If he wanted to be restored to his old life, he would have to get some control of his new life—starting with his new identity.

'Struth, 'twould be less complicated if he really did have amnesia. At least then he truly would have a blank where his past was. Instead, he was compelled to juggle two names, his own and one wholly unfamiliar to him. Unless he contrived to forget his real identity, he would doubtless trip himself up.

Therefore, and from this moment on, he must think of himself as Jocelyn Vayle. Introduce himself as Jocelyn Vayle. Answer immediately to Jocelyn Vayle. Most important, he must not even twitch when someone mentioned "Caine," which was bound to happen eventually.

His family had called him "Val" until he decided that was too unsophisticated for a young man about town. "Vayle" was close enough, he supposed, to catch his attention when people addressed him.

He leaned against the bank of pillows, closed his eyes, and murmured "I am Vayle, I am Vayle" until he almost believed it.

But not quite. "I cannot manage this on my own," he said aloud. "Help me out, Francis."

A sudden noise almost sent him off the bed. Sitting bolt upright, he looked around in confusion, expecting an apparition.

Instead, the door opened and Gwendolyn Sevaric stood there, outlined by the lamplight from the hallway. "Were you calling for someone, Mr. Vayle? If you require a servant, there is a bellpull just beside you."

With effort, he mustered a smile. "Did I cry out? I must have been dreaming. Forgive me for disturbing you."

"You did not," she said flatly, crossing to the wall sconce to turn up the light. "We have brought your dinner. Winnie, you may come in now."

The pudgy chaperone entered the room, glancing at the bed, then ducking her head as if afraid to be caught looking. Quickly, she faded back into the corner, so that Vayle could hardly make her out in the shadows. For such a substantial woman, she was good at effacing herself.

A footman followed with a tray and stood at attention next to the bed.

Vayle gazed at the silver dishes with delight. Food! After a hundred years, the very thought set his stomach rumbling. To taste again! To swirl wine on his tongue, to chomp into rare roast beef and creamy cheese and warm crusty bread. A meal would set all his appetites aflame—and that was how he best liked his appetites.

"You are a ministering angel," he told Gwen as the footman set the tray on his lap.

"Hardly." With a sweeping gesture, she lifted the silver cover from the bowl. Underneath was a pale, lumpy blob, something like paste diluted with glue.

"Gruel." She set the cover down on the night table and looked at the tray with a satisfied smile. "There is cream, and a bit of sugar for sweetening if you like. Also a pot of weak tea."

He stared at her in dismay. "But I don't *like* gruel. Not that I've ever eaten any, but I can tell by looking at it that it is not to my taste."

"You aren't meant to like it, Mr. Vayle. No one does." She picked up the spoon and dipped it into the glutinous mixture, letting blobs of it fall back into the bowl. It was all too clear that she was enjoying this. "But gruel is nourishing and will not overtax your weakened digestive system."

"The carriage clipped me on the head, not the belly." Steeling himself, he looked down again at the mess in the bowl. It was even more repellent now that she had stirred it up. "I assure you that most parts of me are in perfect functioning order. What's more," he added plaintively, "I'm ravenous."

The chaperone crept up to the bedside, her face troubled. "Miss Gwen, perhaps—"

His tormentor shook her head. "Doctor's orders, Winnie. He said Mr. Vayle is to have gruel, and gruel he shall have."

He crossed his arms and gritted his teeth. "I won't eat it!"

"But you will. Because Winnie and I shall stay with you until you've swallowed every bite." She drew up a chair and sat down right next to the bed. Her hands lay poised in her lap, ready at any instant to seize the spoon and force-feed him. "We are responsible for your good health, and it is no more than my Christian duty to repay you for saving my life. Sit down, Winnie. We'll keep Mr. Vayle company while he dines."

He regarded her through narrowed eyes. What kind of woman rewarded her rescuer with a bowl of pap? Gwen Sevaric was determined to punish him, for no reason he could imagine. Those hazel eyes of hers were gleaming with irony and suspicion.

She had suspected him from the very start. In their first encounter on the street, when he had smiled and bowed, she had drawn her skirts in and glared at him as if he had insulted her. What the devil was wrong with bowing? True, he'd been after her, but she could not have known that. Then he risked his very life to shove her out of the path of stampeding horses.

Altogether gallant, in his opinion.

Certainly not deserving of gruel.

Perhaps Sevarics had an inbred dislike of Caines, so instinctive that Gwen felt it without knowing who he was. But Max liked him well enough. And until Gwen, he had never met a woman able to resist his charm, nor one who had tried. Gwen, he suspected, didn't even have to try.

He glanced over at Winnie, who gave him a tremulous smile. When he smiled back, the color rose in her cheeks and she simpered like a girl. Now *that* was more like it. Winnie, he realized, he could twist about his finger. That knowledge might come in handy someday.

But Gwen—no smile was likely to sway *her*. She wouldn't even let herself be distracted from the gruel. When he looked at her beseechingly, she only tilted her head. "Do begin, sir. Your dinner will taste better warm, I suspect."

With a sigh, he picked up the spoon. Making Gwen happy was one of his tasks, and at all costs he must win her over. It was his misfortune that her happiness at this moment seemed to depend on torturing him with gruel.

But then, should he fail, he would wind up in Hell, where gruel was probably the only item on the menu.

"You are most kind," he said, raising his spoon to his lips. The words tasted nearly as bad as the meal. When the first bite stuck in his throat like a clump of glue, he grabbed for the teacup. It was empty.

"Allow me," said Gwen, taking the cup and filling it from the pot while he choked and sputtered. As he swallowed the lukewarm tea, she added cream to the gruel.

His gorge rose, but manfully he plowed in again. It tasted no better, but at least it didn't clot up in his throat any longer. Finally he succeeded in emptying half the bowl without casting up his accounts.

Winnie clucked sympathetically as he gulped at the tea again, and Gwen smiled that ironic cat-smile he was coming to loathe. "It must be rather terrifying," she said, "not knowing who you are. Have you no recollections at all?"

Grateful for a reason to stop eating, he made a vague gesture. "None whatever. When Lord Sevaric told me my name was Jocelyn Vayle, I felt as though I were hearing it for the first time."

She leaned forward, elbows on her thighs, and propped her chin in her hands. "How odd that you speak perfect English and know how to use a spoon. I wonder that you have forgotten some things and not others."

"Should you rather I found myself helpless as a squalling babe?" He grinned. "You'd not have liked changing my nappies, I warrant."

Gwen flushed to the roots of her hair and Vayle knew he'd scored a point. Discomposing the arrogant Miss Sevaric was an achievement he savored.

" 'Struth, I cannot explain what has happened to me," he said in a kinder voice. "And I regret this inconvenience to your family. But I cannot be sorry that I chanced to be passing by when you were in danger."

Get out of *that*, he thought smugly.

But he found that Gwen was better at offense than at defense—or perhaps they were the same thing for her. She turned her head inquiringly to the side and remarked, "Did you truly just 'chance' by? I ask because you appeared to recognize us earlier, when we passed you on the street. Do you remember?"

Vayle assumed an innocent, befuddled expression. "I recall nothing before waking up in this bed. What did I say?"

"You did not speak. But you looked as if you wanted to." She frowned and poured him more tea. "I suppose it meant nothing. Lady Anathea was with us, and there was never a man who didn't want to make her acquaintance."

"Anathea? What an unusual name."

"She is exceedingly beautiful. A true Incomparable."

He agreed completely, except, of course, he wasn't supposed to remember the buxom Anathea. Gwen didn't sound envious, he decided. Only a bit forlorn. Plain as she was, especially with those pursed lips, she was doubtless accustomed to being ignored. Vayle had to admit that he himself wouldn't ordinarily have noticed Gwendolyn, not if Anathea was about.

"I was there, too," Winnie put in. These were the first words she had addressed directly to Vayle, and they were accompanied by another girlish blush.

He turned to her with a wide smile. "That explains why you ladies caught my attention. How could I pass by the Three Graces without making my bow?"

Gwen shot him an irritated look. "You have not finished your dinner, sir."

"Oh, yes, I have." He rubbed his temples, his discomfort real this time. That gruel might as well have been poison. "I seem to have the headache again. Perhaps I will recollect more at breakfast. Don't ask me how I know," he added cunningly, "but I'm certain that I usually dine on beefsteak in the mornings."

Gwen came to her feet and took the tray. "Gruel," she said crisply, "until Dr. Murkin says otherwise. And we don't expect him to call again for several days."

Vayle watched her stalk from the room and could not help observing the well-shaped rump under her drab brown skirt. No beauty, Miss Sevaric, but she did have a trim figure.

Winnie trailed behind, casting a look over her shoulder from the door. "You will let me know if I can do anything for you?" she whispered when Gwen was out of range.

"Perhaps another lamp," he said after a moment. "I'll try to sleep, but I seem to have an aversion to darkness."

Winnie nodded, and soon a footman appeared and set a lamp on the table beside the bed.

"Can you procure a glass of wine?" Vayle asked hopefully.

"No, sir." The footman looked guiltily toward the door. "Miss Sevaric would have my head."

"Is she always such a tyrant?"

Their tentative amity vanished as the footman drew himself up austerely. "We are all fond of her, sir," he said, and left, closing the door firmly behind him.

The man never denied she was a tyrant, though, Vayle thought as he kicked away the covers. Just that her servants were fond of her nonetheless. He could understand that, he supposed. Prickly as she was, Gwen did have some redeeming qualities. She had lovely eyes, and a sharp intellect, and, he admitted, an astute sense of irony. Even her refusal to succumb to his charm was rather stimulating.

Vayle refused to credit Gwen, much less her gruel, but he couldn't deny that he was suffering few ill effects from his encounter with the carriage. Except for a steady throb in his head and a gnawing at his stomach, he felt healthy, even restless—too restless to stay abed.

Throwing off the covers, he swung his legs out of the bed and stood up. The dizziness almost overwhelmed him, but he grabbed hold of the chair back and concentrated on its undeniable reality. After Proctor's incorporeal office, he took great comfort in the substantiality of oak.

He couldn't leave the room without rousing Gwen's ire, so he went to the window and opened the casement. The evening chill was pleasing, for it reminded him yet again that he had a body and that it experienced sensations. He leaned into the darkness, marveling at the lamps lining the street as far as he could see. Even as he watched, a boy raised a long pole to the lamp at the top of one iron post, bringing it to flame before moving to the next. How festive they made the night, glowing like golden halos in the still air.

He'd always loved the night, that time of mystery and excitement. Now the soft hush, the soft glow, beckoned to him, reminding him of how many adventures lingered in the shadows of the evening. The gaming hells would be lively at this hour, and doubtless he'd encounter a willing woman with her own vacant bed.

With a sigh of regret, he drew his head in and closed the window. Ah well. 'Twould have to wait. But tomorrow night he'd sample the delights of this new century, because except for the amnesia he intended to make an immediate and miraculous recovery.

With a sigh, he turned up the lamp on the side table and looked around for entertainment. The stack of newspapers caught his eye. Sevaric had left them in hopes he'd recognize a familiar name. Not bloody likely. But he picked up a copy of the *Times* and began to read.

Just seeing the date gave him a shiver. The 26th of November, 1816. Until this moment, it had not truly struck him. He'd been dead for a hundred years! And six months, for the duel had been fought in May.

After a while he set the paper aside, having learned more than he cared to about a recent war with France. But that was scarcely noteworthy. This one seemed more conclusive than most, though there was much dissension among the victorious allies. At least they agreed about one thing—they were all glad to imprison someone named Bonaparte on a remote island. Vayle knew a moment's empathy for the unknown exile, for he felt himself marooned in an alien century, and his escape home was far from certain.

Distances must be shorter now. This journal was reporting diplomatic events that had occurred only three days earlier in Paris. In Vayle's day, Paris fashions were obsolete before they finally made it to British shores. Now, he supposed, he might be able to order a coat or waistcoat from France and expect it within a fortnight!

Modernity had its appeal, but it was some comfort to learn that human nature had not changed one jot in the last century, just as Francis had predicted. Scattered about the newspaper were snippets of gossip about adultery, extravagant wagers, and other scandals. People were aflutter about one Beau Brummell, a dandy, apparently, who had fled the country to escape his creditors.

Had there been a publication like this one in 1716, Valerian Caine would have been prominently featured. Back then, he was the most interesting person in London, a gossip's dream, in fact. His gaming for high stakes always attracted attention—though he usually won and never once had to flee to the Continent. The most beautiful women vied for access to his bed. And jealous husbands occasionally challenged him even after he established his lethal reputation. Risk, love, and danger—

The perfect life. He could hardly wait to reclaim it.

But first there was the nuisance of completing his task. At least Max Sevaric would be easy to manipulate, because it was clear the man's rigid code of honor had been temporarily diverted by the feud. It wouldn't take much to set him straight again.

The stiff-lipped sister would be more difficult to handle.

Gwendolyn's stubbornness could very well do him in. He'd only just met her, but he understood women, and he could tell this one had never been happy. If there was any joy she wanted for herself, she had long since given up hope of achieving it.

Gwen Sevaric was like a castle under siege, armed for defense. She would let no one come close. He sensed that, without knowing why. Else, he thought, she would have succumbed to his charm before this.

True, she had no looks to speak of. To marry well—and a woman had no other possible aspiration—she required beauty, title, and fortune. Two of the three, at least. The Sevarics lived well, to judge by this house set in front of a parklike square. But there was no sign of an immense fortune to attract a suitor. As for title, Max was a mere baron, and the Sevaric history was nothing to boast of. All in all, Gwen had little to offer a husband but a sharp tongue, and what man would voluntarily wed a shrew?

Supernatural intervention was required to make her happy, but Vayle did not expect Proctor to hand him a miracle. In fact, Gwen put him forcibly in mind of Proctor. Both were the kind to serve up gruel, real or virtual, just to watch him squirm.

With a groan, he stacked the newspapers on the side table and folded his arms across his chest. So far he'd met the Sevarics and taken their measure. One would be easy to handle, the other well nigh impossible.

What of the Caines? From the vision Proctor had granted him, he knew that Dorothea was beautiful. No surprise, since good looks ran in his family, but he'd a faint recollection of intelligence in her eyes. Unfortunate, that. A stupid but lovely woman would be more easily managed.

Somehow he must contrive a meeting with Dorothea without Max knowing of it. That meant venturing into the city on his own, all the while maintaining a residence here. Max would be

sympathetic and buy his pose as a healthy but disoriented am-
nesiac, but Gwen—

"Mr. Vayle?"

Startled, he looked up to see Winnie enter the room, a large
tray balanced on her stomach. The rich odor of juicy beef and
hot bread wafted to his nostrils and brought tears to his eyes.

"Forgive me if I disturbed you," she said in a timorous voice.
With an awkward little dance step, she kicked the door closed
behind her. "I thought you might be hungry."

He opened his arms. "Bless your heart, sweet lady. You are
the answer to my prayers."

"*Shhh.*" She glanced over her shoulder at the closed door.
"I'll be turned off if we are discovered." Tiptoeing to the bed,
she handed him the tray and jerked back as if expecting immediate punishment for her daring escapade.

He'd have come to his feet and hugged her if not for the tray
on his lap. Why was she so frightened? Would the Sevarics cast
her out for so little reason? The Sevaric baron he'd killed in the
duel was of such a disposition, or so his wife had maintained,
but neither Max nor Gwen seemed quite so bloodthirsty.

"This smells delicious," he said carefully, "but not for all the
world would I make trouble for you."

Winnie's hands fluttered. "Please, enjoy yourself. And pray
do not fret about my security. I have no reason to fear dis-
missal—Lord Sevaric and Miss Gwen have been all that is
kind. I only fear to offend them by taking advantage."

For my sake, he thought with a shaft of awareness. "They
are concerned for my health," he said, "but you have seen that
I am well enough except for the headache. Thank you, Miss
Winifred, and this shall remain our secret. Will you keep me
company while I eat?"

Flushing hotly, Winnie drew up a chair.

For all she must be fifty years old, her eyes reminded him of
an alert, wary kitten longing to be stroked. No man had ever
made love to her, he knew with certainty. Almost no one had
ever paid her any attention whatever.

In fact, he'd not have given her a second thought a hundred years ago, not even if she'd brought him a plate like the one he saw when he lifted the silver cover—roast beef smothered in juices, a fat potato slathered with butter, mushrooms stuffed with sausage and cheese. How she had managed this he didn't know. Why she had done so for a stranger he wasn't ready to ask.

Especially as he intended to pry her for information. Guilt tickled at his throat, but still he swallowed the first bite of rare beefsteak. It was delicious. This one bite was more real to him than a hundred years in the Afterlife had been.

"You said that you are new here," he began over a mouthful of potato. "Were you not always Miss Sevaric's chaperone?"

"Only since Lord Sevaric's return after Waterloo," she replied. "I am a cousin three times removed, and resided in Yorkshire with my sister until he asked me to come here. Miss Gwen lived with her father until he died of apoplexy, or some other ailment. I'm not sure. After that she was here by herself in this house until her brother sold out. He thought to launch her into society and knew she would require a companion."

"So you have been dancing at all the fashionable balls?" he asked, raising his fork in mock salute.

She sighed, and gazed off into the distance. Vayle suspected she was envisioning the color and light of a great ball. "Alas, no. Miss Gwen has no interest in balls, or any other gatherings. Oh, please don't think I am complaining. We take walks in the park, and visit the subscription libraries and sometimes stop for ices at Gunter's. In truth, I have enjoyed myself immensely and am ever so grateful to be here in London. I only wish—"

He swallowed a mushroom. "What? What do you wish?"

"They are both so lonely," Winnie said after a long silence. "Miss Gwen, and Lord Sevaric, too."

Vayle regarded her somberly. Winnie, he suspected, knew loneliness when she saw it. She must have experienced it all her life.

The idea sliced through him. A century ago he'd been surrounded by his fellow rogues at the clubs and gaming tables. And there were women, always women, in his arms and in his bed. He had never thought about being lonely.

He didn't want to think about it now. "Miss Sevaric should get out more," he said. "Have you any idea why she is reluctant to go into society?"

Winnie shook her head. "I thought at first it was because . . . well, her best friend is a beauty and she is not. Perhaps she feels cast in the shade by Lady Anathea."

"At first? Have you changed your mind?"

She wrung her hands. "Dear me. I've no right to speak of this, and I beg you to tell no one that I did. It's only that you are like fresh air in this house. Your presence has stirred things up. Perhaps you can help."

"That is my greatest wish," he assured her. "The Sevarics have been kind to me. And you know, I can do little enough for myself until I remember who I am. In the meantime, it would give me a sense of purpose to be of use to them."

Winnie nodded slowly. "I understand, I do. I want to help, too, but I don't know how. The truth is, I have no idea what happened to Miss Gwen. But something did, something horrible, after her father died and before Lord Sevaric returned. Sometimes we share a bedchamber when relatives come to London and require the use of my room. She has nightmares and cries in her sleep. It is only my intuition, but I believe she is hiding a secret."

He swallowed a lump in his throat. "From her brother, too?"

"He knows," she replied despondently. "I'm certain of that. That is why he is so careful of her safety. But neither of them is telling."

"I see." He put down his fork. Gwen's secret must have something to do with the feud, although he could not fathom how a reclusive spinster became entangled in the web. 'Struth, he had no idea how things stood between the Caines and the Sevarics a century after the duel. Nor could he ask. He wasn't supposed to know the Caines even existed. Damn!

"I often wonder," Winnie said thoughtfully, "if Miss Gwen's troubles are connected to her father's obsession. Even in Yorkshire, we used to read in the gossip pages about Lord Basil Sevaric and Hugo Caine. They were feuding, you see, and stopped at nothing to cause problems for each other."

"Indeed?" Vayle perked up at this felicitous opening. Perhaps this would all be easier than he suspected. "What set them at odds?"

Winnie frowned and lowered her voice to a whisper. "As I understand it, many years ago a wicked Caine scoundrel seduced the wife of the third baron Sevaric. Lord Sevaric called him out, of course, and was killed in the duel. By some accounts the villain fired early. But he got his just punishment, because the baron managed a clean shot and cut him down, too."

Vayle suppressed his automatic reaction to that slander. Was he now remembered only as a scurrilous cheat? Then he took a long, calming breath. Winnie had recounted only the Sevaric version, twisted by a century of feuding. Naturally the Sevarics would seek to blacken his reputation, if only to justify their own.

But a *cheat?* Bile rose in his throat. His standards of morality had been somewhat flexible, and he had surely bedded Sevaric's wife. Other men's wives, too. Marriages were made for convenience, and once an heir popped out most women looked elsewhere for their pleasure. He had been more than willing to provide it.

But even so, he had never turned a false card, tossed loaded dice, or refused a gentleman's challenge. By the code of his set of friends, he had been an honorable man.

Until now, it had not occurred to him to question his definition of "honorable." But until now, he'd not been faced with the consequences of his actions, nor charged with setting them to rights.

"Miss Winifred," he began carefully, "how can this ancient quarrel signify? Gwen Sevaric does not strike me as a woman who would pursue a grudge, let alone one originated by people who are long since dead and gone."

"She is not." Nervously, Winnie fingered the fringe of the coverlet. "But her father was possessed by the feud. Although I met him only twice, I always thought him more than a little mad. He compelled Miss Gwen to serve as his assistant and rarely permitted her to go out. She cannot help but have been affected."

Outside in the hall, there was the sound of a door opening and shutting. Winnie came to her feet. "I-I have said far too much, Mr. Vayle. Pray forgive me. This is none of your concern, and you have been most polite, listening to an old woman's troubles."

She hesitated there beside the bed, then added softly, "It is only that I worry for Miss Gwen, and hope you will be patient with her uncertain temper. She does not mean to be . . . that is, there are reasons for her stern disposition. I don't know what they are, but at heart she is generous and sweet-natured."

" 'Struth, 'tis not for me to stand her judge," he said gravely. "And I cannot help but respect any lady wise enough to treasure you, Miss Winifred."

Flushing, she gave him an apologetic smile. "I must take the tray with me, sir."

With regret, he watched his mostly uneaten dinner leave the room. Ah well, he reflected. She had left him food for thought.

Four

Clootie proved invaluable the next morning. Vayle was determined to get out and explore this new century, but his lack of a reflection and unfamiliarity with the garments made his escape dependent on the efficient valet.

"There you go, sir." Clootie stood back, hairbrush in hand, and gestured toward the mirror. "Does it please you?"

Vayle pretended to study the mirror, but a reflected glare from the window was all he could see where his face should be. "Well enough." He glanced down at his front—a white shirt, a blue waistcoat, and a plain dark blue jacket. "Rather neutral, though, don't you think? I'd prefer a more colorful ensemble."

Clootie nodded, surveying him head to toe. "You might sport a brighter pattern in the waistcoat, I'd expect. The ladies like that, you know."

"They do? Well, then, order me a few new waistcoats. One in, say, blue and gold. And perhaps a vivid green?"

"Very well, sir." Clootie opened the wardrobe door and removed a waistcoat. "I'll take this as a pattern for the tailor. Now about your evening clothes. You'll likely want another set made up for your visits to—to the establishments we spoke of, where the young gentlemen go. The ladies there do appreciate fresh linen and stylish dress."

Since Vayle agreed that pleasing the ladies was of paramount importance, he recklessly pledged to be fitted for another evening coat and breeches. His hundred pounds, he realized, wouldn't last long at this rate. Then again, no tailor had ever dunned him for payment. He didn't suppose merchants had changed very much in a century—they would know that outfitting a well-looking man-about-town, even on credit, was good for business.

When he entered the breakfast room, he found brother and sister dividing up a newspaper and a plate of eggs. Max greeted him with a grin. "I could tell last night you weren't going to waste much time convalescing. Sit down and have some beefsteak."

Vayle couldn't resist a triumphant glance across the table at Gwen as the footman gave him a plate of beef. But she merely observed coolly, "If you find yourself convulsed with pain later today, please don't say I didn't warn you."

"Nonsense!" Max said in a bracing tone. "Vayle's no weakling. I could tell that the first I saw him. And no real man will let an injury keep him down. Why, I remember when the medicos took off Bayard Chilton's leg after Vitoria. It'd hardly stopped bleeding before he was hopping around, demanding to join the victory party."

"Max, please," Gwen said faintly, and even Vayle hesitated before chewing up his bite of beefsteak.

"Sorry, m'dear. Forgot where I was for a moment." In an obvious effort to change the subject, Max said to Vayle, "I've been thinking of how we might help you determine who you are. We'll take you about in public. If you're a Londoner, someone is bound to recognize you. And if you're country-bred, you might encounter a neighbor up for the Little Season. You don't seem the rural sort, though."

"Certainly not," Vayle replied without thinking. Recollecting his amnesia, he added more tentatively, "Is it possible that I might be unknown to all?"

Max and Gwen exchanged glances. "We did note your accent. Nothing amiss with it, of course," Max said hastily. "You aren't a foreigner, that's clear enough. But you don't precisely sound—English either. I thought you might have been reared in the colonies."

"The colonies? You mean Virginia?"

"Virginia?" Gwen set her cup down with a clatter. "But Mr. Vayle, Virginia isn't our colony any longer."

"Right." France must have taken it in one of those interminable wars. He smiled apologetically. "I forgot."

"That is a deal to forget, isn't it?" She regarded him through narrowed eyes, and he sensed her skepticism. "Especially when we've only recently concluded hostilities with the United States?"

The United States? What on earth was that? Vayle was too confused to answer, so he stuffed a corner of toast in his mouth and nodded. Gwen sniffed in that skeptical way he knew all too well by now. "Surely you recall that the United States won its independence during Lord North's ministry."

"Right," he repeated. "Lord North. I think I remember the name."

"I don't quite understand this form of amnesia, Mr. Vayle. You have forgotten about the United States, yet you remember that Virginia was once our colony? You can't yet be thirty, and that means that you're remembering a situation that existed before your birth, and forgetting what has been the rule afterward."

Fortunately, Max was impatient with this inquisition. "Gwen, for pity's sake, don't confuse the man. He's told you he doesn't remember. Now," he said with a grin at Vayle, "if he says he doesn't recall who won the Derby last year, I'll be worried."

The Derby. Could he mean the county Derbyshire? But how could anyone win a county? Was that some new way to finance wars—lotteries with an entire county as a prize? Vayle's head was aching again, and he decided only a diversion would extricate him. He essayed an agreeable wave of his hand, and knocked over his coffee cup, and once the ensuing bustle concluded no one thought to mention the United States or Lord North or the Derby again.

But Max was as good as his word. In an effort to determine Vayle's identity, they trooped off to a horse auction, a boxing parlor, and a gentleman's haberdashery. Finally Vayle had to

plead exhaustion and retreat to his bedchamber. But hardly had
he risen from his nap than Max was knocking at the door, inviting him to visit a fashionable club.

A club! Now that was more like it. Vayle rang for Clootie
and donned his evening clothes, thinking to himself that Max
might not be such a dull dog after all.

Two hours later Vayle stared at the remains of his dinner—
boiled beef and overcooked potatoes—and resumed his earlier
opinion of his companion. Max was a sturdy fellow, brave and
honorable, no doubt. But his notion of what constituted a suitable club was sorely misguided.

'Struth, he had never spent a more tedious evening than here
at White's. The dining room was a cavernous place, poorly lit
and overheated, furnished with dark woods and mediocre hunting prints. Most of the members assembled at the tables were
so old that Vayle fancied he saw cobwebs dangling from their
ears. The conversations, from what he could hear, all concerned
tiresome Parliamentary feuds and fusses. To think gentlemen
actually vied for admission to this pretentious graveyard. He
could hardly wait to escape.

"I had hoped for better luck tonight." Max swallowed the
last of his port and gestured around at the other diners. "They
all seem to like you, at any rate."

"No one recognized me or my name," he said, trying to sound
disappointed, "and you must have introduced me to forty men.
Ought we try a somewhat . . . ah . . . livelier establishment?"

"Bored, are you?" With an understanding chuckle, Max rose.
"Not fond of White's myself, but nearly everyone of importance
shows up here sooner or later. There's still hope someone will
be able to identify you. Shall we try the gaming room?"

Gambling! Vayle came to his feet in a hurry, sniffing a chance
to pad his bankroll. The miserly hundred pounds that Proctor
had allowed him would serve as a stake, and he usually left the
tables a winner.

As Max led him down the hall, two uniformed men flushed
with drink erupted from a side room.

"Sevaric! Been looking for you. Trent said you were here, and by God, so you are!"

They each clapped Max on the back, and he returned the gesture with a heartiness that made Vayle glad he wasn't one of their circle. Colonel Trent and Captain McHale were old war comrades, Vayle surmised. After perfunctory handshakes, the men returned their attention to Max.

"Come bend an elbow with us," Trent urged. "Last time we saw you was the night before Waterloo."

"I oughtn't—" Max shot a glance at Vayle.

"Never mind me," he said with a self-deprecating smile. "You go on with your friends. I'll just wander around for a few hours. You can find me later in the gaming room."

For a moment, the battle between duty to his houseguest and a chance to reminisce with his friends held Max in place. Before he could make the wrong choice, Vayle bowed and headed for a pair of doors guarded by two stern-faced footmen. The last thing he wanted was a moralistic ex-soldier hovering over him while he tossed the dice. A good man, Sevaric, but not the life of any party.

The footmen bowed and opened the doors. Vayle entered a large, high-ceilinged room wreathed in cigar smoke and echoing with noise. The edgy excitement of gamesters charged the air. For the first time since waking up in the nineteenth century, Vayle felt right at home.

He ambled from table to table, smiling when anyone glanced his way. For the most part, the men were intent on cards, dice, and one another, giving him a chance to observe the games in play.

After two circuits of the room, Vayle swore under his breath. Now and again a game looked familiar, but closer examination proved otherwise. How was he to join in without knowing the rules?

He decided to study a single game until he learned it. At the first table he approached, however, play was just breaking up. A young man, his head bent as he scribbled on a scrap of paper, muttered, "I'm played out, gentlemen. Here are my vowels, and you may be sure I shall honor them."

The other players gathered in the paper scraps and rose. One cast a disgusted look at the loser. "See that you do. Another delay like the last one and you'll be blackballed."

They moved away, leaving the young man sitting alone, face buried in his hands. Auburn glinted in the brown of his hair. The sleeves of his coat were slightly frayed.

Vayle started to back away, leaving the man to his misery, but then a shaking hand reached for a glass. He saw a pale-green bloodshot eye, a cheek puffy with drink and exhaustion, the corner of a turned-down, sulky mouth.

Robin Caine! He was sure of it when the other hand fell to the baize table, revealing the face of a man about five years younger than he. Give or take a hundred years, of course.

So this is what the charming, devil-may-care Caines had degenerated to—a listless, sotted wretch. No wonder the Afterlife Powers deemed him unsalvageable. At least Vayle didn't have to worry about saving this loser. In contrast, enrapturing the grim Gwen seemed a simple task.

But why was this pathetic young man a hopeless cause while a dedicated sinner like Vayle was accorded a second chance? Curiosity drew him to the table.

"Forgive me for disturbing you," he said with his sweetest smile. "But I am new to London and have no acquaintance among these gentlemen. You appear to be alone, so I thought perhaps . . . ?" He let his voice fade into a hopeful question.

Robin's careless gesture sloshed brandy out of his glass, staining the sheet from which he had torn his IOUs. "You shan't gild your reputation by associating with the likes of me, but sit if you like. I could use the company, and my credit is good enough to buy you a drink. Tonight, at any rate. I don't expect I'll be welcomed at White's in the future."

No great loss, Vayle thought privately as he took a chair across the table from Robin. However high-stakes the play, this gentleman's club lacked an essential ingredient. He preferred a salon that provided an opportunity for gaming with a woman by one's side, her soft breasts catching the light, she on fire at the heady action at the table and the sport to come—ah, that was how a man should spend his evenings.

But as long as he had to wait here, he might as well get to know his great-great-grand-nephew. This was Dorothea Caine's brother, and could provide an address for her. Vayle would have to be careful not to arouse suspicion, though.

As Robin stared morosely at his empty glass, Vayle summoned a waiter. Soon a bottle of aged cognac was delivered. "Sevaric will sign for this," he told the man.

Robin's head shot up.

The servant lifted an eyebrow but nodded and moved away.

"I'll not drink anything a Sevaric paid for," Robin declared with a return of spirit. His bloodshot eyes narrowed as he regarded Vayle. "And what is your connection to that blackguard?"

Caution, Vayle told himself. He would never get information about Dorothea if Robin distrusted him. Casually he replied, "I am his houseguest, but only because he took me in when I was injured in an accident. I scarcely know the man." He filled both glasses and lifted his own in a toast. "To good times. I am Jocelyn Vayle, by the way."

Temptation proved stronger than suspicion. Robin swallowed a mouthful and then another before wiping his chin with his sleeve. "Robin Caine, Viscount Lynton, but call me Robin. My ancestors would turn over in their graves if they heard me use the title. Nothing left of it but an inscription in some old registers anyway."

"Indeed? I fancied that viscounts inherited estates and fortunes as a matter of course."

"They sometimes do, and I might have. But I got only a few derelict properties after my uncle gambled the good 'uns away." He gulped down the rest of his brandy and held out his glass for more. "So I managed to lose most of those and what remained of the family fortune. Hardly matters, does it? When I die, the title will revert to the Crown and there will be nothing left. Nothing at all."

At this bleak prediction, Vayle's heart sank. "Surely matters are not so grim. One day you'll marry and sire an heir."

Robin laughed mirthlessly. "Marry? Who would marry a Caine?"

It was too much to take in. In his day, even Caine younger sons were highly prized on the marriage market. Why, Vayle himself could have claimed an earl's daughter, had he been of any mind to wed. And now Robin, who ought to know, was sneering that no one would marry a Caine.

Vayle wasn't going to waste his concern on Robin, who was no part of his task. Besides, this poor wastrel was likely to put a bullet in his head before he could get to the altar. But Dorothea— How could he be expected to ensure her happiness if no one would marry her?

He couldn't think about that just yet—that the once-proud name of Caine could now make even a beauty like Dorothea ineligible. "Still, the title need not revert to the Crown, need it? Have you no relations? Some distant cousin to continue the line?"

Robin shook his head. "Not a one. Believe me, Vayle, the Caines are done for. But I do have a sister. Dorie. She lives in the country."

"Aha." Vayle leaned forward, propping his chin on his wrists. Dorothea. Finally. "So you still own a country estate?"

"Estate?" Robin laughed without humor. "Not likely. Greenbriar Lodge is a rundown hovel in Surrey, scarcely livable even for m'sister. Dorie always makes the best of things, though. She's spent the last year fixing up the house and trying to help the tenant farmers work the land." He shrugged. "Maybe she'll succeed. I hope so."

"Surrey, you say." At least Surrey was still a British possession, he thought with some relief. "I used to hunt there. Where exactly is Greenbriar Lodge?"

Robin shrugged. "The backside of nowhere, but I send mail

to the Thruppence Inn at Croydon. Give me London any time. Even in the bad times, there is something to do here. I'd go mad on a farm."

"My sentiments exactly." As Robin sank into another brown study, Vayle congratulated himself on his subtle interrogation. Without alerting Robin, he'd learned the whereabouts of Dorothea Caine. And now he could start fixing her life.

Marriage to a rich man was the only solution to her problems. The image he'd seen in the Afterlife vision flashed across his mind. Surely such a beautiful woman didn't need an untarnished name. He'd only need to introduce several potential suitors and let nature take its course.

But first she must be brought to London. Tomorrow he would dispatch a letter to the Thruppence Inn, signed "A Friend," informing Dorothea that Robin was in trouble and needed her help.

To his gratification, the tasks assigned by Proctor were proving rather simple to accomplish. Over dinner, Max had suggested another scheme that played right into his hands. Gwendolyn should get out more, he had said, and Vayle's unfortunate amnesia was a perfect excuse to drag her to balls and such. It was a clever plan, Vayle had to admit, and one that would introduce him to a more interesting crowd.

A crowd that included the fairer sex. He would trade a week in this tiresome club for one hour with a fascinating woman. Thank heavens he would soon be back in 1716, where men were men and proved it in the bedchamber.

He fingered the cards strewn over the table and looked across at his sullen relation. "I don't suppose you'd be willing to teach me how to play?" he inquired into the silence.

Robin regarded him suspiciously. "I'm not such a flat to be cozened by that old ploy."

"Ploy? Dear me no. I am perfectly serious about requiring lessons, although I cannot explain"— he thought a moment— "unless you can be trusted with a confidence."

Looking flattered, Robin nodded.

"The accident has left me a trifle disoriented, but I'd rather

not have that generally known. People would be forever watching
for signs of dementia." When Robin drew away, Vayle waved a
hand. "I'm not truly demented. Not at all. But my behavior might
seem, on occasion, a trifle odd, because I have lost memory of
a few trivial things. Recent history, for one. I do recall earlier
events, say, most everything that occurred before the last century."

"I wasn't a great hand at history either," Robin said sympathetically. "Never missed it much, I must say."

"Alas, I've also forgotten the rules of dice and card games—
and that I *do* miss, as you can imagine. A pity that, because
instinct tells me I was fond of gaming." With nimble fingers
and intense pleasure, he stacked the deck and cut it and shuffled
the cards. " 'Struth, I must once have had some facility with
the pasteboards, as you see."

"I'd be doing you no favor, teaching you to play," Robin said
darkly. "You see what a lust for gaming has done to me. Those
are the Devil's Books. Better you leave them alone."

Vayle tilted his head, surprised. Could there yet be a remnant
of decency left in the boy? Unfortunately, that couldn't be encouraged, or Vayle wouldn't pick up the new games.

"I'll learn to play in any case, or possibly my memory will
improve. I only thought we might seek out each other's company
now and again. For all his kindness to me, Sevaric is something
of a dull dog."

With his thumb, he feathered the deck and then spread it in
a fan on the table. "Of course I'd repay you for the lessons. Not
with money, for I have little, but I'm accounted a good shot and
am a past master at fencing. Does either interest you?"

Robin's face lit up. "I long to fence and shoot. Box, too, if
you know how. But if you've lost your memory . . ."

"A good point." So Robin had never learned the manly
sports? Vayle shook his head, wondering what sort of upbring-
ing the boy had. "I will have to test my skills and see what
remains. Let's start with foils. Is there some place we can meet
for swordplay?"

"Antonio's," Robin said, fumbling in his pocket. "Here is my card. Only let me know when you'd like to begin. For now, I can sketch the rules for quinze. It's by far the simplest of the card games."

Robin was a good teacher. His motions were surer as he dealt out the cards. Even his voice took on some authority when he explained the rules for quinze, which indeed seemed almost childishly simple. Vayle grasped the basics quickly and won the second hand.

"What the devil?" Max's harsh voice broke into his lesson.

"Sevaric." Robin struggled to his feet and stood, swaying from side to side like a small boat in a storm.

Caught between them, since Max was planted firmly behind his chair, Vayle could only raise his hands in a calming gesture. "There you are. What took you so long?" Playing dumb, he looked from Robin to Max quizzically. "Do you two know each other?"

Max's face darkened, and Robin looked mulish. Neither would answer the question. Finally Max declared, "You are my guest, Vayle, and I must ask you to respect one rule. You do not know this man. You will not acknowledge him. Understand?"

With a negligent shrug, Vayle pushed from the table, forcing Max to back away. "I meant no offense. I'd not realized you had a quarrel with him. He seems harmless enough to me."

"He's a Caine. That means all he does is harm." Max was still taut with anger, and his words were sharp as grape shot. "There is nothing more to be said. Let's go."

Turning on his heel, Sevaric strode away with the assurance of an officer who'd given an order and expected to be obeyed.

Vayle looked at Robin, expecting rage in response to Sevaric's insult. But though his eyes blazed with anger, Robin's face was pale and his hands were jammed into his pockets. His voice was barely audible. "You'd best do what he says."

Vayle patted the pocket where he'd stuffed Robin's card. "Our secret," he said softly. "I'll be in touch."

Five

"Absolutely not!" Gwen rose from the couch to confront her brother. He was wearing his implacable face, though experience should have taught him it did nothing but raise her hackles. "Only four days ago he was all but dead. It's far too soon for him to be gallivanting about."

The prospective gallivanter stood by the fireplace with a glass of sherry in his hand, radiating the languid, constrained energy of a healthy cat. Gwen hated to admit it, but his dress was wasted on this simple family occasion. Vayle was resplendent enough for Carlton House.

Impatiently, Max looked up from the desk where he was sorting through invitations. "Come on, Gwen, look at him. I've had him out to the clubs three nights in a row, and even so he's as hale as a horse. So you can't use him as an excuse. We have agreed that your career as a hermit is at an end."

"Fustian. We have not *agreed*. You have made up your mind, that's all." She shook her head, exasperated. "Sometimes you forget that you are no longer Major Lord Sevaric."

Max flushed and looked back down at the invitation cards, and Gwen regretted her sharp words. Not that she was wrong—in his high-handed moments, Max could be as tyrannical as their father.

But she shouldn't have criticized him in front of an outsider, especially one who lounged against the mantel, observing them with ironic detachment. She glared at Vayle and resumed her seat on the couch.

"I don't mean to snap orders at you, my dear." Max took one invitation out of the pack and tossed the rest into a basket. "But our guest must be presented to society if he is to encounter any acquaintances he might have in London. He's been to the major clubs, and yesterday we rode in Hyde Park, but he should be seen at *ton* parties, too. And in company with the both of us, to lend him credit."

He mended a pen and started scrawling a note—an acceptance, she supposed. "You are well aware how newcomers are dealt with by the high sticklers. He requires your help, and you owe him that and more."

She looked over, expecting Vayle to deny it, but he only gave her a seraphic smile.

Contemptible wretch. He was gallant only when it suited him. Still, what did she expect? He was a man. Some few were kind, like Max, while others used force, but all turned despot when it came to getting their own way.

But that didn't mean masculine arrogance should go unchallenged. She crossed her arms over her chest and turned pointedly away from Vayle.

"In fact, *you* are the one using Mr. Vayle as an excuse to drag me where I do not wish to go."

"I won't deny it," Max said after a moment. "But I'm acting for your own good, and on that count you must trust me. Do you doubt I have your best interest at heart?"

She did not doubt it, although she wasn't going to say so. Nor would she object to Max's bullheaded assurance that he knew what was best for her, not while Vayle watched the proceedings with unconcealed fascination.

"Why must it be Lady Sefton's ball?" she asked instead. "Or any ball whatever, since we've no idea if Mr. Vayle can even dance."

She lifted a brow. "Can you, sir?"

Vayle uncoiled from his position and with exaggerated bewilderment looked down at his form in the tight garments. No doubt he found it appealing, for he smiled that sleek smile.

" 'Struth, I've no idea. Perhaps you should put me through my paces this afternoon. And if I fail the test, you can teach me."

"Absolutely n—"

"An excellent idea!" Max interrupted, pushing away from the desk. "There's a pianoforte in the upstairs salon, and Miss Crake is an accomplished musician."

He yanked on the bellrope. "I'll have the servants roll up the carpet. Gwen, find Winnie and put on your dancing shoes."

Ten minutes later Max was still issuing orders, this time from a chair next to the piano. "With only two of you there's no point trying any country dances, so I suggest we concentrate on the waltz. Winnie, play a bit and see if Vayle recognizes the meter."

Frustrated beyond endurance, Gwen went to the window and stared out into a gray afternoon. This was absurd. She had never danced in public, and had endured lessons only when Max insisted on hiring a caper merchant. Mr. Popplewell got on everyone's nerves, even Winnie's, and had been dismissed after a few weeks.

Moreover, on the rare occasions Max had coerced her into joining him at a ball, he never danced either. Hypocrite! Tonight, while he stood on the sidelines as usual, she would be compelled to make a spectacle of herself.

Even here, in this private room, the thought of touching Jocelyn Vayle sent shivers down her back. He was beautiful. And he was dangerous, with those emerald eyes that saw too much and revealed nothing. In his presence she was always conscious of her appearance, like a crab apple set down next to a peach.

She turned her head just enough to see him out of the corner of her eye. He had removed his coat and looked elegantly slender in tight doeskin pantaloons, white shirt, and a peacock-blue waistcoat embroidered with gold thread.

His thick hair shone auburn under the chandelier as he stood, hands clasped behind his back, listening attentively to the music. When he became aware of her regard, he glanced in her direction and smiled.

She gritted her teeth and stared resolutely at the raindrops tracking down the windowpane. But if she squinted just a bit, she could see the entire room reflected in the glass—and Mr. Vayle in the very center.

Winnie arrived at the last chord and looked up expectantly. "Do you recognize it, Mr. Vayle? I'm lamentably out of practice."

"On the contrary, Maestro. Or is it Maestress?" He gave her an elaborate bow. "You play divinely. I was so enrapt I forgot to think about the dance."

Winnie giggled like a girl. It was dismaying how silly women became around that man. Gwen could just imagine the response of the debutantes at the ball tonight. And he would preen under the attention, she knew it. He would preen and glow like a cat getting caressed.

"Ready to have a go?" Max urged, always impatient to get on with business. "Not much to it, really. One-two-three, one-two-three, in circles."

Vayle gazed at him blankly.

"This is a waste of time." Gwen crossed to the door, but couldn't bring herself to walk out. "He doesn't know a waltz from a Morris Dance."

"Oh, but I remember seeing Morris Dancers," Vayle said brightly. "They were peasants, though. Has Morris dancing become the fashion?"

"You see," Gwen said to Max, exasperated. "You can't want him to make a fool of himself in front of Lady Sefton and her cronies."

"I won't." Vayle's tone was soft, but his eyes flashed.

Max regarded his sister with some displeasure. "If you want him to learn, Gwen, just show him how it's done."

She gazed at Vayle's broad shoulders and narrow waist and could not imagine putting a hand anywhere on him. Seizing Max's wrist, she hauled him out of the chair with preternatural strength. "*You* dance with me. He can learn by watching us."

Max gave her an annoyed look, but led her onto the floor and nodded at Winnie to play. For several minutes they circled the room, Max grimly counting "one-two-three" under his

breath. Gwen would have laughed if she hadn't been so aware
of Vayle's bemused scrutiny.

Max held her stiffly, at a distance, like a man embarrassed
to be seen dancing with his sister. He moved as if claiming
territory for the Crown, meticulous and determined, while she
felt like a piece of artillery he was hauling along with him.

Her feet spent more time on his boots than on the varnished
floor, and Max swore under his breath when she landed especially hard on his toes.

Two dancing bears would have been more graceful.

Mercifully, Winnie put an end to the ordeal with a sudden,
decisive chord. Then everyone looked at Vayle for his reaction.

If he laughed, Gwen knew she would lunge for his throat.

"But how spendid!" he said with clear delight. "The waltz,
you say? I know I've never seen its like, because I could not
have forgotten anything so enchanting." With a wide smile, he
walked right up to Max and bowed. "May I claim your lovely
partner?"

Before Gwen could make her escape, Max practically thrust
her into Vayle's arms. Her nose landed in the folds of his cravat
and only the strength of his arms kept her upright.

"Such an eager partner," he whispered before setting her
away, one hand firmly on her waist and the other holding her
right hand in a loose but possessive grip.

For the first time, she realized neither of them was wearing
gloves. She felt the pulse beating in his thumb as it pressed the
back of her hand, his warm breath inches from her temple, the
pressure of his fingers against the small of her back.

All her senses were at needle-point. It seemed forever they
stood there, his scent wafting through her nostrils, his gaze hot
on her face as she stared at his neck.

Winnie began to play, but they didn't move.

"Relax," he said into her ear. "Please, Miss Sevaric. I'm not
sure which direction to go, and I fear that whichever way I leap,
you'll stay rooted to this spot."

She looked to his face and couldn't help but grin. He was so attentive, so concerned, and positively devilish at the same time. "Go whichever way feels natural," she advised. "You are supposed to lead, and I to follow."

Tugging her closer, he stayed in place another few beats, swaying in time to the music. She began to sway with him.

Then, before she was even aware of it, they were in motion. He was a trifle mechanical at first, but not for long. Soon her feet scarcely touched the floor as he whirled her around and around in dizzying circles.

She forgot to be awkward, forgot to be afraid as she yielded to his embrace and gave herself to the music. For the first time she understood why people loved to dance, knew she loved it, too, and wished this waltz would last forever.

Winnie must have read her thoughts because she played a great deal longer this time. At one point the music slowed, and Vayle drew her almost to his chest in an embrace so intimate she wondered fleetingly if Max would call him out for it.

Then they were practically flying again, in great sweeping arcs that left her breathless when the music finally stopped.

Vayle held her a moment longer than necessary, squeezing her hand in approval. "How graceful you are," he murmured.

Heat flamed everywhere in her body. She stepped a careful few feet away, only then hearing the sound of applause from Max and Winnie.

"For a man who claims he never saw a waltz, you're a right dab hand," Max exclaimed.

"All the credit is to my partner, and to our lovely musician." He crossed to the piano, lifted both of Winnie's pudgy hands, and kissed them in turn. "Now tell me, fair lady, do you waltz? I require more practice and wish above all things to lead you out."

"Oh, Mr. Vayle!" She bounced on the bench with pleasure, fluttering her stubby lashes like a schoolgirl.

Gwen snorted. The man was a veritable tomcat, nuzzling up to every female within range. Winnie was behaving as foolishly as she'd just done, mistaking his practiced flummery for genuine interest. Jocelyn Vayle could not be attracted to a plump sixty-year-old spinster, any more than he was captivated by his earlier partner, the plain, freckle-faced shrew.

She hated him all the more because he could turn his attention to a woman, any woman, and make her feel like the only woman in the world.

Max had quite a different reaction, of course. He thought it was all great fun, so long as he didn't have to do the dancing. "If you can suffer my wrong notes, I play a little. Go on, Winnie. Dance with him." He took her place on the bench and, after a few false starts, launched into a creditable waltz.

Gwen watched crossly as Vayle swept Winnie into his arms. To her astonishment, Winnie was light on her feet, for all she must weigh fifteen stone. Or maybe it was Vayle's skill and the strength of his embrace that made her appear agile.

Max's waltz had a somewhat martial beat, but neither seemed to notice. They gazed into each other's eyes as they danced, and chatted, and laughed together. Gwen recalled that she hadn't said a word during her dance, and could not remember looking into his eyes. That would have been too dangerous.

Vayle was having more fun with Winnie than he'd had with her.

When Max hit the last chord like a thunderclap, Vayle hugged his gasping partner and planted a kiss on her cheek. "You were born to dance, Miss Crake."

Winnie could hardly speak through her giddy laughter. "I declare, Mr. Vayle, you do sweep a lady off her feet. I cannot remember when I've enjoyed myself more."

"Promise you'll waltz with me tonight," he implored. If Gwen hadn't known better, she might have sworn he meant it. "The next time will be even better now that I'm getting the hang of it."

Winnie shook her head, her hand on her heaving bosom. "I cannot, as well you know. 'Twould be a terrible scandal if you took the floor with an old woman like me. No, I'll play chaperone and make sure you don't dance more than twice with Miss Gwen."

Vayle turned with a smile to Gwen. "Only two waltzes, Miss Sevaric? I'd have wished for more, but it seems that pleasure is forbidden."

After she swallowed the lump in her throat, Gwen said gruffly, "You don't need me, sir. You can have your pick of the fashionable ladies at Lady Sefton's ball, and they all dance better than I do."

He regarded her enigmatically. "You are wrong," he said flatly. "I want very much to dance with you, twice if you will permit it. And I'll not go to the ball without your promise of at least one waltz."

"That's foolish and you know it." She looked over to Max, expecting him to join her protest, but he was reading the sheet music as if it were a newspaper and studiously ignored her. He could be infuriatingly obtuse at times. "You want to go to the ball, so go."

"I'll be a stranger there." Vayle took his coat from the piano and shoved his arms into the sleeves. "And I'd be excessively nervous dancing a dance I've only just learned with someone I've only just met."

Vayle nervous? What a clanker! Surely he knew he'd be in his element in a grand glittering ballroom. "Are you so vain as to imagine every eye will be on you?"

He shrugged and tugged his lapels straight. "The whole point, as I understand it, is that I am to be seen by all and sundry. And if I am to be seen, I would prefer not to be seen tripping over some unsuspecting young woman's feet. If that is vanity, well, then, I suppose I am vain."

He gazed at her with a look of entreaty. It was very nearly irresistible, especially when he added in a wheedling tone, "But with you, I dance acceptably. I can rely on you to keep me from disgrace, can I not?"

He was so beguiling she almost succumbed. And he was so

infuriating, she nearly told him to go to the devil. But then she glanced at Winnie's flushed, happy face and bit her tongue.

He had made Winnie happy. He had exerted himself, at no conceivable profit to himself, on her behalf. And he would do so again if another opportunity arose. He seemed to genuinely like Winifred Crake, and she suspected that he would once again insist on a waltz with her. And the next time, Winnie would not refuse.

But why was he insinuating himself into their family this way?

She was ungracious and selfish to resent his kindness to others. It was just that she could not trust any man except her brother to be kind to a woman without a hidden motive. And even Max was manipulating her now, on Vayle's behalf.

She almost said no. But then she saw the disappointment in Winnie's eyes, and sighed. "Very well, I'll dance with you to-night. The first waltz, unless you find a partner more to your taste."

"Impossible," he said with that devastating smile, but she didn't believe him. Couldn't believe him. He wasn't real.

Something rang false about Jocelyn Vayle. He had appeared out of nowhere, and he didn't quite fit no matter what identity Max proposed for him. He was too polished for a colonial, too ignorant for a Londoner. And she just knew that this amnesia of his was a pose. No, he had some reason for being here in Sevaric House, and it wasn't to regain his memory. She felt her suspicions soul-deep, and would not give up until she found out what he meant to get from his association with the Sevarics.

Once it would have taken three hours for Vayle to prepare himself for a ball. But this evening Clootie accomplished it in less than an hour. Of course, there was no queue to groom, and no patches to stick on. Vayle did lament that change in fashion, for he always found that a heart placed at the corner of his mouth was likely to garner him kisses.

While Clootie fussed with the neckcloth, Vayle raised his hand to touch his own face and found it closely shaven and reassuringly familiar. He might get a few kisses, even without the patches.

Clootie stepped back, tilted his head appraisingly, and nodded. "Have a look in the mirror, sir. I think you will be pleased."

Careful not to face the mirror, Vayle reached for his white gloves. "There is no need. I'm content to rely on your skill and excellent taste."

"You may do so without fear. But in my experience, no gentleman leaves his chamber until he has satisfied himself that his appearance is all it should be." With a smile, Clootie gestured to the glass over the shaving table. "Do tell me if you approve."

Was he simply fishing for compliments, or was this another of his games? Vayle slanted him an assessing look, but Clootie was busily reclaiming failed neckcloths from the floor.

A very odd fellow indeed.

For the most part he ignored the valet, even his oblique suggestions about places that young gentlemen enjoyed. Not that Vayle wasn't interested, but so far he'd had no time for prowling London's Houses of Pleasure. When Max wasn't trolling him through fashionable clubs, he was stealing away for fencing, shooting, and gaming lessons with Robin Caine.

On several occasions, Clootie had implied that he knew the company his employer was keeping. Vayle suspected those were veiled threats, since Max would certainly object if he found out. But damned if he'd buy the silence of a bloody valet. Could he manage without one, Clootie would have been dismissed days ago.

He was almost certain that Proctor had arranged for him to be tormented by this sly, officious creature. That made firing him all the more tempting, until Vayle remembered that he had enough trouble on his hands without antagonizing the Powers.

He had to put up with Clootie another few weeks, but that

was no reason to be craven. With ten minutes to spare before meeting the others downstairs, he decided to stir the waters.

"A pity, this new fashion for black and white," he said, gazing mournfully at his plain dark sleeve. "I feel rather like a crow. Black is not my best color."

Clootie looked up from the drawer where he was folding stockings. His strange pale eyes glittered. "Ah, you were born to wear ivory lace and purple brocade. But these are plainer days, aren't they?"

Vayle held his breath, waiting for another signal that Clootie knew what an ordinary valet would have no way of knowing. But the valet only smiled thinly and put away a pair of stockings. "You know, an emerald stickpin in your neckcloth would brighten that ensemble."

"You may be right. But I own not so much as a watch fob." He focused on Clootie's narrow face, hoping for a telling reaction to his next statement. "You have wondered, more than once, why I do not examine my appearance in front of the mirror. The fact is, I cannot see my own reflection."

Clootie lifted an eyebrow, his expression one of mild curiosity. "Indeed? Not at all? How strange."

"A trick of the eye, no doubt, like being nearsighted. My image appears as a blur in my vision. That is why I depend on you to see me suitably rigged out." To conceal his disappointment at Clootie's bland response, he pulled on his gloves and chuckled. "One day I must inquire about spectacles to correct the problem."

"Science is working wonders these days." Clootie went to the armoire and pulled out a heavy black cape lined with green satin. "If you *could* see your image, sir, you would know how well I have succeeded. Indeed, you have already made an impression on Lady Melbrook—riding dress does become you. She saw you yesterday in Hyde Park, and I daresay she will seek you out tonight."

Once again, Vayle regarded him suspiciously. The man was

positively infernal with his hints and insinuations. "How the devil do you know that? And why should I care?"

"Information is passed through the servants' network almost before the incident in question takes place. As for why this should interest you, I cannot say."

He draped the cloak over Vayle's shoulders and tugged the folds straight. "Unless you wish me to, of course."

Swallowing an oath, Vayle drew back and picked up his silver-knobbed cane—his first London purchase, it concealed a short lethal sword. No gentleman gossiped with servants.

Then again, Clootie was no ordinary servant, and he, a stranger in this place and time, could use an ally. His instincts clamored a warning that Clootie was no friend to him, but so long as he was on guard . . .

"I recall no Lady Melbrook among my acquaintance," he said in a deliberately casual voice.

Clootie brushed invisible lint from a tall, curly-brimmed hat. "As I understand it, she is a young, wealthy, beautiful, and shall I say *playful* widow. A woman who gives all and makes no demands for the future. Gentlemen who enjoy her favors never regret it, or so I hear."

"I wonder that you are a valet," Vayle said coolly, "when you seem inclined to a less respectable profession."

For the first time, Clootie smiled directly at him. It wasn't a pretty sight. "My only inclination is to serve, and my master decides how I can be most useful. Shall I wait up for you tonight?"

Vayle exited without answering. Obviously Clootie expected him to go home with the Melbrook widow. And maybe he would. A few outings with Max, harmless as they were, had convinced him the soldier was not so straitlaced as he'd first appeared. Max would certainly understand a man's needs and turn a blind eye if his houseguest sought company elsewhere.

Of course, Gwen would despise him for taking up with the willing widow, but she despised him already and he'd done nothing wicked at all. So far, at least. And only because he'd not had the chance. Still, she had already judged him and found him wanting.

Such a caustic model of dull propriety, Gwendolyn Sevaric. Well, he couldn't call her *dull* precisely. When she was discon-certed, she wasn't dull at all.

No wonder he liked to disconcert her, as he had done during their waltz—in his arms she had enjoyed for a few brief minutes the pleasure of a dance. Naturally, that made her despise him.

She would be, he thought suddenly, a perfect mate for Proc-tor. He laughed aloud as he went downstairs to join the others, and the notion was reinforced when he looked down to see her staring at him critically from the foyer.

Pausing at the bottom of the staircase, he regarded her with some surprise. Gwen looked remarkably pretty in a honey-colored dress that brought out the gold highlights in her hair and eyes—her censorious hazel eyes.

He decided then and there that he would annoy her this eve-ning, for disapproval made her eyes glow, and that put her in her best looks. She might even turn that skeptical gaze on other men and garner a few dance partners. Why, if they managed to irritate her, too—and he sensed any man would—she could be well on her way to Incomparability.

The thought made him smile, and as he had hoped, she frowned and looked even prettier. Seizing her gloved fingers, he touched the tips to his lips.

She yanked her hand back and glared at him.

"Enchantress," he murmured, and she turned on her heel and stalked to the door.

"Don't waste your pretty on Gwen," Max advised. "She will just call it trumpery and read you a lesson in vanity."

Vanity wasn't one of Max's faults. He walked past the hall mirror without even a glance at his reflection. Just as well that he had the sort of negligent good looks that looked most dra-matic when windblown and disarranged.

Winnie was fussing with her gloves, and Vayle turned to her with a smile. She wore a blue gown, dark enough to be slimming even around the hips, and the cameo at the high lace neckline drew attention from her double chin. Somehow she had tamed her frizzy hair, and the hint of rouge on her cheeks and lips gave color to her face. He thought her beautiful, in her way, and his smile widened.

This must be a special occasion for Winnie—an elegant ball in the best company. He suspected there had been few of those, if any, in her bleak life, and his heart went out to her. He held out his arm, and with a blush she put her hand in the crook of her elbow. "Tell me you have changed your mind," he begged. "Tell me we shall dance together this night."

"Oh, Mr. Vayle," she said with a girlish shake of her curls. "What a devil you are to tempt me so."

"Devil indeed," Gwen muttered. At her imperious gesture, the footman flung open the door and let in the chill. "Let us go quickly, before we are smothered in his treacle."

Six

According to Major Max Sevaric, a London ballroom bore a marked resemblance to a battlefield. Vayle watched, amused, as he stopped at the top of the staircase to survey the combatants below, then ordered his troops into parade ranks. After steering them through the receiving line, Max marched to a corner of the ballroom for a strategy conference.

"First we'll make a complete circuit so everyone can see Vayle. Later, when we are in company, we will mention his name at every opportunity and point him out." He pulled a small card from his pocket and studied it. "While we were waiting in line, I confirmed the order of the dances. The first waltz is number four, Gwen, and you've promised that to Vayle. I expect you to dance more than that once, so don't hide behind the potted plants with Winnie."

She stuck out her chin. If there was to be a mutineer in the ranks, it was bound to be Gwen. "And what if no one asks me?" She didn't look particularly upset about the prospect.

"I'll take care of it," Max replied ominously. He turned to Winnie. "You will be on your own tonight, as I intend to keep Gwen busy. Have you friends to sit with?"

Winnie came to attention. "I will find some, Lord Sevaric. Don't worry on my account."

He nodded. "And Vayle, you'll stay visible—no retreating into the game rooms."

Vayle agreed. He could gamble any evening, but he would

not always have the opportunity to be surrounded by so many lovely women.

"Well, then," Max said, "let us scout the territory. Stay close to me."

They moved in step from group to group, smiling on cue. Max aimed first for his fellow officers, and within minutes Gwen had dance partners, whether she wanted them or not.

Vayle had to admire the lady's poise. Subtlety was not among her brother's virtues, and she was surely embarrassed when Max presented her to his friends. The tone in his voice was a virtual command. The men were gallant and charming once they got the point, but in the interim Gwen stood straight and calm although Vayle knew she must be aching inside.

At their third stop, when a young lieutenant offered for the waltz, Vayle was quick to assert his own claim. For some reason, that made her more intriguing. Other men stepped forward then to beg dances as Max nodded his satisfaction.

Sister accounted for, Vayle interpreted the look on his face. All well on the left flank.

Gwen and Winnie veered off to greet acquaintances, and Max was soon replaying some battle or other with his friends. So Vayle took the opportunity to look around. He was not impressed.

For one thing, nearly all the men were dressed alike. Oh, a few wore army uniforms and several young blades sported bright waistcoats and starched collars that reached to their ears, but otherwise every man conformed to the standard taste for black and white. Good Lord, they were stamped out like coins.

And the women! The young ones wore white, or pastels that washed them out. His eyes were drawn immediately to the ladies who dared to wear bright purple and red, but most of them were elderly, and their bright plumes adorned gray coiffures.

What had become of style? Panache? A hundred years ago, the men had nearly outshone the women in glittering attire, especially at fashionable balls where the guests made a point

of dressing to show off their personalities. Now, everyone tried
to look like everyone else.

He shuffled uneasily on the flat slippers Clootie had found
for him. The last time he danced at a ball, he'd worn shoes with
rubies sparkling on the lifted heels and gold buckles on the
toes. Lace had drifted over his fingertips. A stiff ribbon held
his long hair in a queue. He usually chose an emerald green
coat, to match his eyes, and a gold waistcoat with russet threads
that mimicked his auburn hair.

More than ever, he longed for his former life.

Soon, he reminded himself. He'd only to endure this drab
society a few more weeks, until his tasks were completed. Then
he would live again where he belonged, as Valerian Caine, wearing brocade coats and drinking and gaming and fencing and
making love to beautiful women.

Raising his quizzing glass to survey the offerings, he found
that magnification improved the view considerably. Those plain
little frocks that passed for ball gowns were as fine as gossamer,
and very revealing. He aimed his glass at a feathery bird gliding
past. Her skirt clung to her thighs as if she had just come in
from the rain. Now *that* was a modern fashion he could approve.

Just then Gwen tapped his shoulder. Wrinkling her nose, she
said, "Max is fighting Waterloo again. Perhaps we should move
on in case there is someone here who knows you. Once the
dancing starts, it won't be so easy to get around."

He took her arm and led her past clusters of chatting men
and women. Now and again someone looked up and smiled,
but Gwen tugged him ahead. He realized she was shy, for all
her spirited temper, and was not eager to approach people she
didn't know. It was enough for him to be seen, so he let her set
the pace.

Winnie had disappeared. It was just the two of them, arm in
arm like old comrades, circling the room. At least one thing
had not changed, he observed with delight. The women still
noticed him. Young or old, they gazed at him through lowered

lashes and fluttered their fans. He could practically hear them calling out, silently, begging him to stop and greet them.

And then one did.

"Is that you, Robert?" called an old woman in a purple turban topped with droopy ostrich feathers. "Yes, you. The redheaded one. Come here, boy."

She pointed a skinny finger at him and jerked it imperiously. "Come *here.*"

With a smile at her companion, he made an elaborate leg to the woman. Eighty years old at the least, he thought, admiring the beauty mark on her wrinkled cheek. She at least kept up the old fashions.

The woman beckoned him closer. "My spectacles, Elspeth. Give me my spectacles."

Beside her, another lady, nearly as antique, fumbled in her reticule. Gwen stepped forward and curtsied. "Your grace, may I present my brother's guest, Mr. Jocel—"

"There now. Let me look at you." She put on a pair of wire-rimmed glasses and peered at him.

"Ah, you are so much like him." She took off the spectacles and passed her hand over her eyes. "For a moment I thought . . . but it was merely the fantasy of an old woman."

"He reminds you of someone?" Gwen put in sharply.

"Yes, indeed. Especially the eyes. Robert had eyes like that, two emeralds set in a face so beautiful he had no rivals among men."

Gwen looked surprised—Vayle realized she had not expected Max's scheme to succeed. For that matter, neither had Vayle, and something like a chill passed through him.

She recovered quickly. "Mr. Vayle has come to London in search of his relations, your grace. Perhaps you could introduce him to your friend."

"Not likely," snapped the woman. She dabbed at her nose with a lace handkerchief. "Robert Caine has been dead these forty years."

"C-Caine?"

The old woman looked at Gwen for the first time, and snorted. "You are the Sevaric chit, aren't you? Well, missie, I'll not hear any attack against my Robert, nor a word about that absurd feud. There is blame enough on both sides."

Gwen, pale as birch bark, lowered her head. "Yes."

"It was quite the scandal when I was a gel, though." The woman laughed. "Gentlemen knew the way of feuding back then. Had some meat to 'em, the Caines and the Sevarics, but their blood has run thin. Your father's, at any rate, and what's left of the Caines. Some pasty boy named Robin, I trow. He does no honor to his name."

"That is my opinion also," Gwen said through tight lips. "But my brother—"

"Compose yourself, girl. I read the newspapers, even now, and I know your brother was a soldier. Mentioned in the dispatches, as I recall. His blood might not be so thin. His brains, though, that's what matters here! Mayhap he will have the good sense not to pursue a quarrel that grew tedious long ago."

Vayle regarded Gwen with concern. She was obviously shaken. Perhaps she was remembering her father's obsession, and her own service in it. He was a trifle disturbed himself, what with this talk of a dead man who could only be a nephew or grandnephew.

"Please excuse me, your grace," Gwen said. "I must make certain Miss Crake is settled with her friends before the dancing begins." With a graceful curtsy, she turned away.

Vayle bowed to the duchess, intending to follow, but she tapped his arm with her fan. "Elspeth, amuse yourself elsewhere for a few minutes. We require your chair."

Recognizing an irresistible force when he met one, he settled next to her with a smile. And he was curious, if oddly wary, about Robert Caine. "I am Jocelyn Vayle, your grace. And you are clearly a duchess, but—"

"Dowager duchess," she corrected with a grimace. "Put out to pasture decades ago, when my son married a birdwit. And m'grandchildren take after their mother, so even the illustrious Rathbones are in decline."

She waved her fan in a gesture that took in the whole ballroom. "For that matter, so is everyone else. Look you at this dreary assembly. Dead bores, the lot of 'em, with water for spines. In my day, people knew how to have fun. We fought and schemed and made love in the grand manner, with elegance and dash. You'd have liked it, Mr. Vayle. I can tell that about you."

"I am flattered, your grace. And 'struth, I often feel I was born a century too late. Now, will you tell me about Robert Caine?" He winked at her. "You were more than mere acquaintances, I daresay."

"Naughty boy." She rapped his hand with the fan. "As was Robert. When I made my come-out, he was the handsomest bachelor in London. But he was only a viscount, and my parents were in full cry after a duke. So Robert and I stole kisses when we could while my marriage was arranged. We became lovers after I'd presented Rathbone with a pair of sons. In those days, such arrangements were understood."

"Just so." He made rapid calculations and decided that Robert Caine must have been his brother's grandson. If he had inherited the title so early in life, that must mean that Vayle's nephew Thomas had died young. Vayle closed his eyes and found an image of the little boy, laughing as his toy boat sailed the Serpentine. Blanche Sevaric had cooed over him that day, and that night Vayle had won her—

And now Thomas was long dead, and his son Robert, too. And Blanche.

"You have the look of him, that's certain." Sighing, the dowager duchess opened her fan and waved it slowly before her face. "I dreamed of him t'other night, and when I saw you I thought his ghost was passing in front of me. No such thing, ghosts, but sometimes I feel his hands on me in my sleep. He would come to me again, if he could."

Vayle gazed at the duchess with fascination. Had he not been killed in that duel, he might have known her. He'd have been in his sixties when she came out of the schoolroom. It occurred to him that he might yet have the chance to meet her when she was young and beautiful . . . be there when she fell in love with his great-nephew. How eerie it would be, seeing the girl and remembering the old woman.

Even as he watched, her eyes drifted shut and her hands fell limp against the purple silk of her skirt. To his astonishment, she emitted a snore.

He felt a tap on his shoulder.

"If you will permit, sir." Elspeth took his place when he jumped from the chair, and put a firm hand on the duchess's shoulder to hold her erect. "She insists on attending every important party, even though she dozes through most of them."

"I admire her spirit," he said quietly. "Take good care of her."

He was only a few steps away when he heard the duchess's voice, querulous now as she pushed aside sleep. "They're all dead. Everyone I knew is dead. All dust."

Vayle didn't turn back. All dust . . . Not I, he told himself fiercely. Not yet.

Gwen was nowhere to be found, and Max was still refighting old battles with a group of uniformed officers. Vayle walked by, glad to be ignored. Wars didn't matter, except to the dead. Life—that was what mattered to the living. And Sevaric ought to be getting on with that, and start looking for a wife, or at least an armful for when the party was over.

That reminded him of his own intentions. Somewhere in this room was a woman eager to warm his own bed, if Clootie was to be trusted. But he couldn't remember her name. It started with "M." Marlborough? Milquetoast?

Lost in thought, he nearly stumbled over a graceful foot planted in his way. He looked up, past long legs outlined by clinging silk to a bosom that rivaled any he had ever cradled in his hands. His gaze remained fixed there for several moments before moving on to the woman's face.

Her knowing smile told him she was well aware of where his

eyes and imagination had been, although she feigned a look of surprise.

"Pray, forgive me, sir. I was searching for a friend and nearly walked into you."

"My fault entirely," he said with a bow. And because she might be someone he ought not flirt with, he swallowed the practiced compliment that rose in his throat and waited for her to make the next move.

At his silence, she tilted her head. "Oh, dear, how awkward this is. Since there is no one to introduce us, will you think me terribly fast if I give you my name? I am Barbara Stuart to my friends, although acquaintances call me Lady Melbrook." Her slow smile became ever more knowing. "I do hope you won't be one of those."

Melbrook! That was the name Clootie had mentioned. Lifting her gloved hand, he brushed a kiss across her wrist, pressing her palm with his thumb in a gesture she could not fail to recognize. "Jocelyn Vayle, at your service. I am a stranger in London and don't know how to go on, so if I violate the proprieties you must tell me."

"I have little patience with rules, Mr. Vayle. You must look elsewhere for lessons in proper behavior. I am so very improper that yesterday, when I saw you in the park, I wasted no time in determining your name. I felt sure we should meet again soon."

Her boldness excited him, and a century ago he'd have taken the lovely brunette straight out the door and home to his bed. But he dared not invite her to Sevaric House, and could not think where else would harbor a bed for them.

Her lips curved into that knowing smile. *"Some* gentlemen," she said in a seductive voice, "would have invited me to dance by now."

"As would I," he replied immediately, "if I knew how. To dance, that is. I have been abroad for many years, and since returning to England I've learned only the waltz."

"I like the waltz above all other dances."

She hadn't yet released his hand, and she was holding it between them, close to her waist, where no one else could see. Not dust, he thought defiantly. Not I.

Just then, the orchestra began to play. For a panicky moment, he couldn't tell what sort of dance it was. Was it a waltz? He tugged his hand loose and turned to look at the dance floor. No, it was some country dance. Across the room, Gwen was taking the hand of a callow young officer in scarlet regimentals. Neither of them appeared very happy about it.

Gwen. Waltz. "I have already been promised a waltz with my host's sister. A matter of duty, you understand." Even as he said it, he didn't like the way it sounded—a duty. Lady Melbrook, though, was looking expectant. "But only the first waltz is confirmed. Perhaps later—"

"Lady Melbrook?" A young man with rosy cheeks and a receding hairline appeared at her shoulder. "I believe this is our dance."

She flashed him a brittle smile. "So it is, Lord Mumblethorpe." Turning back to Vayle, she licked her bottom lip with a slow pink tongue and pressed his hand once more. "I trust we shall meet again, sir?"

"I'll see that we do," he said under his breath as Mumblethorpe led her away.

In the meantime, he had little to do but twiddle his thumbs, since he'd promised not to enter the game rooms. Frustrated, he went looking for Winnie.

What had he come to, when the best entertainment he could find was cozing with Gwen Sevaric's chaperone?

Seven

Vengeance, thought Gwen as Lieutenant Fielding stepped on her toe for the third time.

Her partner, excruciatingly polite, apologized yet again, and she managed a wan smile even as she devised schemes to punish Max. She would get her revenge on him, for forcing this ordeal on her while he bantered with his friends.

She could not entirely blame Lieutenant Fielding, for she was no dancer either. Even Mr. Popplewell had despaired of her. But she could not relax when a man put his hand on her arm, or moved so close she could feel the heat of his body. Only once, during the waltz with Vayle, had she—

Better not to think about that.

Max's intentions were good, although misguided. And singleminded. The war won, he had set out to find his sister a husband, and only then would he consider his own future.

But she would never marry. She could not, even if some poor sod was brought to scratch, and it was past time to reorder her brother's thinking. For now, how could she repay him in kind for this night's work?

The weapons fell into her hands when the cotillion finally ended. Three matchmaking mamas descended en masse, giggling daughters in tow, all angling for information about Jocelyn Vayle.

"I scarcely know the gentleman," she protested. "He is my brother's friend."

"But he is living at your house, or so I hear," Lady Stadler observed slyly. "Surely you could provide an introduction."

"To Max? Certainly. In fact, I expect he would be delighted to partner your daughter, and the others, too. When that is accomplished, it will be quite natural for Mr. Vayle to be drawn into the circle. Please, follow me."

Max was recounting a skirmish involving heavy artillery and damp powder when she broke into the conversation. "Pardon me for interrupting, gentlemen, but I require a word with my brother."

Courteously, the men withdrew and she stood on tiptoe to whisper in Max's ear. "Several young ladies wish to dance with you, but they are extremely shy and you are making no effort whatever to be sociable. Under the circumstances, I decided to take a hand. Put a smile on your face and I'll present them." With glee, she watched color rise to the tips of his ears.

"Wretch. What are you up to?"

"Oh, a little tit for tat. Now try to be pleasant and do your duty." With a bright smile, she introduced the women and made a tactical retreat.

A few minutes later, as Major McKinney led her out for the next dance, she was pleased to see Max and a chirpy blonde take up a position next to her in the line. He cast her a disgruntled look, and she winked back.

Her delight vanished when she saw Vayle and Winnie making their way from group to group. For once, her friend Anathea Renstone had no partner, and when Vayle reached her he went no farther.

From the look on Anathea's face, she was infatuated with the rogue, and Gwen could not blame her. When Vayle turned on the charm, he was well-nigh irresistible. She might have succumbed herself, but she'd had the opportunity to take his measure and found him wanting.

So it wasn't jealousy that made her resent his attention to Anathea. She was only concerned that her friend would mistake his practiced charm for a genuine tendre. While the major led her to a side table for refreshments, she could not help glancing over her shoulder at Vayle and Anathea.

No, not jealous at all. Only worried for her friend, because the man was a fraud. She sensed it in her bones. And one way or another, she would expose him before anyone got hurt.

Honesty reminded her that he had saved her life, and that she ought to be patient while he recovered his memory—if he had truly lost it. She had more than a few doubts about that.

Years of coping with her half-mad father should have given her more forbearance. She was nothing if not self-critical, and she knew that her hostility to Vayle was excessive. But her instincts usually served her well. And her instincts told her that he would make her already difficult life more irksome. The sooner he was gone, the better.

She managed a smile when another of Max's friends—Max had too many friends—claimed her for the next dance. He said his name, which vanished from her memory as she moved with automatic steps and watched for Vayle. He had disappeared. Off with Anathea, she thought peevishly.

She stumbled again and again as she wondered what they were doing. Then she saw Anathea dancing with Lord Mumblethorpe and wondered all the more. Dear God, next would be the first waltz.

Panic rose in her throat. She could not do it. Dared not. Only once before had she been so terrified and felt so helpless. There was no reason a stupid waltz with a man she didn't like should remind her of that occasion. But it did, and she started to tremble.

"Shall I escort you to Lord Sevaric?" her partner asked kindly. "You look a bit pale."

She could scarcely hear him over the pounding of blood in her ears. Confused, she finally realized the dance had ended and the young man didn't know what to do with her.

She didn't know what to do with herself. "Excuse me," she murmured. And then she fled through the open French doors onto the terrace.

It was deserted. A quarter-moon hung low in the sky, outlining in yellow the chimney pots next door. A light damp breeze stirred the dead leaves of potted trees, and she hugged herself against the cold. At least she could breathe again, and Vayle would never think to look for her here—if he remembered that he was supposed to dance with her.

Behind her, the orchestra struck up the first notes of the waltz and couples took the floor. Against her will, Gwen walked to the window and pressed her nose against the glass.

It was uncanny, how her eyes were drawn straight to Vayle, among all the people in the crowded ballroom. He was moving along the edges of the dance floor, skirting the chaperones and glancing from face to face. He was looking for her. He stopped near the orchestra and stood on tiptoe, scanning the crowd.

She felt foolish and ashamed. It was only a waltz. Common sense, not to mention courtesy, required her to go back in and face the music. If Max could dance with those silly ingenues, she supposed she could endure another few minutes in Vayle's arms.

She had made up her mind to go inside when Lady Melbrook came slinking up to him. He shook his head, still looking around, but the widow persisted, putting her hand on his arm and stroking it. It was a pantomime of seduction.

Teeth clenched, Gwen watched as Vayle's attention focused on a woman everyone in London knew to be a slut. He smiled then, and bent his head to hear what she was saying.

Unable to bear it any longer, Gwen turned her back and aimed herself across the terrace, down the marble steps, and into the garden.

Winding through the skeletal rows of rosebushes, she gazed up in despair at the bright moon. What was she to do now? Already she was too cold to stay outside. Nor could she return to that ballroom to watch Vayle sweep Lady Melbrook into a waltz.

Gwen's waltz.

Shivering, she left the garden. Gravel crunched under her feet as she walked around the corner of the house. There she came to a pair of glass doors and peered through the small opening between the curtains. It was a library, unoccupied.

To her relief, the latch turned when she tried it, and the door swung open silently. On the opposite wall was a fireplace where a fire blazed. Two heavy wing-back chairs were angled in front of the hearth, behind an Oriental screen that sheltered the fireplace from the rest of the room.

A perfect hideaway, she thought, warm and private. She would relax here a few minutes, out of harm's way, and later explain to Max and Vayle that she'd torn her skirt and gone upstairs to have it mended.

For good measure, she took hold of the hem and made a creditable rip. Then she settled back in her chair, arms folded across her breasts, and stared into the flames.

She felt so lost.

Max's actions tonight made her realize that she could no longer avoid her future. If she didn't make her own plans, he would do it for her—and she might find herself entertaining the proposal of some poor young officer who owed him a favor. And if she didn't accept . . . well, Max would find another, and another. He wouldn't give up till he ran out of friends. Tenacity was the Sevaric curse.

Gwen suffered from it, too. But hers took a more passive form. She persevered. She had spent the last decade patiently managing the house while her father obsessively pursued his quest to destroy the Caines. When he died without quite achieving it, Max came home from the war. Gwen wanted nothing more than to take care of her brother as she had taken care of their father. It was a comfortable role, familiar, safe.

But Max deserved better than their meager family. He was a simple man, for all his dramatic looks, and preferred simple pleasures—good friends, good food, and a comfortable home. Underneath the soldierly reserve was a warmth and gentleness that would make him a loving father. He needed only a sweet wife and a houseful of children to ensure his happiness.

Instead, he was held in harness by the legacy of an old feud and the unhappiness of a younger sister.

His dependent sister. The sister he felt bound to avenge.

He would never forsake the feud, or forsake her, until he knew she could be happy on her own. But she had no idea how to go about being happy. Her misery would destroy her brother, unless she convinced him to leave her behind.

But he would not, until she was wed, because his rigid sense of honor would not allow it. Barring a miracle, Max would choose a lonely bachelor's life with his old maid of a sister rather than put another woman in her place in the household.

A sound broke into her thoughts—a closing door. Sitting up, she listened intently and heard nothing further but the crackle of the fire.

Just imagination, she thought, relaxing again. But a low sound hummed in her ears, like the murmur of voices. Then she heard a distinct sigh and the whisper of silk.

Good heavens! A pair of lovers had chosen the library for a rendezvous. The night had gone from bad to worse! She could avoid a humiliating scene only if she used the screen to conceal her escape back into the garden. Quietly she came to her feet and tiptoed to the French doors.

"Oh, Jocelyn, please," begged a husky voice. "Yes, like that."

Her hand froze on the latch. Vayle! And, if she was not mistaken, Lady Melbrook.

A rock settled in the vicinity of her heart.

He had every right to seduce women, she knew. But this capricious assignation only confirmed that Vayle was the undiscriminating lecher she suspected him to be. Let them get on with it.

She started to turn the latch when another thought occurred to her. What if someone else walked in on them? She swallowed an oath any soldier would recognize. Vayle had been invited to Lord Sefton's home because Max had vouched for him. If he were discovered *in flagrante delicto* with Lady Melbrook, her brother would be subjected to gossip and criticism. And that she would not permit.

Silently, she slipped back behind the screen, pausing only to verify it was indeed Lady Melbrook she was about to embarrass. Then, fixing a look of worldly indifference on her face, she stepped into full view.

Vayle and the widow were so preoccupied they didn't even notice her. Both were still fully clothed and on their feet, although his right hand was invisible under a swath of lace at her bosom. They were kissing, too, and their mouths were open!

Gwen shuddered in disgust.

Taking no care to be quiet about it, she walked past them toward the library door. And still they didn't look up. She wondered if they'd notice a herd of elephants stampeding by.

"Don't let me interrupt," she said sweetly. "But I suggest you lock the door when I am gone."

At that, the lovers sprang apart.

Immediately Lady Melbrook set to work restoring her clothing. She was calm, as if being caught in the act wasn't new to her. Vayle just stared at Gwen, color rising to his cheeks.

"Obviously you won't be coming home with us tonight," she said with a malicious smile. "I'll make your excuses to Max."

He lifted a hand. "Gwen—"

"Miss Sevaric," she corrected, opening the door. "Do go on from where you were."

She was halfway down the hall when he caught up with her. "You must let me explain," he said urgently. "Please."

Several guests stood in conversation a few yards away, and to avoid a public scene she stopped and turned to him. "Mr. Vayle, your nocturnal activities are none of my concern, so long as they are conducted in private. But you are a guest in Lord Sefton's home. Did you consider how this might reflect upon my brother?"

He stared at the floor. "No. Not for a moment. It never occurred to me."

"Ah."

His gaze lifted, and she was struck by the cloudiness of his eyes, usually such a transparent green. "I was selfish," he said in a somber voice. "Consumed with my own pleasures. Had I thought . . . but I wasn't thinking. Not for the world would I bring trouble on Lord Sevaric."

She wasn't sure she believed in this sudden penitence. "Max assumes that every man is honorable until proven otherwise, and is bound to pay now and again for such misplaced idealism. Fortunately I am the only one aware of your indiscretion, so he will be spared. This time."

"You won't tell him?"

"I should. But I am not partial to those who carry tales and do not care to join their ranks. I only wish men like you did not give me reason to make difficult choices. If you insist on living with us, and persist in carrying on as you've just done—"

"I will not," he said forcefully. "Carry on, I mean. At least, not in any way that will reflect badly on your family. You have my word on it."

Her lips curled. "Why does that fail to reassure me?"

"Because you do not trust me," he replied after a moment. "Until now you had no reason, but from here on I can scarcely blame you for being suspicious."

"Why not from the beginning, Mr. Vayle? By your own account, you do not know who or what you are. Perhaps you fled to England with a charge of murder on your head."

"Anything is possible," he acknowledged with a shrug. "I must say that you counter your brother's optimism with a bull-headed conviction that men are dishonorable until proved otherwise. Why is that?"

"Because I'm a realist? In your case, you must admit that I was right."

He rolled his eyes. "I am to be drawn and quartered because of a few kisses? The woman was willing and yes, so was I. But we chose our time and place unwisely. I take full responsibility, have apologized, and am sworn to be more careful in the future.

What more can I do to win myself into your good graces, Miss Sevaric?"

Drat the man! He was right and she hated him for it. It was so much easier to despise him for cause, but he kept snatching the reasons away.

"Are you angry because we missed our waltz together?" he asked quietly. "I did look for you. Truly."

She knew he had. She'd watched him. "I tore my dress," she said, lifting her skirt slightly, not enough to reveal her ankles. "See?"

"And you thought to mend it in the library." He grinned, and she thought that he looked relieved. "Shall we each confess there are a few matters we had rather not explain in detail?"

"I've nothing to confess, sir, except that I think you a contemptible libertine."

"And I think you a fascinating woman, Miss Sevaric, and an exemplar. Even a contemptible libertine like me can recognize your value. I will henceforth rely on you to keep me out of trouble."

Such trumpery about her fascination and exemplitude made her distrust him even more. Gwen gave him a repressive look as she started back to the ballroom. "Mr. Vayle, I am not in the business of working miracles."

Eight

The sun was descending behind the chimney pots when Max
and Vayle returned from the tailor's shop. It had been a difficult
afternoon, but Max congratulated himself on his patience—
never certain in the best of times. He was no expert on fashion,
having spent most of his adult life in a combat-scarred infantry
uniform. But he'd found himself citing the Gospel According
to Beau Brummell whenever Vayle got that predatory look and
picked up another garish fabric.

"Brummell said only dark colors for evening," Max would
say hastily. "And blue and buff for day wear. And white linen.
No patterned neckwear." At one point, Max appealed to the
obsequious tailor for support. But true to form, he only coughed
and suggested that Mr. Vayle take both the purple satin and the
white waistcoat fabric, and perhaps the emerald green also.

As they entered Sevaric House, Vayle was still sulking. He
cast his sedate beaver hat on the hall table and stared into the
gilt mirror as if it held some secret. "Perhaps, if we both wore
them," he said with sudden inspiration, "we could bring patches
back into fashion."

Max rubbed his aching forehead. "No patches. No powder.
This is the nineteenth century, for pity's sake!" He regarded his
companion with honest confusion. "I wish you could tell me
where you are from. You have the queerest ideas of what's in
fashion. Italy? That's where the macaronis got their start."

The butler, his arms full of their hats and gloves, coughed

discreetly. Max turned with some gratitude from his trouble-
some new friend. "Yes, Wilson?"

"A Young Lady is here to see you, my lord."

The reverence in Wilson's tone set Max on guard. "To see
me? Not my sister?"

"Yes, my lord. A Miss Caine."

Max was too surprised to speak right away, but Vayle made
a strangled sound. No doubt he'd heard about the Caine-Sevaric
feud from a helpful servant and imagined some Romeo-Juliet
tangle. Max felt it necessary to scotch the supposition. "Miss
Caine? We are not acquainted."

Wilson stood his ground with unusual pugnacity. "She is in
the drawing room. I told her you would see her when you came
in."

"She must be quite a lady," Vayle said under his breath. "Why
don't we go see?"

Max had to admit to a bit of curiosity about this heretofore
unencountered member of the thieving Caines, especially as she
had somehow made an ally of his butler. "All right, I'll see
her."

As he started off up the stairs, Vayle was close behind. Max
looked over his shoulder quizzically, and Vayle hastened to remark, "Can't meet with a young lady alone, can you? Not
proper."

Max halted on the landing to consider this. He would rather
deal with Miss Caine in private. But Vayle had a point. Who
could tell what a Caine might do to further her family's interest?
A witness might keep her honest, or at least harmless.

Max said, "Good idea, Vayle. I rely on you to guard my
back."

"From a young lady?"

"From a Caine. They haven't the least notion of honor, and
I wouldn't put ambush past them."

Vayle made that choking noise again, but Max was already
striding through the drawing room door and didn't look back
to see if he was ill. He stopped when he saw a dark-haired

woman before the fire, her cloak and her bonnet draped on the chair. "You wished to speak with me, Miss Cai—"

Max never got that damned name out, because the woman turned to face him. In the silence that followed, he felt the engine of his heart slow and halt, and then take up again with renewed force, the blood pounding all the way up to his head. This was, he thought when he could think again, the cleverest trick yet.

Vayle was no help at all. He'd forgotten to guard Max's back, and somehow managed to get in front. He materialized next to the woman and bent over her hand in that old-fashioned way of his. "Enchanted, Miss Caine."

Other ladies seemed to like Vayle's cozening ways, but this one was tougher. Immediately she withdrew her hand from his. "Thank you for seeing me, Lord Sevaric."

Vayle didn't correct her misperception, so Max had to shoulder past him. "I'm Sevaric. This is Jocelyn Vayle. A houseguest. From the colonies."

She transferred her gaze to Max. She had wary eyes, that mysterious green-gray of deep waters, and they held him for a moment before long lashes swept down to shadow her thoughts. "Mr. Vayle," she said, and favored him with the smile she had withheld when she thought him a Sevaric.

Another malicious trick. That was how she won over his butler—that dangerous curve of red mouth, the advance and retreat of a little dimple there in the right cheek, the green eyes all stirred up now with warmth. Vayle fell for it. He started making a fool of himself, as men usually did in the presence of Beauty, begging her to take a seat, ringing for tea, taking a chair across from her, acting as if he, not Max, were her host.

But Max took up the command position next to the tea caddy, leaning one hand on it and effectively blocking Vayle's view. The tea came in then, followed by a maid, and Vayle sent her back for more biscuits. The man ate like he'd been starved for decades, but at least it kept him from flinging flattery at the Caine woman.

Ah yes. The Caine woman. She held the teacup in one slender

hand, and with the other held back the flow of her hair. Damn. It was maddening, that hair, all red-dark and wavy-thick, and as a lock brushed her cheek he could almost feel it trailing across him, too, careless and caressing. He gripped the edge of the table, hard. "You had something to ask me, Miss Caine?"

The teacup was reluctant to leave her lips, and he thought he understood why: to be in touch with a mouth like that— But then he realized she was afraid. Or something. Her hand shook slightly as she set the cup back in the saucer, and she didn't look up at him, or even at Vayle, who was making encouraging sounds across the table.

"May I speak candidly, my lord?"

Max glanced back at Vayle. "Yes. He's trustworthy. Whatever you say will go no further."

"I know *Mr. Vayle* won't speak of this."

Max was speechless again, but this time it didn't last so long. He couldn't expect a Caine to understand what honor meant, could he? And so he didn't order her out, only said brusquely, "You are a guest in my home. You may be certain I will behave honorably toward you."

"I don't want my brother to know, you see."

"Your brother?"

"Robin Caine." Bitterness flickered over her perfect brow but left no mark. "The man you're trying to ruin."

Ah. This must be Dorothea Caine, the wastrel's younger sister. A woman, thus inconsequential in the larger scheme of things, but of course she wouldn't think so. "He needs little help from me, if ruination is his aim. I haven't forced him into the gaming hells."

"If you wouldn't offer to buy up his markers at a premium, no one would play with him!"

Max shrugged. "Can I help it if he is a dedicated loser? A worse cardplayer I've yet to encounter, and as for dice—"

Abruptly Miss Caine rose, gripping handfuls of lilac skirt until her knuckles were white. Max looked from those small implacable fists up the lace-trimmed bodice, sweet and rounded

and loin-tingling, to the ivory throat where he fancied he saw
a pulse throbbing, and finally to the eyes, stormy now like the
waters of the English Channel. He guessed she was angry; he
knew she was passionate. A woman who stood so straight, so
graceful, with her fists clenched and her mouth trembling—

Another dirty trick. He forced himself to stay where he was,
not stepping back from her fury, or stepping toward her passion.
He wasn't going to lose his head because some Caine woman
bit her full lower lip with small white teeth and glared at him
with those stormy eyes.

"Your brother has chosen his own path to Hell, and I must
say, he deserves it."

"Why? Just because he's a Caine?"

"Among other crimes."

That made her even more angry, but it lasted only a moment.
Then the fire went out of her eyes as if someone had snuffed
it. Those long lashes dropped again, and her mouth drooped in
the most beguiling way.

"Lord Sevaric, I am asking you as a gentleman. Lay aside
this stupid feud. My uncle is more than a year dead. It was his
obsession, not my brother's. Robin—Robin cares naught for
such things, I know it. He has done nothing to further the ani-
mosity between our families—"

"Nothing you know of, that is."

Max didn't look at her beguiling mouth anymore, or any other
part of her that might make him forget again who she was and
what she represented. He stared resolutely out the window and
reminded himself what he knew of Robin Caine.

More than Robin Caine's sister, that was for certain. She said
hotly, "He's done nothing! I asked him. And he said that he
wants no part of this feud of yours."

"He is part of it. And he's chosen to be, whether he's told you
so or not." He couldn't resist any longer, and jerked his head
around to get another glimpse of her. She was still beautiful—
more now, with the late afternoon light gilding her ivory skin.

He couldn't help the way his tone softened. "If you want no

part of it, stay out of it. I don't pursue quarrels with women. Not that your brother is much an example of a man. . . ."

The insult was provocative, but she had, he noted, the good sense to ignore it. Or maybe she agreed with it. At any rate, Miss Caine only said, "I cannot stay out of it," and hunched her pretty shoulders and crossed her arms over her bosom as if she were cold.

Vayle went back into his host impersonation, jumping up to toss another pair of logs onto the fire. When he beckoned to her, she came forward to stretch her hands toward the warmth, and Max found himself wishing that he had that sort of persuasiveness with her. He only set her back up. That was all he cared to do, of course, but still it annoyed him to see Vayle pat her hand in that avuncular manner, and the quick grateful smile she gave him in response.

It was unfair, this playing on his sympathy, on his chivalric tendencies. He wasn't any different from Vayle—he didn't like to see a woman anxious and upset, and in ordinary circumstances would do his best to make her feel better. But it wasn't any of his doing that she had a weak malicious little slug for a brother.

Roughly he said, "I haven't done anything to harm you."

"You think not?"

He couldn't see her eyes anymore, for she'd hunched her shoulders again and her lacy collar hid her face. But he didn't need to, for he heard the hard tone in her voice and knew she had regained her anger. All the better. Her anger was no threat to him.

"A year and a half ago," she said, "I was making my debut. It was the victory spring, do you remember?"

"Of course I remember. I was in the 52nd Foot. We landed in Belgium in May." A debut in 1815? Then she must be about Gwen's age, a bit younger, probably.

"I became betrothed the night after we heard of the great victory at Waterloo."

So she was betrothed, was she? He glared at the back of her

head, wanting to suggest that next time she send her fiancé to fight her battles for her. But perhaps the fiancé wasn't any more of a man than her brother, if he'd already waited a year and more and hadn't yet claimed her as his bride.

"The next month my uncle . . . died. When the estate was settled, there was little left."

There was Vayle again, patting her hand with all the sympathy in the world, as if the bankruptcy and suicide of Hugo Caine had been anything less than divine retribution. Miss Caine took a deep breath and withdrew her hand and bunched it into a fist. She turned toward Max, and pressed the fist against the lace over her breast.

"Uncle Hugo had made some bad investments, in unsound enterprises. Eventually we learned who was behind those investments—your father. He had others acting for him, of course, but his sole purpose was to entice my uncle to mortgage the family properties. The enterprises all collapsed, and the mortgages were called."

"My father had nothing to do with that." Max had heard this accusation before and found it baseless. "He was several months dead by that time, and there wasn't any evidence he ever owned any of those enterprises."

Even if it were true, well, it was only fair turnabout for the previous generation, when the Caines had implicated a Sevaric in the Jacobin rebellion. His head ended up on a pike at the Tower of London, and the family estate was confiscated and sold to the Caines.

Still, Max was a bit disquieted at the thought of such surreptitious doings. He didn't condemn covert action, but he preferred to take credit for exacting revenge. It seemed more honorable somehow.

He was even more disquieted when Miss Caine went on dispassionately, "Once my financial expectations were revealed as limited, my fiancé asked to be released from the betrothal."

"The cad! You are better off without him then," Vayle said,

and Max agreed, though his language would have been less temperate.

Miss Caine nodded soberly. "He wasn't suited for me. I know that now. At the time, though—" She shook her head and took back whatever she had meant to say. "I went back home then. I thought, at least, with my uncle and your father passed on, the feud was ended. But then you returned from the war, Lord Sevaric, and it started again."

"Your brother—" he began defensively.

"I know. My brother gambles too much. And he kept on signing markers, even after it was clear you were the one buying them up. Robin had control of my dowry, so that went first. And last year the lenders took the house our mother left us. I expect"—she added, with a hardness that looked all wrong on that sweet curved mouth—"that you sold it to buy those fine racehorses of yours."

Actually, he'd deposited the proceeds in Gwen's account at the Bank of England, as he'd done with all the funds he'd gotten from Robin Caine. But he had no reason to tell this to Caine's sister, or justify his motives at all. "Your brother should be ashamed of himself. But he hasn't even that much backbone, does he?"

He saw a protest starting up in Vayle's eyes, but Miss Caine beat him to it. "*You* should be ashamed—taking advantage of his weakness this way! Now there's nothing left worth taking, and you won't even agree to stop before you bleed us entirely dry!"

Vayle's usually friendly face was closing up, and his voice came choked with emotion. "Nothing left? All the family properties are gone?"

Max hoped that knock on the head hadn't turned Vayle into some moralizer bent on saving the world from sin. That was unlikely, considering his facility with dice, but Max supposed that pretty Miss Caine had made more than one man repent his sins—at least till they learned her dowry was gone.

He shoved away the stirring of guilt. All he had done was

buy up the markers Robin Caine had signed. That was no crime. "Caine's not been taken up by the bailiffs yet. So there must be something left."

"Nothing but the hunting lodge at Greenbriar."

Miss Caine's words seemed to echo in the sudden stillness of the room. The lodge. Greenbriar. He'd almost forgotten Greenbriar Lodge.

The light was fading into evening, but there was enough from the fire to illuminate the panic in her eyes. Max wondered abstractly what he looked like now, for she must have guessed from his expression that she shouldn't have mentioned the lodge. "You won't—" she began, but fell silent as Vayle spoke.

"Greenbriar Lodge?"

When Miss Caine pressed her lips together and refused to reply, Max said, "In Surrey. We used to own it, but the Caines took it seventy years ago." Another casualty of the treason charge against Joseph Sevaric, along with the London house and Sevaric Hall.

Miss Caine's eyes were wider now, and wary again. She must be imagining—what?

He didn't have time to speculate, for she came forward and seized his hands. Her grip was tight but not intimate. In the early evening dimness, desperation shone in her eyes as she looked up at him.

"Let it end, Lord Sevaric. You've got nearly everything we own. If—if you stop now, if you leave Robin be, I'll—I'll have him sign a waiver. I know I can do it. I need only wait until he's drunk, and give him the paper and tell him to sign. He's got no caution when he's drunk—you know that. He'll sign a waiver."

"A waiver? Of what?"

"Of our claim. We'll renounce our claim. You needn't worry that we'll prosecute then."

A chill settled through Max. It was her hands, he thought. They were cold as ice. He slowly drew his own hands away. "What have you to prosecute us for?"

Impatiently she said, "For keeping the Caine treasure, of course. We'll renounce our claim. You can bring it out of hiding then, and sell it, or give it to your wife, or whatever you want to do with it. You know it's worth far more than—than an old hunting lodge."

"I haven't got a wife. And I haven't got the Caine treasure, in hiding or out."

She made a dismissive gesture. "I don't care, do you see? You can go on saying you don't have it. I don't care. I'll give you the waiver anyway. I'll make Robin keep silent about it, too. You needn't admit that it was ever ours, if you don't want to—"

"How forbearant of you."

The tightness of his voice must have been a signal, because Vayle stepped forward, put a hand on Miss Caine's arm, and gently drew her back out of range. A chivalrous gesture that, if unnecessary. It's true, she'd as much as said he was a liar as well as a thief, and were she a man, he'd call her out for that. But Max wasn't going to hit a woman, even one who piled insult upon insult.

He couldn't stay in the same room with her though, not when she was looking at him with that mutinous plea on her face—a princess forced to beg. Savagely he cursed the brother who had reduced her to this. All the more reason to reduce him to nothing—

"I will consider what you say, Miss Caine. But it's late now, and we have a dinner appointment to prepare for. If you'll excuse us—"

She made it to the door before she gave in. Hesitating there, her hand on the knob, her gaze downcast, she said in a low voice, "Please think about what I said. About the waiver. I promise you, I can get Robin to sign it."

Before he could speak, Vayle had ushered her out of the door. Later, while Max was dressing in his room, Vayle knocked and then entered without waiting for permission. He was already dressed for dinner, and prowled around the periphery of the room as Max fastened shirt studs and pulled on stockings.

Finally Vayle stopped in front of the mirror—Vain Vayle, they must have called him at school—and frowned at what he saw there. "Tell me," he said in a casual tone, "what is this Caine treasure Dorie was talking about?"

"Dorie?"

Vayle started. "I mean, Miss Caine. Dorothea, isn't it? Didn't she say she was called Dorie?"

Max didn't remember that exchange, but then he might not have been privy to everything the girl said to Vayle. She certainly had gazed at him confidingly enough; perhaps she had felt emboldened to tell him not only her Christian name but its diminutive, too. Dorie, was it.

"The treasure," Vayle prompted.

Max shrugged into the waistcoat his valet held up. "It's some frippery thing the Caines say we stole from them. Stole! The Caines are the thieves, not the Sevarics." He shouldered Vayle out of the way of the mirror so he could tie his cravat, and brooded for a while on Miss Caine's implied accusation. "She thinks I'm as dishonorable as any Caine."

Behind him, Vayle started pacing again. "You think the Caines are dishonorable, then?"

"I don't *think* it. I know it."

"You considered Dor—Miss Caine dishonorable?"

Max regarded himself in the mirror, remembering her standing before him, clenching her fists and biting her lip and swallowing her pride. Begging for her brother. That took—courage? Desperation? "Well, no. But then, honor isn't for women, is it? They have virtue; we have honor. And the last surviving male Caine—he has no honor."

"Why? Just because he's unlucky at cards?"

His hands weren't working right, and the cravat came out lopsided. His valet took over, humming happily as he fashioned the sort of elaborate knot Max usually refused to wear. He was too distracted to remonstrate much. "Not so tight, dammit! And, no, I don't think it's a dishonor to be a poor cardplayer, though gambling away your sister's dowry about pushes the limit. No. He's dishonorable because he turned down my challenge. Like a coward."

He shouldn't have said that, but he didn't want Vayle to think that he was some rigid moralist, condemning a man for his cardplay. But Vayle seized upon the information.

"You challenged him? Just because your families have been feuding?"

"Certainly not."

"Then why?"

Max liked Vayle well enough, and trusted him, too. But this wasn't his secret to tell. "I had a reason," he said shortly, and pulled away from the tidying hands of his valet. "He knew what the challenge was about, and cravenly refused to meet me."

"He probably thought you would kill him. You've been in the army. I presume you know how to shoot."

"I told him I'd use a rapier if he preferred. And still he backed down."

"Did he apologize?"

"An apology wouldn't be sufficent." Max yanked his coat on over the pleas of his valet to take care. "Besides, he said he doesn't remember committing the offense, so won't apologize for it."

"Maybe he didn't do it."

He didn't appreciate Vayle playing the devil's advocate, if that was what he was doing. But he reminded himself that Vayle couldn't know what had transpired eighteen months ago. "He did it. There was . . . a witness."

Vayle persisted. "A *credible* witness?"

With sheer force of will, Max held onto his temper. "Yes." Abruptly he crossed to the door. "Come on, if you're coming. And you needn't worry. There's no honor in hurting women. The girl is out of it."

Vayle waited till they were out the door and halfway to St. James before he mused, "Honor. That's important to you, is it?"

Max didn't deign to respond. He was a Sevaric, and an officer in the 52nd Light Infantry—that was answer enough.

"Is there honor in buying up a man's markers? At a premium? Rather indirect, wouldn't you say?"

"It's all I can do. He won't play cards with me any longer, he won't meet me at dawn—he's no more than a worm. And if there's dishonor, it's in having to regard him at all."

He stopped in the middle of the path and glared at his new friend. "Dammit, Vayle, will you let me be? This isn't your concern."

"Ah, but it is." In the yellow light of the street lamp, Vayle looked much older, and much wiser. "More than you'll ever know."

Nine

"Coo, and aren't you the handsome one!"

Vayle glanced at the filthy, broken fingernails gripping his sleeve, and then at the rouged face and bloodshot eyes of the latest whore to accost him during the long evening.

He had his standards, despite a certain physical urgency after a hundred years without a woman. "You flatter me, my sweet." He retrieved a coin from his pocket and pressed it in her hand. "Alas, I am not my own master tonight and dare not claim a stolen hour with you. Perhaps another time?"

With a look of regret, the woman moved on to a fresh-faced youngster just entering the noisy gaming hell.

The Devil's Bedchamber was the fourth den of iniquity they had visited. Even in his wildest days Vayle had patronized only the most fashionable establishments, so this was his first venture into the stews. He might have enjoyed himself, had Max given him the slightest opportunity.

'Struth, the buxom redhead at the Hot Dice had been a lovely armful, with fresh-washed hair and a clear complexion. But he'd barely time to kiss her before his determined escort pulled him out the door and on the way to another gaming hell.

Max insisted this ramble was meant to find someone who recognized Jocelyn Vayle. Yet in each hell, they stayed only long enough to make a circuit of the rooms. None of the preoccupied gamesters would recognize him even if they looked up from the dice and cards, and Vayle had long since realized he was merely an excuse.

Max was here about some business of his own. And whatever
that was, it had taken him off for the moment. Surprised to find
himself alone, Vayle accepted a glass of champagne from a
waiter and strolled around the smoke-filled room.

The roulette wheels had been rigged, he saw immediately, and
probably the cards were marked. This was an establishment that
preyed on young flats, distracting them with drink and women.
At the tables he saw familiar faces, men who gamed at White's
and Brooks's, men with titles and the gaming fever. Stupid men.

Then he saw Robin Caine.

The viscount's cheeks were flushed with excitement. Eyes
bright, he fanned his cards on the table and raked in a mound
of notes and coins, adding them to an already large pile in front
of him.

Vayle's heart sank. Nothing was more dangerous to an ob-
sessive gambler than a lucky streak.

The grumbling losers moved away, leaving Robin alone.

"You are doing well, I see." Taking a chair, Vayle propped
his elbows on the table. "I have meant to thank you for teaching
me the rules of hazard and quinze and macao."

"Nothing to it," Robin said lightly. He was intoxicated, but,
Vayle thought, more from the victory than the brandy. "You
have a knack for games. And you are a positive genius at fencing. I still cannot credit the thrashing you inflicted on Master
Antonio."

Vayle shrugged with false modesty. "I enjoyed our lesson
yesterday, and you did well for a beginner. As for Antonio, he
made the mistake of underestimating a stranger. The next encounter will be more challenging."

"Well, my money will be on you." The coins sifted through
Robin's fingers and clinked together on the felt tabletop. "Your
style with a sword is like nothing I've ever seen, though I've
frequented Antonio's for months. Never dared try my hand until
you gave me the chance, though. Will you continue my lessons?"

"While I remain in London, yes." Three weeks more, he recalled with a surprising pang of regret. He had no future, not

here. Only a future in the past, if he managed to get back where he belonged.

"Should my luck hold tonight, I'll buy my own foil and mask." Robin gestured at his winnings and added resolutely, "And my luck *will* hold."

"Care to put that to the test?" Max Sevaric inquired softly. He had come from nowhere, it seemed, but now he loomed over the table, eyes glittering with malice.

Robin paled and automatically covered his winnings. Jumping to his feet, Vayle put his hand on Max's rigid arm. Now he understood why Sevaric had combed the underbelly of London. "Lord Lynton was just leaving, and we should be on our way, too. No one here has recognized me. Let's try somewhere else."

Max waved him away and put a flat, dusty box on the table. "Settle awhile, Vayle. Better yet, go off and amuse yourself with one of the women. I'm of a mind to play backgammon with this gentleman." The last word dripped acid. "What do you say, Lynton?"

Robin looked apprehensively at the backgammon box. "You've never played me directly. Always bought up my vowels instead. Why now?"

"Because you're here now." Max pulled out a chair and sat across from Robin. "You've been remarkably evasive this last year, scampering from the tables the minute I arrived. It was you who avoided a confrontation, giving me no choice but to come at you by other means. But I'd not have you think I ruined you secondhand. Better we end this thing face-to-face, don't you think?"

He opened the box and began to align the black pips in home position. "From what I hear, you fancy yourself an expert at backgammon. At that game, skill can make the difference. Luck, too, of course. Do you feel skillful tonight? Or just lucky?"

Robin lifted his hands from his pile of coins. "Bloody right I do, on both counts." The heat of expectation sent color to his cheeks as he gathered the red pips and lined them up on the board. "For once, I have something to wager. Put your money on the table, though. I've no faith in a Sevaric promise to pay up later."

With a sigh, Vayle lowered himself to his chair. He had been assigned to end this feud, but couldn't even think of a way to scotch the coming engagement. Or maybe it was the *coup de grâce,* to judge by the look in Max's eyes.

Still, what final satisfaction could Max wrest from plucking a few pounds from Robin Caine?

His intuition said the stakes were higher this night, but he didn't know what they were. "I wouldn't trust dice in this establishment," he advised, hefting the pair Max had dropped on the table. They felt balanced, and he was a good judge, but he doubted there was an honest set of bones in the Devil's Bedchamber.

"That's why I paid one of the ladies to dig out her own backgammon set from upstairs," Max said dryly, drawing his finger along the top of the dusty box. "It belonged to her father, hasn't been used in years, and she swears it's honest. Objections, Lynton?"

Robin glanced nervously at Vayle. "What do you think?"

"If the dice are loaded, I doubt Sevaric knows how to manipulate them," he replied after a moment. Max would not cheat, he knew, even to destroy the Caines. "But I'll be an impartial witness, and speak up if I detect a foul."

He saw nothing amiss through the first swift games. Luck ran evenly, and Robin won about twenty pounds. But the next three games went Max's way. Although the men had been well-matched at the outset, Robin drank steadily while Max left his glass untouched.

After several careless moves, Robin had lost his stake. His eyes were bleary and his hand shook as he pushed the last few coins across the table. "I'm played out," he muttered.

"Are you?" Max sat straight as a lance in his chair. "Have you nothing else, nothing at all, to wager?"

"What's the point of continuing?" Vayle put in. Max was after something that smelled of disaster. "Call it off now. The boy's drunk."

Robin's face set into a pugnacious expression. "I'm sober as a judge. Bad streak, that's all. Take my vowel if I lose the next game."

"I think not," Max said coldly. "I have a great many of your vowels already, purchased from creditors who had no hope of collecting on them. Come up with something solid, Lynton. Shall we say, the treasure?"

"You know damn well I don't have it," Robin shot back with renewed fire. "The Sevarics stole it a hundred years ago. Hell, if I had it don't you think I'd be living at high water? The way *you* do," he added sourly.

Vayle looked from one man to the other. What the devil was this treasure everyone kept talking about? Dorie had mentioned it, too. "Exactly what is the prize in dispute?"

Both men ignored him.

"You are wrong," Max said in an icy voice. "I've no idea what became of it, and am sick to death of defending myself on the subject. Put the treasure, or anything else you still own, on the table now. Otherwise we'll call it quits. Your choice."

Robin took a long swig of wine, his eyes hollow with misery. He made a move as if to stand, and then his gaze fell on the winnings in front of Max. He sat down and refilled his glass. "Greenbriar," he said. "I have title to that."

Max leaned back and crossed his arms, looking ominously pleased. "You still own a property?"

"Not much of one," Robin said through clenched teeth. "A run-down house and a scrap of land. But it's worth more than you've got there."

"I wonder that you gambled away the Lynton estate and your own town house in London while clinging to such a trifle."

"Didn't think anyone would want it," Robin said after a beat.

But his voice trembled, and Vayle knew he was thinking of his sister.

Anger sent heat to his ears and fingertips. Sevaric knew exactly what he was about, an act so repellent Vayle had not imagined him capable of it. Max had set out to win Dorie's home after she'd begged him to spare it.

Killing the last Sevaric male would end the feud, he thought savagely. At the moment it was damnably tempting to call Max out.

But he had been sent as a peacemaker. His nails dug into the palms of his hands as he dredged every ounce of self-control from his limited reserve. "Sevaric, you cannot want to be saddled with a run-down country shack. Let us go. I have the headache again. That accident—"

"I'll put all the markers I've bought against Greenbriar Lodge," Max interrupted. "This is your last chance to come about, Lynton. Take it or leave it."

Robin studied the dregs of claret in his glass. "You aren't that stupid. Why gamble a fortune against a ramshackle farm?"

"It seems I am not ready for the game to be over. So far you've been a tedious opponent, scarcely worth my time. But if you can find your backbone under that yellow streak, have at me. You need win only one match to bring me down."

A tense silence fell over the table. The raucous sounds of drunken men, shrill women, and dice hitting the table faded in the hush. Max Sevaric and Robin Caine locked gazes while Vayle sent frantic prayers to Heaven.

"I'll do it!" Robin blurted. "Greenbriar Lodge against the markers."

From that moment, there was no stopping them.

As the dice rolled across the table and the pips moved around the board, Vayle couldn't determine which man to back. The course of the feud hung in the balance, and his own fate was suspended next to it. If the Heavenly Powers were being fair, they would grant him some way to affect the outcome.

Neither family would concede until the other was in ruins. If Robin won this game, he would have the resources to continue the fight. But if he lost, he'd be left with nothing at all.

Vayle frowned. No doubt Proctor meant for him to reconcile the Caines and Sevarics, but he'd not spelled out the terms. To

the contrary, his instructions had been astonishingly vague—
"On Christmas morning, the feud must be at an end."

A Sevaric victory would accomplish that, his most difficult
task. And it would achieve most of the rest, too, because Max
and Gwen were bound to be happy at the outcome.

That left only Dorie. If Max took Greenbriar Lodge, she
would be left homeless. But not for long, Vayle reflected, his
innate optimism surfacing. He'd only to find her a husband, and
with her astonishing beauty that would not be difficult. Yes,
better for him if Max came out on top.

And yet, what of Robin? He was the last Caine, the only male
heir of a family that had endured for centuries. His own blood,
Vayle thought with a shiver. Robin was not one of his tasks,
though, so why should he care?

But he did.

Still torn, he wrenched his attention back to the game. Robin
was playing like a man possessed. His drunken lassitude had
vanished with the chance of redeeming himself, and the dice
cooperated. At the end, Max was pinned in.

Only a roll of double sixes could save him. One chance in
six-and-thirty.

As Max shook the dice in the leather cup, the gazes of all
three men fixed on the board.

Vayle clenched his fists to keep from grabbing the dice. Only
a disaster could bring an end to the give-and-take that had kept
the two families at odds. If Max lost now, he would pursue the
feud long past Christmas Day. And Proctor would relegate Valerian Caine to—

He didn't even want to contemplate the possibilities.

Double sixes, he murmured under his breath. Help me, Francis.

The dice tumbled from the cup, rolled across the green baize
table, and came to a stop.

Ten

Robin Caine led them up a dark twisted flight of stairs, apologizing under his breath for the broken banister and the steps littered with old newspapers. After skirting the protruding plank on the top step, Max wasn't surprised at the door that shrieked as it opened, and the debris-ridden room revealed when Lynton lit a candle.

It wasn't so much the bare mattress under the taped-up window that confirmed his impressions—Max had lived in much worse accommodations on the Peninsula—but the empty gin bottle on the table, and the pile of clothes in the corner, and the dirty chamber pot left out in the middle of the floor.

The whole place reeked of failure. Weak and wasted—that was the Caine legacy now.

But not in the sister. Max watched for some resemblance as Lynton squatted to root around in the papers under the table. Brother and sister both had that red-tinted hair, though Lynton's was dirty and lifeless. And they shared the fair complexion, only what was ivory and rose in the sister was pasty and florid in the brother.

The slender build, the straight back—there was some similarity. But he couldn't imagine the rosy-cheeked Miss Caine wheezing just from the exertion of rising to her feet. He couldn't imagine her in a room like this, or in a life like this.

Lynton must have been thinking about her, too, for he peered at the Greenbriar deed for a long moment before folding it up again. "I didn't tell you this when I staked the lodge. But m'sister Dorie lives there."

Max only nodded.

Lynton dropped the deed on the table and moved back to let Max pick it up. "You'll give her some time to find another situation?"

Vayle, who had been silent through all this, shot a scowl at Max. "Don't you worry. He'll do what's right."

Whether he wants to or not, Vayle was implying, and Max felt a stirring of anger. But then, it was clear he felt some strange sympathy for Lynton. Max couldn't. He'd spent his own youth seeing boys of far worse backgrounds dying bravely for principles that were only words to Lynton—honor and country and loyalty. Any one of them deserved life more than this worthless sod.

Max pocketed the deed and walked to the door. But Vayle lingered at the table, staring at its scatter of fripperies. Max saw nothing of much interest there—an old snuffbox, a few cufflinks, a woman's ivory fan, things Lynton couldn't pawn or gamble away.

Vayle was transfixed. He picked up the snuffbox and pried it open. There was nothing inside, snuff being more expensive and less essential than gin. Nonetheless, he brought it closer and inhaled. "Where did you get this?"

Lynton had been slumped on the bed, head in hands, but he looked up at this. "Family heirloom." He shot a glare at Max. "One of the few that weren't stolen from us."

Max intended to leave without a fight, so he pressed his back against the door and clenched his fists and kept his mouth shut.

Lynton glanced at the fists and hastily turned back to Vayle. "It's almost a century old."

"More than that," Vayle said absently. "It's from the time of Queen Anne."

"That's right," Lynton said. "I remember now my uncle saying that. How did you know?"

Vayle closed the box and set it gently on the table. "I—I just recognized the style, the Oriental influence. Dragons are—were a popular image then."

Max cut this discussion short by opening the door. Its shriek woke Vayle from his reverie and got him moving. As the two of them emerged into the damp night, Max decided that Gwen was right about Vayle's erratic memory—imagine remembering snuffbox styles and not your own name.

But one glance at his companion's face reminded Max of his resolution to stay out of altercations tonight. Vayle looked to be spoiling for a fight, and Max knew better than to give him one.

Still it was outside of enough, he thought resentfully, to have a blood like Vayle disapproving of him. Max Sevaric was known among his regiment and indeed the entire army as a man who could be counted on to play fair at cards, steer clear of his brother officers' wives, treat his mistresses generously, and keep his given word. A man of honor, in other words. And yet Vayle, who had proved to be a cardsharp and a gallant, was stalking down Storey's Gate, righteous as a rector.

Waving away a hackney driver, he caught up with the tight-lipped Vayle. "You were the one who called it dishonorable to buy Lynton's markers."

"So you fleeced him instead?"

"Fleeced him? *Fleeced* him? By God, if you hadn't saved my sister's life, I'd—" Max broke off, took a deep breath, and got firm hold of his temper. "I did not cheat him. He can't dice any better than he plays cards, that's all."

"You took advantage of his drunkenness."

"If not me, it would have been someone else. The man is begging to be ruined, and I might as well have the pleasure of obliging him."

"You insulted him, too, telling him you'd had enough of his markers and wanted real property."

"He hasn't anything to back up his markers. Nothing left but the lodge. You heard what his sister said."

"Ah, yes." Vayle's voice was heavy with meaning. "His sister.

Who came to you in secret, and asked for your word as a gentleman that you would not betray her—"

"I didn't betray her," Max said sharply. "I never told Lynton how I heard of the lodge."

"No. You just used the information she gave you to deprive her of her home."

It was a low blow, and Max felt it hard. He walked on in silence for a block or so. "I haven't deprived her of her home. I'll—I'll—" He hadn't considered what precisely he would do about Miss Caine, but an image of her face came up in his mind, and he spoke impulsively. "I'll lease the place to her. On favorable terms."

Vayle shrugged skeptically, and Max was moved to add, *"Very* favorable terms. I promise you, I shall be a better landlord than that no-account brother of hers. Did you see the way he kept his rooms? Is it likely he's kept Greenbriar Lodge any better? At least I'll maintain the property."

The only answer was a jerk of Vayle's head, which said, plainly enough, that he would believe that when he saw it. Max was about to take issue with this doubt, but then he heard a tinkle of glass and the street went dark.

At last. A fight he didn't need to avoid.

He still had a soldier's instincts; in the instant before the street lamp went out, he memorized his surroundings—St. James's Park ahead, the dark rowhouses lining the street, the four shadows veering up out of the alley to the right.

His hand went to his belt, but he wasn't uniformed, so his sword wasn't there, nor his sidearm either. From a few feet away, he heard the surreptitious slide of metal—Vayle must have a swordstick in his cane. "Good man," he said under his breath, and dropped into a crouch, his fists at the ready.

It took a moment for his eyes to adjust, but a bit of light came from a lamp in a nearby window, and eventually he made out the street ahead. The shadows blocked their way a dozen feet away, darker than the darkness.

Max considered retreat, but discarded it—at two to one, the

odds weren't great enough to merit running. Vayle must have had the same thought, for he stepped forward brandishing his short sword. For a moment, they all stood there, a tableau of threat, and then came a shout and the shadows leaped at them.

One landed full on Max, but he took the blow on his shoulders and straightened out, hurling the man off. He saw a flash of steel and threw up an arm to block it. As soon as he felt the blade slash through his sleeve, he chopped down with his fist, striking leather.

With a muffled cry, the attacker fell to the ground, moaning and holding his arm.

Immediately another footpad took his place on Max's back. Though he reared, Max couldn't dislodge him nor the hands that tightened around his throat. His vision went red, his breath came choked and useless, and in the clarity of the moment, Max considered the irony of having survived six years of war only to die on a London street.

But then he heard a scream—not his own, he was almost sure—and the hands released their killing grip. Max stumbled back against the discarded body of his attacker. He bent low, grabbing for air, and heard the man's low moan, "I'm cut, lads!"

Alive, then. But no longer a threat, thanks to Vayle, who calmly wiped his blade on his breeches. The two remaining footpads retreated back into the shadows, but Max knew better than to relax his guard. So did Vayle—he held the blade chest-high, flashing a warning in the dimness.

But it wasn't enough. Over the rasp of several exhausted breaths, a shot rang out. The bullet whistled past them and ricocheted against the stone stoop across the street, then clattered into silence.

Diving toward the nearest house, Max readied himself for the next one. But Vayle just stood there in the middle of the path, his blade out as if it could ward off a bullet. He didn't respond to Max's warning shout. Cursing Vayle's habit of going off into trances, he launched himself just as a muzzle flashed red. The bullet went over his head as he knocked Vayle to the ground.

He listened hard, his face pressed against the dirt. When he heard the clatter of a retreat, he looked up cautiously. Only the attacker wounded by Vayle's blade remained behind, curled up in the gutter.

Vayle rose then and held out a hand to Max. Wearily, Max used it to haul himself to a stand. "Good work there," he said. "I owe you."

"No," Vayle said. "You paid me back quick enough. I—I heard the bullet ricochet. Didn't know there would be another after it."

"In my experience," Max replied, "bullets always come in pairs." He crossed the street and knelt beside the footpad. The man's breathing was ragged, but he heard no death rattle.

In the light from the nearby window, the blood was dark on the man's dark green shirt. Max felt in his pocket for a handkerchief, wadded it up, and pressed it to the wounded shoulder. The footpad groaned but came out of his faint and opened his eyes.

"You'll live," Max said. He took the man's hand and placed it against the bandage. "Just keep that tight on the wound. It's not bleeding too badly. They'll be back for you?"

"I think so. Once you've left."

"Right." He pulled off his greatcoat and draped it over the prone figure, and started to walk away. Then he turned back, leaving Vayle behind, and dropped his purse—all he had won from Robin Caine—on the ground beside his coat. The coins clinking on the pavement woke the man again, and he turned a puzzled face toward Max.

"Steady, trooper. The other lads will be here soon."

Vayle was silent for a street or two, but Max knew it wouldn't last. And it didn't.

"Others might have called in the watch."

It wasn't exactly a criticism, nor a suggestion. Max just shrugged.

"You gave him your purse."

Max's throat was sore, and anyway, explanations never came easy for him. He only said, "Did you see his shirt?"

"His shirt?"

"Rifle green. He was in the 95th Riflers. That's a Light Division regiment, like my own." After a moment, he added, "The troopers, the men in the ranks, they didn't have much to come home to, you know. Most only ever knew the army. And once the war was done, the army was done with them."

"Still, he tried to kill you."

He could feel Vayle's questioning gaze and flushed. "What else does he know, but killing? That's what we trained him to do. Not that I condone highway murder. Maybe now, with that bit of a stake, he'll find some other occupation."

They walked in silence the rest of the way home. But as they approached Sevaric House, Max stopped short at the sight on his doorstep. He couldn't see the face, but he knew the slight figure all too well. Wrapped in her cloak, hunched down on the stone step, Dorothea Caine awaited him.

Vayle laughed quietly. "Now you have a real fight on your hands."

Eleven

"What the devil are you doing here?"

Vayle watched, stunned, as Max jabbed an accusing finger at the small figure on the doorstep.

"Have you no sense whatever? It's blasted cold!"

"An excellent point, my lord." Vayle used his cane to push Max aside, bent to one knee beside Dorie Caine, and took her hands. They felt like two small chunks of ice even through his gloves and hers. "Open the damn door," he told Sevaric harshly.

While Max felt in his pocket for the key, Vayle lifted Dorie to her feet. "You'll be right as a trivet, once we get you warm again."

She could hardly stand, so he put his arm around her and supported her into the foyer. Even as he spoke his meaningless reassurances, he heard her teeth chattering and knew she couldn't reply. His heart went out to her, so cold and so vulnerable, a pawn in the murderous game already lost.

He hugged her to his side, cursing himself for playing a part in her ruin. He had wanted this to happen, wanted Max to win because it suited his own purposes. Or so he imagined at the time. Now he couldn't remember why Max's victory was so necessary.

Max had resumed his air of command and led them to the study. The fire had nearly died out. He tossed wood onto the grate and stirred the smoldering embers with a poker as if his life depended on it. "Get some tea," he said over his shoulder. "She needs to drink something warm."

Vayle raised his hands in a helpless gesture. Get some tea? He was about to ask how when Max spun around, scowling at Dorie.

"Why were you sitting outside?" His voice cracked, at odds with a jaw set harder than rock. "It's three o'clock in the morning."

Dorie drew herself up proudly. "No one would let me in. I was informed by a man named Clootie that the gentlemen were not at home and that Miss Sevaric was occupied with a guest. Then he slammed the door in my face."

A long silence followed that pronouncement.

"You mustn't blame your footman for turning away a stranger at midnight, Lord Sevaric," she said in a more subdued voice. Now the fire was blazing, and she moved closer and held out her hands to the warmth. "I ought not have come at all, especially at such an hour. But I had hoped that if we could talk again, one more time, you might agree to put an end to this feud."

Her small body, silhouetted by the flames, was shaking with cold. She pulled her cloak more tightly around her. "Stupid of me, I know, to dismiss the hack and wait for you to come home. It's just that I felt desperate all of a sudden, as if I must prevent something terrible."

Too late, Vayle thought as he drew a chair and urged her to sit close to the fire. "Clootie is my valet," he said, settling her into the seat, "and had no right whatever to turn you away. I'll see that he regrets it." He glanced meaningfully at Sevaric, a warning to treat her more kindly, before turning back to her.

How lovely she was. All the Caine beauty, passed on for generations, culminated in this woman. He felt a thrill of pride just looking at her. Her gaze met his, and he revised his initial impression of Dorothea Caine as a helpless victim. Despite hours alone in the winter night, she remained fearless and determined.

With genuine respect, he bowed. He almost pitied Max for the confrontation to come. 'Struth, she was more than a match for him. "I expect our host has something to explain to you, my dear. Meantime, warm yourself while I brew a pot of tea."

Max shot him a furious look as he headed into the passageway. Tea. That meant the kitchen, wherever the devil it was.

He spent several minutes looking for it, and more time examining the place when he got there. He had never been in a kitchen and didn't know what to expect. The large room was dimly lit with a pair of wall sconces, and a banked fire glowed in an enormous flagstone hearth. Mysterious metal contrivances—stoves, he supposed—stood adjacent to sinks fitted with odd devices to emit water. Exactly how he didn't dare guess.

Vayle feared he would make major trouble here if he truly set out to produce tea. He might set a fire, or start a flood—Max wouldn't appreciate that. Clootie would know the technique for making tea, but Vayle wasn't ready to face him yet. Not while rage churned in his veins, as it had since Max gulled Robin into wagering Dorie's home. The sensation was so unfamiliar it alarmed him.

He could kill—*had* killed—with the lethal calm that assured victory. But temper was alien to him. He considered it vulgar, a waste of the energy best devoted to pleasure, and was astonished to discover this wholly unexpected vice in his nature.

Restless, he prowled the kitchen, opening cupboards and finding contraptions that looked for all the world like instruments of torture. A dented tin caught his eye, and he was pleased to discover an assortment of biscuits inside. Popping one into his mouth, he carried the container to a trestle table and lowered himself on the bench.

When Proctor told him about the feud, Vayle thought it a great piece of silliness, even if, in some measure, it was meant to avenge him. Initially, he considered ending a quarrel sparked by a century-old duel to be no challenge at all. In his experience, such matters were gossip-fodder for a week and forgotten when the next scandal inevitably took center stage.

Vayle himself could not remember sustaining an emotion of any kind longer than a week. If desire, the most compelling of human passions, flowered as briefly as a rose, surely hatred could not endure a hundred years.

But it did, in Max Sevaric. The same man who gave his cloak and purse to a footpad was willing, without a blink, to destroy Robin and Dorothea Caine. It made little sense, at least as Vayle understood the man and his morality.

Robin was a pathetic, harmless sot, and Dorie an unsophisticated girl, unequal opponents to a skilled and experienced soldier. Max could take no triumph in defeating these two. Indeed, he had been bristling with defensiveness all the way back from Robin's, and his rage at Dorie must have been inspired primarily by guilt.

Yet Vayle sensed that if the Caines acquired anything worth owning, Max would resume his criminal course. It was as if his honor and virtue had been corrupted by hatred, and victory only encouraged him.

He bit into his third biscuit, which tasted like the ashes of his foul mood. Damn! What should have been a simple task had become so complex he could not imagine a solution. And if he failed, it was back to the Afterlife and an eternity playing shepherd to dung beetles.

And another century, perhaps, of hatred between the Sevarics and Caines.

With a sigh, he propped his chin on his wrists. Then again, he thought, ending the feud might be easier than that other task—bringing happiness to Gwen Sevaric. He wished he could just prescribe marriage for her, as he had with Dorie. But even dowry-less Dorie could make a man lose his head. Gwen had the dowry, but to get it, a man would have to put up with her sour disposition and plain appearance.

That wasn't entirely fair, he supposed. Gwen had pretty eyes, sad eyes, almost haunting. Still, no man took a woman to bed because he liked her eyes.

Gwen's fate could wait, he decided. Thinking about her made him oddly uncomfortable. Meantime, he had the faint hope Dorie could restore to Max some semblance of Christian charity. Her strong will and his sense of honor must be clashing even now, and perhaps that conflict would make Max see the error of his ways.

It might help that Max wanted her. That must be disconcerting for him, to desire her even as he defended himself from her charges. Honor, guilt, and lust were a volatile mix, and Max was ripe for a detonation. Just as well. As he was the most virulent of the feuders, he must be brought down first.

Vayle devoured another biscuit, and this one was sweet on his tongue. He still had more than three weeks before his deadline, and a better sense of the weapons at his disposal. There was Max's honor, and Dorie's beauty, and Gwen's—well, he would find something to do with Gwen later. For the time being, he might be able to use what he had learned about human nature to his advantage.

But he was accomplishing nothing here in the kitchen. With renewed confidence, he removed his boots, set them under the table, and put out the kitchen lamp. Then he tiptoed upstairs and crept down the hall to the open doorway.

There was no sound from the study.

Had Max tossed Dorie back into the streets? That unaccustomed rage swept through him again, until he peered around the doorway and caught sight of her. She was standing half turned in his direction, holding a piece of paper as if expecting it to burst into flame.

"It's over, then," she said in a voice edged with pain. "You took my home. Oh, God."

Crouching in the shadow of a grandfather clock, Vayle watched the paper drop from her hand onto the hearth. Max swept it up before a cinder could set it ablaze.

"You needn't worry that I'll put you out." He folded up the deed and tossed it onto his desk. "I don't care to hunt, and haven't any use for another house."

"Then why did you— Oh. Now I see." Dorie was quiet for a moment, then continued with eerie calm. "It was because I told you that we had nothing else left. You wouldn't have gone after my home if I hadn't told you that. I never expected—I never thought that you would use that against me."

"It's not against you! It has nothing to do with you."

"It does now. You've stolen my home."

"I've stolen nothing." Max crossed his arms and retreated into haughtiness. But Vayle heard, or hoped he heard, the remorse under the anger. "I'm no thief, and I won't have you saying that I am. Your brother was the one who gambled away the dowry and the home that was rightfully yours. Call *him* a thief, if you will. But not me."

"So you took advantage of his weakness." With a *grande dame's* scorn, she drew back from Max until she was barely visible in the shadows. "And you stole my home as surely as if you'd broken into Robin's desk and made off with that deed. Are you proud of yourself, Lord Sevaric?"

In the light from the fire, his expression was indeed proud, and Vayle knew a certain despair. Max was stoking his anger, probably because it felt better than remorse.

"You reap what you sow, Miss Caine. And your family has sown falsehood and libel about mine. Your brother won't stop gambling, and he won't stop losing. And now that he has nothing else to wager, he will be compelled to bring out what the Caines have hidden these last hundred years. And be assured that when he finally wagers the treasure, the truth will be known."

"The *truth,*" Dorie said icily, "is that your ancestors stole the treasure decades ago. There's no libel involved. And I have proof."

"You can't have any such proof. My family has never had the damned thing."

"Then why did your father taunt my uncle time and again? I saw the letter. 'The treasure is most splendid,' he wrote. 'I am gazing upon it even as I write.' He boasted of possession. Surely that is proof!"

Max took a step back, clearly startled. "I don't believe it!"

"Are you calling me a liar, Lord Sevaric?" Dorie's voice was dangerously low. If she were a man, Vayle thought, she'd be flinging a glove in his face.

Max backed down, as he never would have with a man. "Of course not. If you say you saw a letter, I believe you saw a letter. But that does not mean they were from my father."

"I saw the seal. An italic *S*."

Boldly, she walked over and seized his right hand. He was too surprised to resist as she pulled off his ring and held it up to the light. "There! That is the seal I saw on the letter."

Max grabbed the ring back and stuck it in his pocket. "Perhaps he did make such a boast. But—but it was part of his plan, I'm certain. He must have wanted to disorient your uncle into making some mistake that would reveal the treasure's hiding place. He wasn't . . . precisely in his right mind, near the end."

"Why such a complicated explanation, instead of the simple one? Which is that your family has had the treasure all along."

Vayle shifted uncomfortably, trying to make no sound. A muscle in his thigh had cramped, distracting him from the conversation. Still, it seemed as if he ought to know something about this mysterious treasure. His family's vault had harbored any number of valued heirlooms, but they all belonged to his elder brother. Vayle had given them no mind, caring only that his allowance was paid quarterly.

His brother had been especially partial to a folio of Shakespeare's plays, though. Perhaps that was it.

Max's exasperated voice broke into his thoughts. "We have never had the Caine treasure. If you don't believe me, perhaps you'll believe the inventory that was done when I inherited. Everything we own, down to the last spoon, is listed."

"That would prove nothing. Your father wouldn't list it, would he?"

"The inventory was done by a solicitor's firm after his death. Signed and sworn. Here, I'll show you."

Vayle peered through the open door and saw Max pick up a lamp and walk behind the desk. He raised what looked like a decorative sword hanging on the wall. A narrow panel swung open and Max and Dorie vanished from view.

A secret room! Vayle slipped into the study and surreptitiously moved closer to the desk. As he gazed at the panel door, a thrill pulsed through him. He could solve every problem between the Caines and Sevarics. Dorothea could reclaim her beloved Greenbriar Lodge, and should the treasure surface again, it would belong to the both of them.

All he had to do was close the door without Max or Dorie seeing him, lower the sword to lock it, and they'd be bolted in for the night!

No virile man, and Max Sevaric was surely that, could resist a beautiful woman in an enclosed space. And even if Dorie held him off, as she probably would, they would be compromised.

Honorable men married women they compromised, and Max was nothing if not honorable. 'Struth, he might even see it as a way to make up for stealing Dorie's home. . . .

Padding to the narrow panel door, Vayle gently pulled it shut. Then, with infinite care, he slid the heavy sword into its latch.

"Enjoy yourselves," he murmured as he left the office, closing the door behind him.

He sauntered down the hall, congratulating himself for his brilliant maneuver, imagining Max's face when he discovered their entrapment. He was headed for the stairs to his bedroom when he saw a ghost.

The apparition floated some distance above the floor, draped in white and wavering in the light of a single candle.

A shaft of icy terror held him in place, until he realized a ghost was the last thing he had to fear. By the rood, he *was* a ghost. But he couldn't bring himself to move, even when the spirit descended to the floor and advanced toward him.

"What in the name of heaven are you doing here?" Gwen Sevaric demanded. She set her candle on a table and folded her arms, her small bare foot tapping as she waited for an explanation.

Vayle broke out laughing. Now that he could see her clearly, he realized she had been standing on the stairs that led to the second floor. The white gown was her nightrail, an altogether pedestrian swath of flannel.

"Well?" Her foot tapped double time as he moved closer, still laughing. "Should I call a footman to search your person?"

That brought him up short. "Search my—? Oh, I see. You imagine I've been pilfering the family silver." With a smile, he held out his arms. "Rummage away, Miss Sevaric. Anything you find is yours for the taking."

She took a quick step back, her cheeks flaming. "You are insufferable!"

Repentant, he dropped his hands. "My apologies. It's only that you startled me. At first sight, I actually thought you a . . . well, never mind that. And then you practically accused me of stealing, although that is no excuse for my ill-bred remark."

"I expect rakes to be offensive." The embarrassed color in her cheeks had faded, and her voice resumed its usual acidity. "I am simply not accustomed to having one in the house. And you have not explained why you are roaming the halls without your boots."

He looked down and discovered that he was, indeed, bootless. "They are in the kitchen." He needed to draw her away before she decided to inspect the rooms behind him. By now Max and Dorie were probably banging on the wall and yelling for help.

Fortunately, the hidden sanctuary must be resistant to sound, because he heard nothing. But he spoke loudly to cover any stray noises. "I thought to make some tea and changed my mind, but perhaps we could brew a pot together." He gestured to the back of the house, away from the study. "Or enjoy a glass of wine?"

"That is an altogether improper suggestion, as you well know. Especially tonight, with Mrs. Fitzniggle in residence."

He choked back a laugh. "Mrs. F-Fitzniggle?"

A wicked and, he suspected, unwilling grin curved her lips. "She is a distant relation and has her ear to every scrap of gossip in England. You did not fall out of the sky, Mr. Vayle. If you came here by ship, as we suspect, Mrs. Fitzniggle will soon discover which one carried a passenger matching your description. That's why I invited her."

"So you can be rid of me," he said, finishing her unspoken thought. "I regret that my presence is so distressing, but—"

"Keep your voice down," she interrupted with a scowl. "I came to investigate because I heard noises, and if Mrs. Fitzniggle does the same it will be a disaster. She is the highest of sticklers, and were she to find us alone together, dressed as we are, a parson would be summoned immediately."

"Indeed?" He rubbed his chin thoughtfully. "Then by all means we must take care. Still, I look forward to meeting the redoubtable Mrs. Fitzniggle. The sooner she traces my origins the better, since I am such a burden to you. Perhaps we could arrange a meeting tomorrow morning? Where could we meet? It might help if an atlas and a globe were at hand for consultation."

To his relief, she accepted without comment his notion that in geography lay the key to his identity. Vayle willed her in the right direction, and she didn't fail him. "Max has both in his study, and a map of England on the wall."

"Capital! He shan't mind our meeting there, I'm certain, for I think he meant to spend the morning at Tattersall's." As that latest lie rolled trippingly off his tongue, Vayle reminded himself that it was all for a good cause. He just hoped Francis and Proctor had taken the evening off.

"I'll see that a message is given to Mrs. Fitzniggle by the maid who brings her morning chocolate. Is nine o'clock too early?"

"For a rake?" he inquired with a deliberately ostentatious bow. "Generally, I would say yes. But I'll exert myself this once to accommodate you. Will you join us, Miss Sevaric?"

A smile flickered and vanished before she nodded. Gwen Sevaric had a smile lovely enough to match her lovely eyes. He wished it would remain long enough to be enjoyed.

"I dare not leave you alone with Mrs. Fitzniggle," she said

crisply. "You would charm her into doing whatever you wanted her to do, and I'm not at all sure what that is."

"Is she beautiful?" he asked with a wink.

Gwen picked up her candle. "She is passing sixty years old and has a nose like the beak of a macaw. But I'll be there to chaperone in case you are tempted." Without a farewell, she made her way to the staircase.

A trick of the light outlined her body under the dense folds of flannel, and he noted with appreciation her shapely legs, rounded bottom, and slender waist.

Perhaps a man could be found for her after all.

Yes, a good night's work, he reflected as he opened the door to his bedchamber. With luck, Dorie and Max were even now locked in a passionate embrace, and it remained only for Mrs. Fitzniggle to do her duty and discover them. Then—then the feud would be over.

He couldn't suppress a certain envy. In Max's place, with some other woman, he would certainly be taking full advantage of the situation. As it was, desire hummed in every part of his body. Some parts were practically singing an oratorio.

He stripped off his clothes, random thoughts playing in his head.

Could he have been killed had Max not thrown him to the ground before the robber's bullet hit? He was, after all, dead already.

For a split second, when he heard the sound of the ricocheting shot, he had relived that earlier death. No harm done this time. Perhaps his guardian Francis had been paying attention for a change.

On the whole, he'd rather rely on Max Sevaric when the bullets started flying.

Then there was that blasted treasure everyone was disputing. The Shakespeare folio was a definite possibility. As he recalled, it was a hefty book, not easily concealed. But what if—? A vague memory tickled at his mind and disappeared before he could grab hold of it.

More to the point, had Proctor granted him any supernatural powers? On at least two occasions he had wished for some unlikely occurrence, and willy-nilly his wish had come true.

The runaway carriage that gave him a chance to rescue Gwen and Max's lucky throw of the dice were the most obvious examples. And Gwen had chosen exactly the right place for tomorrow morning's encounter with Mrs. Fitzniggle, who would be a prime witness when Max and Dorie were found together.

Coincidental, perhaps. And he knew damned well that wishing for something didn't make it happen, because he had been wishing for a woman ever since he recovered from the accident. If his wishes had any power behind them, he would not be sleeping alone tonight.

The sheets felt like ice against his naked body as he stretched out in the bed. Within a few hours, the forced union of the Caine and Sevaric families would put an end to the feud. Oh, there would be squabbles galore, but Max's obvious desire for his bride and Dorie's common sense would bring them to terms in short order.

Which left only Gwen.

She should marry Robin, of course. That would complete the circle and join the families forever. Another excellent idea, he thought—Robin and Gwen. The perfect solution.

But he spent the rest of the night with his arms crossed behind his neck, staring at the ceiling, wanting something else entirely. Something as elusive as the missing treasure.

And when Clootie arrived with a basin steaming with hot water for his morning shave, he still didn't know what it was.

Twelve

Dorie could hardly believe it. A secret office, concealed behind a wall! How very like a Sevaric to build such a place, a sanctuary for hiding away and scheming to ruin.

As Lord Sevaric raised the lamp, Dorie could see the extent of this folly. There were no windows, so his was the only light, and the corners of the room were hidden in darkness. She got the impression of ledger books scattered on the bare floor and desk. And she could smell dust everywhere. Probably no maid had ever been allowed in here.

To judge by the disarray, the current Lord Sevaric seldom ventured into this place. Even now, as he looked for the document he promised would prove all, he was straightening the books on the desk. "Here it is," he declared, tugging a sheaf of papers from under the blotter.

But he didn't give them to her. Instead, he set the candle on the table and, bending low over the pages, scanned the document. "Come here and see. There's nothing on this list that resembles your treasure."

Dorie stayed where she was, several feet away. She didn't want to stand there next to him and watch his finger travel down the list of his father's possessions. She didn't want to see how much the Sevarics owned now they had ruined the Caines.

"I don't care."

Sevaric glanced up, startled. "But you wanted proof. Here it is."

"I don't care about what you call proof. Your father could

have hidden it in some drawer somewhere. He had a secret office, so why not a secret drawer?"

Stepping back, Sevaric gestured toward the desk. "There's no secret drawer in here—look for yourself."

"But don't you see, I don't care!" She closed her fists tight again, and her eyes, and finally her mouth. None of it mattered—not the feud, not the treasure, nothing but her home. And he had stolen that, and it mattered naught that he'd done it legally. It was all she had, and he had taken it, and all it meant to him was another item to list in that damned inventory.

Blinded by tears she wouldn't let fall, she ran to the door and wrenched at it. But it didn't give. Cursing her own stupidity, she rubbed at her eyes and took hold of the handle again and yanked. It turned, but the door didn't open.

Sevaric was beside her in an instant. "Let me try."

He had no better luck. "The latch is down on the other side. It must have fallen when the door shut."

"But you left the door open!"

Sevaric studied the door as if it contained some answer to this puzzle. "Perhaps a draft blew it shut."

"More likely," Dorie said bitterly, "it's your father's ghost. His final revenge on the Caines—locking me in here with a Sevaric."

He looked hard at her once and then resolutely ignored her. "It opens inward, so I can't very easily smash the latch. But I might as well try—"

And before she knew what he meant, Lord Sevaric drew back and then shoved himself forward, crashing his broad shoulder against the thick oak door. It shuddered but didn't move. Again and again he tried, resolution and exertion darkening his face. Finally, when the front panels were splintered but the frame itself was unaffected, Dorie cried, "Enough!"

She wouldn't admit that she worried about his shoulder. "Brute force will not work, Lord Sevaric. Else you certainly would have broken through to Portman Square by now! Perhaps we should try using our minds instead?"

He was breathing hard, but managed to reply, "If you have any brilliant ideas, please share them with me."

"Mr. Vayle was going to prepare tea for us. He is probably returning just now. If we shout, surely he will hear us and set us free."

As she might have expected, Sevaric responded to this sensible suggestion with a hint of scorn. "I think if he were about, he would have heard the ruckus I just made. But shout if you like, and I will join you."

She felt foolish, pressing her mouth against the crack between the door and the frame and calling out, "Help!" Her first few cries were a bit ladylike, as if she were trying to signal a chaperone across a ballroom. Then Sevaric added his baritone boom and, emboldened, she took a deep gulp of breath and shouted, "Help! We are trapped!"

A few moments later, her throat was sore and her fists raw from pounding on the door, and her cries became feeble again. Sevaric also quit calling out, and though he didn't say it, she knew that he was thinking "I told you so."

He said only, "Likely Vayle is still in the kitchen, trying to figure how to use the stove. Or perhaps he got halfway there and forgot what he was about and went off to bed. He hasn't much of a memory, has Vayle."

Dorie would have liked to defend Mr. Vayle, who had, in their brief acquaintance, been quite kind to her. But there was no denying that he had failed utterly as a rescuer. "Perhaps he came back and saw the study empty and thought we had gone."

"It hardly matters now. We are stuck here, I think, until morning."

Morning. "What time is it?"

Sevaric found his watch and brought it over to the lamplight. "Nearly four."

It was early December, that time of long grim nights. Dawn was three hours away. The room was cold, with ghostly shadows thrown off by the single lamp on the desk. And Sevaric was standing arms crossed, looking like some vengeful dark god. She couldn't bear it.

She walked around the room, her hand trailing along the wall. There had to be another hidden door somewhere, one that led to a withdrawing room where she could be alone, away from this man who had so coldly deprived her of her home and future. But the walls were bare white plaster, without even a wainscoting to arouse her hopes.

"You might as well take a seat." Sevaric gestured toward the only chair.

Dorie regarded the hard wooden chair balefully for a moment, then its alternative—an even harder wooden floor—and finally did as he suggested, tucking her skirt under her legs and her hands in her lap. With a pang, she recalled the cloak she had so thoughtlessly left in front of the library hearth.

There was a hearth here, too, of course, but the granite fireplace was bare, without even a stick of kindling to burn. If she had to sit in this frigid room till morning, she would die of exposure. That would solve all her problems, she supposed, but she couldn't help but wish for a warmer fate.

Lord Sevaric was keeping warm by prowling around the room, tapping the walls, searching for some second exit. He was fortunate to be a man, thus dressed comfortably enough in his severely cut evening coat and breeches. As he reached to test the plaster cornice, Dorie's gaze lingered on that coat, spread so taut across his shoulders and tight on his powerful arms. He turned and caught her staring, and she quickly bent her head to hide her flush.

But then he was next to her, stripping off his coat. "Here. Wear this."

It was almost unthinkable, accepting this gift from her enemy. And improper, too, although it was too late to pay much mind to propriety. "Oh, no, I couldn't—"

"Wear it." He dropped the coat on her lap and strode to the hearth.

The coat was still warm from his body, and she was so cold.

So she pulled it on, rolling up one sleeve and then the other above her hands. Her fingers caught on a slash in one sleeve, and she considered it with some abstract interest. It must have happened this evening, for his valet would never have let him wear it like that. Perhaps he had caught it on a nail as he was hurling himself against the door to the study.

He had tried, at least, to free them from this prison. And so, huddling there, breathing in the scent of sandalwood from the lapels, she forced herself to say, "Thank you," for the effort as well as the coat.

In his shirtsleeves and white satin waistcoat, Sevaric picked up a heap of old newspapers and transferred them to the hearth. "I don't know why you young ladies always wear such inappropriate garments. Muslin in December—it's a wonder you don't all catch lung fever."

It must be beyond him to be gracious, and she had never been a saint of forbearance. "I can't afford a winter wardrobe. Woolens are expensive—not that you need take any note of that!"

He must not have had an answer for this, for he got very busy balling up newspapers and tossing them into the fireplace. The resulting pile would, Dorie thought, burn for a moment or two. But she reckoned without Sevaric's ruthlessness.

"Get up."

She was too stunned to react, and after a moment he shook his head. "I mean, would you mind giving me the chair?"

It wasn't very gentlemanly of him to demand her seat, but she supposed it was only fair to let him sit for a time. So she rose and stepped away in silent dignity.

Her hauteur dissolved as he seized the chair and dragged it to the hearth. "What—what are you doing?" she asked, but it was plain enough. He took hold of one chair leg and, with adroit pressure from his knee, split it off. Then he tossed it into the fireplace and repeated the butchery with the other legs. Very soon the Queen Anne chair was a crosspatch of splinters surrounded by newspaper balls.

"I'll need the lamp," he said.

Glad for a role to play in their survival, Dorie picked up the lamp and, shielding its flame with her hand, brought it to him. After removing the glass, he held a screw of newspaper to the light, then transferred the flame to the paper balls in the hearth.

She pulled his coat tighter against her. As the flame licked and then ignited the broken wood, she said with an attempt at brightness, "Well done! And with such meager materials!"

He shrugged. "On the Peninsula, we learned to make do. One night, on an Andalusian plateau—not a tree or shrub for miles— we had to burn our saddles to stay warm. Either that or our boots."

He crossed to the oak table and brought a couple of ledgers to her. "Here," he said, laying them down on the floor. "Not much of a chair, but it's all I can offer you at the moment."

He hauled over another ledger and sat a discreet couple of feet away. They waited in silence, watching the flames eat away at the old chair. It was warmer now, but Dorie knew that soon the wood would be consumed and the room would gradually chill again.

She thought longingly of the hot tea Mr. Vayle had gone to make. If only he had arrived with it before they came into this room . . . but then, of course, if he had been about, they would never have been trapped in here.

Once the chair legs and back were mere ashes, Sevaric silently attacked the ledgers, ripping the pages and adding them to the fire. She thought of helping him, but held back. It seemed too private somehow, as, his face intent, he tore up the records of his father's obsession and burned them.

Eventually he ran out of ledgers, and they had nothing to fuel the fire, and nothing but the leather bindings to sit on. The flames were dying to coals when Sevaric finally spoke. "I won't put you out of your home. You needn't worry about that."

She had been drifting, almost asleep in the wisps of warmth, but this recalled her to the painful new reality. "It isn't just my home. There are two families who till the farm that adjoins it."

"They may stay, too, if they like. The rent will be favorable, I assure you."

His offhandedness left her confused. This was Sevaric. He had ruined her brother, and he had no reason to spare her. There must be a trick in this somewhere, she reminded herself. "We haven't much money to pay rent. We haven't had to, as long as my brother owned the lodge."

Bitterness crept into her voice as she realized Sevaric had every right to demand rent in exchange for her tenancy in her own home. "I do make a bit of income from my millinery work, and perhaps I can stretch that to—"

"Millinery work?"

The lamp had long since gutted out, and the fire was almost extinguished, so she couldn't see the expression on his face. But his horror was clear in his tone. A viscount's sister making hats—that must violate one of Lord Sevaric's rules of proper conduct.

She tilted her chin proudly. "We make straw hats and bonnets and sell them to a Bond Street shop. The proprietor pays us a pound and sells each for ten pounds." Staring down at her palms, scratched and callused from weaving the bristles of straw, she added, "I can't afford to purchase my own bonnets. That is some measure of success, I suppose."

"You don't truly make the bonnets yourself?"

"I and the wives of my—your—tenants. We all weave them, and then I trim them with ribbons and such. I was always grievously fond of bonnets, when I was a London debutante, so I have put my weakness to good use."

He said nothing more as the glow of the last coals faded and the shadows deepened into darkness. Finally, gruffly, he said, "You need not worry about losing your home. I assure you, I have no use for the place."

She was tired and cold and wished he would disappear so that she could give way to tears. "Then soon you will tire of paying the maintenance on it and sell it to someone who will have some use for it. And the tenants and I will have to make do."

Sevaric said something under his breath—probably a curse. More clearly he added, "You are wrong to consider me an enemy. I have no quarrel with you."

"But I," she replied softly, "have a quarrel with you, Lord Sevaric. I did not seek it out. You forced it on me. I cannot avoid it any longer."

He swore again. Again she couldn't quite distinguish it, as it was in another language—Spanish, she thought. But his meaning was clear enough, especially when he abruptly stood and strode back to the door.

Dorie was glad of the darkness then, so that she didn't have to see him once again futilely smashing his shoulder against the solid oak. She heard it, though, heard his harsh breathing, and was glad when he finally gave up.

"Come here, Miss Caine."

She responded with automatic defiance to his command. "Why?"

He sighed, a long, weary sigh. "Forgive me. I am cold, and I suspect you are even colder. And since there's no warmth coming from that pile of ash, you might as well join me here. This wall faces my study, and there's a little heat leaking through."

Reluctant and a bit repentant, she followed his voice across the room. She reached her hands out, feeling blindly, fending off the corner of the desk. Then Sevaric seized her hand and drew her safely to the wall.

His hand was cold but comforting as he guided her to sit on a strip of carpet with her back against the wall. Then he arranged himself next to her and without a word took her in his arms.

It happened so quickly Dorie had no time to protest, and once the moment had passed she hadn't the will for it anyway. They would freeze, most likely, if they didn't share body heat, and so, improper as it was, she laid her head on his chest, and told herself it was no different from clutching her hot-water bottle on a chilly night at home.

His body, she thought confusedly, was warmer than his hand, probably due to the exercise he'd just had. Heat radiated through the satin waistcoat and began to melt her. She closed her eyes and thought of a bed heaped high with a satin coverlet, a bed like the one she had slept in until her uncle lost all his money, a bed with hot-water bottles and hot bricks and warm flannel sheets.

She must have dozed off, because the next thing she heard was "Listen!" What, she mused drowsily, was Lord Sevaric doing in her warm bed? Ah, yes, she recalled, he had won the bed in a dice game, and she refused to give it over, and so in stalemate they both climbed in and fell asleep. . . .

"Listen! I think the maid must be laying the fire in my study!"

He released her and rose, and she sat there in the darkness entirely bereft, a crick in her neck, chill seeping into the warm places where he had been against her. When he started beating on the door, she remembered it all.

They weren't in bed together, of course, but something even worse, trapped in a horrid cell of a room that reeked of obsession and failure. And he hadn't won her bed in a dice game . . . or perhaps he had, along with everything else in the house she called her own.

But she couldn't give into despair, not now, when release was only a few oak inches away. She stood, aching in every joint, and added her shouts and bangs to his.

Suddenly, the door creaked, and an inch of faint light sliced across the dark. They stopped banging and stepped back to let the door swing open and let the blinding day in.

When she saw the shocked faces of Mr. Vayle, a young woman, and a dragon of a matron, she realized what they must look like: she with her coiffure coming down and his coat draped over her shoulders, he in his shirtsleeves and tousled hair and needing a shave.

It's all right, she told herself fiercely as the society dragon took a sharp breath. The Sevarics have already ruined me, when they drove my uncle to suicide.

So without once looking at Lord Sevaric, she let his coat drop to the floor and pushed her way past his friends and relatives. I must get home, she repeated silently as he called out after her. Home.

But home, of course, was lost to her. In confusion and sorrow, she halted at the front door. The kind Mr. Vayle was right behind, running down the stairs, calling her name. "You can't go without your cloak!"

It was true. She couldn't face the cold in her flimsy muslin gown. But Mr. Vayle didn't have the cloak with him and when she asked for it, he shook his head. "No, no, we can't let you leave until you're warmed up and rested. What a terrible ordeal that must have been! Come have some coffee!"

His gentleness was like a balm, and she let him tug her up the stairs. But no matter how she tried, she couldn't ignore the scandalized cries of the dragon as she entered the study. And she could not ignore Max Sevaric, scowling by the hearth—he had reclaimed his coat, somewhat the worse for wear—or Mr. Vayle's *sotto voce* message back to Sevaric, "Honor!"

Honor? At first, she was too weary and too cold to question that, and too eager to get her hands around the coffee cup held out by the silent young woman across from her. But as the warmth seeped through her, the meaning of "honor" did, too.

She heard Sevaric telling the dragon in a firm voice, "Yes, my fiancée and I got trapped in there. I only meant to show her the secret room, but a draft slammed the door shut—"

Fiancée? Dorie started to protest, but Mr. Vayle was immediately beside her, pushing a piece of toast into her open mouth. "Just wait," he whispered as she bent over, coughing helplessly. "Don't say anything yet. Just wait till Mrs. Fitzniggle is gone."

Choking brought tears to Dorie's eyes, but through the wavering sheen she saw Mrs. Fitzniggle nod judiciously at what Sevaric was saying. "Considering the circumstances," the dragon matron observed, "it's good that you are to be married—soon, I hope."

"Very soon," Mr. Vayle put in. Dorie was slightly heartened that Sevaric responded to this interference with a glare that matched her own.

But Sevaric did not deny Mr. Vayle's statement. In fact, he echoed grudgingly, "Very soon."

"He's already got the special license." Mr. Vayle was an accomplished liar—he didn't blink as he uttered this falsehood, beaming at her in his avuncular way. "Sevaric realizes that he must make Miss Caine his immediately, for she is too precious to let get away. Isn't that right, Sevaric?"

Sevaric allowed himself a short nod. Dorie was frozen with humiliation and couldn't speak. Just as well—no one seemed interested in anything she might say. No one was even looking at her any longer, except the silent young woman—Sevaric's sister, apparently—whose gaze kept shifting from Dorie to Mr. Vayle, as if she suspected a conspiracy.

Dorie wanted to blurt out the truth, but something kept her silent—the realization that an unwary step could take her over the abyss of ruin. That was what Mrs. Fitzniggle was threatening, in her steely polite way, when she suggested that the wedding take place immediately, "since you already have the license prepared, and tongues haven't started wagging yet."

The Caine family name had been tarnished for a century, since Valerian Caine was killed in a duel by his mistress's husband. Her uncle's suicide and her brother's dissipation only added to the stain. She had never thought that she would bring further dishonor to the Caines—not Dorie, the good little girl, the one who always tried to do the proper thing.

But she had only herself to blame. She should never have come here last night, should never have risked her reputation for Sevaric's charity. She should have known—

She felt his gaze then, and forced herself to meet it. He was calm enough, purposeful, but something like desperation glinted in his dark eyes. He might have been a commander ordered to lead his troops into a certain slaughter. He stared hard at her, as if to infuse a bit of death-defying enthusiasm. Some remnant of discipline made her sit straighter and match his outward composure.

Then Mrs. Fitzniggle made another interfering comment, and Sevaric glanced away.

"A church?" He frowned. "It might be difficult to schedule a wedding at such short notice—"

But it turned out that Mrs. Fitzniggle had a cousin Morton, a vicar at St. Ann's, who would perform the wedding as a favor to her. Dorie's hands tightened into fists in her lap, crushing the muslin of her skirt, as she listened to these strangers deciding her fate.

Mrs. Fitzniggle sailed out to pen a note to her cousin, and Miss Sevaric murmured something to her brother, then went to the door. She stopped with her hand on the latch. "Perhaps you might help me, Mr. Vayle?"

Mr. Vayle was less than enthusiastic, Dorie thought, but he could hardly ignore the hint. He rose and bowed to her and whispered, "Courage, my dear!" Then he left her alone with her false fiancé.

Finally she had a chance to speak, and she did before the words could get caught in her throat. "This is absurd, of course. We did nothing wrong."

"Nothing?" Sevaric smiled, but the light never reached his eyes. "As I recall, we spent the night alone together. We even— we even slept together."

"Only to keep from freezing! And that's hardly reason to— to—" She couldn't say that momentous word "marry," and no ready substitute came to mind. "We can't let the likes of Mrs. Fitzniggle force us into ridiculous actions."

"I do not think we have a choice. She wasn't very subtle in her threats to tell all to all. And the story is volatile enough, considering our families' past encounters. It will spread like a brushfire."

Dorie closed her eyes and waited for strength to return to

her. But there wasn't any to spare. She couldn't even bring herself to rise and walk out. "I don't care. I shan't be coming to Town very often, and so the bad opinions of a few Londoners won't matter to me."

"You think not? The word will reach Surrey before the next stagecoach. In my experience, rural residents are even more judgmental than Londoners. You must know what it would mean, to be deemed a fallen woman. Who would marry you, knowing that?"

"I—" She faltered, but then took a deep breath and tried again. "I would hope that the man I married would overlook such worldly things and value me for my true worth."

"Have you the least reason to expect that?"

Dorie wanted to swear that yes, she knew that some man would trust her and love her even if the world considered her ruined. But she looked past his implacable form to the fire and in the flames saw the face of her betrothed as he told her that, fortuneless, she could no longer be his wife.

Perhaps there was a man in the world strong enough to love her, but she couldn't expect that, based on the men she knew best—her reckless uncle, her weak brother, her disloyal betrothed.

And there was Sevaric, hard as the stone mantel he leaned against, brutally reminding her of the nature of her fellow humans. She couldn't acknowledge the force of his argument, so she put up her chin defiantly. "Then I shan't marry. I can get along quite well without a man."

"And without children, too?"

The breath left her body as if he had snatched it away. Somehow he knew all her weaknesses—her silly pride, her romantic dreams, her desire for babies. Her confusion must have shown on her face, because he smiled ironically and pushed away from the mantel.

"Think about it. I believe you'll come to see that this is the best solution for the situation. If we wed, you will have the security and the status that your birth deserves. And your reputation will be saved. No one—no one—would dare speak ill of my wife."

More gently he added, "I am going off to seek a special license. I hope you will honor me with your hand in marriage."

He left the door open, and a moment later Mr. Vayle appeared as if summoned by some ghostly voice. "My dear, my dear," he said, sitting beside her on the couch and taking her hands. "What a coil this is. To be found out by Mrs. Fitzniggle, of all people! I blame myself, I do, for it was I who opened the door. But when I heard Sevaric calling, what else could I do?"

Dorie thought of asking him just what had become of him the night before, but she was too weary to get into it. Instead, she said, "It isn't right, that we should be forced to marry because of a stupid mistake. We—we don't even *like* each other!"

"But don't you see, that makes it all the more imperative!"

She had already discovered that Mr. Vayle was able to state bald contradictions in the most persuasive voice. But even he could not persuade her that mutual dislike was a good foundation for marriage.

He did his earnest best though. "All the world knows of the enmity between your two families. Imagine what the crim con would be—that Sevaric seduced and abandoned you in further-ance of his vengeance. He will appear a reprobate and a scoun-drel, and you—forgive me, my dear—will be known as a silly lovesick fool."

She swallowed a gasp, then rose to pace the floor. "No! It is so—wrong! I never meant—"

"Of course you didn't," he said soothingly. "But consider the alternative futures. If you don't wed, your reputation will be in shreds. Very likely your brother will feel forced into call-ing Sevaric out, and I can vouch that Sevaric is a crack shot."

Dorie stopped in the middle of the floor and hugged herself to ward off the chill. She didn't think Robin would challenge Sevaric; she had no illusions about the depth of his physical courage. Just as well. She had no desire to have a duel fought over her. But if Robin declined to defend her honor, it could well be the final failure for him, one that would send him into irrevocable dissipation.

Behind her, Mr. Vayle continued in that soft, persuasive voice. "And if you do wed, think of it. The feud would be over, wouldn't it? Sevaric could hardly dedicate himself to the ruin of his own brother-in-law. There might even be a sizable marriage settlement."

"No."

"But—"

"No marriage settlement. I refuse to profit from this travesty."

"But you will participate in this—umm, this travesty? You will wed Sevaric when he returns?"

From deep within her came the despair, and after it, the peace. "Yes. If it will end the feud."

"Thank you." Mr. Vayle heaved a surprisingly heartfelt sigh of relief.

He certainly was a man who regarded the problems of others as his own.

His kindness encouraged her to beg a favor. "I would like my brother to be there at the church, and I know Sevaric will object." She crossed to the desk and searched in vain for a sheet of notepaper without the Sevaric crest. There was nothing to do but scribble on the back of the coal-merchant's bill. "Would you see that Robin gets this note?"

Mr. Vayle took the page from her outstretched hand and said he would convey it to a discreet and fleet-footed kitchen boy for delivery. "And now, perhaps you would like to rest in one of the guest rooms? You must be exhausted."

She was indeed weary, and now that she had made such a momentous decision her mind's working had slowed to molasses. "My bag. I left it under the stoop last night. I meant to leave for home at first light, so I hid it there. There's a dress—"

"I understand," he said, and she knew it was true because his face was so kind and so strangely familiar. "You want to look your best, don't you? Well, your best will be dazzling. I will have the bag sent to your room."

Finally she was left alone, with the weight of her decision resting on her heart. But before she could react to it, a plump woman bustled in and introduced herself as Miss Crake. "Mr. Vayle sent me to take you to a guest room. You must be tired after such an exciting night."

Wearily, Dorie decided to ignore the implications of that last remark and followed the woman up the stairs. On the landing were two large portraits of the most recent Lords Sevaric. The late Basil, her uncle's enemy, had a mouth so cruel and eyes so fierce that even Reynolds couldn't make him attractive.

Next to him was his son—her future husband, by some incalculable mischance. In the sharply cut scarlet uniform of the infantry, he looked both splendid and severe. His fist was balanced on the hilt of his sword. He was as composed and as stern as he had been when he told her she must marry him. Did he never smile? Yes, he did that once, that ironic, unamused smile when he first recognized the trick fate had played on him.

"Come, dear! We haven't much time," Miss Crake called from the floor above. "Mrs. Fitzniggle arranged for a ceremony at three o'clock. And I know you'll want to look fresh as a rose for the occasion."

Fresh as a rose. Well, better that than a funeral lily, Dorie supposed, and went up to ready herself for the ceremony.

Thirteen

Vayle suppressed a sigh of relief as he took his seat near the front of the church. Only a few moments separated him from the fulfillment of his plan—the few moments it would take Dorothea Caine and Maximilian Sevaric to plight their troth and end their family feud.

Oh, there had been some dangerous moments in the three hours since the pair were discovered in their impromptu prison. Young Dorie had remained recalcitrant to the end, arguing with every line in the proposed marriage settlement. Foolishly, she insisted that she didn't intend to profit from this marriage.

Sevaric, of course, couldn't have it said that he didn't provide for his bride, and insisted she accept an annuity and a generous amount of pin money. Dorie just crossed her arms and shook her head.

"Women!" Max said feelingly, but Vayle knew better. Dorie Caine was unique—most women would have taken the settlement and demanded that the family debts be paid off, too. Dorie just wanted what she said was hers by rights, her decrepit Greenbriar Lodge.

It threatened to become a full-scale debate, until Vayle took the groom aside and suggested he set up a suitable trust for her after the wedding, when she could no longer repay his generosity with a jilting.

It was a near-run thing, but soon Vayle could bask in his success. For now he found himself slightly out of breath, as if he had run a long way to get to this seat in St. Ann's. Probably it was due to the unfamiliar environs, the towering sanctity of this sanctuary, especially the huge cross looming over the altar and casting a shadow across the pews.

He couldn't recall the last time he had been in a church. Perhaps when his nephew Thomas was christened?

The two principals were still missing, but Mrs. Fitzniggle sailed in and, nodding at Vayle, took her seat in the first pew. This prominent place was fitting, since it was through her doing that they had the church, the vicar, and the quick wedding.

Miss Crake came next. She started toward the first row, but Vayle smiled at her, and with a blush of confusion she tugged in her gray skirt and slipped into the seat beside him.

"Lovely church." Her timid whisper echoed off the high ceiling, and she blushed even pinker.

"And you are lovely company," he responded gallantly. "Where is Miss Sevaric?"

"Helping the bride. How pretty she is!"

"Miss Sevaric?"

"No—I mean, yes, of course, but I was speaking of Miss Caine. So delicate! So radiant! The perfect bride!"

He let that soothe him. If Miss Caine was radiant, she couldn't be regarding this as a tragedy. And why should she? he told himself righteously. She was marrying a man of wealth, station, and honor—and she was ending the feud. She could hardly expect to do better on such short notice.

"It's so romantic." Miss Winnie sighed. "Love at first sight."

Not exactly, Vayle thought, recalling Max's reaction to Miss Caine's arrival. But it was romantic, in a way. Romeo and Juliet, and all that. "Quite so."

"Ah, the angels must have been with them." Miss Winnie's face took on a glow as she gazed at the cherubs hovering over the Nativity creche near the altar.

Vayle choked back an unholy laugh. "Yes, this is definitely a match made in heaven." Right, Francis? he thought, picking out the fattest, pinkest cherub and imagining it with Francis's face. Tell me yes. A match made in heaven. But the cherub's pursed lips didn't answer.

Miss Sevaric came in the side door and halted in front of the pews. Her gaze rested coolly on Vayle, then passed on to Miss Winnie. Finally she slipped into the front pew, next to Mrs. Fitzniggle.

It was the proper place for her as the groom's sister, but still Vayle was stung. She needn't have made it so clear that she disapproved of Winnie sitting with him—that she disapproved of *him*. More than ever, he wondered what she suspected, for surely she suspected him of *something*. Not the truth, certainly, but something nearly as bad.

Just to discompose her, he leant over the back of her pew. "I see you had some time to prettify yourself as well as the bride."

He meant it as a compliment of sorts, but she stiffened and the nape of her neck, above the white lace color, flushed pink. Without turning, she murmured, "How ungallant of you to suggest that Miss Caine requires any 'prettifying'."

He couldn't win, so he subsided back in his seat, glaring at the little twist she had made with her hair. Just as well he had completed his work early. This girl was spoiling for a fight, and he was just about ready to give her one. Francis would do well to spirit him away as soon as the ceremony was over, leaving Miss Sevaric to gape and gasp while he returned to the embrace of more agreeable women in 1716.

As if prompted from above, the vicar entered, a solemn bridegroom in tow. Envy shot through Vayle, for Max sported a spectacular scarlet ensemble, complete with sword, that would have been admired in Queen Anne's court. Apparently only soldiers could wear real colors, while civilians were expected to dress like parsons.

From the organ in back came the strains of a stately hymn. A long moment passed, during which time Vayle grew more and more anxious. The church doors remained stubbornly closed as the vicar's wife brought the hymn to a close, and then, in some confusion, began it again. Where was Miss Caine? Gwen should never have left her alone, for fear she might scarper.

Perhaps Dorie was standing on the church steps, waiting for her brother to escort her. Vayle felt an unfamiliar twist in his chest as he realized that Robin wouldn't be coming. He might be drunk yet, or hung over, or just too angry or frightened to give his sister away to the enemy.

Vayle longed to tell her that she had another Caine here to sustain her and wish her well. He couldn't tell her they were related, but at least he might provide his arm as a support as she went to become a Sevaric.

He rose, but just as he was excusing himself past Miss Winnie, the door opened and the cold air slid in. Vayle sank down, murmuring a distracted apology as he edged off Miss Winnie's skirt. Dorie didn't need support after all.

She walked up the aisle as if she were a queen at her coronation—or her execution. Somehow she contrived to make a tedious pastel gown look like court attire. She wore no jewelry, but in her hand was a single hothouse rose. Her head was high, her bearing dignified, and her gaze on the altar.

She did not deign to look at the meager collection of guests, at that empty space where her brother should be, at her groom splendid in his unchurchly uniform. When she reached the altar steps, she gathered her skirt in one hand and gracefully ascended the first stair. Max pushed his sword out of the way and followed suit, and the obsequies began.

The vicar did a proper job, as far as Vayle could tell, getting through Max's six names without a trip, and pausing dramatically as he asked if any man present had cause to doubt the lawfulness of the marriage. As that pause wore on, Vayle's nerves grew taut. What if Robin burst in and shouted his objections? What if Proctor didn't approve of Vayle's scheme and materialized as a bishop before them?

But just as his jaw began to ache from the tension, the vicar turned to the business at hand. "Wilt thou," he said, fixing Max with a stern look, "have this woman to be thy lawfully wedded wife?"

Always the trooper, Max agreed to honor her and comfort her and even to forsake all others. When similarly taxed, Dorie allowed that she would likely do the same, though she didn't sound quite so positive about it.

The vicar cleared his throat, and Max fumbled in his pocket and pulled out a ring. The light from the big rose window glanced off it and directly into Vayle's eyes, no doubt accounting for the sudden pricking behind his lids.

Echoing the vicar, Max said, "With this ring I thee wed." His voice took on a bit more enthusiasm as he added, "With my body I thee worship," and then with defiance, "With all my worldly goods I thee endow."

Dorie only lifted her head higher at this reference to their latest squabble, stuck out her hand, and accepted the ring without a whimper. Good girl, Vayle thought, and cleared his throat and blinked his eyes as the vicar wrapped things up expeditiously.

Winnie sighed and sniffled beside him. Remembering himself, Vayle pulled out a handkerchief and passed it to her as the bridal couple turned on their heels and marched down the aisle. They both looked ready for the firing squad. But that was all right, he told himself. They were wed, and the feud was over, and he was headed home.

Mrs. Fitzniggle and Gwen followed, Gwen looking back at him with one of those indefinably challenging looks. Winnie rose and, still sniffing, waited for him to join her.

"No, no, you go on ahead. I would like to spend a moment in—in contemplation."

Winnie nodded understandingly and left him alone in the church.

When the others were gone, Vayle moved to the communion rail. He stood transfigured in shafts of blue and red and yellow as sunlight poured through the elaborate rose window.

"Francis?" he said aloud. "Where are you?"

Behind him, wood creaked as if someone had lowered himself to one of the kneelers. He glanced around, but the small church was deserted. Shaking his head, he gazed up at the cross over the altar.

"Have you kept track, Francis? Max Sevaric and Dorothea Caine are married. The feud is over. I'm ready to go now." He held out his arms expectantly.

Nothing happened.

"Did you hear me? The feud is past history. And we have a deal, right? I'm supposed to wake up in the garden after the duel. The bullet missed me this time. You promised."

As if a cloud passed across the sun, the church grew dim.

It occurred to him that he ought to be more humble. Dropping to his knees, he templed his hands in a prayerful gesture. " 'Struth, I appreciate the second chance. And I did what you asked. So what are you waiting for? I want to be Valerian Caine again. Take me back."

He bowed his head, closed his eyes, and waited for a long time. The stone was hard and cold, and he began to shift uncomfortably from knee to knee. Finally he rose and addressed the cross again. "What the devil—I mean, what in *heaven* is happening here? If I can't take the word of God, whom can I trust?"

"Think again," a voice whispered at his ear.

There was no one behind him.

"Think about *what?* I was told to end the feud, and so I did. What else—"

He leaned against the altar rail on both hands. How had he forgotten the rest? In his great good luck at orchestrating the marriage allying the Caines and Sevarics, he ignored the second of his tasks. Dorothea and Max, and Gwen, too, must be happy and at peace on Christmas Day.

So far, not a one of them was content.

Vayle closed his eyes. The wedding had been all but a farce, both parties unwilling and still at odds. Gwen faced a lonely future playing spinster aunt to her brother's children, assuming Dorothea ever allowed Max to consummate the marriage. And from the look on her face as she walked down the aisle, that was not a good bet.

He had thought his mission over and done with, but it had only just begun.

Why were people so complicated? Was this another idiosyncrasy of modern times, or had he always been out of touch?

In the old days, he drank when he was thirsty, and took a woman to bed when he felt the need. He had gambled for the challenge of beating the odds and fenced to experience the exhilaration of besting a worthy opponent. Life was simple. Straightforward. Or so he had always imagined . . . until now.

"This is not *fair*." He opened his eyes and glared at the cross. "I cannot manipulate feelings. How the deuce am I to make Max and Dorie happy? They have to do that themselves. And Gwen has long since made up her mind to be miserable. She won't listen to me. In case you haven't noticed, I've done everything in my power to win her over, but she loathes me still. She is the only woman I ever met who despised me, but she does. And you knew she would, didn't you?"

His words echoed off the vaulted ceiling. But there was no other sound.

"Speak up. I'm calling on you, Proctor. Francis? Answer me!"

"And who, pray tell, are Proctor and Francis?"

He whirled around.

Gwen stood by the door of the church. "Have you run mad, Mr. Vayle?"

After a last, frustrated glance at the altar, he made his way down the aisle. "I was . . . praying."

She regarded him skeptically. "To Proctor and Francis?"

"My favorite saints. Martyrs. Lions ate 'em in the Colosseum."

"Francis being, of course, a traditional Roman name."

He gritted his teeth. "It was Fr-Franciscus back then, but he and I are on familiar terms. What of it?"

"Nothing at all, sir. I am merely astonished to discover a religious streak where it was least expected."

" 'Struth, I am rather deeply concerned with matters relating to the Hereafter. How much did you hear?"

"Not much, I'm sorry to say. If you were making your confession, I arrived in time to catch only the last few words." She grinned. "Well, it could not have been a confession. You weren't here long enough to recount all your sins."

He shuffled uneasily. "If you are referring to that unfortunate incident with Lady Melbrook—"

"I am not your conscience, Mr. Vayle. Now do come along. The carriage is waiting, and we have a wedding to celebrate."

He could not mistake the bitterness in her voice. Gwen Sevaric had never said a word against the forced marriage of her brother, but it was clear she resented it deeply. Another complication, especially if she lived with Max and Dorie.

Vayle groaned inwardly and followed her through the door.

Just outside the church, Mrs. Fitzniggle was engaged in a lively conversation with the vicar. She waved a hand when her charges appeared. "My cousin has invited me to tea with his family. Pray, make my apologies to Lord Sevaric and tell him I'll be along later."

Gwen looked appalled. "But that means—"

"The two of you will do well enough for the ride home," Mrs. Fitzniggle ruled, dismissing the proprieties as swiftly as she enforced them when it suited her. "But keep the curtains drawn over the windows, lest anyone see you alone together."

Gwen huddled against the paneled door as far away from Vayle as she could manage. He was not a large man, but he seemed to occupy most of the space in the carriage. A combination of long legs and vibrant personality, she decided, though he had yet to say a word.

And that suited her just fine. She didn't want to talk to him either, nor to anyone else. What was left of her life had come to an end when her brother married Dorothea Caine.

Now she would be the spinster relation, a ghostly presence in the house where she had been mistress since she was thirteen years old. Dorothea had replaced her, literally overnight, and from now on Lady Sevaric would order the staff and tend to Max's comfort.

Perhaps she could convince him to buy a cottage for her in some quiet village. She'd live there with Winnie, another castaway, tending the garden and knitting shawls. She knew nothing of gardens and knitting, but she could learn. What else was left to her?

She glanced at Vayle. He sat staring out the window, his arms folded across his chest, a sulky downturn to his lips. He'd forgotten to draw the curtains, of course, but then he cared nothing for her reputation.

No one would suspect them of impropriety in any case. The elegant Mr. Vayle would never be attracted to homely Gwen Sevaric. Even Mrs. Fitzniggle had rejected the possibility with a wave of her hand.

While he was distracted, she took the opportunity to examine his face. Ever since the dowager Duchess of Rathbone appeared to recognize him, she had looked for some family resemblance to the detested Caines. Like Robin, he had green eyes, but his were a deep, transluscent emerald while Lord Lynton's eyes were paler and invariably bloodshot. Both Vayle and Dorothea Caine had high cheekbones and a natural grace, but so did many others.

Besides, Jocelyn Vayle could not be related to the Caines, even distantly. Her father had traced every branch of the family, down to the last twig, and only Robin and Dorothea remained of the once-flourishing Caine dynasty.

From the time she was old enough to notice, Papa had huddled like a spider in his secret office, dispatching hired agents to track down everything of value the Caines owned so that he could snatch it from them. When his eyes grew dim, he dictated to her as she wrote in his heavy ledgers, and for ten years she recorded all there was to know about the Caines.

Not even a bastard child would have escaped his attention, although that was her first thought when the duchess beckoned Vayle to her side at Lady Sefton's ball. Later that night she had gone to the hidden office and scoured the ledgers, searching for some hint of a Caine by-blow. At one point her father had worried about that possibility, too, and paid a great deal of money for a diligent search that led nowhere.

It was mere coincidence that the unwelcome houseguest put her in mind of the Caines. And maybe she was only scrounging for an excuse to despise the man, for reasons she did not want to examine too closely.

"Why do you so dislike this marriage?" Vayle asked suddenly.

Startled, she gazed directly into those iridescent eyes and knew exactly why he disturbed her. Seizing a deep breath, and then another, she managed a careless shrug. "What makes you think I do?"

"Is it because you are concerned for your own future? I well understand, because everything will change for you now."

"Yes, but Max had to marry eventually. I am only dealing rather abruptly with a situation I'd have faced sooner or later. I shall come about."

He gazed at her for a long moment. "I am sure you will. 'Struth, I can't remember ever meeting any woman so determined to fend for herself."

"But you can't remember anything at all. Or so you say."

He gave her a quizzical look. "You doubt my loss of memory?"

"I have . . . reservations. When it suits your convenience, you seem remarkably perceptive. But I am no expert on mental disorders."

"A neat change of subject, Miss Sevaric. But I'm not of a mood to defend myself on the subject of amnesia, except to say I truly recall nothing that happened in the world for the last hundred or so years before I came awake in your house. And since I am only seven-and-twenty—"

"How is it you know that?" she interrupted. "If you remember how old you are, why can you not remember where it is you came from?"

"God knows," he replied softly. "Quiz me at your pleasure, but later if you don't mind. For now, I wonder how you feel about your brother's alliance with a Caine. There are rumors of a feud, but I have met Robin and he is too dissolute to be a threat. Dorothea is certainly harmless. What set your families at odds?"

She closed her eyes as the memory swept back. But she couldn't tell him about the incident that transformed her dreams to nightmares until she dreaded going to sleep at all, nor the reasons why Max had taken up the old quarrel.

He had tried to escape it, years ago, buying a commission in the army before Father's obsession with destroying the Caines caught him up. At the time, she resented Max for leaving.

Men had choices. Even a war was cleaner and more honorable than what she experienced in her father's house and later, when she was taken from it. Or so she had thought, until Max came home and she saw the fathomless pain in his eyes.

And then, to her never-ending regret, she had drawn her brother into her own nightmare and set him on the poisonous trail of vengeance.

Damned if she would repeat that mistake by sharing the tale with a frivolous stranger. An account of the feud's origin was safe, and distant enough to be practically irrelevant now. She would tell him that, and hope the old story satisfied Vayle's galling curiosity.

"Caines and Sevarics have been at each other's throats for a hundred years," she said in a flat voice. "And all because a degenerate rakehell seduced the wife of my great, great . . . some number of greats . . . grandfather."

Vayle sat forward, his eyes glittering with curiosity. "When was this?"

"In 1716." Even after a century, she supposed, it was entertaining gossip. And perhaps it would be a lesson for this present-day rakehell. "By all accounts, Valerian Caine was a libertine who thought nothing of bedding married women. But this time, Richard Sevaric returned home unexpectedly. There was a duel then, and both men were killed."

Vayle shuddered, or did she imagine it?

"Surely that ought to have put an end to the quarrel. Why carry on, with both of them dead? Were they not sufficiently punished?"

"Valerian Caine got his just desserts, that's true. But Richard Sevaric didn't deserve to die, just for having an adulterous wife."

"Would she have strayed had Sevaric not neglected her? Why settle all the blame on her lover?"

She raised her hands in exasperated surrender. "I'll agree that Blanche Sevaric was no innocent. She took vows to be faithful, and whatever the temptation, she was honor-bound to keep those vows. I'll not defend her, but I despise even more the lecher who sniffed out an unhappy wife and lured her to infidelity."

He smiled then, although his eyes were shadowed. "You Sevarics set a great store by honor. But where's the honor in that sordid little story? Why pursue a feud that ought to have died with the men who began it?"

"If it were merely the duel, perhaps you would be right." She disliked conceding even that much, though she had once been of the same opinion. "The duel, though, wasn't all of it. Soon after that, the Caines accused my family of stealing a treasure of great worth. And when the Sevarics denied any knowledge, the battle was joined. There have been any number of offenses on both sides ever since, and I expect the contenders lost track of how the hostilities began. They simply took vengeance for the latest outrage."

He fixed her with a penetrating gaze. "And just what *is* the latest offense, the one that put you and your brother at odds with the Caines?"

She swallowed the venom that rose to her throat. It had taken every ounce of courage she possessed to give Max the truth. And she would not have done that, had he not commanded her when she was too disoriented to realize he ought never hear the story at all.

But it was too late. Now he knew, so the feud persisted through yet another generation. He wanted vengeance, and so, most of the time, did she. The trouble was, no matter how much vengeance they got, she felt no release.

Now he was married to a Caine, and no good could come of it. Max would always be torn between loyalty to his sister and the duty he owed his wife.

She thought she could not cry any more, but a tear streaked down her cheek. Surreptitiously she wiped it away with the back of her hand while she pretended to cough.

When she dared to look at Vayle again, he was gazing at her with a somber expression.

"Don't worry about Max and Dorothea," he said gently. "This was meant to be. Now there can be peace, and an end to the feud."

She wanted to believe him. At least, she hoped Max would find happiness. She felt some pity for Dorothea—she didn't seem to be pretending when she said she didn't want the marriage. But Gwen found it hard to trust her. She was a Caine, and her late-night arrival at Sevaric House was suspect, especially in light of the consequences.

Max would not have invited her, or welcomed her presence. And the entrapment in the secret office was all too convenient. If only she had not let Vayle distract her this morning, Gwen might have been the one to find them. Unlike Mrs. Fitzniggle, she would have kept her mouth shut.

For that matter, why had Vayle been wandering the halls in the middle of the night? Some deep instinct told her he knew more than he was telling, but she could not imagine why he would want her brother and Dorothea together. He'd nothing to gain, and Vayle was the kind of man who acted exclusively in his own interest.

When the coach drew up in front of Sevaric House, Vayle descended and turned back, holding out his hand to help her alight. She slid across the leather squabs and was about to step down when she saw a cloaked figure emerge from the side door and hurry down the street.

Dorothea!

She nearly called out, then bit her tongue. Vayle had not seen the new Lady Sevaric making her escape, for he was looking into the carriage. And Gwen saw no duty to object if the bride chose to flee before the marriage was consummated.

Dorothea must have decided that a coerced marriage was no true marriage, and took the sensible way out. Now there might be an annulment, if Mrs. Fitzniggle could be bought off.

With a smile, Gwen took Vayle's hand and allowed him to lead her into the house.

Max didn't like to be thwarted, so he would likely be furious. But it wasn't as though he loved the girl. He hardly knew her. Gwen needed only persuade him this was for the best, before he did something stupid like chasing after his unwilling bride.

Fourteen

From the drawing-room doorway, Wilson coughed discreetly. "The wedding breakfast is prepared, my lord. And may I say," he added, a smile breaking over his face, "that I and the staff extend our heartiest congratulations on the occasion of your marriage. You are fortunate in your bride."

That was some relief, Max thought as Wilson bowed out. The staff, following the besotted butler's lead, would ignore the two families' long enmity. Would that society follow suit, but this match between Caine and Sevaric would likely be a nine-days' wonder—the talk of the Little Season.

From the sideboard, Max picked up the special license and scowled at his bride's neat signature: "Dorothea Mary Caine." No longer. He wasn't going to think of her as a Caine any longer, and neither was anyone else. The sooner she was established as a Sevaric, the better for them both.

At least they were doing the wedding breakfast right, if a trifle late—after four o'clock. It would be private, as befitted the unusual situation, but congenial enough, since the interfering Mrs. Fitzniggle had chosen to dine at the vicarage. The rest, Gwen and Winnie and Vayle, were gathered by the fire, talking in low voices.

The bride was still upstairs "resting."

Max dispatched a maid to rouse her, and waited restlessly by the door, gripping and releasing the hilt of his sword. Soon the maid was back, looking frightened. "Miss—I mean, Lady Sevaric doesn't answer, milord."

She had been up all night, or near enough, he reminded himself. Perhaps he should let her sleep—

"The bride?" Gwen broke in. "I thought she had gone out."

Max's hand dropped from his sword, and he turned to his sister. "What do you mean?"

Gwen's face took on the innocent expression that she wore when she wanted to trick him. "Oh, didn't you know? I saw her leaving the house as I returned from the church."

"When you returned—" For a moment, Max couldn't find breath enough to speak. "But that was more than an hour ago! You should have said something!"

Gwen shrugged. "I thought it odd that she didn't take a carriage, but then, nothing a Caine does surprises me."

The thought must have occurred to the others at the very moment it occurred to him—she had scarpered. Max Sevaric had a runaway bride. And his own sister had as much as abetted her.

Gwen met his scowl briefly, then looked away, and he knew it was true. She had deliberately kept quiet to give Dorie a head start. His own sister had schemed against him.

Hardly had the anger gripped him than he understood. His marriage would displace her as the chatelaine of the household. She would not grudge that, of course, but to have to give way to a Caine—

In all the chaos of the last few hours, he hadn't given a thought to how that would affect her. Now he knew. She wouldn't look at him, but her jaw was set in that way that always reminded him of his father.

He rubbed his forehead with his fist. None of his army friends would believe it, but he was the milksop of the Sevaric clan. He'd rather face a battalion of Imperial Guards than his sister or his father in an obstinate mood.

His new bride appeared to be just as forceful, though in a subtler way. She didn't rant or rave like his father, or glare like his sister, but she got her way nonetheless.

Gwen took his arm, standing on tiptoe to speak in his ear.

"Listen, Max. She's deserted you. You can get an annulment on the grounds of nonconsummation."

For just an instant he considered the idea. He wouldn't admit it, even to Gwen, but Dorie's escape hurt him, and scared him, too. To run away like that, without a word—what sort of life would he have, with a wife like Dorothea Caine?

Dorothea Sevaric, he told himself fiercely. Dorie.

"Never." The force of the exclamation surprised Max himself. But it felt right. And so he knew it was right. "I took vows before God, and by God, it's my duty to fulfill them. I'd have no honor left if I disavowed her now, just because she's proving a bit difficult. Couldn't look at myself in the mirror in the morning."

And besides, though he couldn't say such to his sister, an annulment was only obtained by claiming incapacity to consummate. And that a man of the 52nd Foot would never say, even if it were true. Which it most decidedly wasn't. Or wouldn't be, anyway, if he ever got a chance at a wedding night.

Gwen opened her mouth as if to argue the point, but Max cut her short with a harsh "Enough." He didn't look at her again as he crossed to the door. "I'm going after her."

Winnie called, "Oh, no, my lord, shouldn't you do better to wait here? Surely Miss—I mean, Lady Sevaric—only went out for a bit, perhaps to collect her things from her rooms. Or—"

"Or she went to see her brother," Vayle put in. "She might have wanted to explain the marriage to him, before he had time to misunderstand."

That made sense. Max halted with his hand on the door handle. "You're right. I'll look there first."

He flung the door open, and it banged against the wall, knocking a miniature portrait of his mother off its nail. Cursing under his breath, Max strode down the stairs, calling for his horse to be brought round.

Vayle followed him to the hall. "Perhaps I ought to go with you."

It was clear Vayle didn't think Max capable of controlling his temper. But he was in complete control. Absolute control.

He didn't want Vayle there to hold him back when he found Robin Caine concealing his wife. . . .

"No."

A bewildered Wilson came in with Max's hat and gloves, muttering about the ruined wedding breakfast. Max ignored him and yanked on the gloves. "I want you here, Vayle, in case Dorie's gone to cover. It will take some time to track her down, and I need you to watch over my sister. Caine might decide to retaliate."

"Retaliate?" Vayle looked as if he didn't know the meaning of the word.

"Yes, dammit, retaliate. If he thinks I've forced his sister into this, he might take revenge by—by hurting mine."

"Surely not!"

Max was silent until Wilson trudged disconsolately away toward the dining room. "I wouldn't put it past him to try."

Vayle shook his head, but with a glimmer of humor he said, "I'd back your sister against Robin Caine, in a fair fight."

"Well, a fair fight is just what you won't get from a Caine." He shrugged into his coat and went to the door. "So I have your agreement? You'll stay here to protect Gwen?"

"If I must—but it'll be decidedly improper, if you're gone for more than a day, me here alone with your sister."

"Propriety be damned." Max pulled open the door, noting with displeasure the shadows deepening in the square. He didn't have time to deal with Vayle's prim sensibilities. "For God's sake, I'm trusting you with her life. I can surely trust you with her virtue. And anyway, Mrs. Fitzniggle and Winnie will be here, and that'll be chaperonage enough."

Vayle raised some other objections, but Max ignored them and mounted his horse. The groom handed him the reins, and he turned toward Piccadilly and Westminster Close, where Robin Caine holed up.

When Max finally got a response to his door banging, he knew immediately that he was out of luck. Robin Caine suffered from more than just the night's excess. He still wore his stained evening clothes, hanging onto the open door and blinking his red eyes as if the wan sunlight might blind him. Still drunk. Or drunk again, to judge by the bottle of blue ruin he clutched in one hand.

Max shoved past, scanning the room for any evidence that his wife had been there. But the place was as decrepit as the night before. Dorie would have tidied up; he somehow knew that.

Caine was different though, slumping there against the door. He looked as sorry as ever, but a light had gone out in his eyes. Max had seen it happen to the cockier recruits facing their first artillery barrage. They collapsed like a scaffolding that had lost its legs.

"Whaddaya want?" Caine spoke carefully, but the gin showed in his slurring. "You got the damned deed last night. And you did the deed today, didn't you?"

It was no use talking to him, but Max tried anyway. "Where is your sister?"

"M'sister?" Caine swung his bottle to his lips and groaned when he found it empty. He stumbled to the night table and with a shaking hand poured a glass of water and gulped it down. When he turned, he was clutching a screw of paper. "Ah, yes, my sister. My sister. My little baby sister Dorie."

He opened his hand and let the paper drop. A draft from the hearth sent it scuttling along the floor. Max caught and untwisted it to find a bill made out to him from a coal merchant. In some confusion, he turned it over. There he saw a message in a neat round hand: "Robin—I must marry Lord Sevaric. There is nothing to be done about it. But do please come to St. Ann's, one o'clock. I need your support."

The plea was restrained, but only the most heartless of fools could have missed it. Max balled the note and dropped it on the floor, then booted it toward the bed. "You miserable worm. She's a Sevaric now, and I'll see to it that she doesn't turn to you for aid again."

He slammed the door behind him, and only then did he hear Caine's reply. "You'll have to find her first."

* * *

Back in the street, he reached into his pocket and pulled out the marriage contract his solicitor had hastily prepared this morning. He narrowed his eyes in the fading light and read the fourth clause: "And upon the marriage of Dorothea Caine and Maximilian, Lord Sevaric, will be conveyed to Dorothea the property Greenbriar Lodge, west of Croydon, Surrey, and all its contents and grounds."

She must have taken refuge at the lodge she regarded as her home. Without letting himself think about why she might need refuge, Max guided his horse to the Brighton road. Croydon was just twenty miles northeast of his Sussex estate, so he wouldn't need to spend more than a few moments at Greenbriar Lodge. He would just collect his runaway bride and take her home.

Near Croydon, his mare threw a shoe, and he had to walk her two miles to a village and wait out the darkness in a stable. His service pelisse was warm enough, and the hay a better mattress than he'd known on some Peninsular nights, but he couldn't sleep in the gathering chill.

He'd experienced worse—much worse. There was the night he crouched in a trench, sniper fire overhead and, next to him, a trooper whispering for his mama, bleeding to death despite Max's frantic amateur doctoring. And the night after Waterloo, when he searched the battlefield for what remained of his regiment, stepping from body to body for there was no bare ground between them.

But peace had weakened him. Now the discomfort of two consecutive cold sleepless nights made him reflect on his misery and wonder how his life had taken this turn. A simple quest for vengeance, a victory at backgammon—nothing untoward, and yet here he was, far from his bed in the iron dark, chasing a woman who didn't want him.

There would be a bed at Sevaric Hall, he told himself drowsily, and a woman to go in it, and if she didn't want him, well, she was his wife. She would have to make her peace soon enough, or . . . or else.

He was too weary to decide what "else" would be, so he closed his eyes and imagined her face. When first he had seen her, he thought that face another dirty Caine trick—she was too pretty, too dangerous to his cause.

But by happenstance and by law, they were allied now, and that face, that sweet stubborn mouth and those wary eyes, gave him comfort more than caution. It would be pleasant, and something more than pleasant, to see that face every evening in the candlelight, to caress it in the darkness, to kiss it in the night.

Of course, bringing her round would likely take some persuasion, and he wasn't much good at that. He was a soldier, used to issuing orders and commanding obedience. He didn't think that would work with Dorie.

No, she would need some lighter touch, a bit of cozening. For a moment he wished he'd brought Vayle along to argue the case—there wasn't anyone better at cozening than Vayle. But that would have been the milksop's way, to let another fight his battle.

About seven, the blacksmith arrived, yawning and scratching. Setting to work, he directed Max to the local taproom where hot coffee and warm crumpets might be attained. Mindful of a bride's sensibilities, Max bespoke a room and cleaned up as best he could.

He gazed at his dark-stubbled face in the mirror and thought he had never looked so un-cozening. But he had no razor nor even a change of clothes. At least none in his regiment would ever know how grossly unprepared he set out for this battle.

The sun was full in a pale blue sky when he saw a newly painted wooden sign announcing Greenbriar Lodge. He reined in on the rutted lane. Seeing the name made the anger rise in him. That his wife would live here, of all places—but, he reminded herself, she couldn't know what dark memories Greenbriar Lodge held. It was just the last refuge she had, once her brother lost all else.

In his mind, the lodge was malevolent, dark and squatting

and evil. But as he crossed a bridge and the grove of trees parted to reveal the house, he saw it was just a building after all. The evil he had expected to feel wasn't there. Perhaps it had died with Hugo Caine, or vanished when Max won it.

Or perhaps it withered away when Dorie moved in.

This was just a hunting lodge—a compact, two-story stone cottage, square and masculine and dwarfed by its nearby stables, surrounded by rocky fields ineffectively plowed for farming. But there were signs of feminine activity in the newly swept circular drive, the neat flower beds, the freshly painted window boxes, the Christmas greenery over the door.

Max, a landowner himself, could interpret the state of this small farm. There wasn't money or manpower for any real improvement—graveling the lane, replacing the roof, grading the fields. But Dorie had achieved a good deal with hard work, limited materials, and gallantry.

He felt an unfamiliar twist of remorse; remembering the blisters on Dorie's hands. She had tried so hard to make this a home, and he took it away from her.

Well, he could make it up to her now. Never again would she have to scrape paint and weave straw. Sevaric Hall awaited her, with its army of gardeners and maids, and she need do nothing more than approve menus and greet guests.

An old man shuffled out to take the mare. He jerked his head toward the house. "She didn't 'spect you till tomorrow."

That was heartening—at least Dorie hadn't lost her senses and forgot their wedding entirely. Indeed, when she appeared in the front doorway, lovely and guarded, he took a conciliatory approach.

"I'll have no more of those Caine tricks, madam."

She sucked in her breath, then withdrew inside and slammed the door. On the front steps, Max paused in some irritation to evaluate what had gone wrong with his strategy. Perhaps the "madam" was too coldly formal? But he could hardly call her Miss Caine, could he? There was always Lady Sevaric. He imagined he'd get used to that eventually. But right now, the title still signified "mother" to him. And he didn't feel very filial, not after catching a glimpse of his wife's bare arm when the shawl fell away from it.

Dorothea. He could call her that. Or Dorie. She shouldn't take offense at her own name, not when they were wed.

That decided, Max knocked on the door and, receiving no answer, tried the handle. The door swung open. Deftly avoiding the greenery tacked along the frame, he entered a narrow hallway. Ropes of evergreen branches hung along the curved staircase, and a gilded cone dangled by a ribbon from the sconce. The house smelled not of evil but of Christmas—pine and cinnamon and wood smoke.

By instinct Max found his way to the parlor. In this cheerful, light-filled room Dorie sat militantly, surrounded by dangerously feminine paraphernalia—a sewing box, a basket full of straw hats, ribbons and bows, and a tabby cat.

Compared to the cat, Dorie seemed almost approachable. At least she didn't hiss when Max entered the room. As she bent over her ribbons, her cheeks were a bit flushed, though that might have been a reflection of the flames in the hearth.

She wore an old faded gown, but she was still pretty with her curls falling about her shawl. He decided she would always be pretty, in any circumstances, and that thought was chased by another—you are lost, old sport. Lost.

If he had to lose himself, best to do it with his lawfully wedded wife. She was legally required to find him.

He maintained an awkward but he hoped authoritative silence until she finally deigned to look at him. "Please sit down, sir."

Put that way, it sounded like a challenge. Max reminded himself that he was being conciliatory. "Thank you." After a moment he added, "Dorie."

That startled her, and she flushed more deeply. "Molly is bringing tea. You must be chilled from your ride."

This could go on for hours, this careful *politesse*. But Max was already weary of it. "Look," he said abruptly, "you shouldn't have run off like that. I was worried."

"You mean you were embarrassed that the bride missed the bridal breakfast."

He dismissed this with a shrug. "The staff was disappointed. Wilson especially. He would have liked to show off the Charles II china to you, I think."

Too late he recalled that the Charles II china had come to them fifty years ago, along with other contents of the Caines' secondary estate, when Robert Caine's card turned up red instead of black. But Dorie only said, "I am sorry then. Had I know that Wilson was so kind to honor me that way, I would have—"

"Stayed?"

"I would have thanked him especially."

"You can thank him yet." He pulled out his watch and glanced at it. It wasn't yet ten o'clock. "I will send word for him and the rest of the staff to meet us tonight at Sevaric Hall."

"Sevaric Hall?" She frowned as if he had suggested she follow him to the Black Hole of Calcutta. "No, I mean to remain here."

"But—" He forgot all about conciliation. "But we are wed, dammit. We are supposed to live together."

Dorie went back to her plaiting, her eyes cast down, her fingers moving in controlled agitation over the straw. "I didn't say we couldn't live together."

"You said you meant to stay here."

"You are my husband. You may stay, too."

Max took a deep breath and held it until he was certain he could moderate his voice. Even so, his tone almost made the arriving Molly drop her tea tray. "Stay here? When my own home is hardly a dozen miles away, and far more comfortable?"

Dorie sent Molly on her way and set aside her plaiting to pour tea. "Oh, well, if *comfort* means so much to you, decidedly you should go to your own home." The barest hint of reproach entered her voice. "I have tried to make Greenbriar comfortable, but no doubt you are used to finer places. So I will not plead with you to join me here. I wouldn't want to deprive you of any *comfort*."

That galled him. Max Sevaric was not a man enslaved by his own comfort. Far from it. Someday he would tell her about those cold and wet nights in the trenches around Lisbon—but for now he wanted to get one thing straight. "You are my wife. You are coming with me."

"I am staying here. I have work to do." With that, she pushed her teacup to the side and took up the unfinished bonnet.

"My wife has no need to work, dammit. Put that down."

Dorie slanted him a defiant look. "I have an order for ten bonnets. And I am one who keeps her promises."

He wanted to argue the point, but he'd always believed in keeping promises, too. Grudgingly he said, "When you're done with those, that will be an end to it."

"But I've other work, too." She waved her needle, and he noticed now the cracks in the plaster, the gaps in the wainscoting, the threadbare carpet. "I am pledged to restore this lodge. I've spent the last year on it, and I have much left to do. It's not just for me," she added, "but also for Molly and Tim, who live in back. I promised they would always have a home here."

More promises. He could hardly tell her she shouldn't keep promises, since he always did so himself. "I've no objection to that. And as for restoring this place, well, I'll hire workers to do it. You shan't be needed at all and can take your rightful place at Sevaric Hall."

"No!" She looked startled at her own vehemence. "Forgive me, but I do not want or need hired workers. This is my responsibility, and I shan't delegate it to another."

Max suppressed a groan. She was impossible. But she was his wife, even if she preferred to ignore it. "I am going to Sevaric Hall. And you are coming with me."

Her mouth set mutinously as she stabbed her needle into a ribbon. She tied up the thread before replying, "I will not go willingly. If you mean to force me, to abduct me, well, then you are no gentleman."

This enraged him more than anything else she had said. *Sevarics* did not force women, or abduct them from their homes— With a wrench he returned to the present, to his lady wife and her lady's parlor. "I do not force women. But we are wed. There is nothing to be done about that. I have no wish to live separately from my wife."

The frown between her brows unwrinkled. More quietly, she said, "I understand. It's just that I was not anticipating becoming your wife. The lodge restoration has been my—my constancy. I have devoted everything to it, and I cannot simply quit this and start another life. Not yet. Not till I'm ready."

He didn't want to wait. But she was regarding him with those gray eyes, half hopeful, half wary, and he remembered the words they had spoken only a day ago. Till death do us part. That was what marriage was, he thought, permanence.

Already he knew his strategy—send to Sevaric Hall for clothing and supplies, and write to Gwen to tell her he was—no, he couldn't tell her he was at Greenbriar Lodge. He'd just tell her he was safe, and not to expect him back for a week or so. This campaign wouldn't take more than a week, surely.

"If I must," he said ungraciously, "I will stay for the time being. Help you with this restoration."

Dorie opened her mouth to speak, then closed it tight. A blush crept up her cheeks. "I thank you. But—you understand, when I said I am not ready to assume the duties of your wife, well, I also meant"—she screwed up her face and blushed redder and in a strangled voice concluded—"conjugal duties."

It was a not-unexpected setback, but hard to take nonetheless. "I understand," he said stiffly. "We shall have separate beds, you are saying."

"Separate rooms," she whispered.

Courage, he told himself. Persistence will win the day. "As you wish."

In all his years of soldiering, Max had never expected to make such an unconditional surrender. But then, he never expected to gain such a victory either.

For just a moment, her eyes glowed, and then she had to lower her head to hide from his appraisal. She was glad he was staying.

Fifteen

After repeated knocks, Robin finally opened the door. Vayle took one look at his unshaven face and listless eyes, pushed him aside with his cane, and stalked into the dim room. "Don't you ever clean this place?"

"What for?" Shoulders slumped, Robin went to his cluttered desk and lowered himself to the chair. "No one ever comes here."

"Indeed? And what am I—a *ghost?*" Vayle swiped his arm against the tattered curtains, sneezing as dust billowed in gray puffs. But the afternoon light revealed what was better kept in the dark. "This room is a disgrace. And so are you."

"Then go away. You weren't invited, and I prefer to be alone."

Vayle regarded him with disgust. Robin had been making progress until he lost Greenbriar Lodge to Max, but now he'd reverted to his former dissolute state. "Are you drunk?"

"I would be, could I afford so much as a bottle of Blue Ruin. But I'm damnably sober, and have been wondering how many days before the landlord kicks me into the streets. Months behind in the rent, you know. He is making threats."

"Then he hasn't heard the good news. Look lively now. A carriage waits for us and the horses must not be left to stand. We require hot water for your shave. How is it obtained?"

"What good news?"

"Water first. See to it and then I'll explain what you should have figured out for yourself." When Robin failed to stir, Vayle prodded him in the ribs with the cane. "I am an impatient man, sir."

Muttering under his breath, Robin rose and went downstairs.

At least he was easily manipulated, Vayle reflected as he wandered back to the window and gazed into the filthy alley below. Not like Gwen, who had a will of steel. After Max went haring off after his bride, Gwen had closeted herself in her room and even Winnie could not gain access.

Nodcocks, the both of them. Gwen and Robin should grasp every ray of sunshine and any chance to laugh, even at life's bad jokes. Too soon they would be shades in a murky void, subject to Proctor's mean-spirited whims.

If only they knew what it was like to be dead.

Life was the most precious thing in creation, to be savored because it was so very brief. Vayle had learned that the hard way, and he would pry Robin from his misery, at swordpoint if necessary, before the boy wasted another minute that should be cherished. Gwen, too, if he could think of some way short of violence to reach her.

Robin returned with a basin and plunked it on the desk, water sloshing over the greasy papers formerly wrapped around the street-fare he'd brought home to eat. "What good news?" he asked again, belligerently this time as he rummaged for his razor.

Vayle gave him a wide grin. "Why, the alliance of Sevarics and Caines after a century of conflict. As we speak, the *ton* is ravenous for morsels of gossip about the wedding. We shall dine out for weeks on this story."

Robin regarded him balefully. "I know nothing whatever about that wedding, and I don't want to."

"Shave! Your ignorance is a blessing. You will smile and shrug and be discreet, which will enhance your reputation. Meantime, I'll sprinkle a few particulars about the ceremony to whet their appetites. This, Lord Lynton, is your chance to reclaim status among your peers. We shall be, for a time, the most intriguing fellows in London."

Robin's razor slipped, and he swore and pressed a filthy handkerchief to the cut on his chin. "And what do you suggest? Shall I sneak through the servants' entrance to balls where I've not been invited, or thrust myself into Almack's on Wednesday next?"

"Almack's?" Vayle frowned. "Is that a place we ought to go? Well, never mind. For now, put on your best clothes. We have much to accomplish this afternoon."

While Robin pulled on a marginally clean shirt and breeches, Vayle wandered to the littered desk. Though he could not explain why, his fingertips itched as if something familiar was buried there. He fumbled through the rancid mess of paper and uneaten food until his hand met cold metal.

Brushing the papers aside, he picked up the gun. "What is *this?*"

Robin glanced over his shoulder. "A dueling pistol. Been in the family a hundred years. Somebody took it from a dead man's hand and gave it to his brother, who happened to be my great-great-grandfather. If I knew how to prime the thing, I'd have put it to my head."

"I'll have none of that sort of talk," Vayle said automatically. He regarded the pistol with mingled fascination and nausea.

It could only be the gun he'd taken from the velvet-lined case offered him just before the duel. The pistols had belonged to Richard Sevaric, and in his youthful pride he'd not bothered to examine them closely. Honorable men fought honorably, after all, and the affair was so rushed there was no time to procure seconds for either of them.

But how had he imagined himself an honorable man? He'd thought nothing of seducing a married woman, although in truth Blanche Sevaric had been more aggressive than he. She was a passionate beauty, and he'd often bedded her before that fateful night.

What happened to her after they were discovered together? he wondered for the first time. She was not present in the garden when he fought Sevaric. A young servant had brought the pistols and faded into the half-light of dawn, counting off the paces in a trembling voice.

He remembered the pierce of gravel under his bare feet, the frightened boy calling eight, nine, ten. The jump of the pistol as he pressed the trigger. The bark of the gun when it fired. A searing pain at his temple, and then . . . nothing.

Chilled, he ran his fingers over the carved handle and smooth barrel of the pistol that killed Richard Sevaric A gun exactly like this one had killed him, too, with the help of an ill-placed stone.

Pointless, all of it, beginning to end. No woman was worth dying for. "I'll keep this awhile," he said to Robin, "until you are out of the mopes."

"Give it to Sevaric." Lethargically, Robin pulled on a pair of battered riding boots. "He has everything else we ever owned."

Including the mate to this pistol, Vayle thought as they made their way to the carriage.

Entering the coach, Robin knocked over a stack of parcels wrapped in brown paper. "What the devil are these?" he said, pushing them to the side and slumping down on the seat.

"The beginnings of your new wardrobe. Our first stop is a tailor who will recut them to fit you. We are nearly the same height, but you are of slighter build."

"You are offering me your cast offs? I'll not take charity, Vayle. You insult me."

"Pah! What you are wearing is an insult in itself. Think you to cut a dash in clothes a ragpicker would spurn? I wore one of those coats for a few hours, and the other items are new. Max chose them, and he has a lamentable partiality for drab colors. They do not suit me, and would hang in the armoire until doomsday had I not bethought me of this plan. For the rest—shirts, boots and the like—we'll go to the shops where the proprietors know me."

"And pay with what? I'm quite done up, and could not muster credit to buy so much as a pint of ale."

"Ah, but now you have *expectations*." Vayle pulled the door shut behind him and winked at Robin. "Gentlemen have been known to live for years on their expectations. Your brother-in-law is a wealthy man, and the shopkeepers extended me credit on his word. They will do the same when I vouch for you."

"Sevaric hates my innards." Robin kicked sullenly at the other seat cushion. "And all of London knows it. What's more, think what he'd do if he learned I had borrowed against his bankroll."

"I daresay he would commend your pluck." When Robin snorted, Vayle couldn't help but laugh. "Very well, not immediately, but neither will he skewer you. Dorie would not permit it."

"Blast it, now you want me to hide behind my sister's skirts. Let me out of here. I want no part of this scheme." He started to rise, but the coach lurched into motion and he fell back to the seat.

Swallowing his irritation, Vayle settled against the cushion and folded his arms. "Did you imagine there would be an easy escape from the hole you have dug for yourself? Now a lifeline has been extended and you must grasp it, even if certain factors offend your delicate sensibilities."

His voice grew serious. "Heed me, bantling. We are on a mission to make you respectable so that you will not further shame your family. Lord Sevaric is now part of that family, and he will eventually respect your efforts. Besides, you'll borrow only enough for a decent wardrobe. If you dare extend Max's credit for gaming or to buy spirits, I'll skewer you myself."

Slowly Robin's face brightened. "Will this please Dorie, do you think?"

"She will be proud of you," Vayle assured him. At least Robin cared about his sister's approval. "Once we give her something to be proud of, that is. She worries about you, do you know?"

Robin hung his head. "I know."

"You must restore yourself to full health, so that when she sees you next her anxiety will be relieved." Vayle regarded him sternly, then let an encouraging note enter his voice. "When

we've done at the shops, we'll fence at Antonio's. You have a
decided flare, and because every eye will be on you, I shall
contrive to make you appear more skillful than you are. For that
humiliation, because I'm not fond of losing even a staged bout,
I expect your full cooperation in all other matters."

Robin nodded briefly and then stared out the window, maul-
ing his chin with a shaky hand. "Why did she marry him?" he
asked suddenly. "Why Sevaric?"

The question had been inevitable, but Vayle still had not come
up with a plausible explanation. He shrugged. "Love at first
sight, I suppose. Who can understand women?"

"It's because I left her no choice," Robin said dully. "When
I gambled away her home, she had nowhere to go and no way to
live. How she must despise me. Now her life is ruined forever."

"I suggest you never express that ridiculous opinion in front
of Sevaric. Most likely he fancies himself a good catch. Is it
beyond all reason they might be happy together?"

Robin laughed without a hint of humor. "Happy? After what
he did? You were there that night. Sevaric is as guilty as I am.
He played on my weaknesses and stripped Dorie of the only
thing left for her to care about. She must hate *him*, too."

"Dorie does not strike me as a women who carries grudges.
I agree that Max has earned whatever punishment she metes
out, if any, but that is for him to deal with. It's nothing to do
with you."

He poked his cane at Robin's chest. "If you care anything for
your sister, you will do everything in your power to make up for
your blunders. Max and Dorie are wed and will come to terms
with each other. That you cannot control, but you *can* take charge
of yourself and give her one less thing to worry about."

Robin gazed at him with unsettling awe. "How did you come
to be so wise?"

Vayle broke down in laughter. Proctor would be grinding his
teeth if he heard that, which he probably did. And if he actually
had teeth.

"That was a compliment, not a jest," Robin said plaintively.

Unable to speak, Vayle waved a hand.

Robin scowled. "Sometimes I don't understand you at all. When you're done making fun of me, I wish you'd tell me about the wedding."

That sobered him immediately. "And where were *you?*" he demanded. "Dorie sent you a message and badly wanted you there. Why did you fail her?"

Lowering his head, Robin admitted, "I w-went to the church, but could not bring myself to go inside. So I waited around the corner and saw them leave together. She did not look happy."

"Does that surprise you? She had to walk down the aisle alone because you were too cowardly to lend your arm and your support."

"I know. I was not there when she needed me." He covered his eyes with his hand. "I have been nothing but a trial to her since we left the nursery. She will never forgive me now, and I'll never forgive myself either."

"Oh, cut line, you stupid child! I weary of this mewling." Robin was only a few years his junior, but right now Vayle felt every bit of a century older. "Concentrate on what you can do to redeem yourself. Imagine how pleased she will be to return from her wedding trip and find you have become a lion of society."

There was a long silence.

"Perhaps a cub," Robin said finally, with a diffident smile.

Vayle clapped his hands. "A sign of life from you at last! From henceforth we look to the future. I shall bring you into fashion, a neat trick since I'm not precisely in fashion myself. But we will shine with such dazzling light that I defy anyone to turn us away. 'Tis all in the presentation, you know."

"If you can carry me off, you'll have worked a miracle," Robin said skeptically. "But I give you my word to do my best."

Vayle suppressed a groan. If only he *had* been granted miraculous powers. 'Struth, he could scarcely think what to do next, let alone how to do it.

In fact, he ought to be concentrating his efforts on Gwen.

He'd been assigned to make her happy, an impossible feat. Without question Proctor was resolved to see him damned, or at the least damnably *bored*, for all eternity.

And he would probably have his way. Less than three weeks remained until Christmas, and Gwen was holed up licking her wounds. Deep wounds, Vayle had begun to realize, although there was no explaining them. Certainly she'd no intention of confiding in *him*. He had to find some way to draw her out.

Once Lord Lynton was cleaned up, he'd make an acceptable escort. Gwen was stubborn, acid-tongued, and no beauty, but neither did Robin have much to offer. They would be an ideal match, or at least they were unlikely to do better by themselves. And if the two of them fell in love—ah. That would be a miracle indeed.

Yes, a husband, however unsatisfactory, would provide Gwen with more than she could now hope for. She'd have a home of her own to manage as she saw fit, and children. For all her inexplicable bitterness, Gwen might be a wonderful mother. It was unfortunate she could not marry and give birth before the Christmas deadline!

A child would make her happy.

He wanted her to be happy. There was little chance of finishing the job by Proctor's deadline, but perhaps he could help Gwen make a good beginning.

"You needn't be concerned about invitations," he said to Robin. "They arrive with regularity at Sevaric House, and now that you are Max's brother-in-law it will not be questioned if you attend balls and routs in company with his sister."

"No! Th-that is out of the question."

Vayle gazed at him in surprise. Robin's new spirit had vanished. Perspiration streaked his brow, and he wrung his hands as if he'd just been invited to put his neck on the guillotine.

"Miss Sevaric despises me," Robin said tersely. "I'll not force my presence on her. Nor will she come along if I am one of the party. Trust me about this."

What was between them? Vayle wondered. When pressed,

she agreed it was irrational. But it was somehow connected to the families' enmity, he would warrant. And from the determined look on Robin's face, there would be no swaying him on this point.

"As it happens, Miss Sevaric doesn't much care for me either," he confessed, with a grin. "No accounting for it, but as I said before, who can understand a woman? Well, we shall spare her the ordeal of our mutual presence and fend for ourselves. When she chooses to go out, I'll endure her scorn and stand in her brother's place. But whatever invitations she refuses the two of us will accept. Hold yourself ready."

"I have promised." Robin sounded as if the concession pained him. "But if you attempt to foist me on Gwen Sevaric by surprise, damned if I won't call you out."

Serious indeed, this puzzling hostility. Smothering the arrogant response that rose in his throat at the idea of Robin's challenge, he managed a pacific smile. "Be still, cub. I've enough trouble dealing with the young lady without tossing you into the mix. Unless you care to tell me how you came to be at odds with Miss Sevaric?"

"None of your bloody business, Mr. Vayle." Robin's eyes narrowed suspiciously. "And for a houseguest, you meddle rather too much in Sevaric affairs. I wonder if he would approve this errand, in his carriage, with his name bandied to tailors and bootmakers as payer of the bills we intend to run up."

"What does it matter? Sevaric is leagues away, and won't hear about it for weeks," Vayle said seraphically. "Relax and enjoy yourself for a change."

Elation at Robin's show of spirit fired the gloomy afternoon and his own natural optimism. The cub had some lion in him after all.

Sixteen

A week after his arrival, Max retired to his room under the eaves and wondered if this siege would ever be won.

The fortress was inhospitable, the place of his angriest nightmares. His opponent was baffling, alternately defiant and conciliatory.

She liked to undermine his defenses when he was supposed to be undermining hers. She might frown in that sad pretty way and he would suddenly feel an urge to lay down his arms and make a separate peace. Then he would retreat to restore some order to his tattered forces, only to weaken again when he saw her smile.

The fight was telling on him. Especially now that he was so weary, his every muscle aching from his day's work replacing shingles on the ancient roof. Both thumbs throbbed from encounters with the hammer, which had also worn calluses in his palm. With a groan, he climbed into bed.

There it was, more undermining from Dorie—a hot-water bottle warming the sheets. She never gave up these little tricks designed to win him over to her side. But if she thought that a bit of comfort might reconcile him to separate beds, well, disappointment awaited her. When they finally negotiated their treaty, the conjugal bed would be Item One.

He stared at the flickers the candlelight cast on the ceiling. The big crack in the plaster seemed to wriggle in the play of light and shadow, and the brown stain undulated obscenely.

Even the weather was unfavorable for his cause. The rain had started again, pattering against the windows. Perhaps, he thought with treacherous weakness, he might be spared the roof work tomorrow. Dorie wouldn't expect him to work in the rain. . . .

Of course, Dorie didn't expect him to work at all. She never assigned him tasks, and when he took them on she always shook her head and said, "Pray don't bother, really. This isn't your sort of work!"

This image of him as an effete aristocrat, too dainty to dirty his hands while his wife blistered hers, goaded Max into Herculean labors. Her startled praise and anxious cautions only made him more determined to prove himself. Max Sevaric could handle anything this house threw at him, even if he had to retaliate with the unfamilar hammer instead of the sword he preferred in battle. He refused to fail, with Dorie observing his every move.

The patter of rain became a pounding, and the old windows shook. Now the ceiling crack was glistening ominously. The moisture congealed into a single drop. It grew and grew and drooped and finally dropped off and splashed onto the comforter beside his arm.

At least today he'd managed to get the shingles over Dorie's room replaced, he thought as another drop, splendidly aimed, doused the candle. Her bed would stay warm and dry, cozy and comfortable.

The thought—and a raindrop on his forehead—made him groan, and he pulled the pillow over his head and ordered himself asleep.

He came bolt awake when something hit him. My arm, he thought, too blank to panic. Artillery, grape shot, shrapnel. He felt his shirt near his shoulder and found it wet with blood. There was no pain, no cut. His shirt wasn't even torn. Distractedly he felt around him and came up with the projectile. It crumbled in his hand.

Plaster.

Where the hell am I? he thought, struggling to a sitting position.

Indoors. In Dorie's house. Not in her bed.

Right. The missing shingles, the glistening crack. Rainwater, not blood, on his shirt.

The ceiling was breaking apart.

With a curse he lit the candle and surveyed the damage. A hole about the size of his fist punched through the stain on the ceiling. What a capital night he had ahead of him, waiting for the roof to cave in on him.

But in the morning, when he told Dorie, she would be apologetic and offer to help him clean up the mess, and—

He lay very still, contemplating that sagging stain. Then he leaped up, ignoring the creak of the bedsprings under his stockinged feet. He didn't need to stretch to reach the ceiling, and his hand fit nicely in the hole.

This plaster was an unworthy opponent; with the slightest yank, it came apart at the crack and collapsed, showering him with dust and the comforter with chunks. The hole, grown a dozenfold, gaped, and through chinks in the roof he could see the gray-black sky.

Coughing, he dropped back to the bed and inserted himself under the laden comforter. Then he cleared his throat and let out a bellow he hoped resounded with affronted dignity, and then a fluent string of Spanish curses.

His reward came quickly to the door—Dorie, petite and irresistible in her flannel robe, a candle held trembling in her hand. "Max? What is wrong?"

His Christian name. That almost made up for the humiliation of being plastered into his own bed.

"The ceiling caved in. I—" He knew a moment's regret for his abandoned ideals, then called himself sternly to account. All's fair in love and war; even Wellington would agree with that. "I think a piece might have hit me in the head. I'm a bit dizzy—can't see very clearly."

Instantly she crossed to the bed, her bare feet crunching the bits of plaster on the floor. As she sat the candle on the night table, her face was anxious. "What can I do?"

He pressed his hand to his forehead and managed an artistic groan. "Help me out, will you?"

With a soothing murmur, she pulled back the comforter, spilling more plaster and revealing more Max. She looked startled at his open-necked cotton jersey and trooper's woolen trousers, worn more for warmth than fashion or modesty.

A tactical error. He should have gone to bed in his uniform, or at least hunting garb. But there was no help for it now. He sat up, remembering to moan and clutch his temple, and swung his legs over the side of the bed.

She put her arm around his shoulders, and gazing into his eyes, asked tenderly, "Do you think you can walk out of here?"

"Yes, of course. Of course. I'm fine." Taking shameless advantage of the support her body offered, he levered himself to a stand.

"It's just that I'm so tired. And my head aches. And my arm . . ." That came out rather like a whimper, so hastily he straightened into a more heroic, yet still wounded posture, with only one shoulder drooping. That let his arm hang loose and brush innocently against her sweet, flannel-covered bosom.

She clasped him about the chest with both arms, as if she thought to carry him to safety. She was very warm, and soft in that lovely place between her arms. "Yes, yes, you must rest!"

"But where?" he asked piteously, glancing in a disoriented way around the room as she led him to the door.

"I—I don't know! I haven't got the linens mended for the blue room, and the yellow room's mattress is being reticked."

He heaved a martyred sigh. "It will have to be the couch in the parlor, I think."

"The couch? Oh, no, that will never do! You're far too tall to be comfortable there. And you must rest comfortably, after such an ordeal."

He allowed himself the briefest of moans and let a bit more of his weight rest on her. "Yes, I would like to rest. My head—"

She pressed tighter to him and guided him into the dark hallway. "You must come to my room. The fire is out, but the bed is warm and—and I will be able to monitor your breathing as you sleep. Head injuries so often result in concussion, you know."

"But—"

"No more protests. I shan't sleep at all, if I must worry about you in the drawing room, suffering with your poor head!"

And so Max finally entered his wife's bed, unbloody but bowed. He held his head heroically and cut short a cry of pain as he lay back on the sweet-smelling pillow slip. There was another pillow next to his, on a bed big enough for them both. And the sheets were warm with the memory of her body.

As he gave in to the wonder of this, Dorie bustled about, fussing with a water glass and a hot-water bottle and a compress for his forehead. She drew a chair to the bedside.

"You're not going to sit there?" Max had no need to invent panic. His strategy would fail if she slept sitting up.

"I thought—I thought you might be more comfortable alone."

He knew he would be ashamed of himself in the morning, but it was night still, so he pulled out all the stops. "What if I get feverish? You won't know it, because you will be so far away, there in that chair."

She hesitated, her hand on the arm of the chair, her eyes on him. Then she tied the sash more tightly around her waist, blew out the candle, and slipped into the bed beside him.

He held his breath. Yes, she was between the same sheets he was, only scant inches away. His hand almost made it to her hip when her fingers clasped his arm.

At least she didn't push him away. Instead, her fingertips rested lightly on his wrist. "There," she whispered. "I'll know if you get agitated. Oh! Your pulse is racing! Perhaps I should send for the doctor!"

Muttering something brave to forestall her escape, he closed his eyes and concentrated on calming himself and his heartbeat. An impossible task, given the way she was leaning toward him and radiating that sweet warmth in his direction. But the men of the Light Division specialized in the impossible, and eventually she pronounced his pulse normal and lay back down, only her fingertips touching him.

It was Hell. And Heaven, too.

Seventeen

Vayle had become a positive Nemesis, tracking her through the long cold days and haunting her restless nights.

Gwen stirred her tea till it splashed out on her napkin. It was after dinner, and the Nemesis was due elsewhere. But still he lingered in the drawing room, lounging back in his chair, his teacup balanced negligently in his hand.

The laughter of Winnie and Mrs. Fitzniggle filled the room and must have gratified Vayle no end. When they begged, he immediately produced another outrageous story for their amusement.

Sycophants, the both of them, hanging on his every word and singing his praises at every opportunity. They could not understand why she disliked the man. Nor could she explain, because only a deep instinct told her that he was a charlatan.

In the two weeks since Max's wedding, they had conspired to throw her into Vayle's company with treats she could not resist. But every lure came with a hook. They would make up a party to see *Hamlet,* but only if she agreed to go to Lady Jersey's ball the night before. Mrs. Fitzniggle detested opera, but would endure *The Magic Flute* if Gwen accepted the Duchess of Argyle's invitation.

One way or another, she found herself on Vayle's arm almost every night. And she resented him all the more because she inevitably enjoyed herself.

He had made a great many friends in London, and like Max

he saw to it that young men solicited her hand for every dance, except for the waltzes. Those he reserved for himself.

In his embrace, she felt almost beautiful. Although he never complimented her, not since she told him how she disliked his flummery, he had a way of looking at her that sang of silent praise. Some nights she came home nearly drunk with the heady wine of popularity, her feet aching and her spirits soaring.

Unaccustomed to attention, she found in herself a surprising store of witty retorts and conversation that others seemed to find appealing. The effect was so disorienting that sometimes she regarded herself from a distance, as if the real Gwen hovered near the ceiling, looking down on an almost pretty young woman holding court in a circle of admirers.

And always she saw Vayle, a proprietary smile on his face as if he'd orchestrated her success. She supposed he had, at the beginning. But as her confidence grew, she was able to walk into a crowded ballroom with assurance of a warm welcome, even on the rare occasions when Vayle did not come along.

To her vast surprise, she had attracted a pair of devoted suitors. Lord Mumblethorpe never failed to dance with her twice, and it was all she could do not to laugh at the ardent expression on his sweet face.

The Honorable Barry Leftbanks, heir to a great fortune, asked her at every opportunity when her brother was expected to return. Clearly he meant to make an offer, which she would naturally refuse although she'd not been able to dash his hopes. No man had ever courted her before, and she had no idea how to deal with adulation.

That was the price of social success, she supposed. Always she had to guard herself. She dared not truly speak her mind because her witty remarks would be repeated, out of context, in parlors across London. And humor didn't travel well. On a tabby's tongue, Miss Sevaric's most casual observation might be transformed into a poisonous, hurtful attack on someone she barely knew.

Only with Vayle could she relax and be herself. He took no

offense at her sharp tongue and sarcastic wit, even when it was directed at him. And he didn't expect her to be a ninnyhammer just because she was a woman. In her experience, men didn't approve of intelligence in a female, but Vayle seemed to delight in it.

As she rang for another pot of tea, she felt his gaze on her, inquiring and amused. No doubt he was piqued that she had failed to attend to his every *bon mot*. How flattered he would be if she confessed where her thoughts had led.

With his natural grace, he came to his feet and crossed to the game table. "Up for another clash at chess, Miss Sevaric? I believe you are down ten matches to nine."

Her heart took a leap, but she forced it back into place. "I thought you had an appointment this evening."

"It can wait." He opened the drawer and began setting pawns and rooks and knights precisely in the middle of their squares.

She joined him at the table, watching his long, graceful fingers align the ivory and onyx pieces, and wondering if his plans for later included a woman.

Or perhaps he intended to join up with Robin Caine again. Now that she was in society, she heard all the gossip, and this particular rumor had not escaped her. Vayle and Lord Lynton fenced together, patronized fashionable clubs, and were all too often mentioned in the same breath. It was a good reason, if she needed one, to distrust Vayle and his attentions.

Of late, Lynton was accounted good *ton*. She knew that was because Max had married his sister, and she loathed him all the more for taking advantage of the situation. When Max returned to London, with or without Dorothea, he'd soon put Robin Caine in his place.

For now, she could only wait and watch as Vayle played his enigmatic games with them all.

Tonight, though, chess was the only game that mattered. As the elderly ladies plied their needlework by the fire, Gwen took a white pawn and made a deliberately provocative opening move.

Vayle chuckled. "No prisoners, I gather."

"None."

While he studied the board, plotting his strategy, she thought about her father and the chess lessons that began when she was scarcely out of leading strings. Craving his approval, she had taken care to master the game, but Papa lost interest when she was good enough to beat him. By that time, he was wholly obsessed with the feud.

Although she was out of practice now, Vayle had come to respect her skill after their first few matches. He even admitted it. And she played her strongest against him, probably because she wanted so much to best him at something.

How she envied his self-assurance. It was all the challenge she needed, if only to prove Jocelyn Vayle could not control her as he controlled everything else, bending them all to his will with that offhanded charm and those luminous green eyes.

To his credit, he never permitted her an easy win. On the contrary, he fought her tooth and nail, and this evening was no different. Finally, with the evening far advanced, they agreed to a stalemate.

"What a reckless and tenacious creature you are," he said, as he returned chess pieces to their drawer. "I wonder at the contradiction. First you lured me into outrageous positions with daring gambits, then you pulled back and waited for me to make a mistake."

"You never did," she said with a rueful smile.

" 'Struth, this devilish encounter took all the concentration I could summon. And yet I cannot recall respecting an opponent more." He didn't let her enjoy that compliment long. Shaking his head, he added, "It is a pity, however, that you lost the gamester's edge when you might have seized the advantage. Had you been a bit less cautious at the end, you might have taken my king."

True, she admitted to herself. But caution had become second nature, at chess and at life. Still the praise warmed her heart. And she was grateful for his advice, because it meant he saw her as an worthy adversary who could stand up to constructive criticism.

"You might have won," she reminded him, "had you refrained from sacrificing your bishop in that doomed assault on my queen."

He closed the drawer with a snap. "Bishops are meant to be martyred. What surer path to Heaven, after all?"

That was heresy, or something like it, but so very *Vayle* that she could only sigh. He seemed peculiarly fond of martyrs, with his devotion to . . . what were their names? Proctor and Franciscus?

"Nevertheless," he said with a wide grin, "I declare us evenly matched—for now. Next time I shall be more ready for your astonishing lack of restraint in the early game."

"And I shall befuddle you with an altogether different strategy," she retorted, pleased when her comment drew a laugh.

Sometimes she could almost like him. He seemed to value her for the same qualities she valued in herself. But then he took out his watch to check the time, and she remembered how that slender hand had cradled Lady Melbrook's breast.

Did he plan an assignation with her tonight? Would he touch Lady Melbrook again, even more intimately, and forget all about the plain girl who only inspired him to the passion of a victory at the chess table?

At least Gwen had no illusions. She was nothing special to him, although sometimes he made her feel that way. She had to keep reminding herself that he was not to be trusted on any count.

His association with Robin Caine was evidence of that. And somehow, she suspected, he was implicated in the events that led to her brother's disastrous marriage. By now, Vayle fully understood the state of war between the Sevarics and the Caines, never mind that her brother had deloped by marrying Dorothea.

In that aspect Vayle was likely to be disappointed. An annulment was the only logical conclusion to the farce, and once Max had run his bride to ground, he would see to it. So far he had sent only the briefest of notes, very like the ones he had sent from the Peninsula: All is well. Don't worry.

She refused to believe he might have caught up with his wife. The possibility that they might consummate the marriage, making it real, was too horrible to contemplate.

No, the battle wasn't over. It had just moved to more treacherous ground, with Vayle serving both sides, consorting with her worst enemy while living in her house and exploiting her brother's good name.

She wanted him gone. She wanted him to disappear in a puff of smoke. She wanted, above all things, to stop wanting him.

Suddenly cold to the bone, she stood and gave him a false smile. "Surely you must be on your way, Mr. Vayle, or you'll miss your engagement. And I have developed a slight headache. Good night, sir."

After making her farewells to Winnie and Mrs. Fitzniggle, she made a somewhat breathless escape into the passageway.

To her annoyance, Vayle followed, looking concerned. "Can I be of help?" he asked with unmistakable sincerity.

Leave this house, she wanted to scream. Leave me alone. "It's nothing," she said evenly. "I'll be fine after a good night's sleep."

His green eyes shone like emeralds on fire. "Dream of flowers," he said mysteriously. "Flowers and children and love."

And then he bowed and turned away, leaving her to wonder what he meant as she tripped over the first step on her way upstairs.

Flowers and children and love!

Vayle wondered what he'd meant by that, even as he tossed the dice at White's. Gwen had looked so sad as she left him that he was impelled to offer some comfort—and that, alas, was the best he could do. Mayhap it would work. Better that she dream of love than of revenge.

Robin sat behind him, drinking soda water and pretending

not to care he wasn't one of the gamesters. They had agreed to test his restraint at a venue most likely to tempt him to folly, and so far he was behaving admirably. A young man-about-town could not entirely escape liquor and gaming, because they were everywhere, and Robin knew he had to content himself with watching. It could not be easy.

But addiction had nearly destroyed him, so he had no choice but to avoid the clubs altogether or to learn to be an observer. As the stack of markers and scrawled vowels mounted in front of him, Vayle wondered if he ought to stop winning. Robin might be more inspired to forsake gaming if he saw his best and only friend run aground.

Still, Robin knew very well how to lose. The best test of his resolve was to contemplate success and decide to forgo it.

Vayle stacked markers worth several hundred pounds and pushed them in front of Robin. "Care to play?" he asked casually. "Free money, since I began with practically nothing and have won rather a lot."

Robin looked at the markers, at Vayle, and back at the markers. He nibbled the inside of his lower lip.

"Have at it, Lynton," Lord Halbersham encouraged with a hearty laugh. "That's my blunt and I want a chance to win it back. Vayle here is unbeatable."

Vayle swirled brandy in his glass, pretending to be transfixed by the play of candlelight on amber liquid. "What have you got to lose?" he asked softly.

Unsteadily, Robin came to his feet. "You know the answer to that. Sorry, gentlemen. You must wrest your funds from the Devil while I call it a night."

Vayle caught up with him at the main door. "I'm leaving, too, Simpson," he said, tossing the porter a sovereign.

While Simpson went to the cloakroom, Vayle clapped Robin on the back. "Excellent," he began, his voice fading as Robin turned on him with a murderous expression.

"Damn you! Was that meant to be a test? A deuced cowhanded one, and I'm not so ungrateful as to break my re-

solve in your presence. If and when I fall, you'll not stand witness."

Simpson returned with greatcoats, hats, and gloves before Vayle could reply, and the men remained silent until the carriage pulled up in front of Robin's flat.

"I never thought you'd actually join the game," Vayle said mildly. "But I wanted to know your feelings when the chance was given you. Is the compulsion vastly strong?"

"Bad enough," Robin admitted after some thought. "It's not the money, you know. It never was. But I love the action. And I despair of finding anything to replace the exhilaration I felt at the tables, even when I was losing. Tonight was easy, or nearly so with you standing watch, but how am I to go my whole life without gaming?"

Vayle understood weakness and temptation, but full-fledged addiction was beyond his power to imagine. He had no answers for Robin, and his support had to be limited to a few more days. Come Christmas, the boy would be on his own.

"Could *you* give it up?"

Vayle frowned as he considered this for the first time. "If necessary. Unlike you, I game for the money. Well, partly, because I, too, have a need for competition. But I can find challenges elsewhere, in a fierce game of chess, for example." He smiled as he recalled his match with Gwen. "Or fencing. Once I determined to be the best, other interests took second place."

"Perhaps I'll set myself to beat you with the foils."

"You have talent," Vayle said. "Enough to defeat just about anyone, eventually, if you put in the work."

"Does *anyone* include you?"

When Vayle laughed, Robin opened the carriage door. "I thought not. Will you come upstairs for a moment? I've something to show you."

After instructing the driver to circle the block, Vayle followed Robin to his rooms and was astonished at what he saw when he stepped inside. The tiny flat was neat as a pin.

"I borrowed from the cent-percenters," Robin explained.

"Only a trifle, to hang new curtains and hire a maid twice a week. She is a harridan and complains if I leave so much as a cravat out of place."

He pointed to the desk, now covered with books. "I also joined a subscription library and am trying to repair my education. Dorothea was furious when I left Oxford after one term, but I'd gambled away the funds she wrung from our uncle to put me there. Now I want to make it up to her. There is an elderly man down the hall who was once a schoolmaster. He is tutoring me."

Vayle gazed around him at the transformed room, his heart swelling with pride. Robin was trying so hard to redeem himself.

In many ways, Robin had more raw courage than he could claim for himself. Vayle had never needed courage, because everything had come easily for him. Proctor had the right of it—"a useless, self-absorbed mortal wasting gifts that should have been put to better use."

He looked up through burning eyes to see Robin in front of him, grinning boyishly.

"I have a Christmas gift for you," he said. "It's early, I know, but I couldn't wait. 'Tis little enough after all you have done for me."

Vayle lifted his arms, intending to protest, and into his right hand Robin dropped a small, smooth object.

As his fingers closed, Vayle recognized the oval shape, the familiar weight, the cool feel of solid gold. He ran his thumb over the cloisonné lid where the Lynton crest was marked out in red, black, and silver. Around the body two dragons were engraved, their tongues of fire meeting to form his initials.

VC, for Valerian Caine. His brother had given him the snuffbox on his coming of age. Now his brother's descendant gave it to him again, more than a century later.

Unable to speak, he shook his head.

"I'll not hear any objections," Robin warned. "Many were the times I thought of selling it, but could never bring myself to let it go. Until this moment, I did not know why. Probably you don't believe in such things as fate and destiny, but I am convinced it was meant for you."

Caught in a whirlwind of emotions, Vayle struggled to pull himself together. "I am most grateful," he said in a husky voice. "And I will treasure this all my life."

"Well then." Robin cleared his throat, as if such sentiments made him uncomfortable. "Good. Never cared for snuff myself. Makes me sneeze."

"I am partial to it," Vayle said, matching Robin's nonchalance. "Tomorrow we'll go to a tobacco shop and select a special blend. After that, you can have another try at me with the foils."

"Done. But I expect you should go before the horses wear a rut in the street."

"Yes. I should. Good night. Thank you."

When the door closed behind him, Vayle stood for a moment, pain and pleasure washing over him in waves. He lifted the lid of the snuffbox and held it to his nostrils. Was it his imagination, or did he catch the fragrance he'd delighted in a hundred years ago? Surely the snuffbox had been used since, by other Caines, before it came into Robin's hands, and yet it conjured memories of the splendid life he wanted more than ever to reclaim.

The memories were all the sharper because he had little more than a glimmer of hope of completing his tasks to Proctor's satisfaction by Christmas.

He could not regret neglecting them in favor of Robin, who was coming, slowly but surely, into his own. But Robin was well launched now, and his own goal more elusive than ever. Counting on his fingers, he realized a mere eight days remained to him.

Without question he was doomed. He might have succeeded with Max and Dorie—he had great faith in Max's persistence and in Dorie's appeal. But he had only to think of Gwen's bleak face this evening to know that her happiness was outside his control.

Yet no matter what his fate, he was no worse off than before Proctor sent him here. How many souls got the chance to live again? Eight more days and nights to be human, he reminded himself. Enjoy yourself while you can, Valerian Caine!

He trotted down the stairs and whistled for Max's coach. Robin would get the snuffbox back in just over a week. The boy could have his clothes, too, and anything that remained of his winnings at the tables. Vayle resolved to write a will when he got home, making sure of it.

And before he was reabsorbed into the bloodless Afterlife, he would make love to a woman. His body ached constantly with the need. Perhaps he could find Lady Melbrook again. If not, he suspected Clootie would be eager to point him in the direction of entertainment.

Not tomorrow, though. He was promised to Robin for the afternoon, and planned to escort Gwen to a ball in the evening. Such a virtuous schedule played havoc with sinful intentions, he reflected with a chuckle. But there were always the hours before dawn. He *would* sin, while he could—and the consequences be damned.

So long as he had a body, he'd use it to best advantage. And nothing else he'd experienced, in his former life or the shadowy interim or the few weeks allotted him now, surpassed the delight of pleasuring a woman and taking pleasure from her.

Except, perhaps, the moment Robin handed him the snuffbox and thanked him for being a friend.

Eighteen

Her new husband was a gentleman, Dorie learned, but a man nonetheless. When it was time to dress or undress, he would linger hopefully in their room, until she glanced toward the door to indicate she couldn't proceed in his presence.

By the end of the third week of December, Dorie was torn by his expression of regret as he exited. What would happen, she wondered as she dressed for dinner, if someday she failed to announce her intention and simply began to strip off garments?

No need to speculate. As she tugged her chemise over her head, she remembered the heat in Max's eyes that morning when the bodice bow on her nightgown came undone. It revealed no more than an evening gown might, but somehow it was different—they were in bed, and she was undressed, or at least less dressed than she ought to be. If she hadn't slid out of bed on the pretext of getting more wood for the fire, he might have—

Well, he might have, it was true, but in fact Max merely dug his head under the pillows and groaned. Max was a gentleman. Gentlemen didn't insist on consummating a marriage begun under awkward circumstances, even if subsequent awkward circumstances required bed-sharing.

And Dorie was a lady. Ladies didn't tease gentlemen with glimpses of the forbidden, or promise what they could not fulfill.

That was why she was surprised to find herself opening the door and calling to her husband that she needed his assistance.

He appeared with pleasing alacrity. But when he entered the room and saw her, fully dressed to her pumps, his face fell.

Ladies did not disappoint gentlemen either. So she held out her hand, palm upturned. "Would you mind fastening this bracelet for me? I can't seem to do it one-handed."

It was not, probably, the request he had hoped for, but Max took the bracelet and did his duty with his battered and bandaged fingers. In fact, he did a bit more than that, bending to kiss her wrist just under the clasp.

It was the most gallant gesture he had ever made, and as Dorie took back her tingling hand, she murmured her thanks and turned to hide her blush. But Max didn't take the hint and move away—or perhaps he thought she was hinting that he should stay next to her? She didn't quite know herself what she was hinting, or why she was hinting it, for that matter.

The space between the bed and the door was so limited that she could feel the brush of his evening coat against her bare arm, and a comforting warmth that she recognized as radiating from his—well, there was no other word for it—from his body.

She had no reason to object, she told herself firmly, for after all, she had once spent a few hours right up against that body, though only under threat of freezing. And each night this last week she lay a few inches from it. Any objections at this point would be moot. And besides, he was speaking now and it would be rude not to answer him.

"Scent? Yes, I did apply a bit of scent." Glad of an excuse for action, she grabbed the crystal bottle from the night table and showed it to him. "It was my mother's. She always used this scent, you see. Always."

The expression on his face was so arresting that she thought she had better go on talking to distract them both. "She loved this scent. My mother. She had it made special by a perfumer on Bond Street. But it's gone now. The perfumer. I don't mean the scent is gone."

She knew her words were tumbling out in no particular order. Now he had taken her hand again and brought it up to his face, intending, she supposed, to sample the scent again but accidentally missing his nose and instead touching her wrist to his lips.

"But I have just a bit left. Just a bit. Once Mama had simply quarts of it, because we—Robin and I—we always knew she would welcome it as a gift. So each Christmas that's what we got her. This scent."

"It's—it's lovely." Max's voice was husky, and his warm breath caressed her wrist. "Did you—did you apply a bit to your, umm, your throat also?"

She caught her breath, wondering what he might do if she said yes. But she couldn't lie. "No. I haven't enough to spare. It's almost gone."

"Too bad." His whisper came in a stroke up her arm, and he had reached the inside of her elbow before she panicked.

"Speaking of Robin—"

He dropped her hand and stepped back. "Let's not."

She hadn't intended him to withdraw quite *that* far. Piqued, she said, "Speaking of Robin, I'm going to write to him and invite him to visit for Christmas. He hasn't anywhere else to go, and I hate to think of him alone for the holiday. Your sister and her companion, and Mr. Vayle, might join us, too."

If she had hoped that this last remark would soften him, she was disappointed.

"No." It was his major's voice, and he was wearing the matching expression—cold and commanding.

Dorie stiffened. Setting the perfume bottle firmly on the table, she said, "I do not take your meaning."

"My meaning is that your brother is not welcome in my home."

"Not welcome in your home?" Suddenly what was only an attempt at distraction had become a struggle for authority. "But my dear Sevaric, perhaps you are forgetting. This is *my* home."

He had no response to this, unless she counted his taking two steps and seizing the doorknob and yanking it open. He was leaving—just the room, or her house? "Max!"

He stopped but didn't turn around.

"He's my brother." She pressed her fist against her mouth, then dropped her hand to her side. "Oh, I know he isn't the best of men, but we were children together. He taught me to ride a horse. And he's the only one—he's the only one who knew my parents and remembers them as I do. Sometimes, when he hasn't been drinking so much, he will talk about Mama. He remembers more than I do, for he is the elder—" Her voice faltered, and she said softly, "He is the only family I have."

"You have me."

Her heart stopped, then picked up again, beating more rapidly than before. "Thank you. But it can't be at such a cost. Surely you know that. I would never ask you to abandon your sister—"

"My sister has done nothing to merit that."

"But even if Gwen had, you wouldn't! You would still try, as I have with Robin."

"I shan't have my sister's name mentioned at the same time as his."

"Just because he is a Caine?"

"It starts there, yes."

Max's voice was gritty with suppressed emotion, and Dorie knew a moment's despair. He hated Robin. Hated him. And it made no sense.

Once she might have thought her husband capable of impersonally carrying out the feud of his ancestors. Now that she had spent a fortnight in his company, she knew better. He was a hard man, no doubt, and in the war he had known violence and brutality. But he had integrity, too, and honor. He didn't condemn men because of their ranks or stations in life. He wouldn't condemn Robin for his name.

Now, looking at his rigid back, his tense shoulders, she knew this rage had to be more than family prejudice. "But I am a Caine, too. And you have treated me well. You do not hate me."

"You are a Sevaric now."

"My blood hasn't changed. Only my name. And you—you don't hate me."

"No." His voice was so low she could hardly hear him. "I didn't want this. It was my father's fight, not mine."

"Then why fight Robin? What has he done to deserve this?"

For just a moment, she saw a slight relaxation in his tension, and she thought he might tell her the truth. But finally he said, "I cannot betray a confidence."

He let go of the door and turned slowly. But still he didn't look at her. He just picked up the perfume bottle and held it to the light, as if some answer might be found in the rainbow it cast on the scarred wall. Then he set it down. "You are my wife. Your loyalty must be to me now. And you must believe me when I say I cannot welcome your brother. If you invite him nonetheless, I will leave this house."

In the silence that followed, the striking of the clock startled them both. Max glanced at the time and in a normal tone, told her, "We must go, or we'll be late for the squire's dinner."

Subdued now, she agreed and gathered up her wrap and reticule and followed him out to the carriage. They did not speak on the drive to Squire Willett's house, but by tacit agreement both made an effort to be sociable during dinner.

As they were readying to leave, Mrs. Willett took Dorie aside, and on the pretext of straightening her bonnet, gave an assessment. "He is a handsome one, that husband of yours! And so kind, too. Not a drop of arrogance, either, considering he's a lord and an officer, too. You did very well for yourself, capturing a man like that!"

Dorie glanced over at her husband and suppressed a sigh. If she had "captured" him, she was finding him rather hard to tame.

They spoke no more about Robin, or anything else of substance. But later that night, sleepless in her not-quite-conjugal bed, Dorie turned on her side and studied the bulky dark outline of Max's shoulder.

His breathing came in the light regular rhythm of sleep, and she was almost resentful. Here she was, relentlessly wakeful, and he slept as quietly as a child. But she supposed a soldier must learn to rest no matter what the turmoil in his environment.

At least, she thought, snuggling down under the covers, his body kept the bed warm on this cold night.

She couldn't love a man who hated her family, could she? For didn't that mean he hated her? She was, as much as Robin, the scion of the Caines.

She never wanted the feud, though. A moderate, conciliatory child, she distrusted obsession, and tried to ignore her uncle when he cursed the Sevarics and plotted their downfall. Robin liked to join in and mutter a few curses of his own, but that was no more than a fatherless boy's search for masculine approval. No matter what bitter sentiments Robin echoed, he was harmless, except to himself.

But Max wasn't. He had proved how dangerous he could be by completing the ruin of her family. And now he posed a special danger to Dorie. He offered her what she had always longed for—a home, a family, a beloved—but only if she surrendered herself and her past. And then what would she have left to give him?

Quietly, without waking him, she pulled on her robe and slippers and left the room. Closing the door gently behind her, she found her way by memory down the stairs through the dark. In the chilly parlor, she lit a candle and sitting at her desk, took up her quill.

The candlelight flickered on her blank page as she hesitated, wondering what salutation to use. "My dear Miss Sevaric" suited the young lady who had given her breakfast with a neutrality that bordered on scorn. "Dear Gwen" suited better the girl who helped her dress for the wedding. But neither suited Dorie's purpose—to reach out to the one who knew her husband best.

Finally, in a rush, she wrote:

My dear sister,

   I pray you don't mind that I call you sister, but we have by some chance become related, and I hope to make that true in heart as well as law. You were kind to me before my wedding, and I beg your kindness now.

I have learned these past weeks that my husband esteems you, for he speaks highly of your wisdom and good sense. In that spirit, I turn to you for aid.

Lord Sevaric has been kind to me, kinder perhaps than the circumstances of our marriage merit. I would like to return that kindness. I beg you to join us here at Greenbriar Lodge to celebrate this first holiday of our life together. That will make this truly a family occasion, and more joyful for Lord Sevaric.

Stopping to mend her pen, Dorie had time to reflect on the meagerness of a family holiday with only three persons in attendance. What would the rest of the London household do for the holidays? The dragon Mrs. Fitzniggle had her own family, and probably they would have no choice but to take her at Yuletide. But Miss Winnie and Mr. Vayle, she suspected, had nowhere else to go. On impulse, she added,

Perhaps Miss Winnie and Mr. Vayle could be persuaded to come also. Lord Sevaric has said that Mr. Vayle should consider Sevaric House his home, and I extend him the same welcome to my house.

Before she went on, Dorie had to gather her courage. She wasn't used to confiding her troubles in others, much less a new acquaintance who, she suspected, disliked her. But she had nowhere else to turn. Courage, she told herself sternly, and took up her pen again.

Now I appeal to you as a sister. You know your brother best. I had hoped that our marriage would diminish his anger toward my family, but that has not occurred. Instead, his hatred of my brother seems only to have increased, so much that he expects me to prove my loyalty to him by abandoning Robin. As a sister yourself, you must understand how difficult that is.

Perhaps you have some insight into his antipathy? If so, I beg you to share it with me. I feel certain if I knew why he feels this way about my brother, I might find some way to conciliate them.

Please understand that I mean only the best for your brother. This union began inauspiciously, but I have the greatest respect for Lord Sevaric, and mean to be a good wife to him. If you can find it in your heart to help me, I would remain always,

Your grateful sister,
Dorothea Sevaric

Nineteen

"Thank you, Clootie." Vayle folded the scrap of paper and slid it in in his pocket. "I'll make good use of this address tonight."

The valet produced the cheerless twist of his lips that served him for a smile. "I'll send word ahead so that Mrs. Benson will be expecting you. Her clients are selected with discretion, as are the women she provides. You will not be disappointed. And if you prefer diversions of a more unusual sort—"

"The usual will suffice," Vayle assured him. "First I must endure a tedious musicale with the ladies and contrive an excuse to leave early. You needn't wait up for me tonight."

Clootie might have winked, if his face weren't so tight. "Should she ask, I shall inform Mrs. Fitzniggle that you retired with the headache and cannot be disturbed."

Vayle chuckled. "She runs a tight ship, when it suits her. I rely on you to cover my tracks. See that the butler has my hat and the rest, will you? I'll take a glass of sherry in the drawing room while I'm waiting."

He chose brandy instead, to dull his senses for the amateur performances at the musicale, and consoled himself with thoughts of what was in store when he made his escape.

At long last, he would have a woman in his arms. A naked, willing woman intent on pleasuring him. After a century of celibacy, every nerve in his body ached with longing.

Proctor's censure was inevitable. But he'd begun this enterprise expecting the worst of Valerian Caine and would not be surprised when his least-favorite charge fell from grace. No matter. Whatever the wages of sin, the erstwhile Valerian Caine intended this night to sample liberally from the garden of earthly delights. And on that thought, he poured himself another glass of brandy.

'Struth, he was already doomed. Only five days remained until Christmas, and for all he knew Max was still in hot pursuit of his bride. Dorie was wily enough to elude him for several decades if she set her mind to it. And as for Gwen—Gwen remained distant, obstinate, and mysterious.

Women! Outside of bed, what man could satisfy any one of them?

Wonderful creatures, though. They never failed to intrigue him. Even Gwen Sevaric, with her waspish personality, made him long to explore the source of her unquenchable spirit. More times than he could count, he'd put aside other interests to coax a smile from her.

He never could resist a challenge, he reflected, pulling the snuffbox from his pocket. Only arrogance explained his determination to win her over. He'd a better chance of securing Proctor's respect than Gwen's affection, which made his efforts all the more ridiculous. Proctor would determine his fate, and Gwen could never be part of it.

He sprinkled a bit of redolent powder on his wrist and inhaled deeply. After several failed efforts, Fribourg and Treyer had created a blend similar to the one he used to favor. The scent of snuff would be his last and only bond with his former life, unless Francis produced a last-minute miracle.

For a Guardian, Francis certainly kept his distance. And he wasn't likely to show up at Mrs. Benson's establishment either, although the idea of Francis at a brothel tickled his fancy. Perhaps he'd rush in to—

"Mr. Vayle?"

Gwen stepped into the room, wearing the dark, plain sort of dress she favored when she stayed at home. Her hair was down about her shoulders and her eyes were cloudy with distress.

"Oh, my dear," he said, moving toward her.

She lifted a hand, effectively holding him at a distance. "I'll not be joining you this evening," she said without inflection, as if she'd rehearsed the speech. "I see that you are already dressed. Mrs. Fitzniggle has no great interest in the musicale, but Lady Cameron does not admit unaccompanied bachelors. If you wish to attend, Mrs. Fitzniggle and Winnie have agreed to make up a party."

"Indeed they must not. I can amuse myself elsewhere." He knew the precise location of "elsewhere," and his spirits soared in anticipation. "You will require their company if you are ill."

"I'm perfectly fine!" After that brief outburst, she regained her self-control and stared down at her clasped hands. "There is one bit of news. I had today a letter from L-Lady Sevaric. She and my brother are at Greenbriar Lodge, her former home, and have been these last few weeks."

"Ah."

"So now we need not worry about them. And she conveyed a message to you from Max. You are to regard Sevaric House as your own for as long as you choose to remain."

"Most kind of Lord Sevaric," he said quietly, "but I'll be here another few days at the most. I daresay you'll be pleased to see the last of me."

She regarded him steadily. "Do you expect me to deny it? If your vanity requires a token protest, I shall prepare a speech of flattery and regret to be delivered on the occasion of your departure."

He would have laughed, if not for the unhappiness in her eyes. "Is there anything at all I can do for you, Miss Sevaric?"

"Of course not." She turned, and then looked at him over her shoulder. "But thank you."

As he watched, her shoulders slumped. Her hand shook when she reached for the latch. And then she emitted a small sound, like a hurt kitten.

Without thought, he rushed to the door and put both hands

against it, imprisoning her with his body and arms. "Not yet," he said firmly. "If you are to cry, you will not do so alone."

She went rigid, making herself narrow so as not to touch him. "I am not a weepy female," she said in an icy voice. "I have never been that."

He lifted a hand and stroked it down her cheek. "I know, Gwendolyn. You are brave and strong to a frightening degree. But this is unmistakably a tear."

"*My* tear, and none of your business. Nor have you leave to call me Gwendolyn."

"True, but I am an impertinent fellow, as you have often remarked. And—"

Her elbow planted itself in his ribs.

With a loud Ooof, he took an involuntary step back and dropped the snuffbox he'd been holding. It landed directly between Gwen's feet.

Expecting her to flee, he was astonished when she gazed at it for a long moment. As if in a trance, she lowered herself, crouching on bent knees. Her hand went out, slowly, and picked it up.

He waited in silence, wondering why it fascinated her so. He could see only the top of her bent head and her fingertips moving over the enameled crest.

Then she uncoiled with the speed of a striking snake and slapped his face so hard black spots danced in front of his eyes.

"Where did you get this?" She swung again, but this time he was quick enough to catch her arm and use it to pull her against him.

"That's enough, my dear. You have full leave to rip me to flinders if I merit it, but not before you tell me why." Ignoring her protests and careful to evade her kicking feet, he pulled her to a divan and sat her down.

As her fury subsided, the tears came in earnest. She let the snuffbox fall onto her lap, and didn't protest when he drew her into his arms.

Face buried against his shoulder, she wept hot tears he knew had been stored inside for a very long time. He felt them against his neck and held her close, rubbing her back gently, saying nothing. He had no idea how to deal with such profound grief. All he could do was give her safe harbor.

She would not rest there long, he feared. She would emerge like a spitting cat, furious because he had seen the vulnerable woman under the prickly image she presented to the world.

So proud and fierce, Gwen Sevaric. He admired her courage all the more now that she had yielded, momentarily, to her desolation.

Obviously he was connected to it, beyond his unwelcome presence in her house, but how? Yes, he was a Caine. The originator of the feud, in fact. But she could not know that.

Without question she had suffered because of the antagonism between the families, as had Robin and Max and Dorothea. And yet, more than the others, she had always seemed to him detached from the quarrel.

Then he remembered what Winnie had said that first night he spent in this house. Until her father's death, Gwen served him as housekeeper and secretary. She was permitted no life of her own, no come-out in society, no suitors. She never had a chance to live any of the dreams young girls cherish.

All she had was her position here as mistress of the house. Dorie's letter must have reminded her that soon she would be replaced. No wonder she was overset.

But that wouldn't reduce her to this storm of tears.

Gwen had the strength and resilience of Toledo steel. Under ordinary circumstances, he was sure, she would take her brother's marriage and its consequences without flinching.

There had to be more to it. Something to do with that damned snuffbox.

So much for his evening plans. His lips curved in an ironic grin. Proctor would not even credit him for resisting temptation, because given a choice, he would be writhing on satin sheets at Mrs. Benson's brothel. But he didn't have a choice. He couldn't leave Gwen alone.

She had gone still, and with a sigh he leaned away from her, holding her shoulders with both hands. "Tell me what is wrong," he said sternly. "I'll not let you go until I've heard the whole of it."

When she failed to respond, he shook her gently. " 'Struth, Gwendolyn, you cannot stay in hiding."

"You've no right," she protested, pushing ineffectually at his chest.

"I know. But I am here, and you must speak of this."

Her head lowered. "I already did, to Max, and that was a mistake. It only hurt him. Now—now his wife has asked me why he cannot let go of the feud while she is willing to end it. But he can't, because of me. And if I tell her the reason it will bring her even more pain. Oh, damn."

She was making little sense, but at least she was talking. He let go of her and gave her his handkerchief. "We could both use a drink, I believe."

On the way to the sideboard, he stopped at the door, turned the key, and slid it in his pocket.

"You needn't lock me in!"

"Merely assuring our privacy. Will Mrs. Fitzniggle succumb to the vapors when she hears of this, do you think?"

She managed a faint smile. "In her judgment, I am too commonplace for scandal."

"Then she is a fool." He handed her a glass of brandy and resumed his seat beside her. "Under the circumstances, that makes her an ideal chaperone."

The distraction had done its work, because Gwen's hand was steady as she sipped from the glass. Her eyes widened in surprise. "It burns." She took another drink. "But I quite like it."

He smiled, wishing they could simply play chess or talk of inconsequential things. He was good at easy social congress, without expectations on either side. But Gwen needed more, and he knew he could not give it to her in the short time that remained to him. Besides, whatever was tormenting her, she had already told her brother, and if anything could be done to help her, Max would have seen to it.

He gazed at the snuffbox on her lap and at the initials winking at him in the light of the chandelier. However distantly, he was responsible in great part for her unhappiness. His throat tightened.

"I am sorry for attacking you," she said. "Your cheek is still red. Are you injured?"

"Only my pride. Well, perhaps a bruised rib or two. In my defense, you rather took me unaware."

"I was not expecting it either," she said. "You will find this difficult to understand, but it's as though I was transported to another time and place when I saw this." She lifted the snuffbox. "How came you to have it?"

" 'Twas a gift," he said carefully. "From Robin Caine."

"I should have known that. The two of you have become great friends. For that reason, I mustn't tell you anything more. This is not your quarrel."

"No? However much you wish me to mind my own business, I'm as meddlesome as an old aunt. And more relentless than your brother, Gwendolyn. I doubt you have told him, or anyone else, the entire story. You struck out at me because you were unable to fight back in that other time and place. Am I right?"

She regarded him warily. "On all counts. Has Robin spoken of—"

"Certainly not. But he is convinced you despise him and takes care to avoid your presence. 'Struth, that is why he failed to attend his sister's wedding."

"I do despise him, with reason. But I regret more than ever that this has affected Max and Dorothea. Because of me, they'll never be wholly free to make a new life for themselves." She stared broodingly at the snuffbox. "If only I could disappear as if I never was."

"You wouldn't say that if you knew what it meant, my dear." Gently, he took the snuffbox from her hand and put it on the cushion behind him, out of her sight. "What did Robin do to you? You still dream of it—Winnie told me you have night-mares—and a few minutes ago you relived a terrifying experience. Fear will continue to haunt you, I believe, until you face what happened straight on. Only then can you put it behind you."

"Telling you will accomplish that?"

"Probably not," he said honestly. "But it will be a start, and you may rely on my discretion. Give me everything, Gwen, from the beginning."

For a long time she was silent, staring into the brandy like a fortune-teller reading messages at the bottom of a teacup. He was casting about for some way to prod her when she began to speak, tonelessly, never looking at him.

"My father died almost two years ago, and I was alone except for the servants until Max came home. One afternoon I was returning from the shops, without my maid because she had a cold. A carriage pulled over and I was swept inside. I tried to scream and was quickly gagged. Then something, a pillow slip I think, was pulled over my head."

Her hand was trembling so hard that he had to take the glass from her and set it on the table. She didn't seem to notice. "The trip took forever, and I was sure I'd suffocate. I did lose consciousness for a time, because the next thing I knew I was being carried up a flight of stairs. I was still gagged, although the pillow slip was gone, and I recognized Hugo Caine, Robin's uncle."

She paused to draw a quick breath, and went on. "He was my father's greatest enemy, and the two of them fought like rabid wolves for as long as I could remember. He tossed me into a small, sealed room. There was no furniture, and no light because the windows were boarded over."

She flushed. "There was not even a chamber pot. What I remember most, in my dreams, is the stench of that room. And the cold. He took my pelisse and gloves, and even my shoes. Only by a crack of light through a knothole could I tell day from night. I was left alone for a long time without food or water. Then he came back with an enormous manservant who tied my hands and feet. I remember lying there on the floor with his filthy boots inches from my face."

She hugged herself, her arms across her chest, but her face remained calm. "He wanted the treasure, you see. The Caines are convinced our family stole it, and he thought he could bully me into handing it over. I'd have done so in a flash, were it possible, but we've never had the treasure. And I would have known, because I kept all my father's records for years and years."

Her shoulders shook, as if she were sobbing, but there were no tears in her eyes. "Caine did not believe me, though. He took a horsewhip to me that night, and the night after that."

Vayle held still, his face impassive, though it took every bit of strength he could summon. Not that his reaction mattered—Gwen stared into her own private vision—but he longed to horsewhip Caine until pieces of him were scattered over Greater London. Even more, he wanted to hold Gwen and absorb her pain into himself.

And because he could do neither, he sat quietly and listened, while his heart pounded in his chest like a creature separate from his body.

"The third night he tried to ravish me," she said with staggering calm. "He tossed my skirts over my face and lay on top of me. I thought I must surely die then, of disgust, but I did not."

Vayle's fist clenched uselessly at his side. Stop, he wanted to tell her. Don't say any more. But she continued in that remote voice.

"And he could not. Whatever was required of him, he was unable to do it. I remember him standing over me after that, taking snuff. He dropped the box, and it fell near my eyes. I saw the crest on top, and the dragons carved around the sides."

For the first time, she looked at him. Gazing into her eyes, Vayle felt as if he saw the fires of Hell. But her lips curved in a mirthless smile. "That's why I reacted as I did when I saw the snuffbox again. You took a bit of the punishment I've longed to visit on Hugo Caine." Her head tilted. "Are you sure you wish me to continue?"

Unable to speak past the rock in his throat, he nodded.

"By now you must be wondering how Robin figures in. He was not there at the beginning, or perhaps he was and I didn't see him. I soon lost track of time, although I was later told by the servants that I vanished on a Monday and found my way home the following Saturday."

She sighed then, as if remembering wearied her. Drawing her feet under her skirt, she leaned back against the sofa cushions.

"At some point Robin appeared. I was delirious by then, and recall little of what happened. Suddenly he was in the room with the door locked behind him. He told me he'd been instructed to rape me but had rather not. If I would promise to tell his uncle that he succeeded, he'd not touch me. I was beyond promising anything, but I remember that he sat in the corner and vomited. He was probably drunk."

Locating her brandy glass, she leaned over and picked it up. "He was there another time, too, when his uncle whipped me again. He stayed when the others left and begged me to hand over the treasure. He said something else, but I don't remember what. I don't think I heard him."

She stopped and took a tiny sip of brandy. Her color was coming back, and she seemed more peaceable. The worst of the story was done, he realized.

"I woke up with the idea I'd pretend to know where the treasure was. I had some vague plan that would not have served. But I stumbled to the door and tugged at the latch. To my astonishment, it loosed and the door came open. The passageway was dark and no one stopped me as I found my way outside."

She tilted her head to the side. "Someone had been careless—left a saddled horse near the front door. I thought to make use of it. But I'd the notion my absence would be discovered more quickly if the horse disappeared, so I made my way to a copse of trees and walked from there. I must have stumbled onto a road because a mailcoach nearly ran me down the next morning. The driver was kind enough to take me up and brought me to this house."

She turned to him and said, "So now you have heard it all, Jocelyn Vayle. What think you now? Did the telling of this story achieve anything beyond satisfying your curiosity?"

With effort, he focused on her eyes. They were at once defiant and pleading, shimmering with new tears she would not allow to fall. Moving slowly, he set down the glass of brandy he'd clutched for what seemed like a lifetime, and silently wrapped her in his arms.

This time there were no tears, and no words.

At first she was stiff as a suit of armor, but he pressed his cheek against the side of her head and held her with all the respect and concern he felt for her. How splendid she was, this brave young woman. After all she had endured, she worried more for the consequences to her brother and his new wife than for herself.

She put her hand on his chest and pushed him away. "You needn't feel sorry for me. Hugo Caine died soon after, by putting a bullet to his head. I content myself with thinking his suicide was brought on by my escape and his failure to win the treasure he'd spent his life trying to reclaim."

"I expect you are right," he murmured.

"As you guessed, I told Max the barest details of the abduction—nothing about the beatings and the attempts to do worse. Even so, he immediately called Robin out. Nothing came of it because Robin was too much the coward to face him. And I thank God for that, because I'd not have his death on Max's conscience. My brother endured too much of death in the war and has earned peace of heart. But how can he attain it, married to Robin's sister? Will there never be an end to this hellish feud?"

Vayle let out a ragged breath. What a fool he'd been to think marrying Max Sevaric to Dorothea Caine solved anything. That wedding only upped the stakes for everyone concerned.

His own failure to accomplish his tasks was nothing compared to the mess he would leave behind him. Already he had resigned himself to whatever fate Proctor chose. But he wished he could return to the miserable Afterlife knowing at least one person was better off because he'd spent a month in the nineteenth century.

Sighing, he picked up Gwen's glass of brandy and held it out. "Drink this. It will help you sleep."

When she finished it, he gave her the remains of his own brandy, and she swallowed that, too. Then she handed him the empty glass and managed a valiant little smile. But her eyes were so forlorn he'd have gladly died to spare her another minute of pain.

Except that he was already dead. And from experience he'd learned that a mortal's death meant next to nothing in the universal scheme of things. Better he figure something of worth to do for her in the last few days allotted him on earth.

He stroked her lips with the tip of his finger, wanting to kiss her but knowing he must not. "Thank you for confiding in me," he said somberly. "Although you care nothing for my opinion, I admire your courage more than I can say. And I hope you are a little tipsy from the brandy."

When she nodded a bit absently, he helped her upstairs and fetched Winnie. "Take care of her," he directed.

And then, sword-cane in hand, he set out for a reckoning with Lord Lynton.

Cold with fury, Vayle banged his cane on Lynton's door. With Gwen's tear-streaked face a haunting vision in the dim passageway, he felt more like Valerian Caine than peaceable Jocelyn Vayle.

This time there would be no escape. Robin had eluded Max's honorable challenge, but now he would face a man with nothing to lose. Valerian Caine, already damned, was hellbent on vengeance.

Robin opened the door, smiling as he recognized his unexpected visitor. Vayle regarded him for a moment with contempt. Then he jabbed his cane into Robin's stomach.

When he doubled over, Vayle hit him again, this time with a hard fist to the jaw. Robin landed on his back with a thud.

Stepping inside, Vayle closed the door and locked it. He planted a booted foot on either side of Robin's waist and glared down at him.

Robin gazed back, stunned. A stream of blood escaped the corner of his mouth. "Why'd y'do that?" he mumbled between swollen lips.

"So that I wouldn't kill you." Vayle twisted the silver hand piece, slid the sword from his cane, and pressed the tip against Robin's chest. "But I still want to. Give me a reason to change my mind."

Closing his eyes, Robin turned his head to one side. "I have none. Obviously you have spoken to Miss Sevaric. I was a fool to think you'd never find out. I hoped you would not. But every morning, when I awoke, I wondered if that would be the day my one friend discovered the truth. Now it has come."

"By God, Lynton, for all your sins I never thought you capable of what you did to Gwendolyn. You were ever weak and dissolute, but cruel? No, that never occurred to me."

Robin sucked in a raspy breath. "Sevaric called me out when he learned of it, but I refused to meet him. I won't meet you either, Vayle."

"Did I propose a duel? Easier to run you through now and be done with it. You are not worth an honorable challenge."

"I'd not defend myself in any case. There is no defense for my cowardice." His face contorted. "But I never hurt her, I swear, except by failing to protect her. That was cruelty enough, I suppose, although I wouldn't have had a chance against my uncle and Bouchard."

Tears poured down his cheeks, mingling with the blood from his cut lip. "I should have tried, though. Damn my black soul, I should have tried."

With a grunt of disgust, Vayle moved away and sheathed the blade. "Oh, get up, you sniveling boy. Wipe your nose." He reached for his handkerchief, remembered he'd given it to Gwen, and headed for a stand of drawers in the corner.

Robin sat forward and wrapped his arms around his bent knees, sobbing uncontrollably.

Tossing him an unstarched cravat, Vayle began to pace the small room. "This paltry display of remorse will not serve, Lynton. Get hold of yourself and act the man for once in your life."

"Wh-what do you want of me?" He held the swatch of linen to his mouth, and a red stain spread from his split lip. "You already know what happened. I cannot change it now."

"I have heard from Gwen what she experienced, as much as she can recall or is willing to tell. You give me the rest. Why in bloody hell did you join your uncle in this monstrous scheme?"

There was a tense silence. "I've no explanation that will satisfy you," Robin said finally. "It's a long story, from when I was a child."

"Find a way to make it short. And spare me a litany of excuses."

"I know there is no excuse for what I've become." He wiped his eyes. "Where to start? My father died when I was eight years old, and Uncle Hugo became my guardian. He had control of the money, and me, and Dorie, too. But all he cared about was the feud, and he set himself to destroy the Sevarics."

Robin's voice became bitter. "Mostly he ignored us, but when things went wrong he'd beat me. I was terrified of him. When I got older, I discovered the best way to hold him off was to pretend an interest in his obsession. So long as I was in league with him, I could anticipate his rages and hide myself until they blew over." He drew himself up. "You won't believe this, but I was more concerned for Dorie than myself."

"You're right. I don't believe it."

"Even so, I fancied myself her protector. When he put me in charge of household expenses, I made certain she had nice clothes and a governess. And I hid money in a secret account for her come-out."

Vayle nearly hit him again. "This from the loving brother who gambled away her home?"

"That was unforgivable. But after the incident with Miss Sevaric I lost what little hope for the future I had. Gaming has been my escape since Uncle Hugo taught me to help him cheat. He would deliberately lose, but I was to palm false dice later in the game because no one would suspect a clumsy boy. Bit by bit we robbed Basil Sevaric." With mordant humor, he added, "I stopped cheating when my uncle died. That's why Max has since won everything back."

Losing his last hold on patience, Vayle whacked his cane against the wall. "Cut to the night Gwen was abducted."

Holding his head, Robin rocked back and forth as if buffeted by the rush of memories. "I swear it, I knew nothing of his plans. He was desperate, though. Basil Sevaric had died a few months earlier, and then we got word of the victory at Waterloo. That meant Max Sevaric would soon be on his way home, and he was bound to be a fearsome opponent."

"He didn't want the feud, you fool."

"Maybe not. But Uncle Hugo couldn't count on that. Dorie was about to get married, but her fiancé had demanded a rich settlement. My uncle proceeded to lose much of what he'd won from Sevaric trying to come up with the money, and figured he could only come about by finding and selling the treasure."

Again, that bloody treasure! Vayle shook his head. "Gwen swears the Sevarics never had it."

"Maybe her father never told her where it was concealed, but my uncle was convinced she knew. He sent a message, instructing me to come to a place in Surrey where I'd never been before. He didn't say why, and I was in no hurry to obey. By the time I went through all his papers to find the directions and made my way there, Miss Sevaric had been imprisoned for several days. He put me in the room with her, and ordered me to r-ra—"

Vayle swore profoundly. "I know all that! Why didn't you get her out of there?"

Robin made a helpless gesture. "They would have stopped me. My uncle's valet was enormous, and he carried a pistol. That first night, I went to a nearby inn and bought a stock of smuggled brandy for Uncle Hugo and Calvados for Bouchard. He's from Normandy and could never resist Calvados. I thought if they were drunk I could spirit her away, but I passed out before they did."

"You might have restrained yourself for once," Vayle said coldly.

"They watched me. But they started drinking earlier the next day, and I managed to unlock her door without them knowing it. I had told Miss Sevaric that I would, and asked her to be ready to leave. Late that night I saddled m'horse and left him tied up outside. I meant to go upstairs and get her, but Bouchard woke up and saw me in the hall. I went back to the kitchen and drank with him until we were both grogged. The next morning, she was gone."

Vayle's killing rage was gone. Nausea remained. He straddled a chair and folded his arms across the back. 'Twas a wretched effort, Robin's endeavor to rescue Gwen. But she'd managed to escape anyway, delirious from starvation and torture, without shoes or a cloak or money . . . dear God. A wonder she ever made it home.

He took a long, calming breath. "It seems I must permit you to live, although I wish otherwise. You merit a worse beating than I gave you, Lynton."

Robin laughed harshly. "My uncle took care of that. Miss Sevaric failed to take the horse, you see, and I could not explain why it was saddled and waiting. He'd have beaten me in any case. Uncle Hugo always vented his rage on whomever was near to hand."

"Ah. Then I'm not even to have the pleasure of hitting you again."

"Do so if you must, Vayle, if only for the weeks you played friend to a despicable cur. I should have warned you off."

" 'Struth, I never heed warnings," Vayle said with a rueful shrug. "What's done is done. Now we must look to the future and how you can make amends."

"My uncle put a bullet to his head," Robin said dejectedly. "Should I do the same?"

Vayle gave him a withering look. "Enough of your puling, infant. It sickens me. Tomorrow afternoon you will present yourself to Gwen Sevaric and apologize."

With a plaintive cry, Robin buried his face in his hands. "N-not that. Anything but that. I c-cannot face her. And what good would it do anyway?"

Vayle came to his feet, seizing his cane. " 'Tis a beginning. And you *will* face her, Lynton, if I'm forced to drag you there in chains." He crossed to Robin and lifted his chin with the tip of the cane. "Look at me!"

Robin gazed at him through lashes clumped with tears. *"You* tell her how sorry I am. You can find the words. Besides, she won't admit me if I go to the house."

"I'll take care that she does. Now listen closely. You will make no excuses for yourself, nor lie to her on any count. Miss Sevaric has an unerring sense of truth. If she asks questions, answer them honestly. If she calls you every vile name in creation, accept it as your due. Remember, your goal is to provide her whatever satisfaction she can derive. You are there for her sake only."

Eyes hollow with pain, Robin nodded. "I-I'll try."

"You'll do better than that!" Vayle tapped him lightly on the cheek with his cane before moving to the door. "Fail to appear, Lynton, and I will track you to the ends of the earth."

Twenty

Dear Sister.

Gwen, her elbows propped on the writing table, stared at those words. She couldn't seem to read past them.

But she had to, because Dorothea would be expecting a reply to her letter. With effort, she skipped to the part about coming to Greenbriar for Christmas. The answer had to be *no*, but there was no graceful way to phrase it.

She could pretend to be ill, of course, but that would likely bring Max rushing home. And that wouldn't be right. Max should be with his wife on their first Christmas together.

There was that word again—*Sister.* Dorothea appealed to her as a sister. Begged for her counsel, as if she had any to offer. Of course Gwen knew why Max hated Lynton, but she could not tell Dorothea anything of the truth. It was a wonder she'd managed to speak of it to Vayle last night.

Leaning back in her chair, she gazed blankly at a portrait of her father on the salon wall.

Vayle knew. Dear God, she had confessed every shameful moment to a . . . a *houseguest!* A rackety ornament of a man whose sole virtue was his unquestionable charm.

And kindness. The servants adored him. Winnie and Mrs. Fitzniggle were in his pocket. Perhaps it wasn't kindness at all. Perhaps it was just that he knew how to win people over so he could use them to his advantage.

She shifted uncomfortably on the hard-backed chair. The old arguments for disliking him, the ones she'd used to convince herself since he took up residence in Sevaric House, sounded empty to her now. Every instinct screamed that he was not what he seemed, but everything he said and did put the lie to that.

Except his friendship with Lynton. That alone was reason to mistrust him. Her father's eyes glared back at her from the portrait as if in warning.

Could Lynton and Vayle be in league together? she thought suddenly. What if Vayle had deliberately planted himself in the Sevaric household to gain access to the treasure? They might have prearranged the accident when Vayle supposedly saved her life. It was possible.

It was ridiculous. She was nearly run down by that carriage, and no one could have planned for her presence on that particular street at that exact moment.

Besides, Max was a superb judge of men. He'd had to be, as commander of a battalion, and he held Vayle in regard. She knew nothing of men at all, except what she had learned from her father and the Caines, and none of that was good. Still, her brother proved that men *could* be honorable. And if he trusted Vayle . . .

Oh, damn. Nothing made sense to her anymore.

A familiar dizziness clouded her mind, the same dismal confusion she experienced whenever she tried to fathom the mystery that was Jocelyn Vayle.

She picked up the pen and began to write. "Dear . . ."

Even the correct way to address Dorothea eluded her. "Lady Sevaric" was too formal and "Dorothea" felt wrong. She lacked the courage, or the optimism, to write "Dear Sister."

How wonderful it would be, to have a sister, someone to confide in and feel close to. She'd never had a friend, except Anathea, but they were not true intimates. They had met in a bookstore only a few months ago. For the first time in her life, Gwen had a female of her own age to shop with and take an ice at Gunter's. But Anathea was the daughter of a duke, and once she married there would be no more excursions.

Gwen nibbled at the tip of her pen. What was the use? She could not give Dorothea what she wanted, on any count.

Maybe she ought to write a letter to Max instead, suggesting he tell his wife about the Incident. She knew he would never do so until she gave her consent. On that thought, she put "Max" after "Dear" and was beginning a sentence wishing him well on the marriage when a scratch at the door interrupted her work.

Vayle stepped inside and gave one of his elaborate bows. "Pardon me for disturbing you, Miss Sevaric, but I wished to assure myself of . . . that is . . . well, after . . ." He came to a halt and held out his arms in a gesture of surrender.

Vayle at a loss for words was so astonishing she could scarcely muster a reply. They gazed at each other for a long moment.

"You mean, after I cried into your neckcloth," she said finally. "For that you must forgive me, sir. I am generally in better control of myself."

"Too much so, I fear." He clasped his arms behind his back. "I'd not have you regret sharing a confidence with me, Gwendolyn."

She nearly protested his use of her first name, but then bit her tongue.

"I'm glad you did," he added in a soft voice. "But the aftermath is awkward, is it not? Do you feel uncomfortable with me now?"

"No more than usual," she lied.

" 'Struth, you can barely look me in the eye. I'd rather you ring a peal over me than fob me off with sarcasm."

The pen she was holding fell from her hand. She fumbled for it under the writing table, glad for an excuse to hide her reaction.

He had the right of it. Telling him the story, all of it, had eased her mind considerably. Even though she'd cried herself to sleep, the night was untormented by the horrible dreams that had plagued her since the abduction. It appeared that sharing the experience with another person had indeed lessened her burden, and she was grateful.

Why was it so hard to tell him that?

She found the pen and pretended to examine it, as if a fall to the thick carpet might have dulled the point. The intimacy of last night had not ended when she went to bed. She woke up with the memory of strong arms holding her close, the scent of him in her nostrils, and an ache at the core of her body. He had replaced the nightmare with other dreams, with longings so futile she dared not admit they existed.

She wanted him to hold her again, and if she showed him any weakness at all, even a careless expression of gratitude, he might discover it.

Lost in thought, she didn't notice he had crossed the room until he was right behind her.

"Will you go to Greenbriar for Christmas?" he asked.

She glanced back to find him looking at Dorothea's letter. In a swift motion, she turned it face down. "This is private correspondence, Mr. Vayle. You should be ashamed."

"I've greater sins to account for than reading over your shoulder," he said airily. " 'Tis a good idea, you know. Families should be together at Christmas."

Her hands clenched. "I can't go there. It's out of the question."

"Ah." He came around the table and stood directly in front of her. "I hadn't realized."

She looked into his eyes, which were gentle with concern, and quickly lowered her gaze. He saw too much. Understood her too well. He threatened the small secure place she was trying to build for herself. "Go away."

"It was to Greenbriar that Caine took you," he said as if she'd not spoken. "Naturally you do not wish to return there. Perhaps Max and his bride will come to London for the holidays if you suggest that in your reply."

"I may. If you ever give me the opportunity to pen a response."

"I daresay Max is aware you were imprisoned at the very house his wife so values," he continued thoughtfully. "No doubt that is making their situation all the more difficult. What a coil. As long as you refuse to set foot in Greenbriar Lodge, it will be an issue of conflict for them. Have you considered—"

"Mr. Vayle, where I go and what I do is not your affair. One day, for my brother's sake and when the memories are not so raw, I'll doubtless pluck up the courage to go there again. Meantime, have you no one else to disturb?"

"You have the courage now," he said bluntly. "I wonder why that has escaped your notice."

She gave him a direct look. "How many times must I ask you to leave?"

"You wish to be alone?" He feigned an astonished expression. " 'Tis snowing, you know. Not a day for excursions. I was just about to send for refreshments and challenge you to a game of chess."

Before she could make another objection to his presence, there was a knock at the door and the butler stepped inside. His face wore a look of grim disapproval.

"Miss Sevaric, Lord Lynton begs a few moments of your time."

All the air went out of her in a whoosh.

"Thank you, Watson," Vayle said smoothly. "Allow us another few minutes to finish our business and then show him in."

Her cry of protest came out in a squeak, and Watson was gone before she found her voice again. "How dare you!" She lurched to her feet, the chair toppling over behind her.

Vayle took a step back as she came at him, raising one arm to protect his face from her long fingernails. He had known Gwen would not take this well.

Gritting his teeth, he allowed her to pummel his shoulders and chest until the first fury was spent. She subsided rather more quickly than he'd expected, and with relief he drew her into his arms.

"How *could* you?" she murmured into his lapel.

" 'Twas necessary, Gwen. Your brother is married to Robin's sister. The two of you must come to terms if this feud is ever to end."

"C-come to terms? This is not a business transaction. Have you forgot already what I told you last night? What the Caines did to me?"

He drew in a breath. "I will never forget. But Robin wishes to beg your forgiveness and explain a few things I believe you should know. Listen to him, please. Only that. Then tell him to go to the devil if you wish, or have at him as you just did me."

"You deserved it."

"Agreed. And Robin deserves worse." He lifted her chin with his fingertip. "This is really for you, Gwen, but you can't see that now. So do it for Max."

"Damn you. That's not fair."

"I know." After a hug, he set her back. "Should this become too difficult, or if you are on the verge of killing him, call for me. I'll wait in the passageway, and I promise not to listen through the keyhole."

Watson appeared again, still frowning. "Mrs. Fitzniggle and Miss Crake are not at home. Shall I instruct Lord Lynton to return on another occasion?"

Vayle regarded him with concealed impatience. "That won't be necessary, as Lynton is family now. I'll see to it the proprieties are observed." Behind him, Gwen made a strangled noise.

"Very good, sir." Shaking his head, the butler withdrew, and a moment later Robin Caine stepped into the room, moving with conspicuous difficulty. The left side of his face was a startling shade of purple, and so distended he might have been harboring a tennis ball in his cheek. When he bowed, a low moan escaped his tight lips.

"My heavens! What has happened to you?" Gwen shot an accusing look at Vayle.

He shrugged.

"Forgive me for intruding," Lynton said, his words mushy

and barely audible. "I had an accident and cannot speak well. Perhaps I should come back another day."

"I think not," Vayle said before Gwen jumped in to agree. "No time like the present, I always say."

Gwen clutched at her skirt and Robin at his lapels. They looked everywhere but at each other, putting him in mind of rabbits—noses twitching and eyes casting about for a place to hide.

"Since a spectator would be *de trop*," he said, "I'll be off. But should you require assistance, Miss Sevaric, I shall remain in the vicinity." He took his time closing the door, but Gwen and Robin maintained a stony silence. Just as well. The first wrong word from Robin and he'd have rushed back in.

Restlessly, he paced the long passageway, checking his time-piece so often that he finally kept it in his hand instead of returning it to his watch pocket. Time did not always fly, he decided when what had felt like hours counted to a mere fifteen minutes.

In silent acknowledgment of their mutual anxiety, Watson brought him a large glass of brandy. Whenever he passed the open door of the dining room, he saw the butler lurking just inside, making a show of polishing the silver. Soon the upstairs maid found an excuse to dust the library, and even the tweeny invented errands to keep her nearby.

The cook, a large kitchen knife in her hand, hurried into the dining room, muttering something about checking the dumb-waiter. She sent it up and down, up and down, while Watson stood nearby, rubbing on the same tray he'd begun polishing a half hour ago.

The entire staff hovered within calling distance of the salon, poised to rescue their mistress from the scurrilous Robin Caine.

Servants always knew, he reflected. Gwen thought only Max was aware she'd been abducted, but these people had lived with the feud, too, and shared bits of information below stairs. Now, silently, each one confirmed a deep affection for her.

He could well understand their regard. Although he bore the marks of Gwen's rage on his body, the pleasure of holding her afterward had more than compensated for the bruises. If all went as he hoped, what excuse would he find to take her in his arms again?

Surprised at where his thoughts were leading, he checked his watch. Sixty-seven minutes. 'Struth, if a man wanted to taste of eternity, he'd only to care deeply about a result for which he was forced to wait.

And wait.

Just when he was ready to launch himself into the salon, Gwen opened the door. Her eyes narrowed to see him standing inches away, but after a moment she stepped aside and gestured him to enter.

Robin stood by a window, one hand clutching a limp handkerchief. There were traces of moisture on his cheeks. Vayle had never seen a man weep in his former life, and until now he'd not thought it a manly thing to do. But of late, he was changing his mind about a great many things.

"My brother-in-law," Gwen said quietly, "has explained what happened at Greenbriar. And some of what his own life has been like as a pawn of his uncle, in the same way I was my father's unwilling servant. We have agreed to start afresh."

Vayle took his first painless breath in several hours. "You will cry friends?"

"I dare not hope for that," Robin said. "Miss Sevaric has forgiven me, but—"

"You must call me Gwen," she interrupted. "Remember our plans."

"G-Gwen. I'll try not to forget."

"What plans?" Vayle inquired, feeling left out.

"I have decided to accept Dorothea's invitation, and Robin will come with me to Greenbriar for Christmas. That will be rather a surprise to Max, because we don't intend to let him know in advance."

"He's apt to put a bullet in me before I step out of the coach," Robin said glumly.

Gwen sighed. "As you see, Robin does not anticipate a warm

welcome. And I fear he is right. Nevertheless, we both think Christmas is the best time to effect a reconciliation between our families. When Max sees for himself that we are in accord, he will come around."

"If he hasn't shot me first."

When Gwen fired him a dark look, Robin held out his hands. "I've promised I will go, whatever the consequences. Thing is, for the first time since I can remember, I value my life and have a strong desire to keep it."

Vayle knew exactly how he felt. " 'Tis an excellent plan. When do we leave?"

Gwen regarded him with surprise. "You wish to accompany us?"

"Of course he does," Robin exclaimed.

"It will be deadly dull for you," Gwen warned. "A small country house, little entertainment, and probably a good deal of tension as we adjust to one another."

A ball of ice lodged in his throat. She didn't want him there. The family was closing a circle from which he was excluded.

I made this happen, he wanted to protest, but he knew that wasn't true. He'd set a few events in motion, but Robin and Gwen—mostly Gwen—were the true architects of peace. On her own, Gwen had overcome her fear of returning to Greenbriar for the sake of her family. Robin had summoned the courage to face Max at the scene of his own crimes.

Jocelyn Vayle was not family. He had no place with them, not anymore. And why should he care, really? In four days he would be gone and soon forgotten.

He managed an indifferent smile. "As you say, Miss Sevaric, I'd only be underfoot at Greenbriar."

To his surprise, she came up to him and put a hand against his chest. "Please think about it. You will be most welcome if you choose to join us."

"I can vouch for that," Robin said fervently.

Vayle let out the breath he'd been holding and put a hand over Gwen's. Her eyes blazed up at him, wide and guileless, sending heat through his entire body. "Thank you," he murmured. "I want very much to be with you at Christmas."

As if disturbed by the singular intimacy of the moment, Gwen tugged her hand free and marched to the writing table. "In that case, I must send word to Dorothea, omitting Robin's name. We think it better to arrive on Christmas Eve, Mr. Vayle, in hopes the spirit of that holy night will work some magic for us all."

"And that allows two more days for this swelling to go down," Robin said, rubbing his cheek.

"Yes, yes," said Gwen, waving a hand at both men. "We'll leave Tuesday morning, but for now do take yourselves off while I write this letter. It has been a long day." Then she looked over at Robin. "But a good one."

After a few words with Robin, Vayle sent him on his way and headed upstairs to his chamber.

Clootie was there, brushing a bottle-green coat. He bowed, a speculative look on his dour face. "Good afternoon, sir."

Vayle nodded to him absently, trying to decide what to do with himself for the rest of the day. Gwen wished some time alone, and Robin could not appear in public with that monstrous jaw.

"I was sorry to learn you did not venture to Mrs. Benson's establishment last night," Clootie said in a sour voice. "The young woman selected for you was most disappointed."

"What?" Vayle glanced up. "Oh, yes, the brothel. I'd forgot about it."

"Indeed?" Clootie raised an eyebrow. "Perhaps tonight then. Shall I send word?"

Vayle opened his mouth, but the *yes* he'd begun to form failed to emerge. Surprised, he went to the window and gazed outside. His room overlooked the street, usually a dreary sight, but transformed now by the gentle snowfall. Barely an inch so far, he observed, but enough to dust tree branches and the tops of passing coaches with a mantle of purest white.

The compelling desire to bed a woman, any beautiful woman at all, was unnaturally absent. He felt as if a mantle of snow enveloped him, too.

But underneath he remained warm, the memory of holding Gwen and comforting her a steady flame near his heart. It was too rare and precious a thing to extinguish in a casual tumble with a whore.

"Thank you, Clootie, but I've other plans for the evening. And while I'm thinking of it, we shall leave for Greenbriar Lodge two days hence, to spend Christmas with Lord Sevaric and his wife. Make sure my belongings are packed."

Clootie made a rumbling sound in his throat. "You cannot mean to rusticate in the country! The house is practically a ruin, and there will be no entertainment. It's not to be thought of."

Vayle turned in astonishment. Clootie had never been a conventional servant, but for a valet to question orders was beyond the pale. And what made him think Greenbriar was in ruins? How could he possibly know such a thing? "On the contrary," he said stiffly. "The decision has been made."

"I see." Clootie dropped the clothes brush on the dressing table. "That is unfortunate, because I have been at some pains to secure for you a coveted invitation to . . . but never mind. Your plans are set."

Vayle couldn't help himself. "To where?"

Clootie's thin lips curved. "The patrons call it a Saturnalia. For a stranger to be admitted is unheard of, but I have connections. You might have been one of the favored few."

Casting back to vague schoolroom memories, Vayle recalled an ancient pagan festival by that name, devoted to unbridled licentiousness. The Roman version of a Bacchic Revel.

In plain English terms, an orgy.

He pulled out his snuffbox, running his thumb over the carved initials. Valerian Caine would have loved an orgy. And he, devil take him, *was* Valerian Caine.

"The Saturnalia begins at noon on Christmas Eve Day," Clootie said in a dusky voice, "and ends at midnight on Boxing Day. Do not imagine this a tawdry carouse among vulgar folk. The patrons serve up the finest of everything—music, food, drink, dancing, masques, and spectacles—all that delights the senses. Women, too, of course, the most beautiful and skilled in the kingdom."

Inhaling deeply, Vayle savored the heady aroma of snuff and the tingle of anticipation at every nerve ending. 'Twould be his last night in mortal flesh, the only chance he'd have for all eternity to enjoy pleasure before Proctor snatched him back to the Afterlife. Why not go out in style? Snub his nose at Proctor and raise a little hell?

He looked up at Clootie, who was poised on tiptoe, head tilted, waiting for his decision.

"I—" he bit his lip. How, really, did he want to spend his final hours on this earth? What was the very last thing he wanted to see before he eyes were closed forever?

Images of richly colored costumes, laughing faces, plates with butter-drenched lobster, fountains bubbling with champagne, and voluptuous women danced in his head. He smelled perfume and the musky odor of sex, and felt warm flesh meld with his in a burning drive to climax. He wanted all of these things, and more.

But the phantasms drifted away, leaving in their wake a slender young woman with short curly hair, a pert nose, a stubborn chin, and two bright hazel eyes that gazed into his very soul.

He turned back to the window. "I am for Greenbriar Lodge," he said before he could change his mind. "That is final. And for now, I fancy a walk in the snow. Fetch me some bread, Clootie. I've a notion to meander through Hyde Park and feed the ducks."

"F-feed the ducks?" Clootie said in choked voice. "Greenbriar Lodge and *ducks?* Have you gone mad?"

"I have just possibly gone sane, for once in my existence. Will you do my bidding, or would you prefer to seek employment elsewhere?"

When he heard no reply, Vayle swung around.

Clootie had vanished.

Twenty-one

The day before Christmas, Dorie awoke in near darkness. Today the man's body beside her seemed almost familiar, the quiet breathing, the man-warmth a few inches away.

She reached to touch his shoulder, but then drew back. He might wake, and then—

Between them lay more than a few inches of comforter and sheet. There was also that terrible feud. She could give that up, indeed, she was eager to give it up. But she couldn't get past her husband's stubborn insistence on hating her family, especially her brother.

At least Max refused to hate her—but the price, apparently, was that she give up being a Caine entirely. And that was too much to ask . . . wasn't it?

He stirred, and she held her breath. But he only drew his hand to his neck and rested it there. Poor dear, she thought, his muscles ache from all that lifting. In the gray early light, the gauze on his thumb was tattered and grimy. She would make him change the bandage before he picked up that blasted hammer again.

Though he would clearly rather be in London or his own manor home, Max was still here, trying to help her with the lodge. Surely that argued some emotion deeper than just conjugal regard?

As if he felt her gaze, he rolled onto his back and opened his eyes. The drowsy warmth in them deepened into heat as he looked at her. She almost wished he would reach out to fulfill the promise in his eyes, but she had made him pledge to wait for her. And he would keep his word.

That meant she would have to be the one who decided to make their marriage real. Soon, she promised silently, soon. But just now there was too much between them. Perhaps after the family arrived for the holidays. . . .

But when Max realized she had defied him and invited Robin, he might not want her anymore.

To distract him, and herself, she announced cheerily as she rose, "Christmas Eve! And we have so much yet to do!"

Max got up, too, and limped to the door. He'd injured his leg yesterday when he tripped on the cat as he descended the ladder. But after the initial blast of Spanish curses, he hadn't said a word of complaint.

"I have to go into Croydon this morning. I'll get the post for you. Still haven't heard if Gwen and Vayle are coming for the holiday. You're sure you sent them an invitation?"

"Last week. They must have received it by now."

When he was gone, she dressed slowly, pulling on woolen stockings to ward off the chill. She, too, was worried by the lack of response to her letter. She had meant well, but she shouldn't have relied on Gwen's goodwill. Her new sister-in-law justifiably resented the enemy who displaced her in her own household.

For just a moment, Dorie let herself imagine what she and Max might have been if their families were not at war. He was such a good man, strong and brave and uncomplaining. And handsome, too, she had to admit.

She longed to touch his dark curling hair, trace the square line of his jaw. . . . He was all she had hoped for, in fact, when she was a romantic young girl, dreaming of a knight errant to rescue her from her erratic family life. But instead, here she was plunged into yet more family trouble.

That trouble would be even worse if everyone arrived today, expecting the house to be ready for celebration. She shook the

cobwebs from her brain and went to make up the beds in the
two rooms that still had ceilings.

Until she heard the clatter of hooves in the courtyard, she
didn't realize that she was longing for Max to return. She told
herself it was because there were a few shingles still loose on
the roof, and pine boughs unhung on the staircase, and Christmas only a dozen hours away. But her breath came shorter as
she gathered her shawl tight and ran down the front steps to
greet him in the courtyard.

She was as surprised as he when she ran straight into his
arms. But he hesitated only a second before pulling her close.
She pressed her cheek against the wool of his coat and breathed
deep—

And then, outraged, she pulled away. "I smell—perfume!"

There was no mistaking the flush on his face for a response
to the cold. He was embarrassed, even ashamed. "It's not what
you think."

"And what do you think I think?"

He must have known better than to indict himself. "I don't
know. But I've done nothing wrong."

Dorie regarded him suspiciously. He was still flushed, but his
jaw was set and he wasn't afraid to meet her gaze. She felt the
stirring of something—trust?—but didn't give into it. "When
a husband comes home smelling of perfume, a wife can be
forgiven for wondering if he's been in a bordello."

He scowled at her. "I haven't been in a bordello."

She wanted to give him the benefit of the doubt, but then
she remembered that he had once been a soldier, and soldiers
were notorious. "Never?"

His scowl deepened, but dishonesty was foreign to him. "Perhaps once or twice. But—but not in the morning! And not on
Christmas Eve!"

She stifled a laugh, and felt much better. It was such a Max
response. Of course he wouldn't visit a bordello on Christmas
Eve. "There is still that question of the perfume."

Max stood there, straight and uncompromising. Her inner

laughter stilled. She had seen that look before, on her uncle's face. It spoke more clearly than any words that she was intruding on territory forbidden a mere female. She braced herself for a harsh rebuke.

Then Max held out his hand, palm up. "Will you trust me, just for a little while?"

Dorie closed her eyes, waiting for her defenses to go up. But despite herself, she trusted him. She opened her eyes and took his hand.

She was rewarded by his smile, open, warm, happy. What a wonderful gift trust was, she realized. It changed everything.

They stood for a moment, holding hands, smiling at each other. Then he cleared his throat and reached into his pocket. "I did get the post for you. Here."

While he went back to his work mending the roof, she sat down on a bench in the wan sunlight. Please don't let him fall, she prayed, stealing a glance as he climbed the ladder.

When she saw the cat slinking closer to the bottom rung, Dorie called to it sharply to come away. Tabby had taken a liking to Max, and was forever following him about and getting underfoot. Sullenly she stalked away toward the house, to await her master by the hearth.

When Max was safe on the roof—well, he would never be *safe* up there—she tucked her skirt double under her bottom, to ward off the chill of the stone seat, and resolutely began sorting through her letters.

Nothing from Robin. Perhaps it was best, the coward within her suggested, if they postponed that confrontation for another time.

Then she stopped and stared at the unfamiliar handwriting on one letter. A woman's hand—Gwen's. She broke the seal and opened the sheet. Mr. Vayle and Gwen would be arriving Christmas Eve, but Miss Winnie would be in Bath with Mrs. Fitzniggle. There was more of that sort—Dorie sensed an attempt at casual cordiality—and then, stark, in postscript, a single sentence. "Tell Max I said he should tell you what happened at Greenbriar Lodge."

Dorie stared at those final words. Greenbriar Lodge? What could have happened at Greenbriar Lodge that Gwen thought she should know? It must have something to do with the feud, but she couldn't imagine how.

Oh, according to family legend, this is where the feud began a century or more ago. The lodge had belonged to the Sevarics then, and one of their wives trysted here with a Caine younger son. There was a discovery, and a duel, and a death or two, and then decades of war. The Caine treasure disappeared early in the feud, and the Caines, in retaliation, somehow won the lodge. But that was the last time the lodge figured into the feud, wasn't it?

She closed her eyes, listening to the echo of Max's hammer blows through the cold air. Her uncle used to sit her and Robin down and recite all his grievances against the Sevarics—story after story of Sevaric cruelty and Sevaric craft, of deceptions and double-dealings. Robin would remember better than she, for she had been a daydreamer, and as her uncle ranted she would stare out the window and envision knights and ladies and brave white steeds cantering in the courtyard. Yes, Robin would know—

But Max knew, too. That was the question Gwen's postscript was meant to answer: why Max hated Robin, why he had challenged him to a duel last year, why he was bent on ruining him. And it all had to do with Greenbriar Lodge.

Dorie opened her eyes and gazed up at the roof. The shadow of a tree obscured Max's figure, but she could see his arm rise and fall, pounding nails with force if not skill. He was very good at force, Max was.

Then she remembered his harsh avowal when he first came to Greenbriar. "I don't force women." He hadn't done so, either, not in all this time. And that was so much at odds with his implacable attitude toward Robin—

She didn't want to startle him by calling his name. So she waited patiently, her cold hands gripped tight around Gwen's letter, until he climbed down the ladder and set his feet securely on the ground.

Dorie went to him then and without a word, gave him his sister's letter. Absently he hung the hammer from his watch fob and opened the single sheet. She could tell by his frown the moment he reached the postscript.

"Tell me."

He balled up the letter and pushed it into his coat pocket. "You don't want to hear it. It doesn't reflect well on your—on your family."

That last word dripped with contempt, and she had to fight off her instinctive defensiveness. She took hold of his fist and uncurled the fingers. When she could slip her hand into his, she said, "I want to hear it. Tell me."

And then, staring down at their clasped hands, he told her.

It was the worst story of all the stories she had heard about the feud, and she couldn't believe it. Would her uncle truly have abducted an innocent girl just to win back that benighted Caine treasure?

Yes, a seditious voice whispered. Yes, he would.

But not Robin.

She didn't say that, though. It would be tantamount to calling Gwen a liar. Dorie remembered Gwen's austere face, her sharp clear eyes, and knew she would not lie.

She could only repeat, "I'm so sorry. I'm so sorry." And when that finally faded into a whisper, she took a breath and released it slowly. "Is Gwen—has she recovered?"

"I don't know. I didn't get back from France till a month later, and I could see she was different. Calm. But different. She says she's fine." His voice was tight with anguish. "But since then, she never goes out. Oh, she'll go to the shops, and visit friends, but all those things other girls do—the dances and the parties and the courtships—she wants no part of. She should want a man and a family, shouldn't she?"

Cautiously Dorie replied, "Most girls do."

"She doesn't. Or she says she doesn't. I don't know if she

always felt that way—she was a child when I left for the Peninsula. But she told me she just wanted to keep house for me till I married. I don't know what she'll do now."

His voice hardened. "So now you see why I can't welcome your brother. He won't even admit to what he did and accept the responsibility. I might let it go if he apologized. But when he fled like a coward and—"

"He didn't flee."

Max let go of her hand. "What?"

She knew she would regret it, but Robin's part in this was so strange she couldn't let it go unexamined. "Robin. He didn't flee. He stayed in London and let you ruin him."

He made a harsh sound. "He turned down my challenge. That was the act of a poltroon."

"But he could have gone back to the country, or to the Continent. He knew you were set on ruining him, and he let you do it." Almost to herself, she added, "He seemed to want to lose it all. I kept begging him to stop, but he wouldn't, even when it became clear you would win everything. It was as if he welcomed it."

"He knew he deserved no better."

"Perhaps. . . . Max, tell me, why don't you hate Greenbriar Lodge?"

The change in subject disconcerted him. He glanced over his shoulder at the ivy-covered brick wall where he had left the ladder. Finally he said, "I meant to. I was going to win it and then tear it down, brick by brick. But then I learned it was your home, and I saw how hard you had been working to repair it—the window boxes and the new gravel and the curtains and all the rest. And I reckoned you'd made it yours, and that made it clean. I can't hate what is part of you."

He gave her a sharp look. "You are thinking that your brother is part of you, too, and that I shouldn't hate him. Well, I shan't forgive him either. You can't ask that of me."

"No." She gathered up the other letters and started back to the house, but then stopped a few feet from Max. "It's so strange. I know Robin talks against the Sevarics, but I think he never wanted the feud. Oh, when he was a boy, he listened to the stories and vowed vengeance for the lost Caines. You must understand, our father died young. He was weak and sickly, Uncle Hugo always said, and not fit to carry on the fight. Robin didn't know any better than to look up to our uncle. He was so fierce, you see. A warrior, Robin called him."

"Warrior? He didn't deserve the title! Kidnapping a girl— that's not a warrior's action!"

"I know. I knew it then, even when we were children, that he was just angry. He hadn't anything but his anger, you know— no ideals, no principles. He didn't fight for anything but himself. And Robin came to see it, too. He tried to protect me from it. Uncle wanted to use me against the Sevarics someday, I'm not sure how. But he often spoke of my destiny. It sent a chill through me. Whenever he spoke that way, Robin would try to divert him. He used to ply Uncle with spirits, to get him too foxed to carry out his plans."

She glanced at Max's forbidding expression. "Oh, I know it's not honorable. But it was all he could think of to do. That is when Robin began drinking too much."

Max walked back to hoist the ladder in one hand and started toward the stables. Over his shoulder, he said, "I will not doubt my sister's word."

His tone was implacable, and she could not fault him. "I don't doubt it either." But she thought he was too far away now to hear her.

Everything had changed, she thought helplessly as she watched him go. Now she knew why Max resumed the feud when he returned from the war, and why Gwen had regarded their marriage with such antipathy.

Perhaps she even understood why Robin had been so self-destructive these last two years. It must have been guilt that drove him—

She just couldn't imagine her brother hurting an innocent girl. He would have to admit it himself to persuade her.

But in the meantime, she had to finish preparing the house to welcome her new sister. Gwen mustn't be besieged by bad memories, not at Christmas, not with her family. "Max!" she called out as her husband returned from the stable. "We need more pine boughs to decorate the hall."

He made some comment under his breath, something about denuded pinewoods and junglelike halls. But he went to exchange his hammer for an ax, and she forgot everything she had to do inside the house. She trailed him to the shed. "Dearest—you will be careful, won't you? Perhaps I should go with you. I'll carry the ax."

He didn't have a chance to respond, because a carriage came clattering over the bridge.

"Oh, no! They're here already, and everything is unfinished!"

Max said bracingly, "You've done enough for now. I'll help you once we get them settled. Just put on that pretty smile, and they'll feel right at home." Then he took her arm and led her out to meet their first houseguests.

Gwen emerged first from the carriage, a fur muff dangling from one hand. Now that Dorie knew what had happened here two years earlier, she understood why Gwen remained near the coach and avoided looking directly at the lodge.

Impulsively, Dorie detached herself from Max and went forward with her hands outstretched. "I'm so glad you have come!" And then, bending so close her forehead brushed Gwen's bonnet brim, she whispered, "Thank you."

Gwen managed a smile and replied gently, "Thank you for inviting me," then turned to accept Max's greeting kiss.

Mr. Vayle had climbed down from the carriage also, and came up beside Gwen. Interesting, Dorie thought, seeing the comforting smile he gave to her sister-in-law, and the ease with which she accepted it. Was it just Mr. Vayle's native kindness, which Dorie herself had experienced? Or was it something more intimate?

She slanted a glance at her husband, wondering what he

would think of a connection between his sister and Mr. Vayle. It would solve several problems—

Mr. Vayle left off shaking Max's hand and came to greet Dorie. "Welcome to Greenbriar Lodge," she said, smiling up at him. But Mr. Vayle had frozen, his eyes on a point beyond her shoulder. Automatically she turned to see what had so paralyzed him, but there was nothing there but the house and garden and the road leading back to the stables.

"Has this place—has it always been called Greenbriar Lodge?" Mr. Vayle huddled into his greatcoat as if chilled.

Dorie was puzzled, but answered readily enough. "I don't think so. We've only owned it for fifty years or so."

"It belonged to the Sevarics before that. It had another name then."

"Yes, I think so. Max would know." She wasn't certain she wanted Max reminded of the lodge's history, but Mr. Vayle was so pale she had to reassure him. "We could ask him—"

"No, no, don't bother. There's nothing to be done." He transferred his regard to her, peering at her as if to decipher something from her face. "You called him Max."

"Well, yes." Why this should make her blush, she didn't know, but the heat rose in her cold cheeks.

"Good. You two are happy then?"

She looked at her husband, a few yards away with his sister. It was a most improper question to a new bride. But Mr. Vayle had been instrumental in getting them married, and somehow she felt she owed him the truth. "We are aimed in that direction."

"You haven't reached it yet? But you've had three weeks!" Mr. Vayle shook his head at her as if he were a schoolmaster and she a blockheaded student.

She found herself making excuses for disappointing him. "It's—it's just our families, you see. The feud," she whispered, glancing back to make sure Max didn't overhear. "He still won't accept my brother—and I can't truly fault him."

"We shall see." Mr. Vayle fixed Max with a severe gaze. "We shall see about that."

This was her first Christmas as a wife, and she already had enough to worry about, given the state of the house and the newly mended linens. She couldn't have one of her guests preaching to her husband—it would ruin everything. But Mr. Vayle ignored her half-formed plea and flung open the carriage door.

"You can come out now."

From the carriage, abashed and defiant, came her brother Robin.

Instinctively she started toward him, but stopped. She no longer knew where her loyalties lay—with her brother? With her husband and his sister?

Max said in an icy voice, "Vayle, I told you to keep him away from my sister."

For a moment, they were a brittle tableau: Robin with a foot still on the carriage step, Max with fists clenched, Mr. Vayle with a hand out to warn or arrest—

And then, clear and calm, Gwen spoke. "Don't blame Vayle, Max. I invited Lord Lynton along."

The moment broke. Max spun around to look at his sister. Robin came forward a few steps and smiled apologetically at Dorie. Mr. Vayle crossed his arms and leaned back against the carriage. Gwen stood, pale but resolute, and said to her brother, "We are all family now, you know."

Max's silence was so resonant Dorie strained to hear some change in his breathing that might presage trouble. She knew that silence—it meant he was struggling with his principles.

Under Max's intense regard, Robin straightened to his full height. He was still slighter than Max, but for once he held his head up, and she felt a stirring of pride. It took courage to come here and face the ghosts of the past. She just hoped Max wouldn't punish him for it.

Max strode up to Robin and stopped only a foot away. Robin didn't flinch.

"I can't say I would have invited you here, had I anything to say about it. But apparently you've apologized to Gwen's satisfaction. And Vayle's no fool. If he thinks my sister is safe in your presence, I won't dispute it."

Robin let his shoulders relax as he exhaled a relieved breath. "Then I may stay?"

Max shrugged and turned to help the coachman with Gwen's luggage. "Ask your sister. It's her house."

Max's rash words came back to haunt him. Here it was, after dark, after dinner, and Dorie was expecting him to make good on his promise to finish decorating the hall. Hauling the stepladder up to the landing, he wrenched it into position under the plaster ceiling medallion. He gave reason one last try, not that it was likely to have any effect on his wife.

"Sweeting, everyone's gone to bed. By the time they see this, it'll be Christmas already, and the whole display will be unnecessary."

Dorie dragged the long rope of pine up the last three steps and coiled it into a snake on the battered oak floor. Then, as he knew she would, she put a slippered foot on the first rung. "You go on to sleep then, if you're so tired. I will hang the decorations."

Sighing, he tugged her away from the ladder and took her place. "I'll do it. I'll do it. I will do it. You just hand that rope to me, and the hammer, and the nails—"

"Oh, no, the rope I'm just draping over the banister. This is all I want on the ceiling." From the pocket of her dress, she pulled out a twig. "The kissing bough."

He scaled the ladder in a second or two, and without another word got the twig established in the center of the medallion. "There you go," he said, handing her the hammer and climbing down. "We should try it out, don't you th—"

When his leading foot touched the lowest rung, the ladder bucked. He heard a crunch as the old oak plank gave, saw the surprise in Dorie's eyes as he fell past her, felt with relief the solidity of the floor against his head and back. The ladder had just poked a hole in the floor, he thought as he lost consciousness; the landing hadn't given way under them. She was safe.

He must have died in the fall. For surely he was in Heaven now—held in Dorie's arms, his face pressed in the warm valley between her breasts.

"Max? Is your forehead very badly hurt?"

It would have been uncivil to point out that the injury was on the *back* of his head, and besides, this way his mouth was closer to interesting areas. "Not very," he said huskily. "I—I might feel better if there weren't so many layers between me and my poultice."

He felt her laughter against his head. It hurt a bit, but he didn't complain.

"Is that what I am? A poultice?"

Now that he heard it back, he realized that didn't qualify as much of a compliment. "I guess I'm not very good at being romantic," he said into her bodice.

She released him then to shove the ladder off his legs. But she kept her hand comforting on his forehead, and her eyes warm on his face. "You are good, and brave, and strong, and true. You are kind and generous. And"—she brushed her fingers across his cheek—"very handsome. Even bruised and battered."

Leaning over him, her dark hair falling over her shoulder, she was too lovely, too sweet, to resist. And besides, up above, tacked on the ceiling in the flicker of lamplight, was that kissing twig.

He tangled his hand in her hair, slid it along the back of her neck, and pulled her down for his reward. It was a real kiss, the one he'd been dreaming of for weeks now: her lips were soft and surprised, sweet and welcoming, and he felt her warmth radiate through him.

"Max," she whispered against his mouth.

Reluctantly he let her go, just far enough so that she could speak. Her words came gentle against his chin. "I am grateful that you have been so patient with me. But I think you've waited long enough. I am ready now."

It was too good to be true, and Max armed himself against disappointment. "Ready for what?"

She made an annoyed sound and pressed closer so that she was almost lying against him. "What do you think? What—what will make us truly married." She rose to her knees, then stopped. "Unless your head hurts too much."

"Doesn't hurt at all." But when he leapt to his feet, his head started swimming and he had to lean against the banister. It was poetic justice—he had feigned a head injury to get into her bed, and now a real head injury might keep him out. "Just dizzy from the kiss."

"Liar," she said. But she didn't protest any further.

After securing the area—setting the ladder down against the wainscoting, and pulling off his boot and sticking it in the hole in the floor—he picked her up and carried her to their bedroom.

With his bare foot, he pushed the door open and then hesitated. There was something he had meant to say, before the bed filled his vision and he forgot his own name.

She said something inarticulate but impatient against his shirtfront, and he recalled what had slipped away in the haze of anticipation and concussion. "I love you, Dorothea Caine."

She squirmed closer in his arms. "Max," she whispered. "I'm so happy. But—"

He set her down gently on the bed, her head on the lace pillow. "But what?"

"But do you know what would make me even happier?" In the soft light from the fire she smiled a secret, womanly smile. "If you would give me a baby for a Christmas gift. Maximilian Caine Sevaric. Or," she added, "perhaps it will be Maxine."

He took a deep breath and glanced back over his shoulder at the mantel clock. It read twenty of nine, which meant nine—it always ran a bit slow. That left three hours till Christmas. Plenty of time.

"As you wish, madame. We men of the Light Division never disappoint a lady."

Twenty-two

Yawning, Gwen glanced at the clock on the mantelpiece in her room. Nearly midnight, only a few minutes before Christmas.

Everyone had retired early, pleading weariness from the journey or, in the case of Max and Dorie, disappearing without a word. Except for a mysterious rasping noise, rather like a branch scraping against the roof, the house was silent. She put aside her book, extinguished the lamp, and burrowed under a thick down comforter.

All her Christmases had been lonely. Her father deplored celebrations and mocked her for attending church, but she always went to St. Martin-in-the-Fields for midnight services. There she lost her melancholy for a time in the joyful music and the promises of hope in the gospel readings. During the war years, she had prayed especially hard for her brother, bivouacked in a place even more hostile than Sevaric House.

Everything would be different when Max came home, she told herself year after year.

And so it was. Max was safe tonight, in the arms of his wife, and Gwen's heart was lighter since the reconciliation with Robin Caine. Tomorrow there would be a Yule log and presents and laughter and her first taste of Christmas Pudding.

But she was lonely still. And would be, she feared, for the rest of her life.

A clicking sound, so tiny she scarcely heard it, was followed by a positive roar from somewhere down the hall.

What in heaven? Bewildered, she went to the door and

cracked it open just in time to see Vayle, holding a candle, emerge from the room he shared with Robin. He was in stock-inged feet, with a dressing gown draped over his shirt and breeches.

Stealthily, he closed the door and the latch clicked into place. Immediately the roar subsided to the steady drone that had disturbed her all evening. She stifled a laugh.

No wonder Vayle was anxious to escape that room! Robin's snores could wake the spirits of the dead.

But Vayle was behaving oddly for a man in search of a quieter place to sleep. Instead of proceeding immediately to the staircase just beyond his room, he moved slowly along the wall in her direction, pausing every now and again to rap softly against the wood paneling.

Before the light of the candle came within range, she closed the door and pressed her ear against it. Vayle drifted past her room, still rapping on the opposite wall until he came near to the chamber where Max and Dorie slept.

Then he padded back toward the staircase, tapping on her side of the hall except when he passed her room, as if taking care not to wake her.

When the sounds faded, she slipped into the dark passageway and followed him on tiptoe. What was he looking for? He spent a long time on the staircase, knocking every few inches while she hid in the shadows beyond the top step.

Once she heard him swear, and guessed he'd entangled himself in the branches of greenery piled in a corner of the landing. She'd caught her skirts on the spiky holly earlier, when she made her way to bed.

She strained to hear more, but he had gone still. Curiosity made her incautious, and she leaned out just far enough to see him on the landing below. The pool of light widened as he held the candle above his head, and she saw what had tripped him up—a boot of military cut. That was strange. Max wasn't one to leave his possessions lying about, especially not where someone could get hurt.

Even odder, when Vayle pulled at the boot it resisted him. When it finally came up, he immediately dropped it, set the candle down, and knelt. Gwen couldn't see what he was studying, for he was blocking the candlelight with his body. But whatever it was, it fascinated him. He even stretched out full-length across the landing, peering at the floor.

Jumping to his feet, he grabbed the candle and ran down the stairs, his candlelight casting eerie shadows on the wall. In the ground-floor hall, he resumed his tapping on the plaster.

He had run mad. It was the only explanation. Gwen hung over the railing, holding her breath until her chest ached, watching him test for—for what?

Just under the staircase, he stopped tapping.

Then he looked around, and Gwen ducked back into the passageway. When she inched along the wall to the railing, the hall was dark. He was gone.

Heart in her throat, she crept down into the darkness, her bare feet noiseless against the oak steps. Enough moonlight came in through the window to outline the newel post at the end of the banister. She took hold of it and felt her way around the bottom of the staircase.

Weak light sliced through the wall under the stairs. She had to move closer to discover the two-foot-wide opening in the wall panel.

Pausing several feet away, she gazed into the space under the stairs. The room, if it could be called that, was no larger than a pantry cupboard. Against the opposite wall was a low, shadowy piece of furniture, long and narrow. A table, perhaps, or a trestle bed.

Vayle stood with his back to her, slightly bent over the wooden frame, the candle in his left hand.

How had he known about this odd cubbyhole, concealed in a house he'd never visited? Her skin prickled, as if phantoms hovered about her in the gloomy passageway. Suddenly Christmas felt like Allhallow's Eve, with gauzy spirits floating in the amber light of a single candle.

What if she closed the panel? Would he be sealed inside long enough for her to summon Max?

She bit her lip, annoyed at her timidity. This was only Jocelyn Vayle, after all—a liar and a womanizer, but surely harmless.

The damage he'd done to her heart was her own fault.

She had been weak, yielding to impossible hopes he could not help but rouse. It was his nature to be charming, and her folly to wish his attentions meant he had come to care for her. Air dreams. Insubstantial fantasies. She could sooner capture the smoke of his candle than win his love.

"Come in, Gwen," he said quietly. "You'll want to see this."

At the unexpected sound, she jumped back with a squeal.

"Don't be frightened," he continued in a calm voice. "You have trailed me from the first, I expect, although I thought the sounds I heard were the creakings of this antique house . . . until I felt your presence."

Anxiety became anger. "Why are you creeping about in the middle of the night?" she demanded. "Tell me or I'll call for my brother!"

He turned then, and she gasped.

In the flickering candlelight, he was transformed. The planes of his face were edged with shadows. Fire blazed from his eyes. She did not know him.

He lifted a hand. "Please, Gwen. You must know I would never hurt you. Later you can show Max what I've found, but for now just come inside and look."

She held back as memories of torture in another small room, in this very house, nibbled at her courage. Damn the Caines for turning her into a frightened rabbit. She'd forgiven Robin everything but the loss of her mettle, which even her father's constant rages had never eroded.

But now she feared Jocelyn Vayle, if only because he was not the same man anymore. Not at all.

Still, she'd followed him because he was up to something, as he had been since the moment they first encountered each other on a London street. It was time to find out what that was.

As she moved inside, cobwebs brushed across her face and the stale odor of rotting wood assailed her nostrils. Vayle stepped aside and gestured to a grimy heap on the worm-ridden planks.

"I believe you call this the treasure," he said.

She blinked. It looked like a mound of decaying garbage until he held the candle closer, and then she saw light reflecting from dust-covered sapphires and diamonds. Barely, she could make out the shape of a tiara standing above the other gems.

Her hand reached out, hovering over the jewels, but she could not bring herself to touch them. The treasure. It must have lain in this spot for decades. "How did you know?" she whispered. "How could you possibly know it was here?"

"I did not. It was a guess only. Had Max been more adept at carpentry, I'd never have found this room. The hole he created led me here."

Whirling around, she jabbed a finger at his chest. "So you *are* a thief! I've always suspected you insinuated yourself into our household for some devious purpose. Now you've been found out. All this time, you were searching for the treasure."

He gave her a smile touched with irony. " 'Struth, Gwen, these jewels are of no earthly use to me. By rights they belong to Robin, but Max may wish to claim them on behalf of his wife. I suggest we leave them here for now, buried under a century of dust. Tomorrow you can show proof that Caines and Sevarics have clashed for years over something neither of them possessed."

"Dear God." Unable to help herself, she brushed the filthy glaze from an enormous sapphire. "To think of the pain for so many people while the treasure lay hidden in this room."

Vayle's hand shook, and he swore as hot wax slopped onto his hand. "A century of hatred. All for these baubles."

"You haven't answered me. How did you know?"

With a long sigh, he set the candle beside the treasure and clasped his hands behind his back. "You won't be fobbed off with moonshine, will you? You are readied for a fight, set to go for my face if I serve up another trumped-up story. But you needn't clench your fists like that. Lying to you has become unbearable."

Now that he finally admitted that he had lied, she felt no triumph. The pain in his eyes was too real for her to give way to accusations or caustic comments. "Then tell me the truth."

"The last time I saw these jewels," he said evenly, "they were draped on Blanche Sevaric's body. All but the tiara, which would not stay in place when we began to make love. She had taken a fancy to them after seeing a portrait of my mother in full court dress, wearing the gems presented our family by Queen Elizabeth. Blanche was unrelenting when she wanted something. I broke into my brother's safe-box and carried off the trinkets. 'Twas meant to be for one night only, and I saw no harm in obliging her."

Gwen swayed, her cheeks drained of color. He reached for her but she backed away, both hands raised to hold him off. "Oh, God," she murmured. "Oh, God."

When her shoulders met the wall, she leaned against it, needing the support. Her toes curled against the cold floor.

This wasn't Jocelyn Vayle. This man was older and more wise. Stronger, too, like one who had passed through fire. And she sensed honesty in his words. "Who *are* you?" she asked in a choked whisper.

He regarded her silently for a moment. With the candle behind him, his face was all harsh line and shadow. She could not see his eyes.

"You already know," he replied gravely. "Unless you've decided I am mad."

She wanted to believe that, but madness could not account for the treasure, or for the sincerity in his voice.

"You should run from a madman," he advised. "Do so if you wish. I'll not stop you."

She shook her head. "N-no. Not yet."

He smiled. "You always amaze me, Gwendolyn Sevaric. Until we met, I never understood how beautiful a thing is truth.

But you burn with it, like a clear, bright flame. And you may be the only creature alive who could understand and accept this improbable tale."

Stepping forward, he bowed, lifted her icy hand, and pressed his lips to her palm. "I am Valerian Caine."

Her vision blurred then, and her knees gave way.

With a swift motion he caught her up, pressing her body against his, murmuring something at her ear. She was too dizzy to make out the words, but aware enough to feel solid muscle and the strength of his arms.

"B-but you are real," she managed from a constricted throat. "You are here. I am touching you."

"To my profound delight," he said. " 'Struth, holding you has been the most pleasurable of my experiences in this century. But my time here has nearly run out, and you are cold. Can you stand without my support?"

In reply, she loosed her arms and let them fall to her sides.

He released her, shrugged out of his robe, and helped her put it on. She felt the warmth of his body in the folds of velvet as the dressing gown settled around her, and the elusive scent of lemony soap and fragrant snuff.

"That's better," he said, securing the tie at her waist. His hands lingered there as he gazed into her eyes. "Do you understand, Gwen? I truly am Valerian Caine, the same man who died here at Greenbriar Lodge a hundred years ago."

She could not explain why she believed him. Perhaps they had both run mad. And yet, for the first time, she trusted him, her instincts stronger than the logical part of her brain that told her everything he'd said was impossible—a bizarre ploy to let him snaffle the treasure and escape.

"Will you explain?" she asked helplessly. "*Can* you?"

"That's my girl! And I shall try, if allowed to do so. Do you know what time it is?"

"Just after midnight, I think. The clock in my room showed close to twelve when I went after you."

"Ah." He exhaled slowly. "In that case, I may well disappear at any moment. But let us go someplace warmer and more comfortable while I'm still here. The kitchen? I don't wish to rouse anyone as we talk."

Her heart jumped to her throat. "Why would you disappear?"

"Because I've failed," he said after a moment. "Or so that I cannot tell you things you are not supposed to know. Or just because it's Christmas." He picked up the candle. "If I vanish, 'tis not because I wish it. But don't be surprised."

She took hold of his hand. "As if anything could surprise me now."

When they got to the kitchen, Valerian stirred the banked fire and added wood from the brazier. Then he sat across from Gwen at a trestle table, both her hands resting in his.

It was his fault, the hundred years of feuding. After the duel, when the first grievances faded, only the treasure kept the vendetta alive. And he was responsible for its disappearance. Locating it in this century was a meager achievement, considering the damage he'd done. But at least his brief new life had some meaning now.

How much time did he have? Knowing Proctor, not much, so he started with the most important thing on his mind. It did not translate well into words.

"Miss Sevaric—Gwen—you are splendid and . . . that is . . . if only I'd met you when I was truly mortal, I would have—" his voice faded off.

'Struth, he'd have been too caught up in his own pleasures to bother with a slender, bright-eyed chit whose beauty of spirit lay beyond his vision. The man he'd been would not have made the effort to know her, or appreciated the intricate personality that enthralled him now.

"It doesn't matter," he said finally. "We were born in two different times and are not permitted a future together. Not that you'd put up with a scoundrel like me in any case. I only wanted you to know of my . . . er . . . deep regard."

He couldn't say the word "love." He'd never said it before, to any woman. And now, what good would it do?

If only her eyes were not so clear, fixed on him with unwavering trust. At this moment, she was ready to believe anything he told her and brave enough to accept what no one else would—

"Valerian?"

He squeezed her hands. That she used his name said more than a thousand words.

"We should get on about this while we can," he said gruffly. "Stop me when you have questions, because I scarcely know how to tell the story. Where should I begin?"

Her brow furrowed. "With the easy part, I think. I'd rather work up to—well, how you came to be alive again. What happened before, with the treasure and the duel?"

"Ah." Unfortunately, Gwen's *easy part* cast him in an ugly light. Swallowing his pride, he let go her hands and propped his chin on his fists. Staring down at the table, he recalled the events that took place here a century ago.

"I had been Blanche Sevaric's lover for several months. Her husband was supposedly in Dorset on business, but I expect he knew he was being cuckolded and decided to put an end to it. That particular night he galloped into the courtyard with sufficient clatter to make his presence known."

Gwen's silence worried him. At least she was still there, waiting for him to resume his story.

"Blanche panicked, insisting I conceal myself while she fobbed him off. But I dressed and went outside, ignoring her directions to the priest hole. Only a coward would hide. And Sevaric had the right to meet me, although my reputation with sword and pistol made it virtual suicide to call me out. 'Struth, I didn't expect he would, but the man was ever a fool."

He closed his eyes, and as if on Proctor's screen, the scene played out before him. "Within minutes we were faced off in the road. I chose pistols, thinking to wound him only. But he raved on and on about the vile ways he'd punish Blanche for her infidelity. So I shot to kill."

"And so did he," Gwen said tonelessly.

"That was his intent, but Sevaric fired wildly. For a split second I thought he'd missed. Then his bullet ricocheted off a stone and struck me in the temple. Or so I've been told. At the time I felt a sudden pain and nothing more."

She gave him a stricken look. "I cannot bear to think of you dead."

"But I've been dead for a hundred years," he reminded her. " 'Tis long over and done with, Gwen."

"That is difficult to apprehend while you are sitting here in front of me." With obvious deliberation, she changed the subject. "Do you look now as you did before?"

"I think so. The parts of me I can see directly, like my hands and legs, appear the same as they were. But I'm unable to see my reflection in a mirror." He chuckled. "Ever since I dismissed my valet, Robin has been shaving me."

She leaned over to look, and her finger brushed the side of his jaw. "He missed a spot, just here."

That touch, so intimate, sent heat coursing through his body. If he hoped to make it through whatever time was left without betraying himself, he had to put some distance between them. Summoning a neutral smile, he came to his feet. "Robin's hand was shaking like an aspen through the entire procedure," he said lightly. "I'm surprised he didn't slit my throat."

She blinked. "Would you have died again?"

"Devil if I know. It's been guesswork since I awoke in Hyde Park a month ago, tempted to imagine I'd dreamed everything of the past and was truly alive. But whenever I pass by a window or a mirror and fail to see my image, I'm reminded that I do not belong here and will not be allowed to stay."

"Why is it others can see your reflection? I've done so." She flushed. "Sometimes I looked at your reflection so you wouldn't be aware I was really looking at you."

He halted his pacing, arrested by the significance of her confession. "Have you now?"

"I could not help myself," she said in a tiny voice. "You are excessively handsome."

His chest swelled. That artless compliment touched him in a way all the flattery he'd grown accustomed to had never done. But he was unable to recall a single one of the facile responses that had always come with ease to his lips when a woman praised him. Just as well, since Gwen had no patience with elaborate duplicity.

"Thank you," he murmured.

She tilted her head. "I'd like to have seen you with lace at your neck and wrists, wearing rich velvet coats and embroidered waistcoats. Did you powder your hair? Or wear a periwig? I've always hated those. In portraits, they make a man look downright silly."

"My thoughts exactly," he said with a laugh. "I wore my own hair, unpowdered, long and tied back in a queue. 'Twasn't the fashion, but I was vain enough to set my own style."

"I don't doubt it," she retorted. But then her face grew serious. "What about the treasure, Valerian? Did you put it in that room?"

"Not I. Apparently Blanche hid the jewels in the priest hole while her husband and her lover were busy killing each other. Looking to her future, I expect. The gems would have brought her a fortune, even pried from their settings and sold individually. I've no idea why she failed to reclaim them."

"She never had the opportunity. Lady Sevaric died of influenza not long after the duel. From all accounts the house was then closed up, until a Caine won it on a wager some years later. It stayed in your family after that."

"Ah. That's why I'd no idea Greenbriar Lodge was the same place I often met with Blanche It had another name then—I cannot recall what it was. Until the coach drew up yesterday, I never realized that I was coming back to the last place I had seen on this earth."

He leaned his shoulders against the wall and folded his arms. This house was his own gateway to the Afterlife, a hundred years ago and again within the next few hours. Or seconds. Such irony, he thought. Proctor might have a sense of humor after all.

Gwen was silent for a long time, staring at her clasped hands resting on the table. She looked small and defenseless in the velvet robe. It had slipped over one shoulder, pulling the collar of her nightrail with it, and her bare skin was nearly translucent in the dim light of the candle. Behind her, fire from the kitchen hearth transformed her tousled hair to a red-gold halo.

He would love her, if he could.

Perhaps he already did. It was difficult to know because he'd never loved anyone, not that he could remember. Both his parents died when he was in leading strings, and his brother was cold-natured even as a child. A stern uncle raised them until William was old enough to take the reins. From then on, William discharged his duty as heir to the title with zeal, while his irresponsible younger brother ran wild.

He had admired William, distantly. And he'd been infatuated with women from the very day his voice began to change, pursuing any number of them with genuine passion over the years. Even so, the notion of choosing one woman and being faithful to her had never occurred to him.

Until now, when it was impossible.

Gwen lifted her head. "Can you tell me what happened after you died?"

"I'd rather not. Most is so vague in my mind I could scarcely begin to describe it, and if telling you is forbidden, I might be called back immediately."

"Then do not," she said firmly. "I want above all things for you to stay as long as possible. But is it prohibited to explain how you came to be here now?"

He gave it some thought. In fact, he could be snatched away at any moment, for any reason or no reason at all. Proctor had never outlined the rules.

Why not tell her as much as he could? Not about the foggy, tedious Afterlife, though, because Gwen was a virtuous woman and would certainly experience something altogether different. A just God would not permit her to fall into Proctor's clutches.

"I was offered a second chance," he said. "Not that I deserved anything of the sort, given my record before and after I died."

"Indeed?" She regarded him owlishly. "Were you very wicked?"

"I fear so. Not malevolent, 'struth, but assuredly selfish and dedicated to my own pleasures. If I ever did a truly virtuous deed, I cannot recall it. Nevertheless, I was assigned to put an end to the feud between your family and mine. And if I succeeded, there was to be a reward, although—"

"But you *did* succeed," Gwen interrupted. "Some wounds will take awhile to heal, but none of us will pursue this idiotic quarrel another inch. The Caines and Sevarics are reconciled." Her eyes grew wide. "So what is your reward? Will you now go to Heaven?"

He laughed. "Not likely. As I understand it, Heaven is far beyond my reach."

"Oh dear Lord. Surely not *Hell.*"

"Oh, I'll likely find my way there by one route or another, but not immediately. Eternal damnation, like salvation, apparently requires considerable dedication. As a reward I was offered something that I, in my ignorance, valued even more than paradise—the chance to reclaim my former life."

"As Valerian Caine?" She frowned. "But how is that possible?"

"How is it possible I am here now, a hundred years later? Believe me, Gwen, I've not a clue. Had I accomplished the tasks assigned me, I was to survive the duel and continue from there, doubtless finding more inventive ways to sin."

She cast him a dark look. "And will you?"

"I'll not have the opportunity. If the feud is now ended, I had precious little to do with it. And that was only the first of my tasks. By Christmas day, Dorothea and Max were to be happy and at peace."

"But they are! Did you see them tonight, Valerian? They are so in love the air around them fairly burns."

"As you say. But that was their doing, not mine."

"You'd a hand in it. I've always suspected you shut them in my father's sanctuary just so they'd be compromised."

Smart girl. He bowed in acknowledgment.

"So there you are. Max and Dorothea are happy now because you gave them no choice but to come together. Your reward is assured."

"And *you*, Gwen," he said gently. "You were to be happy, too."

"Me?" Her brow furrowed. "You cannot claim your reward if I'm not happy?"

Then she popped from the bench and held out her arms. "But I am," she said brightly. "Or I can be. I will be. Behold the happiest woman on earth."

He smiled. Precious Gwen, so determined to give him what he'd once thought of value. But if there was ever a useless existence, it was the one he'd set himself to reclaim. Better he take his chances with Proctor in the Afterlife than wreak more havoc as a mortal.

On earth, Valerian Caine was nothing but trouble.

Lifting his shoulders from the wall, he took a step forward. "My dear, you cannot fleece God. He knows, as do I, that you are not truly at peace. Pretending won't help me, but your generosity is beyond any gift I've ever received."

With a fierce look in her eyes, she came directly up to him. "Valerian, I can never in this life be happy if you don't get what you most want. Surely God will know that when he searches my heart. And if I am the only thing standing between you and your reward, what can I do to remove myself? For my soul, I'd give anything to help you. *Anything.*"

He could barely hear her last words. The pulse of blood drummed in his ears, and her sweet, earnest face seemed to dissolve before his eyes. "Wh-why?" he murmured. "How can you say that? You are young and lovely, with a new life ahead of you now that the feud is ended. Gwen, after tonight you must forget me and look to the future. You'll find a man to love, have childr—"

"I have already found him," she said with a tremulous smile. "And any future I have is with you, Valerian Caine, be it only for a minute or an hour." Her hands moved to his chest, near his heart. "You may not care, and it cannot matter when you are transported to wherever you must go, but let these be the last words you hear. I love you."

Tears welled in his eyes, blinding him as he took her in his arms and held her so close no Power from the Afterlife could have separated them at that moment.

Distantly, he heard her say the words again and again. "I love you. I love you." He tried to form a response, but his lips wouldn't move. He could do nothing but hold her, absorbing her warmth and vitality and unconquerable spirit into the bleak desert of his own existence.

Too late, this unexpected, impossible bliss. A century lay between them. Eternity would seize him, carry him away, and whatever his fate, Gwen would have no part of it.

Never had he been so happy, or in such despair.

She lifted her head, and he recognized the stubborn expression on her face. "We have *now*," she said. "And if you were charged with my happiness, Valerian Caine, why are you wasting precious time? Make love to me!"

Dumbfounded, he gazed into her eyes. They were positively radiant. And resolute. Gwen had made up her mind.

"Is that such a repellent idea?" she demanded when he failed to respond. "It's what I want. It will give me a memory to treasure. It will make me happy. And just possibly, the joy you give me will assure your own reward. Will not a born gamester toss the dice this one last time?"

He swallowed hard. "Gwen, with all my heart, and all my body, too, I want you. Believe that. But—"

"Then what are you waiting for? The clock is ticking."

"I'll not compromise you," he said staunchly. "Tonight is out of space and time for both of us, but come the morrow you will regret this generous impulse. And I'll not be here to console you."

"Rubbish!" She fixed him with a pugnacious glare. "Of all the times for you to stand on high principles! You are supposed to be a rake. And for once in my life, I want to be a wanton woman." She put a hand against his cheek. "I want you."

His last ounce of willpower dissolved like honeyed butter. Lifting his gaze, he made one last try to do the honorable thing. "Francis," he whispered, "if this is wrong, take me now."

Gwen clutched his waist as if her strength alone could keep him earthbound. "Whoever you are, Francis, don't listen to him! He is mine. For this one night, *please* let him be mine."

Twenty-three

In his dreams, Vayle heard a voice call his name.

"Valerian?" it whispered.

Not yet, he begged silently. Please, not yet.

But the voice persisted, and he opened his eyes to see the first light of dawn streaming through the window. Christmas morning.

The reckoning was at hand.

For a last moment, he cradled the sleeping Gwen against his chest. His beloved, for one unutterably beautiful night. How ironic to receive love, and find himself capable of giving it, when it was too late for either of them.

Hours ago she had been brave, promising to face his departure without a single regret. She would try, he knew.

But love was not so easily cast off. He had been unconscionably selfish, taking her virginity and accepting her heart when he'd nothing to offer in return.

Gwen should not suffer for his transgression. By the mercy of Heaven, she ought to awaken with no memory of him, her innocence intact, free to love and marry a man wise enough to value her.

He had never prayed before, not sincerely, but he prayed now for Gwen. In her name and for her sake, because he'd not earned the right to ask on his own behalf, he implored God to grant a miracle.

And almost immediately he felt foolish and unworthy. Why should God listen to *him?* Gwen's heart was pure, tempered by fire. A loving Deity would take her into His arms on her own merits.

Meantime, he had been summoned to his own dreary fate. Careful not to wake her, he rose and pulled on his breeches. Proctor the Prude would not approve if he reentered the Afterlife in the altogether.

He expected to disappear immediately, and when he did not he padded to the window and gazed outside. Below him was the garden where he had died a century ago.

It was spring then, and the last thing he remembered was the scent of roses as he turned, lifted his gun, and fired. Now the courtyard was marked out with patches of withered bushes and leafless trees.

The garden was as bleak and empty as he felt. Somewhere down there was the stone responsible for his death. He'd meant to look for it, but by now a hundred years of English rain must have smoothed the place where Richard Sevaric's bullet struck before angling at his temple.

"It is time," said a gentle voice.

Valerian turned to his right and saw Francis's sweet, chubby face. And saw right through him, to the armoire in the corner. Obviously Francis had yet to perfect the art of materializing himself. "I've been expecting you," he said crossly, "although I rather hoped you and Proctor would forget about me."

"I am your Guardian," Francis reminded him. "I have been with you every moment."

"Then you already know I've botched everything. Proctor is doubtless chaffing to rub an *I told you so* in your face, and for that I apologize because I'm sure you did your best. As he predicted, I was a hopeless cause."

"Judgment is not mine to pass. Nor Proctor's. Tell me, Valerian, how do you evaluate your own accomplishments and blunders? Have you achieved anything of worth?"

Valerian sighed and turned back to the window. "A few good things have happened. The feud is at an end. Gwen has forgiven Robin. Max and Dorothea are married, and I have some hope they will do well together. But I cannot say that any one of them is truly happy. And since I was charged to make sure they were, I have failed."

"Perhaps not altogether. At the least, you can take credit for reconciling the Caines and Sevarics."

Valerian rested his forehead against the cold window glass. " 'Struth, I spent more time pursuing my own pleasures than tending to my tasks. I wrote a letter to Dorothea, which brought her to London. I locked a door when she and Max got themselves into a compromising situation. I did a bit of shuffling and tinkering when opportunities fell into my lap. My contributions were trivial, and if anything good came of my presence in this century, it cannot be credited to me."

Francis chuckled. "Remarkably humble of you, I must say."

"Out of character, you mean." Valerian glanced over his shoulder to the bed. "May we go somewhere else for this discussion? I'd not have Gwen wake up."

"She cannot hear us," Francis said. "Now, think carefully. If you stood as judge of your own actions, what would be your verdict? As you pointed out, we have come to the sticking point. What should be done with you?"

"Dung beetles," he said frankly. "I belong with the dung beetles."

Francis clucked his tongue. "That is no longer an option, although Proctor is vastly disappointed. He was so certain you would founder. But you have not, Valerian. Some would have done better, others worse, in your situation, but you did not disgrace yourself."

"No?" Astonished, Valerian pointed out the window. "Does that mean I wake up down there, after the duel, still alive? I go back to where I came from?"

"That was the original agreement, and yes, you may reclaim your former life. Say the word and you will be Valerian Caine again, moments after your bullet struck down your opponent. His shot will have missed. You will be left with a difficult situation, of course, and must deal with the consequences of dispatching Lord Sevaric, but I've no doubt you will smooth things over." Francis smiled with something that looked like affection. "You've always had a way of eluding punishment."

Valerian's eyes burned. Soon he would be where he belonged. It was what he had most wanted.

So where was the elation? Why the bitter taste in his mouth, and the dread of going back?

"Will I be as I was?" he asked in a halting voice. "In all respects?"

"Yes, indeed. Your life will proceed exactly as it would have done. You'll remember nothing of what transpired since, not me, nor Proctor, nor the month just past."

"Not Gwen? I won't remember Gwen?"

"How could you?" Francis asked reasonably. "She won't have been born."

"You are wrong." Valerian fixed him with an icy gaze, not easy to do since Francis was transparent. "I don't begin to comprehend how I can have lived then, and now, and then again. But I will never forget Gwen. Through all time and space I will remember her."

"Not if you go back," Francis said firmly. "I sympathize, but rules are rules. You will be the same man you were, and must learn again what little wisdom you acquired from this extraordinary venture into the future. I can only hope you stumble upon friends like Max and Gwen Sevaric. As I recall, you rarely spent time in the company of decent people. And without a mission to compel you—" He winced. "Perhaps you will come about. I will still be your Guardian, although I am not permitted to interfere."

"Never mind me. What about Gwen? Will she remember that we met? Will she remember what happened tonight?"

"Oh, yes."

Valerian grabbed for Francis's white robe, but his hands closed on empty air. "Why the devil must she remember when it can only hurt her, while I forget everything I've learned? What's the sense of that?"

Francis shrugged. "Now you understand why we don't like

sending souls back and forth in time. With God there is no past or future, so anything is possible. He merely grants a disturbance in the continuum of the universe. And when He approves a petition, He leaves the petitioner to clean up the inevitable mess."

"In that case, let me recall what I've learned and permit Gwen to forget she loved me. Why not?"

"I agree, in theory," Francis acknowledged. "It would be better for the both of you. But precedents have been established, and I've no authority to overrule them. Gwen must live with the decision she made this night and all the consequences. You, on the other hand, have a choice for yourself—if you'll stop objecting long enough for me to tell you about it."

Hope surged in Valerian's chest. "I am tamed," he said, bowing his head. He saw Francis's hand settle on his shoulder, although he felt nothing.

"In truth, my son, you hedged the tasks assigned you, but that we expected. Max, Dorothea, and Gwendolyn had ultimately to choose for themselves. You . . . how shall I say this? . . . dredged them from their rut by your mere presence and occasional interference." A smile lit his plump face. "And you did more, Valerian. Although tempted, you did not revert to your former bad habits."

"I wanted to," Valerian confessed in a shadowed voice. " 'Struth, I can't imagine why I didn't bed Lady Melbrook or spend the entire month drinking and gaming. That was my intent."

"Don't I know it," Francis replied with a shudder that made him flicker like a candle flame. "I almost despaired of you time and time again. But you resisted, and took upon yourself a responsibility Proctor did not assign. Robin Caine."

Valerian looked up in surprise. "He had nothing to do—"

"Exactly! You could not profit by helping Robin, but you befriended him and guided him to a better life. For that, you are now permitted to Move Forward."

"To Heaven? For teaching Robin to fence and giving him a few items of clothing I've earned *Heaven?*"

"Good heavens, no." Francis drew himself up in affront. "Do

you imagine a handful of few good deeds merit an eternity in the embrace of God? But you did care for someone and gave with no hope of reward. For that you will be rewarded, but certainly not with the Beatific Vision. At most, and only with delicate negotiations on my part, you are now permitted to escape Proctor's clutches. And I assure you that your next Monitor will be more understanding."

"A kindlier jailer, you mean."

"On the contrary. Given your poor start, it would ordinarily take eons for you to come within reach of what I can now offer you. Only by the combination of Proctor's impatience and God's mercy can you seize a chance to come wondrously near the ultimate goal. Measure this against your other option—the Earthly Life you wanted more than anything to reclaim. I pray you choose wisely."

The choice ought to be simple. Even automatic, or so Francis appeared to think. But It wasn't, because he wanted neither alternative. Not anymore. Not since Gwen. Whichever way he went, to his former existence or a loftier position in the Afterlife, Gwen would still be compromised and without comfort. Alone.

She deserved better. How could he claim reward and leave her to be punished with a life of dreary solitude?

Perhaps in the eternal scheme of things a few earthly years meant nothing, especially to Beings who had never experienced what it was to be mortal. But he had lived twice. He knew. And he cared about what Gwen faced when she woke up, and the day after, and all the days after that.

Valerian Caine had always been a gambling man, and without another thought he folded both the winning hands Francis had dealt him.

"Send me back to Proctor," he said flatly. "Let him do his worst, even if he crowns me king of the dung beetles from here to kingdom come. I'll take whatever he metes out in exchange for your promise that Gwen will be happy."

Turning, he took a long last look at her slender form curled under the blankets, her disheveled hair against the pillow. Once he had thought her unlovely. Now her face was so beautiful to him his stomach clenched at the awareness he'd never see it again.

"If I did anything good," he said when there was no response, "give me this. Make sure Gwen is happy. If that requires dispatching me straight to Hell, *do it.*"

The room brightened, as if lit by a thousand candles. He turned to Francis, whose head was lifted although his eyes were closed. Heat radiated from the mass of light that had been the Guardian's pudgy form. Now his image, except the cherubic face, was enveloped in golden rays.

After a long time the light faded, leaving the familar, transparent outline. "It appears that Gwen can only be happy with you," Francis reported. "Objections were raised, and her discrimination questioned, but He has ruled that you may remain here."

Valerian's mouth dropped.

"You are now removed from all authority but your own," Francis said solemnly. "Henceforth you are Jocelyn Vayle, a man without family or history, but still a man. What you make of this new existence is wholly up to you."

"You mean I get to stay here, with Gwen?"

"Oh, do pay attention," Francis said with unaccustomed impatience. "And I must say that if it weren't easier leaving you here than returning you to your former life . . . but never mind all that. This unnatural reordering of the physical universe is so blasted confusing!" He began to shimmer.

"Wait! Will I remember you and Proctor? Will Gwen remember who I was a hundred years ago?"

"In part. You will know who you were, and Gwen will know everything you have told her. You will gradually forget the details of your existence in the Afterlife, though, including Proctor. And me."

"But I don't *want* to forget you, Francis. You have been immeasurably kind."

"It's my job, but thank you. And I shall be with you still, as Guardian, although you won't know my name or feel my presence. Just as well, since you have a lamentable habit of addressing me aloud where others can overhear and then lying to cover your indiscretion. Eaten by lions indeed! My powers are virtually stripped away, Jocelyn Vayle, until you pass on again. I will pray for you, but henceforth you are fundamentally on your own."

And then Francis was gone as if he'd never been there.

Vayle shook his head, wondering if he was dreaming. But the floor was cold under his bare feet, and the soft sound of Gwen's breathing tickled at his ears.

Sweet Gwen. Could it be true? Was he now permitted to live with her? Even make children with her? Grow old in this century, dandling grandchildren on his knees?

That would be Heaven enough for him.

For a last moment, he gazed out the window and bade farewell to Valerian Caine. Never again would he be the carefree, self-indulgent rake he'd been a century ago. Although that would require an act of will at every moment, he realized. Valerian Caine was gone in name only. Jocelyn Vayle had not shed any of his weaknesses for drinking or gaming or women, and temptation would ever dog his tracks.

But for Gwen, he could change. 'Struth, she would keep him in line whatever his fleeting inclinations to wander. And he was glad of it.

As the sun of Christmas morning gilded the room, he turned away from the garden. He would walk that path again, the one he'd paced with a dueling pistol in his hand, but this time with Gwen on his arm. They were both too curious to resist exploring the place where he had died.

Meantime, he'd a new life to begin, and he couldn't think of a better way than making love. He started for the bed, but from the corner of his eye he caught a glimpse of a bare-chested man wearing rumpled breeches. Curious, he approached the cheval mirror and studied his reflection.

By heavens, he could see himself! And he looked exactly the same, save for the short hair that was unfortunately fashionable these days. At least he was still a handsome devil, with the lean muscled body of a fencer and rather exceptional green eyes. Women had always found him attractive, and he hoped that Gwen did, too.

He'd little else to offer her.

Gwen awoke to find herself alone in the bed. Valerian had been snatched away while she slept!

Her heart turned to ice.

Rolling over, she clutched to her breast the pillow where he'd laid his head. And then she saw him. He was staring out the window, head bowed as if in prayer.

Silently, she formed a grateful prayer of her own. Now she would have a chance to say goodbye and thank him for the most wonderful night of her life. She could tell him, again, how very much she loved him.

As she watched through lowered lashes, he turned and started for the bed. But he paused, a look of surprise on his face, and swung around in front of the mirror.

If she hadn't known he was unable to see his own reflection, she'd have thought he was admiring himself. He ran long fingers through his tousled hair, flexed his muscles, and nodded as if in approval.

What in heaven's name was going on? She sat up, clutching the sheet over her naked breasts. "Valerian?"

Without turning, he held out a hand. "Come here, Gwen, and look at this."

She retrieved the green velvet robe from the floor, pulled it on, and crossed the room. Immediately he drew her into the circle of his arms, and they stood facing the mirror.

"What do you see?" he asked softly.

Confused, she studied the reflection and could find nothing out of the ordinary. "You and me, of course."

"That's what I see, too, Gwen. You and me." He hugged her warmly. "It's proof, I think. Now I am really here, all of me firmly planted in this century. Tell me you are glad of it."

Her knees gave way as a wave of dizziness swept over her. Distantly she heard his voice calling her name. She sagged in his arms, fighting for air. "Wh-what do you mean?" she whispered when the earth stopped shaking and she could breathe again.

"Forgive me, sweetheart. I'm not handling this as I ought, but I'm more than a bit stunned myself. Come, let's sit down and I'll explain everything." He led her to the chair beside the dressing table and tugged her onto his lap. "Are you all right?"

"I think so. Did you mean it, Valerian? You are to stay here?"

"Yes. Never mind how it all came about, because it doesn't matter and I'm told that I will soon have no memory of the details. But while you were sleeping, judgment was rendered and here I am from now until I die again." He grinned. "In old age, of natural causes, I hope. No more duels for me."

"Oh." Her mind was spinning with a thousand words, but that was the only one that came out.

"I thought you'd be pleased," he said after a moment. "Did you prefer me to vanish after all?"

He looked so downcast she was sure she'd hurt him. Still, how could she be excited about what must be, for him, a disaster? "But this isn't what you wanted, Valerian. Did you not wish to go back to what you were before? Take up your former life again?"

"I found something better," he said simply. "And by the mercy of God it was granted me."

"Oh," she said again. A heavy lump seemed to have lodged in her throat.

"I did have a choice, Gwen. Several, as a matter of fact." He put his hands on her shoulders. "I chose you."

Tears pooled in her eyes. "You have no obligation to me, Valerian. Truly. When you made love to me, we both assumed it to be for one night only. I never expected more. If you are to make a new life for yourself, do so freely. You are not bound to me in any way." She willed a smile to her lips. "England is rife with wealthy, charming, beautiful women, and I expect they'll all be vying for your attentions within a fortnight."

He gazed at her somberly, shaking his head. "What a foolish girl you are, Gwen Sevaric. Did last night mean nothing to you? Or have you forgot how we were together?" He pulled her into his arms. "Allow me to remind you."

There was nothing gentle about his kiss. And she could not mistake the passion of it as he claimed her with his lips and tongue, his hands seeming to touch her everywhere as they moved over her body. He struck fire at her waist and back, on her thighs and her breasts, until she burned for him again as she had done during their long night of love.

And when he set her back, she felt beautiful again. This incredible man wanted her still. She gazed into his clear green eyes and was sure of it.

"I'll have no more of your bird-witted nonsense," he told her firmly. "If you cast me off, do so for good reason. 'Struth, I cannot imagine why you'd have a man without history or title or fortune. I've a hundred pounds to my name, Gwen, and no skills to acquire more except at the gaming tables."

He gave an exaggerated smile. "I would suggest you look elsewhere for a more suitable husband, my sweet . . . had you not compromised me."

Flustered, she gazed into his eyes. "I beg your pardon?"

"And so you should. I was a virgin, in this century at least, until you had your wicked way with me. For honor's sake, you must now offer marriage." He grinned. "If you propose, I'll say yes."

She broke out laughing. Insufferable man! "Why the devil should I propose to *you?*"

His expression grew serious. "So I'll know you really want this, Gwen. A few minutes ago you were at pains to set me free. I mean you to have the same freedom. You must decide if you can bear to spend the rest of your life with a rather useless fellow who has nothing to give you but his love."

She gasped. For his love, she would do anything, but the very notion took her breath away. Drab, homely Gwen Sevaric, married to a rake. A charming gamester. A rogue.

God save her, the bride of a *ghost!*

She reached to touch his face. The stubble of whiskers, faintly auburn, shadowed his chin. She touched the high cheekbones, the arched brows, the forehead creased with a troubled frown.

Then she ran her fingers under the thick hair at his right temple and felt the traces of a scar where the bullet had struck him down. Valerian Caine.

"What shall I call you?" she asked faintly. "When we speak the vows. I, Gwendolyn, take you . . . ?"

With a groan of relief, he kissed her deeply. *"My love* has a nice ring to it," he whispered in her ear.

"Y-yes," she agreed, "but you'll require a name, too. Is it to be Valerian? Shall we tell the others who you are?"

"Were," he corrected. "The truth must remain our secret, and there will come a time when it does not signify to either of us. Henceforth, I am plain Mr. Jocelyn Vayle." Laughter danced in his eyes. " 'Struth, Jocelyn is a foul name. I daresay 'tis Proctor's notion of a jest."

Gwen started to ask and then thought better of it. Proctor and Francis were supposedly his favorite saints—eaten by lions, as she recalled—and she was willing to go along. Whatever he chose to tell her about his century in the Afterlife, he would confide in his own good time.

For now, there were more immediate problems to deal with. "You must return to your own room," she said urgently, "before Max discovers you spent the night with me."

He stopped nibbling at her throat long enough to grumble a mild oath.

"I am serious, Val—Vayle!" She tugged at his hair. "Whatever his personal inclinations, Max is a dedicated moralist where I am concerned. Men set one standard for themselves and quite another for sisters and wives. Unless you are keen to fight a second duel at Greenbriar Lodge, you must leave immediately."

With a last, fervent kiss, he set her on her feet. "If you insist, my sweet, but—"

A knock at the door cut him off.

Twenty-four

The pounding at the door continued, like a carpenter hammering nails. It could only be Max.

Swallowing an oath, Vayle put a finger to his lips. "Shh. Maybe he'll give up."

"Max never gives up," Gwen mouthed silently. "Quick, put on your shirt."

His lips quirked, and she glanced down at the velvet robe, far too large for her slender form, now gaping open from breasts to toes. Under his appreciative gaze, her entire body flushed hotly.

From the hall, Max called out in a rousing voice. "Rise and shine, slugabed! It's Christmas morning, and we're ready to light the Yule log."

"Never fear," Vayle murmured as he untied the knot at her waist, drew the folds of the robe around her, and secured the belt again. "Last night I stood at the brink of Hell, and believe me, my love, compared to Proctor your brother is a lamb. Say something to get rid of him."

She cleared her throat. "M-Max? I'll be down in a few minutes."

He did not, as Vayle had hoped, take the hint. "I've a cup of chocolate for you. Let me in before it goes cold."

Gwen turned anxious eyes to Vayle's face. "What shall we do? You won't think him a lamb over pistols in the courtyard."

His heart gave a lurch. Dear God! Was this another of Proctor's bitter jokes? Time seemed to collapse around him as a sudden vision possessed his senses—a door crashing against the wall, another enraged Sevaric charging into the room, a woman's scream—

"Cover yourself, Gwen," Max warned. "I'm coming in!"

"No!" she squealed, but it was too late.

The door swung open and Max stepped inside, smiling cheerfully as he looked toward the rumpled, empty bed. Then he turned toward the window and saw Gwen, and the bare-chested man standing beside her, and the cup and saucer he'd been holding shattered against the floor. The chocolate splashed on the rug and the wall.

In the frozen silence that followed, Vayle reached for Gwen's small cold hand. Max was the very image of Richard Sevaric, lips curled in a snarl, eyes flashing with murderous intent. It's not what you are thinking, he wanted to say, but 'struth, it was exactly that.

Beside him, Gwen let out a tiny breath and he tightened his grip. It was up to him now, but he couldn't think what to do. Was he to die again, in the same garden, at the hands of another avenging Sevaric?

"Max?"

The soft voice from the hall was followed by Dorie herself, and Vayle's heart returned to its normal place in his chest. Even Francis would not have been more welcome than the imperturbable Lady Sevaric.

She gazed briefly at the awkward tableau and moved next to her husband, the top of her head level with his shoulder. "Oh, there you are, Mr. Vayle!" she said, as if they had met on the staircase. "I tried your room, but the only response was Robin's snore. Do finish dressing and hurry on down, will you? I've already set the table for breakfast."

Max shot her an astonished look, but she only locked his arm in hers and pulled him out of the room. He found his voice just as she closed the door firmly behind them, cutting off what promised to be a ferocious oath.

"At least he didn't run for his horsewhip," Gwen said with a gallant attempt at a smile.

"Of course not! Max is a reasonable man." And doubtless on his way to prime a pair of dueling pistols, Vayle added to himself as he reached for his shirt. "Dress for Christmas breakfast, love. I'll talk to him."

"But you mustn't! Not alone, while he is so angry. We'll face him together. Max won't hurt you if I'm there, I know!"

He swallowed his first response to that unintentional insult and busied himself pulling the shirt over his head. On no account would he hide behind a woman, but Gwen was frightened for him. It was oddly touching, if unnecessary.

" 'Struth, I can take care of myself," he said gently. "Without bloodshed," he amended when she flinched.

With a light kiss on the tip of her nose, he navigated past the shards of porcelain and set out to meet his fate for the second time in a century.

Max was in the parlor, standing at the holly-bedecked window, looking out at the gray day. He turned as Vayle came in. "I had thought you an honorable man," he said in a voice both reproving and sorrowful. "I trusted you with my sister."

Prepared for anger, or even a challenge, Vayle stopped short. There was a strange glint in Max's dark eyes, and his posture was almost too relaxed for a soldier, let alone one readying for battle. What was going on? The man had every right to be furious. Why was he not?

Vayle had the eerie sensation he'd just wandered into an ambush of sorts, and virtually unarmed since the whole truth was not his to tell. Not that it signified, of course. Unlike his sister, Max would never accept the truth, or credit that his former houseguest was really Valerian Caine.

He assumed a pose designed to reveal nothing of his tension, hands clasped behind his back, bare feet set a little apart. "I cannot deny I have betrayed your trust, Lord Sevaric. I accept the consequences. But I am not wholly without honor, and must certainly delope—"

"Delope?" *Now* Max looked angry. "What the hell will that accomplish? And how is it honorable to make Gwen a widow before she's a wife? You, sir, will not squirm out of this so easily!"

"S–squirm?" What the devil was he talking about? "I had no intention of, uh, squirming out of whatever you think I'm trying to squirm out of." He frowned. "Exactly what is that?"

From behind him came Gwen's cool, clear voice. "Yes, Max, what is it you mean?"

Max made a disgusted sound. "It's perfectly obvious. I expect Vayle to wed you, immediately if not sooner."

As relief swept over him, Vayle turned with a smile to Gwen. But her gaze was fixed on her brother, and he watched with interest as she ruffled up like an offended owl. By now, Max should have learned it was no use ordering her about like a raw subaltern.

She stepped forward and planted herself by Vayle's side, her slipper nudging the side of his foot. He recognized a warning to keep his mouth shut.

"And *I* expect, dear brother," she said in a tone so sweet it was surely concealing poison underneath, "that if there are any decisions to be made around here, it is my right alone to make them. I am of age, and you have no say in this matter. None whatsoever."

"The devil you say!" Max looked so stunned Vayle almost laughed aloud. "I am your brother. What's more, I am the head of the Sevaric family, had you forgot? If I say the fellow's going to wed you, by God he will. And if you don't like the idea, well, that's a pity, but you will nevertheless do as you are told."

Major tactical bungle, old boy, Vayle thought.

Gwen marched straight up to her brother and jabbed a finger at his chest. "Hear this, Lord Head of Family. Just because you had to force your bride to the altar doesn't mean you can do the same to me!"

This was almost too entertaining to interrupt, but Vayle knew from experience what Gwen in a temper could do to a man.

"Now, now, Miss Sevaric, you know Max only wants what's best for you."

They both looked at him as if surprised he was still in the room. Disconcerted, he cleared his throat. "Perhaps it's time for us all to be reasonable. Miss Sevaric, I'm sure you meant no insult to your brother and his wife. And you, Lord Sevaric, would not dream of compelling your sister into a marriage she does not wish."

When Max looked ready to object to that, Vayle hurried on. "Thing is, whatever my personal inclinations in this matter, I am demonstrably *not* the best of all possible husbands."

"You're good enough," Max ruled immediately. "She must have thought so last night, or she'd not have admitted you to her b-bedroom." As his voice faded on the last word, a flush stained his cheekbones.

Gwen gave him a decidedly fiendish grin. "But Mr. Vayle was there as my *lover*, Max. Nothing more. And what is agreeable in a lover does not necessarily qualify a man for anything else."

Vayle was fairly sure she meant to tease, but her words stung nonetheless. "If I'm to be disqualified, could you be more specific as to the reasons why?"

"There are no reasons," Max said with a wave of his hand. "You're a good enough husband for me."

"Then you marry him," Gwen retorted.

This was definitely getting out of hand. With Gwen more bent on outmastering her brother than achieving her goal, they could all wind up in the soup. "I am more than willing to wed her," Vayle declared staunchly. "If she will have me, of course."

"Not to offend," Gwen said with an unholy gleam in her eyes, "but what have you to offer beyond a remarkable talent for making love?"

That question silenced both men for a long time.

When Gwen tapped her foot, clearly expecting an answer, Vayle cast about for something to say.

"I am charming?" he ventured.

"Not at the moment," she informed him. "But let me be of assistance. You are handsome. You have been kind to Winnie, and while Max may not appreciate this overmuch, you reconciled Robin to our family."

"Good enough for me!" Max put his hand on Gwen's shoulder. "Kind heart, good looks, accomplished in the bedchamb— well, never mind that. What more could you want?"

"The man doesn't know who he is," she pointed out. "We had to tell him his own name. He has no past, or none he'll admit to. No family either."

Max shrugged. "At least he won't come trailing any derelict relations for me to support."

There was some expression playing in his eyes—irony? Amusement? No, Vayle told himself. Max wouldn't be amused, not with his sister ruined and vociferously objecting to the obvious solution. Unless he was playing some deep game of his own, of course.

Just in case, Vayle hurried to enlist himself on Gwen's side. "I hesitate to bring this up, having already been found wanting on several counts by Miss Sevaric. But 'struth, I've no way to support her."

"Not to mention," Gwen put in helpfully, "any skills of note. None likely to earn you a decent income, at any rate."

"Thank you." His mock-humility was rewarded by his beloved's quiet chuckle. "I cannot support your sister—not in Sevaric fashion. And you cannot honorably send her to virtual exile in a hovel with me."

Max drew back, as if considering his countermove. "I don't know about that," he said slowly. "You're handy enough with the cards and dice. Besides, Gwen's got dowry enough for four brides. Everything I won from the Caines—except this house, of course—goes to her."

Vayle mentally totted up what that was likely to be and gave a long low whistle. "That casts a whole new light on the situation. A fortune, you say?" With an amused glance at Gwen, he bowed to Sevaric. "All my objections are silenced—brother-in-law."

"I rather expected you'd come around," Max said. Now there was no mistaking his irony.

Gwen planted herself between them. "Wait just a minute! I have nothing to say about this?"

"No," Max and Vayle said together.

Just then Dorie came in, and with a single glance took in the situation. Linking arms with Gwen, she established a feminine barricade and turned a smile to Max and Vayle in turn. "Exactly right, my dear. The final decision is your own, and this pair of mutton-heads will not bully you into a marriage with a man who does not please."

She raised a perfectly shaped eyebrow. "I must confess, however, that he certainly *appears* to be worth any amount of trouble. But looks are often deceiving, and if he failed to please you, nothing more need be said. Now about breakfast—"

Gwen detached her arm from Dorie's. "I didn't precisely say Mr. Vayle failed to please me."

"Indeed? But why then are you not eager for a return engagement? That you don't mean to keep him does, well, rather indicate disappointment."

"Now just one moment!" Vayle fixed her with a stern look, then turned in time to see Max hiding a laugh behind his hand. Just who was playing games with whom? he wondered. It began to appear all four of them had pretended to be at odds, even that straightest of arrows, Lord Sevaric.

He felt a surge of elation. For Gwen he'd have endured a troop of sober-sided nitwits when relations gathered for holidays, and schooled himself to conceal his impatience for her sake. But this, he realized gratefully, was a family he wanted very much to join.

Thank God, they appeared to want him, too, even though he came to them without title, fortune, profession, or even the name that died with him a hundred years ago. But they trusted

Gwen, who would never give herself to a man without love in her heart.

Jocelyn Vayle loved Gwen Sevaric. And they knew it, Max and Dorie both. They opened their arms to him, with sly wit and outrageous cunning, to ease his discomfort at being found in Gwen's bedroom on Christmas morning.

Not that he was in the least embarrassed, of course. Well, not terribly, now that he'd twigged to their jest. And now that he'd found his balance again, with the threat of another duel lifted—and another death. Max would not have required an ill-placed rock to aim his bullet home.

He looked up to see everyone staring at him, and remembered he was the one who called for their attention. What was it he had meant to say? Ah yes. "Can it be my imagination, Miss Sevaric, or do I sense a conspiracy here?"

"Several, I believe. Is it not shameful, my own family turning on me like wolves in the fold? I'm almost of a mind to deny them their pleasure."

His mouth opened to protest and closed again. From Dorie's calm expression, she had matters well enough in hand.

She crossed to her husband's post, looking up at him with a secret smile. "That would be a terrible sacrifice on the altar of pride, Gwen. You might even discover pleasure for yourself, if you wed."

Vayle looked to Gwen for her reaction and was pleased to see crimson rise to her cheeks. Last night she had found pleasure again and again, no wedding required.

"It's agreed then," Max said briskly, with an expression on his face that dared anyone to correct him. "We can make use of that worthless brother of yours, Dorie, and send him off for a special license. He needs the exercise—pasty-looking fellow. Spends too much time in gaming hells. Do you know he's still abed, and with no good reason to keep him there?"

"Darling, he'll not find a special license today! It's Christmas, and bishops are otherwise occupied. The wedding will have to wait until tomorrow."

Vayle thought it past time to wrest back his life from these two. "If you don't mind, I'd rather not wait another day, no, not another minute, to make my intentions clear."

He took Gwen's hand and dropped to one knee before her, speaking in a low voice only she could hear. "Will you have me, fair one? I've waited a century to find you. And I want above all things, even Heaven itself, to spend the next century making myself worthy of your love."

Gwen's eyes were glowing golden as she gazed down at him. But all she said was, "I expect I should like that." Then she tugged him to his feet and came into his arms.

Max was a decent fellow, all things considered, and gave them a minute or two before intervening again. "There's still the matter of tonight. You'll have to find another bed, Vayle, for you shouldn't be making merry unless you're married. Last night was all well and good—"

Vayle looked at him in surprise. "Do you mean to say you condone my . . . er, our . . . that is—"

Max waved a dismissive hand. "It was clear enough that you two were smelling of April and May. Well, it wasn't clear to *me,* but Dorie noticed. And knowing my sister's willfulness, I suspect you hadn't much of a chance to refuse." He granted them both an understanding smile. "You hadn't the benefit of army training, Vayle, so you can't truly be blamed. It takes military discipline to fend off an importunate female."

"Time for breakfast!" Dorie announced before Max could elaborate.

Robin was summoned, and joined the others in the dining room, still rumpled from his bed but looking ruddier already in the fresh country air.

When informed of the impromptu betrothal, he regarded Vayle with admiration. "I never imagined—and you won her so quick!" He shook his head, then recalled himself and pumped Vayle's hand vigorously. Finally, his eyes downcast, he turned to Gwen. "Vayle is a fortunate man. May I wish you happy?"

"Thank you." She gave him a warm smile. "And truly, I am the fortunate one." Under the table, she squeezed Vayle's knee.

He put his hand over hers, humbled by her words. It had to be true—Gwen never lied—and his heart soared in response.

After breakfast, they trooped back to the parlor to burn the Yule log and exchange gifts. As he settled next to Gwen, he rather wished his redemption hadn't taken quite so well. Virtue was burden indeed for a man who wanted to forget all about Christmas and take this passionate woman straight back to bed.

The perfect hostess, Dorie had a gift for each of them—a bonnet for Gwen, initialed handkerchiefs for Robin and Vayle, and, for Max, a framed sampler embroidered with his regiment's bugle insignia. After handing all these out, she sat on the floor at her husband's knee, beaming with their reflected pleasure.

Max admired his sampler for a while, then, as if in afterthought, reached into his pocket and pulled out a small flagon.

"Here." He dropped it into Dorie's lap.

Slowly she raised the crystal bottle and held it to the light. "It's my mother's."

"Unstop it," Max commanded.

She pulled off the top and brought the bottle to her face, breathing in the scent. "It's the same perfume! But—but it's no longer made! How did you—"

"I had the perfumer in Croydon match it. Took him a week to get it right. It *is* right, I hope?"

Dorie dabbed a bit on her wrist and held it up for him to test. "What do you think?"

Max wasn't one to ignore such an advantage, and enjoyed a few kisses before he admitted the perfumer had done a good job. "See," he added obscurely, "you were right to trust me."

"Yes, I was right to trust you." With a smile, Dorie stoppered the flagon and put it away in her pocket. Then she gazed expectantly around her. "Is everyone hungry for luncheon now? I have a lovely plum pudding."

"Good Lord, wife! We just left the table."

The others agreed that lunch would be *de trop* so soon after breakfast, and the talk turned to what the bridal couple meant to do with the future. Vayle looked at Gwen, perched on the arm of his chair, for an answer. But she no more than he had planned for a future neither thought to share.

"Feel free to use the London house as long as you like," Max offered. "We mean to rusticate for a bit."

Robin glanced dubiously at his sister's parlor, scarcely large enough to contain a man, much less a family. "Here?"

"Heavens, no. We'll move over to Sevaric Hall." Dorie looked suspiciously demure. "It's so much *safer* there for Max."

To Vayle's amazement, Max laughed and held up his hand with its four bandaged appendages. "It wasn't easy, but I have convinced my wife how unsporting we have been, denying honest carpenters a chance to make a living. In future, more adept laborers will restore Greenbriar while we reside in comfort at Sevaric."

Gwen nodded, a smile playing about her lips. "Thank you, Max. I do think Vayle more suited to London than the country. Indeed, I rather suspect he is already longing for a night on the town."

"Not so," Vayle said, offended. "With you to entertain me, I daresay all my evenings will be spent at home."

That declaration was greeted with skeptical looks.

"You can't mean to stop gaming!" Robin blurted. When four pairs of narrowed eyes turned to him, he waved a hand. "I know, I know. But it's different for me. I've the sickness and will not play again. What's more, I was never any good at it. But Vayle is a true gambler, ever in control of the game and of himself. He plays with skill, sniffs luck when it's on him, and has an uncanny sense of when to take a risk. His talent must not go to waste."

Vayle acknowledged the compliment with a nod before turning a smile on his bride, who looked a bit concerned. " 'Struth, cards and dice are little challenge compared to the gamble I took last night. And no victory will ever be so complete, my love, nor any prize so treasured."

Gwen was shy yet, at least in public, and only pressed his hand. But her eyes promised more later, and when she bent to whisper in his ear, he readied himself for a detailed description of what that "more" might be.

So low that no one else could hear, she said, "You have just reminded me. What about the treasure? The other one, I mean."

He sighed. Once again, that damned pile of stones was making a nuisance of itself. But Gwen was right, so he cleared his throat to get everyone's attention. "Last night, I chanced upon—"

Just then his gaze fell on Robin, standing apart by the fire, shoulders hunched, the odd man out in a room glowing with other people's happiness. Robin Caine needed a victory of his own.

Smoothly he finished, "—that snuffbox you lent me, Robin. Come up with me and I'll return it before I forget."

Robin began to protest that he had meant it as a gift, but Vayle took his arm and towed him into the passageway. He'd every intention of keeping the snuffbox, of course. It was engraved with his monogram—his original monogram—and he took delight in this souvenir of his former life. For the moment, though, it served as a ruse to get Robin out of the parlor.

Near the staircase, a few feet from the hidden priest hole, Vayle glanced up at the landing, hoping to see Francis there to give him one last miracle. Instead he saw only Max's boot, sticking up to mark the hole in the floor, and a ladder turned over on its side. In a flash, it came to him what must have happened last night . . . what he had not been able to make out in the dim light of his single candle.

When it fell, the ladder punched a hole in the wood of the landing. And when he took care to examine it on his search for the priest hole, the secret of the house was finally revealed.

Without another thought, he pretended to stumble on the uneven floor and pitched headlong toward the wall under the staircase. With a mighty effort, he scraped his fingers along the wainscoting as if trying to break his fall. There! He had it, and the panel slid an inch or so sideways. Then he let himself crash to the floor.

Ignoring a stab in his knee, he bounded to his feet before Robin tried to play nursemaid. "I'm not hurt," he declared, bravely suppressing a wince. "But I seem to have damaged the wall."

As he had hoped, Robin bent to examine the wainscoting. "That's odd. There's a gap here." Gingerly he slipped his fingers inside and edged the panel open another foot. A musty odor leaked out. "It's a door! A secret door!"

The others were emerging from the parlor, drawn by the crash. Quickly, Vayle seized the low-burning lamp from the hall table and thrust it into Robin's hands. "You've found a priest hole, I'll wager. Go in and look."

From the doorway, Max objected that he was the man of experience, the one who knew how to scout and evaluate. He should be the one to investigate the discovery.

Vayle swore under his breath. Just what he needed—eagle-eyed Max spotting fresh footprints in the hundred-year layer of dust. "But consider the spiders," he warned.

Max hesitated just long enough for Robin to crouch down and insert himself through the opening.

"I'm not afraid of spiders," Max declared belatedly.

"Shush!" Gwen slipped past her brother and bent to peer into the priest hole. "What do you see?"

Robin's voice echoed slightly in the empty space. "Spiderwebs. Nothing else. Wait. There's something— Good God!"

Max dropped to his knees beside his sister and looked in. "What is it, Lynton? A skeleton?"

"Oooh," Dorie exclaimed. "A skeleton!"

"Not a skeleton," Robin called back. "Something else. Sevaric, let me out."

They all fell back so that Robin could emerge and straighten up. With one hand he brushed at a cobweb trailing from his nose. In the other hand he held—

"The Caine treasure," Dorie said in an awed voice. "Robin, what else could it be?"

The stones clicked as he shook the dust off the necklace. "It looks like it, right enough. Do you remember, Dorie? The portrait at Caine Manor, with Lady What's-er-name wearing the Elizabethan jewels?"

Vayle almost confirmed it. He had been there when the portrait of his mother was painted, four years old then, making as much noise as he could to annoy the artist. This time he held his silence while the young Caines drew together to buff at the necklace and marvel.

Finally Robin raised his head. "I expect we owe you an apology, Sevaric. It's obvious no one has touched this in decades."

"A century perhaps," Gwen put in with a mischievous glance at Vayle. "Not since that wastrel Valerian Caine prowled these halls with his mistress."

"But how did it wind up in the priest hole?" Max took the lamp and bent to peer again into the darkness. "Did you know this place existed, Dorie?"

"No, of course not. I would have cleaned it up and stored painting supplies here. I wonder—do you think Valerian Caine really did bring the treasure to the lodge? Perhaps he stole it from his brother, intending to sell the gems." She bounced with excitement, caught up in her story. "Then Richard Sevaric found him hiding in the priest hole, and took him out and shot him, and got shot, too, and so the treasure lay hidden for a hundred years."

This Vayle couldn't allow, even as speculation. "A fanciful tale, but I expect the truth is somewhat more pedestrian. More likely it was the lady Blanche who put the jewels in the priest hole while the men were fighting."

Gwen picked up her cue. "Very like. From all accounts, she was both greedy and concerned only for herself. But she died not long after the feud, and never had a chance to reclaim the treasure." When Dorie gave her a quizzical look, she shrugged. "Under my father's command, I became somewhat expert at tracing the history of our families. By the way, wasn't there also a ring?"

Robin shoved the jewels in Dorie's hands, dove back in and scrabbled around. "Found it!" he crowed, returning with the ring on his little finger." Now let me see that necklace again." He wrapped it around his hand. "Just look at those diamonds! This must be worth a fortune now."

The glitter in his eyes faded, and slowly he untangled himself from the twist of gold and diamonds and sapphires. "I suppose it's yours, isn't it, Sevaric? We found it in your house."

"As my wife keeps reminding me," Max said, "it's her house, not mine. But I imagine a solicitor would tell you that even after a century, the treasure belongs to the Caines and is a legacy to the nearest heir. That's you, I believe."

"Yes." With a look of resolve, Robin turned to his sister and held out the necklace. "Are you sure you don't want this, Dorie? The bracelet and other stuff, too. You could wear them."

She looked down at the wealth she was already holding and shook her head. "Thank you, Robin, but my tastes are rather more simple. The necklace alone is positively garish, and this tiara would give me the headache."

"The ring is lovely though," Gwen observed. "Just a single sapphire and only a dozen or so diamonds."

Dorie smiled at her husband. "I've all the treasure I need, and Max has already given me the only ring I'll ever want to wear."

Max took the tiara, bracelet, and earbobs from her hands and held them out. "Yours by default, Lynton."

Robin's eyes shone again as the fortune dropped into his open palms. "I shan't lose this by gambling, I promise. In fact, I'll sell every last piece and buy a bit of land. I've always wanted to raise horses." When Dorie and Vayle looked surprised, he grinned. "Well, it will keep me out of trouble, at any rate. And I do like the nags. From now on I'll breed 'em instead of losing blunt at the races."

Vayle clapped him on the back. "Capital notion. You'll have

income and respectability as a country squire, and will always be welcome at our home when you visit London."

Suddenly Robin wrenched the ring from his finger and gave it to Vayle. "Here. You'll need this for your wedding."

When Vayle tried to give it back, Gwen seized his arm. "That's a lovely gesture, Robin." She lifted her hand, and Vayle obediently fitted the ring on her finger.

"It feels as if it belongs there," she said thoughtfully. "Almost as if Valerian Caine, wherever he is, meant for me to wear it. This is a symbol, don't you think? The feud is ended, our families united, and each one of us is wonderfully happy."

Then, with a sigh, she returned the ring to Vayle.

Dorie patted her hand. "Tomorrow he will give it to you again, when you take your vows. Now come, gentlemen. Let us permit these two some privacy. Robin, you can clean the dirt from your treasure while Max helps me wash the breakfast dishes."

When they were gone, Vayle took Gwen in his arms. "By the rood, tomorrow seems an eternity away. And you know I am an impatient rascal. Could I persuade you, dear lady, to become mine on this miraculous Christmas day?"

"You know I wish it above all things, but as Dorie has pointed out, we cannot possibly get a license. And besides, it would be unkind to pluck a vicar from his Christmas goose."

"Even more unkind, to consign me to a bed without you to share it." The corners of his mouth turned down. "What's more, you cannot begin to imagine the noises that boy can make with his nose and throat. Robin's snoring would drown out a cannon barrage."

"Max might relent," she said. "He's in a very good mood."

"Let us not put it to the test. I have in mind another solution, and wonder that none of us have thought of it ere now." He smiled at the puzzled look on her face. " 'Tis perfectly obvious, my love. Handfasting!"

"I beg your pardon?"

His heart sank. "Don't they do that anymore? Lord, sometimes I despise this modern age. So much of value has been tossed aside. Patches, for example. And now handfasting, too?"

"I can't say I'd care for patches," she admitted, "but tell me about the other. What is handfasting?"

"A simple way for a man and woman to plight their troth when vicars and the like are not to be found. Hand in hand, they affirm their love in front of witnesses. 'Struth, marriage is naught but promises made one to th'other, before God. All the rest is legal claptrap."

When she was silent, he stepped back and folded his arms. "But perhaps you wish a formal wedding, in a church, and of course you must have it. I can endure Robin's snoring one more night. 'Tis not as if I will sleep anyway, for wanting you in my arms."

"Gudgeon." She ran her fingers down his whiskered cheek. "As if I'd give up even one night with you for a silly wedding. But we must have one eventually, because nowadays a vicar and our signatures on the marriage lines are needed to make the union lawful and our children legitimate. For now, though, a handfasting sounds absolutely lovely. Our own vows, spoken privately, with our family standing witness—it's just what I would like."

When he was done kissing her, she took his hand and led him toward the kitchen. "We'll tell the others and get on with it. Max is weakening, I think, and will likely seize the excuse to let us share a room tonight."

Or maybe this afternoon, he was thinking as Gwen announced their plans. He'd a century of abstinence to make up for, a woman he both desired and loved, and the memory of last night's passion to spur him on.

Robin and Max responded with enthusiasm, but to everyone's surprise, Dorie put down her foot.

"This is an auspicious occasion," she declared, "and we'll not go one step farther in this havey-cavey fashion." Max lifted his brow at the cant and she fired back a haughty glare. "Don't be missish. It's perfectly obvious a suitable place must be made ready for the ceremony."

Vayle watched, bemused, as his gentle great-great-grand-niece issued crisp orders and implied dire punishment for laggards. Dorie the Hun, he thought as they all marched dutifully to the parlor.

Max, no stranger to autocratic superiors, did not complain as she pointed an imperious finger toward the furniture in the center of the room. At her direction, he shoved the oak table against the wall and carried the wing chair to a spot beside the couch. Then he paced the expanse of threadbare carpet and back again, frowned his way through some mental calculations, and reported to his commanding officer. "Plenty of room now for the vow-taking, ma'am."

The field marshal turned her attention from the room to its occupants. "You are a disgrace, the lot of you. Mr. Vayle, you need a shave. Robin, did you sleep in those clothes? Upstairs, and don't come back until you are properly dressed. That includes you, Max, but not until you've finished helping me here. Gwen, I'll join you shortly to help with your hair."

Everyone stared at her, not sure she was through. She clapped her hands. "Move!"

They moved, Max to her side for his next instructions while the others scampered to the staircase.

"My heavens," Gwen said just before she left Vayle at the door to his room. "I rather think my brother has met his match."

"And then some," Vayle agreed, seizing one last, swift kiss. "Do you know, this will be the first time I've shaved myself in a hundred years?"

"Take care then," she advised over her shoulder as she moved away. "I couldn't bear to lose you now."

A half hour later, Vayle stood in front of the hall mirror, admiring his reflection. His *reflection*—clear and sharp, without a shimmer of insubstantiality. He had even managed to tie the starched white cravat over the blue-and-gold-striped waistcoat that was, unfortunately, the only bright note in his wedding garb.

"What a coxcomb!" Max said from the parlor door. "Always primping in front of a mirror."

Vayle grinned at him. "I don't want to disappoint your sister. And I rather feared you'd cast me in the shade with your splendid scarlet regimentals. 'Tis a relief you chose a plain blue coat."

"Dorie chose it," Max confessed. "She would rather I leave the army behind me, although I fear in that one regard I'm likely to disappoint *her*. After ten years, it's in my blood."

Vayle understood exactly. After a hundred years, Valerian Caine was in his own blood. Why else would he have just been mourning his drab gray coat and, most of all, the absence of his long hair? Gwen might disapprove of patches, high-heeled shoes, and rings on every finger, but she'd have liked his hair.

He turned back to the mirror, wondering how he'd look in a crimson uniform. "Any chance I could get a commission in your regiment?" he asked impulsively.

Max opened his mouth, apparently thought better of what he was about to say, and closed it again. "A commission?" he said finally. "Well, the 52nd hasn't many spots for officers, since the war's ended. And you are rather—rather old to be a subaltern, you know."

Vayle nodded. At one hundred and twenty-seven years, it was somewhat late to enlist. And while he'd have liked the fighting, and certainly the uniform, taking orders was not in his character. A legitimate profession, though, had some appeal.

The notion was so astonishing he turned it over in his mind. Valerian Caine would not, in his wildest dreams, have entertained such a thought. Perhaps he was more Jocelyn Vayle than he realized, if he was considering some way to be more than an ornament at Gwen's side and a lover in her bed.

Max patted his shoulder. "If you're worried about running through Gwen's income, you needn't be. It's substantial as is, and since I won't be supporting Lynton after all, you can apply to me. Without hesitation, Vayle. Don't let pride stand in your way. I love my sister and she deserves the best of everything."

Yes, Vayle thought. But *he* wanted to be the one to give it to her. He could teach fencing, he supposed. Or game, in moderation, and only for the money. With a goal, and Gwen depending on him, he could well earn a fortune at the tables. But he would discuss it with her first. She'd not like him bankrupting callow boys or addicted dicers like Robin. Still, guided by principles of fair play—

His planning was cut short when she came down the stairs, a slip of lace on her hair and a red mum in her hand. Dorie was right behind, beaming as if she had crafted the bride as she did an exquisite bonnet.

"Doesn't she look lovely, Mr. Vayle?"

Eyes fixed on Gwen's, he made an elaborate leg. "Like a sunrise."

Robin arrived, somewhat breathless, and Dorie led them all into the parlor. It had been transformed.

With the furniture out of the way, the little room was intimate instead of cramped. The curtains were open, offering a glimpse of the golden meadow outside, and from the hearth a fire warmed the rays of the winter sun streaming through the glass.

Dorie must have collected every potted plant in the house. Red ribbons adorned each ceramic pot, and she had crafted an arbor of evergreen branches and holly near the window, just high enough for the bride and groom to stand underneath.

" 'Tis splendid," Vayle said as he led Gwen to the spot Dorie indicated. "Thank you."

Blushing, Dorie took her husband's hand and beckoned Robin to join them. She held her left hand to her brother and he grasped it, clearly grateful to be included in the close family circle.

Vayle paused a moment, took a deep breath, and put his hands on Gwen's shoulders. Looking deeply into her eyes, he spoke from his heart. "Beloved, it was my destiny to love you. Across time, lonely and without purpose or hope, my soul searched for yours. You are my saving grace, and from this moment and forever, I swear to prove myself worthy. All that I am, I give to you."

Tears shone in her eyes, but her voice was steady. "Beloved, you come as a gift from Heaven. I never thought to share such love, but you have found your way home to me and I welcome you to my heart. From now until forever, I swear to be a true and faithful wife. All I am, I give to you."

The sun seemed to brighten then, a new light gilding the man and woman who stood, silent and wholly absorbed in each other.

Then Vayle drew Gwen into his arms, her head against his chest, her soft breath warm against his throat. "Thank you, Francis," he murmured into her soft hair. "Thank you, God." He barely managed to stop himself from thanking Proctor.

"Aren't they supposed to kiss?" Robin piped.

"Perhaps not, with handfasting," Dorie replied doubtfully. "Come to think of it, Max, we didn't kiss either, did we?"

"Not then, but we've made up for it since. Don't forget, we were practically strangers when we wed. These two know each other all too well."

Vayle lifted Gwen's chin with his thumb. "Shall we?"

Gwen smiled, mischief dancing in her eyes. "I expect so. It appears the audience is getting restless."

"Do we care?" He bent his head and whispered against her lips, "This is for us, my precious, beautiful wife."

After a minute, or an hour, because he couldn't let go the kiss that sealed them for all time, the sound of a shot nearly sent him diving for cover.

"What the devil?" He jumped in front of Gwen, eyes searching the room for an assassin.

"Good reflexes." With his handkerchief, Max wiped the steaming lip of a dusty bottle. "My apologies, Vayle, but we were all growing old waiting for you to break off that kiss. This is champagne, by the way. Found it in the priest hole."

He poured it into the glasses on the sideboard. "Well, it may be vinegar by now, but at least it's bubbling."

Dorie took her glass and raised it. When she had everyone's attention, she said, "To the miracle of love." She sipped her champagne, nodded approval, and stood on tiptoe to kiss Max.

Vayle and Gwen touched glasses, and looking deep into each other's eyes, drank to love.

"And to the miracle of the season," Robin put in. He lifted his glass in toast, but set it down without tasting it. "Think of it. Just last month"—he glanced at Max—"we hated one another."

"And we'd never met," Dorie said, smiling up at her husband.

"And Vayle was—well, we don't know where Vayle was," Max said. "Nowhere worth remembering, I expect."

"And the treasure was still missing." Robin reached in his pocket and pulled out the necklace. He let it sift from hand to hand and laughed quietly. Then he looked at Vayle. "It must have been the angel of Christmas that sent you into our lives, to solve a mystery that kept Caines and Sevarics at each other's throats for a century."

Vayle lifted his glass again. "To Francis," he said so only Gwen could hear.

Robin shook his head with wonderment. "No doubt about it, my friend. You are a godsend."

Gwen took her husband's hand and brought it to her lips. "Sent from God indeed," she whispered. "And I do love you, Valerian Caine. 'Struth."

Dear Reader,

Like our Ghost, Valerian Caine, we both feel a deep connection to the past. The Regency is our special love, and research a splendid way of reliving history without giving up central heat, indoor plumbing, and chocolates.

To celebrate meeting our deadline (almost), nothing would do but a trip to our spiritual home! Together, we explored London, Brighton, and Bath, and the Cotswolds, seeking the Regency still left in England and gathering ideas for future novels.

Still, it is modern technology that makes our long-distance collaboration possible. Proctor and Francis (yes, we've named our computers after the Ghost's guardian angels) are linked by modem, which lets us send chapters cross-country in the wink of an eye. 'Struth, miracles come in all forms. And wouldn't Prinny adore going electronic?

We hope you enjoyed *Gwen's Christmas Ghost,* and appreciate hearing from readers—Snail-Mail or E-mail.

Lynn Kerstan   Alicia Rasley
PO Box 182301   2138 E. Broad Ripple #143
Coronado, CA 92178–2301   Indianapolis, IN 46220–2132
l.kerstan@genie.com   a.rasley@genie.com

ZEBRA REGENCIES
ARE
THE TALK OF THE TON!

A REFORMED RAKE   (4499, $3.99)
by Jeanne Savery
After governess Harriet Cole helped her young charge flee to
France—and the designs of a despicable suitor, more trouble soon
arrived in the person of a London rake. Sir Frederick Carrington
insisted on providing safe escort back to England. Harriet
deemed Carrington more dangerous than any band of brigands,
but secretly relished matching wits with him. But after being
taken in his arms for a tender kiss, she found herself wondering—
could a lady find love with an irresistible rogue?

A SCANDALOUS PROPOSAL   (4504, $4.99)
by Teresa DesJardien
After only two weeks into the London season, Lady Pamela
Premington has already received her first offer of marriage. If
only it hadn't come from the *ton's* most notorious rake, Lord
Marchmont. Pamela had already set her sights on the distin-
guished Lieutenant Penford, who had the heroism and honor that
made him the ideal match. Now she had to keep from falling
under the spell of the seductive Lord so she could pursue the man
more worthy of her love. Or was he?

A LADY'S CHAMPION   (4535, $3.99)
by Janice Bennett
Miss Daphne, art mistress of the Selwood Academy for Young
Ladies, greeted the notion of ghosts haunting the academy with
skepticism. However, to avoid rumors frightening off students,
she found herself turning to Mr. Adrian Carstairs, sent by her
uncle to be her "protector" against the "ghosts." Although,
Daphne would accept no interference in her life, she *would* accept
aid in exposing any spectral spirits. What she never expected was
for Adrian to expose the secret wishes of her hidden heart . . .

CHARITY'S GAMBIT   (4537, $3.99)
by Marcy Stewart
Charity Abercrombie reluctantly embarks on a London season in
hopes of making a suitable match. However she cannot forget the
mysterious Dominic Castille—and the kiss they shared—when he
fell from a tree as she strolled through the woods. Charity does
not know that the dark and dashing captain harbors a dangerous
secret that will ensnare them both in its web—leaving Charity to
risk certain ruin and losing the man she so passionately loves . . .

*Available wherever paperbacks are sold, or order direct from the
Publisher. Send cover price plus 50¢ per copy for mailing and
handling to Penguin USA, P.O. Box 999, c/o Dept. 17109,
Bergenfield, NJ 07621. Residents of New York and Tennessee
must include sales tax. DO NOT SEND CASH.*